DEAD-END ROAD

Richard Kunzmann is a native South African whose passion has always been African myths and mythologies, and their associated occultism. He majored in criminology, and has worked as a bookseller in London. This is his third novel.

RICHARD KUNZMANN

DEAD-END ROAD

PAN BOOKS

First published 2008 by Macmillan

This paperback edition first published 2009 by Pan Books
an imprint of Pan Macmillan Ltd
Pan Macmillan, 20 New Wharf Road, London N1 9RR
Basingstoke and Oxford
Associated companies throughout the world
www.panmacmillan.com

ISBN 978-0-330-44648-8

A CIP catalogue record for this book is available from
the British Library.

Typeset by SetSystems Ltd, Saffron Walden, Essex
Printed in the UK by CPI Mackays, Chatham ME5 8TD

Visit **www.panmacmillan.com** to read more about all our books
and to buy them. You will also find features, author interviews and
news of any author events, and you can sign up for e-newsletters
so that you're always first to hear about our new releases.

This is for

Peter Lavery

who has not only been
a great editor and mentor,
but a good friend, too

Acknowledgements

I'd like to thank the following for their careful reading of this manuscript's first drafts, and for their enormous support and necessary honesty: my parents, Julius and Silke, my most valuable critics, Erica, Willemien and Nicci – and Phuti, for challenging many of my preconceived ideas about Jo'burg street-life.

I owe much to the various Macmillan teams in the United Kingdom and South Africa, who have rolled up their sleeves and gotten their hands dirty, polishing my work and getting it out to the booksellers. In particular I'd like to thank my editor, Peter Lavery, and also Terry Morris and Dusanka Stojakovic in South Africa. To Stefanie Bierwerth, Vivien Bassett, Rebecca Saunders, Liz Cowen and Katie James – great work! Many thanks to my agent at Aitken-Alexander Associates, Mary Pachnos, for her stellar work keeping an author's head above water.

Last, but certainly never least, I'd like to thank the many booksellers and journalists who have supported me all these years. To say that a book is an author's labour alone is a mistake. It's the collaboration of writer, editor and reader that makes it such a rewarding experience.

ONE

1

The cold air bites as Detective Captain Harry Mason steps out on to the landing and watches the bleak forecourt of the rural police compound through the fog of his own breath. A single spotlight illuminates shadowy human figures moving about in the pre-dawn darkness. Army, local police, and men of the Serious and Violent Crimes Unit spill out of military-issue camouflage tents, carrying duffel bags, metal detectors, bulletproof vests and automatic weapons towards mud-splattered all-terrain vehicles. The ones who could not sleep this late-August night have already packed and are now huddled in small groups, sipping steaming coffee and chain-smoking cigarettes as they talk in hushed voices about what lies ahead. On the purple horizon a slice of sun tints the rust-coloured coal-smoke suspended over a township. It has been burning Harry's eyes and lungs ever since he stepped off the helicopter last night here in Maclear, Eastern Cape.

A heavy boot scuffs the bare concrete doorsill behind him and a gloved hand lands on his shoulder.

'Have you decided what you're going to do yet?'

Harry shrugs the hand off. 'No.'

'I want you to know there are other people's lives at stake in this. Children. And a wife.'

'They are the only reason I'm still weighing things up.'

'That's a harsh thing to say, Harry.'

'I don't think so.'

Senior Superintendent Russell Swarts lets the conver-

1

sation drop off into a silence that makes them both uncomfortable.

'*Jirre*,' he eventually says again, 'I miss early mornings like these, especially out on the farm. You should come sometime. Nice drive up to Limpopo, it is.'

Harry steps aside to make room for the man to pass. 'I'll think about it.'

'You ready for this?' asks Swarts.

'Just about.'

'Have you seen Naidoo this morning? The rest of my Ballies?'

'They're down there, talking to Moraal.' Harry takes another sip from his mug of instant coffee, which would taste little more appealing than brake fluid if it were not for the freezing dawn. He has not been this cold since his childhood in England. A short way off, the rest of the men from Harry's task team, or at least Swarts' inner circle – his Ballies, as he calls them – are studying a map with an army officer.

'Looks like we'll be able to head out by five,' he says.

'*Ja*. Looks like,' replies Swarts. 'I'm surprised by the locals; I wouldn't have thought they'd be up for an operation patched together this quickly.'

Harry glances at the man slurping coffee next to him. Swarts is almost a head taller than himself, and his well-kept beard framing an egg-shaped face shows more grey than brown. From the glow in his superior's cheeks, Harry guesses there is a liberal dash of brandy already floating in the coffee.

Swarts turns to him. 'Now all we need is for your informant to be right, and the darkies up in those hills not to know that we're coming for them.'

'My guy hates my guts, but he wouldn't bullshit me on this.'

'The first thing you learn working narcotics as long as I did is this: don't ever trust someone based on his past record, especially if he's in the business of leaking information.'

'I'll bet on this one,' replies Harry, hoping he sounds more confident than he feels. This is by far the biggest operation in which he has participated. That they are here based on information that was supplied to him, and only him, means that if something goes wrong, it will be him taking the fall.

'A hundred grand and extras is a lot of money for a rat.' Swarts laughs. 'If those guns are there, your guy's going to earn more than I will get out of my goddamned pension. Jesus, imagine that: thirty years on the force doesn't beat a rat's confession.'

Harry smiles non-committally.

'You're still not going to tell me who it is?' asks Swarts.

'I don't think so.' Harry shakes his head, feeling more amiable now that they are back on familiar terrain.

'You're not planning to walk off with all that money yourself, are you?' But before Harry can reply, Swarts slaps him on his back. 'Only joking, Bond! Don't justify that with an answer, please!'

It was one of the first things Harry Mason had to come to terms with when he rejoined the service: the abundance of quirky and fickle nicknames that police officers give each other. And the Serious and Violent Crimes Unit, or SVC, was no different. Sometimes you got lucky, with one like 'Bond', or 'Super Supe Russie Swarts'. You can live with those. Others were not so lucky. Like the German,

Gustav Vok, who started police college with him. That Vok sounded like 'fuck' in Afrikaans did not help him at all, and he dropped out after only a year of service once the pimps and prostitutes on their beat in Rosettenville learned of his surname.

'Well then,' says Swarts. 'Let's hope it's not our funeral.' He tosses the remainder of his coffee out on the weeds growing up against the wall of the station. 'Let me go talk to that idiot Naidoo. Snored like a blimming sawmill the whole night, I tell you.'

His heavy boots clomp down the remainder of the concrete stairs. At the bottom Swarts turns around and faces Harry with a childlike grin – the first smile Harry has seen in days. 'I love it!' He stretches out his arms. 'All of this, Harry – I don't want to give it up.'

'Maybe you don't have to,' he replies. 'Just do what needs to be done.'

'An end comes to everything, even to us.' Swarts shakes his head and his face becomes serious. 'If one of the yokels manning this shithole for a station hasn't already ridden ahead to tell them we're coming, they'll see us from miles away, if they know what they're doing. These *dagga* growers are as used to raids as I am to my wife's blimming Tuesday *bobootie*. We're heading into deep shit, Harry, no matter which way you look at it. It's this kind of thing that decides whether you're fit for the SVC. Remember that. And remember who has your back.'

Harry acknowledges his commander by raising his coffee mug in a silent toast. The sudden chill he feels prevents him from opening his mouth, however.

Swarts shakes his head, then turns towards Captain Sameer 'Sammy' Naidoo and the other Johannesburg SVC task team members, Franklin and Combrink. Just then the police helicopter that was parked overnight on the gravelly soccer pitch next door fires up its engines. Within seconds dust engulfs the temporary camp. Turning his back on an eruption of expletives from the forecourt, Harry re-enters the station to fetch his gear from an empty jail cell which had doubled as his field bed. As he checks his pistol and extra ammunition clips one last time, his mind returns to the dossiers he has in his possession, and what they mean to him.

2

The investigation had begun in earnest when Supe Russie Swarts, whom some even called Super Supe, strolled into Harry's new office one morning, barely three months after he had finally accepted Director Molethe's cajoling offers to join Johannesburg's Serious and Violent Crimes Unit. At first he was not inclined to do so, preferring to rejoin his old unit, where his friend Jacob Tshabalala was still stationed, but when he heard he would be reunited with the legendary Swarts, with whom he had briefly worked in the late nineties, Molethe soon had him hooked.

The office was replete with a new computer, internet connection and fax, and was his and his alone. The pitted brown wood and bare steel furnishings he had grown accustomed to during his first fifteen years of police work did not come close to the equipment he found here. The moment he had settled into the new office chair behind the L-shaped desk, and surveyed the clean expanse of its surface, something had felt right.

'Mason,' said Swarts, this being back before he had given Harry his nickname, 'you're the primary on this one.'

He lobbed a docket on the crowded desk, which already looked like a magpie's nest with three months of accumulated paperwork, and made himself comfortable in one of two padded visitors' chairs. Harry fished up the docket, briefly glanced at the address written on a yellow slip pasted on the front, and flipped it open.

'That's been floating around at station level for ever, but now it's found its way to you, my friend.'

The report detailed how a family of three had been barricaded in their small four-room home in Diepsloot before it was set alight with petrol bombs. The man, his wife and sixteen-year-old son had absolutely no chance of escape: the two exit doors had been jammed shut, while burglar-proofing already barred the windows. Paging through the sparse statements and investigative notes, Harry finally asked, 'Why has this ended up here? It's not our mandate to solve what the local precincts can't crack, is it?'

'Usually no, but the father was Christof Mohosh, a minor ward representative for the ANC, so the fact that he was a political player, coupled with the organization now suspected of ordering the killing, adds up to enough cause for the case to get diverted to SVC.'

'Yes?'

'I reckon you've already heard of the Abasindisi? Well, rumour has it they were responsible.'

The name 'Abasindisi' hung between them for a moment; so the group had shown its face again. 'The Saviours' was an organization formed in the mid-nineties, born out of the frustrations of migrant miners from the impoverished Eastern Cape. Angered by infrequent reports that their livestock back home was being stolen, that their wives and children were being assaulted and their houses razed to the ground while they were working away from home on the distant goldfields of the north, they decided to take the law into their own hands. They wanted someone more dependable than the police to watch over their families and meagre properties while they broke their backs underground. So they pooled their money and armed themselves by resorting to struggle-era arms dealers who had never entirely quit the trade. Largely by coercion they figured out who was raiding their homes, and finally retaliated by sending into the Eastern Cape assassins who were fellow miners unknown to the residents of the targeted villages.

It was not long after this that the raiders figured out how the Saviours were operating, and formed their own covert assassination units to strike back. Back and forth between remote villages these attacks continued – a see-saw of violence that turned an entire province into a war zone of retribution. And when families threatened to cancel their membership fees to the Abasindisi in an effort to stop this escalating violence, they themselves became targets.

'I thought they'd been wiped out, the big boys put paid to.'

Swarts laughed as he leaned forward to pour himself a mugful of coffee from Harry's percolator. 'Not a chance, my friend. That won't ever happen. Once the ground-work's been laid for a successful racket, it won't ever disappear. When the Gambino family was taken down in New York City, that didn't mean the end of organized crime, did it now?'

'But even back then, the Abasindisi's activities always focused on settlements in the Eastern Cape; so you reckon they've finally moved on?'

Swarts nodded over a loud slurp of his coffee. 'It was only a matter of time before all the blood spilled down there would creep back upriver to its source. We now know the orders to kill and raid came from the safety of the mining hostels up here on the Rand. Our victim, Mohosh, though himself of Tswana descent, had Xhosa family connections from near Tsolo, and could therefore easily have picked up a mark if he interfered too much with the Abasindisi or their allies. That's if he wasn't directly involved himself.'

Harry flipped through the docket again. 'And so that's for me to find out.'

Swarts toasted Harry with his own purple mug, which read I ♥ DAD, and winked. 'You've got it, *boet*. This investigation isn't one for the instant-coffee cops you get these days; I need an experienced officer with an open mind on the case. It's not just the murderers we want, because we need to burn the entire spider's web before this city becomes entangled in all the violence that's been happening down there. You up for it, captain?'

'Sure, Supe,' Harry had said readily, without considering what he might find himself up against.

'Good.' Swarts nodded approvingly. 'Their bloody little war isn't spreading to my city, I'll tell you that much.'

3

The sun has finally clawed its way over the horizon, shedding weak light over a world of long dry grass and broken rock. The bleak grey air reminds Harry of London, though this expanse of golden wilderness all around him could not be more different from the city where he was born.

In the police pick-up with him are Swarts and the Maclear station commissioner, a man by the name of Moqomo. Three soldiers dressed in brown bulletproof vests which read SANDF in white letters are racing ahead on their scramblers; slung across their backs are R4 semi-automatic rifles. Occasionally their wheels kick up gravel from the heavily rutted road that hits the pick-up's windshield. From behind them comes the dim growl of a heavy military engine.

'Can you believe this place?' asks Harry over the heater's roar and the clatter of loose rock in the wheel wells. Back at base his nerves had been pretty steady, considering what they were driving into, but now, with a deep ravine to their left, so close to the narrow track, they are touching on shaky. He has never been a great fan of heights.

'What about it?' asks Swarts.

'Bloody sunshine one minute, fog and rain the next.'

'They say it's Saddam and the Americans who've screwed up our weather,' says Swarts. 'Warmest winter we've ever had. The bugs weren't all killed by the cold, and now malaria is slowly creeping up the escarpment. Down towards Durban, too, that's what they say. Cholera in our water, Aids blimming everywhere . . . I'm telling you, Bond, there's no future here but pestilence.'

The station commissioner nods sagely. 'This weather, she's two months early now. Not a good sign.'

'Reminds me of when Moses called up the plague in Egypt.' Swarts fishes out a silver hipflask, unscrews its top and offers it to Harry. 'Time to head for the Promised Land is what I say.'

Harry nods at the flask. 'You sure that's a good idea?'

Swarts offers him a broken smile. 'Nothing's sure, Bond, not any more. But I can assure you that it'll keep you warm and calm the nerves a bit. A drop might do you good.'

'No thanks. Maybe later.'

'Suit yourself, city slicker.' Swarts takes a shot that makes him gasp and he thumps his chest with a fist. 'Take that! Makes you wonder, all these signs, doesn't it? What's the Almighty trying to tell us, hey?'

'No, you mustn't think like that.' Moqomo shakes his head. 'This is a good place.'

'Bullshit, my friend,' says Swarts. 'That's what everyone says who's too lazy to get out of here. I'm *gatvol*. Got my eye on better things. Civilized work.'

'Like what?' asks Harry.

'I'd rather not say till I know which side of the fence you're standing on, my friend.'

Harry decides to ignore this comment, and turns his eyes back towards the steep incline on his side of the car, but not before he notices Swarts shake his head. '*Ja*, what can you do, hey?'

The pick-up's engine suddenly whines as it hits a patch of soft sand and the tyres lose their grip. To Harry's alarm the car begins a slow slide towards the abyss clearly visible from his window.

'Moqomo!' barks Swarts.

'Don't worry! I've got it.'

Far below, white water is churning against jagged boulders the size of houses. The engine screams as the wheels spin out of control in the sand and their slide quickens.

'Christ, I thought this was a four-by-four!' yells Swarts.

'It is!'

'Then get the goddamned thing under control!'

Rocks shoot out from underneath the pick-up and bound over the edge of the track to plunge down the side of the canyon into the foaming river.

'I've got it!'

Somehow Moqomo manages to swing them back into the middle of the road, fortunately without over-compensating and throwing them into another slew, this time to the right. Behind them the other vehicles seem to have negotiated the same slippery patch with relative ease.

Swarts bursts out laughing and digs a sharp elbow into Harry's side. 'Will you look at that, Bond?'

He takes a long draught from the hipflask before handing it to the local commander. 'Well done, sir! That was blimming well *done*.'

Harry forces himself to relax his grip on the plastic safety handle above his head. 'How the hell did they get a bulldozer up here to scrape this shitty track in the first place?' he asks.

Moqomo bursts out laughing. 'I don't think they've ever seen the bulldozer up here.' He takes a swig from the flask, leaving only one hand on the unsteady steering wheel. 'Horses and donkeys, they have those aplenty, and the two feet God gave us all. But that's it.'

The station commissioner hands the hipflask back to its owner, then flicks on the windscreen wipers. Dust and moisture on the window soon turn into a brown slush that reduces their visibility to near zero. With a growing sense of unease, Harry watches a dense bank of fog roll in under the distant mountain crags, blanketing the foothills up ahead. Heavy static suddenly screeches from the police radio, momentarily drowning out the engine's din. It is the helicopter pilot: the sudden change in the weather has made it impossible for their air surveillance to continue any further inland. They are turning back to base.

'I don't like the sound of that,' remarks Harry as Swarts replaces the receiver.

'*Ag*, they were just back-up anyway, in case the cache left the village before we could get to it. These *dagga* farmers have hiding-places all over the escarpment.'

Despite the lightness in his voice, Harry can see disappointment in the superintendent's face. With all the resources that have been pumped into the operation, the top brass back in Johannesburg are expecting results.

'I just hope our walkie-talkies work in this fine English weather.'

'Will you relax, Mason?' says Swarts. 'This is a search-and-seizure, not a blimming tactical assault. It's not like we haven't done it a hundred times before.' Scratching under his blue bulletproof vest, with SAPS stamped on to it in bold gold letters, he adds, 'At least the fog will mask the sound of that Casspir a bit.'

Harry's mobile vibrates in his pocket and he fishes it out to check the incoming message.

'You still getting reception up here, Bond?'

'Shouldn't happen,' mumbles the commissioner.

The inbox on his phone blinks open.

I love you. Be careful.

Smiling to himself, Harry pockets the phone without considering how important a reply might be.

For no apparent reason Swarts suddenly laughs out

loud. 'Don't you love it, hey?' he remarks to no one in particular and shakes his head. 'To hell with it. To hell with all of us.'

Harry thinks that a curious thing to say. Even for the Supe.

4

Harry had been running late for his last lunch date before he left for the Eastern Cape. They were meeting at Route 69, an American-style diner in the leafy suburb of Greenside, Johannesburg. Flustered, he stormed into the restaurant, almost getting the flowers he had picked up on the way caught in the closing door. The place was done up in the classic style of 1950s America – all chrome and booths and red-and-blue counter chairs. On the walls were mounted giant photographs of the American West's endless highways – Nevada, Arizona, California – along with the grilles of Buicks, Plymouths and Mustangs. Waiters clothed in air force-style caps and pressed white aprons loudly conveyed orders which mingled with the clamour of a roiling restaurant and the rockabilly music of Buddy Holly and Jerry Lee Lewis banging out of speakers everywhere.

'Hey, officer, over here!'

Ignoring the many faces that suddenly turned towards him, Harry felt a bolt of joy hit him square in the chest as he spotted a lean woman with wild black hair tamed only by a bright orange sash. She waved him over to a booth underneath an oversized, airbrushed Elvis, doing his twist in a sequinned white jumpsuit.

'Sorry I'm late. The bloody—'

Two palms cupped his face and pulled him closer for a

quick kiss on the nose, then on the mouth. Tanya Fouché laughed and ruffled his hair as though he were ten years old.

'Look at you! That hair of yours is always standing up in all directions. Are you sure criminals take you seriously? And these, they're for me? Harry, they're beautiful! Just look at them!'

He slid into the seat opposite her and she continued talking away. He did not mind at all. He was happy to keep silence and listen to her lilting voice.

They had met only four months before, at a jazz club in Newtown, where the legendary Willie Pick was giving a rare solo blues performance. Neither had been expecting the sudden attraction that bloomed between them. The crowded venue might as well have thrown a glaring spotlight on just the two of them – that is how much attention they paid to anything else going on. Tired acquaintances eventually began to desert the table's wreckage of empty beer bottles, spilled wine and overflowing ashtrays, but the two of them went on jabbering, unwilling to let go of this moment's magic. When the stark fluorescent lights were finally thrown on, and staff began sweeping up cigarette butts and empty beer bottles around their feet, Harry had walked Tanya to her car, which was parked two blocks away, at the Market Theatre. There they had clumsily hugged and said their reluctant goodbyes. A week later he plucked up enough courage to give her a call, and discovered that she had been waiting for it.

Tanya interrupted his reminiscing. 'So when am I meeting that little sweetheart of yours?' she asked between mouthfuls of a tyre-sized monkey-gland burger.

'I don't know. When would be a good time for you?'

'Now that's the problem, isn't it?' Tanya looked up at

the ceiling. 'Jeez, this week's a bit hectic. I'm still fighting with Isaacson to get funding from the local council for the kids.'

'Tell me about it. This bloody operation I'm on is bleeding me dry for time.'

'Oh – my – God!' Tanya held a hand over her mouth in mock surprise. 'Harry, we're not putting this off, are we? Jesus, we *are*, aren't we?'

He thought about it. He had not yet told Jeanie about Tanya; but that was because he had not been sure of how things would turn out, and not because he did not want his ten-year-old daughter to meet her. He did not want to shake Jeanie's life up unnecessarily; there had been too much of that in recent years. Or at least that's what he kept telling himself.

'I guess we could be.'

The air in the restaurant suddenly felt stifling with the smell of fried onions and the throb of people. They were heading into uncertain territory here, which he had been carefully skirting these last two weeks. In truth, he was still enjoying the freshness of what he had going with Tanya right now. Introducing Jeanie to her? It felt like the encounter would inevitably weigh down the relationship and finally bring everything down from the clouds.

Harry shrugged. 'Yes, we are . . . or I am.'

'When is it that we adults started getting so nervous around kids?'

He thought about this. 'I guess when we realized they're more honest than we are.'

Tanya laughed and wiped her hands with a red-and-white-chequered serviette. 'In that case, we should let our toddlers run for office.'

Harry leaned over, brushed an errant strand of hair

from her face and tucked it behind her ear. 'I guess we could do it next week – maybe Friday night? I'll hopefully be finished with this Tsolo thing by then. How does that sound?'

'Good.' Tanya grabbed his hand and pressed his palm against her warm cheek. 'Dinner and movies?'

'She's always loved going to the cinema.'

Her deep brown eyes grew serious. 'Friday it is then, officer.'

Her fingers tightened around his, and he could feel echoed in their touch the nervousness he himself felt. So far neither of them had admitted it, but Jeanie's opinion of Tanya would be their relationship's first real test.

'When are you due back from the Eastern Cape?' she asked.

'Wednesday, at the latest. It all depends on whether we find what we're looking for right away.'

'Can I call you while you're down there? I mean, you won't be upset if someone says "I love you" over the phone while a tent full of beer-swilling policemen are listening in?'

Harry smiled. 'No, I won't. But I don't think there's any phone reception where I'm going.'

Tanya touched her upper lip with the tip of her tongue and winked at him. 'Any chance I can tempt an officer of the law into my den of iniquity tonight?'

He winked back at her, with a foolish grin on his face. 'As much as this detective here would love to be corrupted by a woman like you, there's my daughter to think of. I won't see her for a week, so I have to go home, OK?'

She pouted like a spoiled teenager who can't get her way, and sighed. 'Fine, but that means I have first dibs when you get back.'

'Deal.'

'You be careful out there, you hear? And I'll see you next Friday.'

5

Harry shakes his head at this memory. He is already missing Tanya's laughter. It is the kind of exuberant guffaw which women of his mother's generation likened to the sound of a harbour whore hitting the jackpot, but for him it is the sound of a new and liberating joy.

'Looks like shit out there,' Swarts interrupts his train of thought.

'*Ja*,' agrees Moqomo.

By now the fog has completely enveloped the convoy and turned the world beyond into little more than a roiling grey barrier. With only about a metre of dirt track visible ahead, they can neither see nor hear the outriders moving ahead on their scramblers. A little while back, Moqomo had slowed their advance to a crawl, whilst Swarts turned down the heater, as if by doing so he could better sense their position within the hostile landscape. Harry glances over at the local station commissioner, a man who has spent the greater part of his life either herding cattle in these hills or patrolling them on foot in search of stock thieves. His face, which had been so jocular an hour ago, now looks drawn. Swarts has remained silent awhile now, though still taking regular nips from his hipflask.

Harry scans the mist behind them for the rest of their column, but spots nothing, not even a headlight.

'What are you thinking, Bond?'

Before he can answer the radio flares up.

17

'You, wallah, come in!' It is Naidoo, who is bringing up the rear with Franklin and Combrink in a four-wheel-drive. 'How long is this going to go on for, hey? You waiting till someone *bliksems* off this cliff before you call a halt, man?'

Swarts reaches for the transmitter. 'Are you going soft on us back there, Sammy? I'm almost a decade older than you and I'm sitting here cosy as St Peter on a cloud.' He winks at Harry, but the gesture seems a little forced.

'Well, St bloody Peter, you can't see the rockslides being caused by this fucking Casspir ahead of us. Whose idea was that thing anyway, hey?'

'Calm down, Sammy.'

'Hey, fuck you, Russie! I was born in a city; I'm not some *plaasjapie*, man. I didn't take this job to fuck down some cliff and die in a puddle of mud and cowshit. You call a halt, wallah, or I'm *walking* back.'

Harry winces. Not many lower-ranking police officers would call Swarts anything but Supe, even when they've worked with him for a few years, let alone swear at him. But then, Naidoo and the Supe have known each other a long time now, ever since they were partners in the narcs.

Swarts laughs out loud. 'I've seen you take three bullets in the line of duty and now you're telling me you're afraid of heights?'

'Hey!' yells Naidoo. 'You hear that? That's the car door opening, you know? I'm out of here, you hear me? I'm gone.'

A red scrambler suddenly leaps to a halt in front of them, and Moqomo nearly collides with the outrider. Though the soldier sitting astride it does nothing more than rev the accelerator, the questioning tilt of his head and the persistence of his gaze seem to confer one clear message: *Do you seriously expect us to drive on in* this?

As abruptly as he appeared the soldier is gone again, with a raggedy scream from the motorbike's small engine.

Swarts grimaces. 'I'm not abandoning this operation, not after getting this far. Christ, I crawled on my knees to that blimming national commissioner of ours to get this raid off the ground!'

'If we leave this till tomorrow, there'll be nothing to confiscate, not even a matchbox of *dagga*,' Harry agrees. 'And then we won't have any leverage on the Abasindisi.'

Swarts turns to the Maclear station commissioner. 'Moqomo, what do you think? Can we go ahead on foot?'

The man's response is quick, as if the suggestion has been hovering on his lips for the past hour. 'Yes. This track, it will only get worse from here.'

Grabbing the police radio, Swarts passes the order to halt down the column. 'Let's hope those *troepies* up in the hills are still all right, and haven't been turned into popsicles in this blimming weather.'

'I'm sure the soldiers are fine, Supe.'

Harry makes to get out, but a hand grabs his shoulder. He turns back to find Swarts staring at him with a frustrated look of appeal twisting up a face not used to asking favours. 'What?' he asks.

Swarts lets go of him and pats him on the back. 'Nothing, captain. We're going to bag this one together, right?'

'I thought that was the idea,' replies Harry.

'*Ja.*' Swarts slides out of the driver's side of the car. 'It was.'

The task team piles out of its vehicles, and when all

the engines have been switched off and the doors have slammed shut even the soldiers are taken aback by the sudden impenetrable silence. Only the thin wavering whistle of a chill wind driving the fog over sharp cliffs can be heard. To them, it is the sound of danger waiting, the sound of eyes watching, and it does not sit well with any of them.

6

This investigation into a triple homicide in Diepsloot had progressed at a snail's pace, and it had frustrated Harry no end. Being the first complex case he had been assigned in the SVC, which normally worked in tightly knit task teams, Harry had hoped to show his superiors that he was up to the job after a five-year absence from the police service. He quickly realized, however, that he had underestimated the investigation's sophistication, even with the likely suspects already identified. Statements from the victims' neighbours regarding the night of the petrol bombing were conflicting, and the mysterious address on the case docket's cover had led to an open stretch of dirt where a shack had literally been packed up overnight, the recent occupant unknown to his neighbours by any other name than simply 'Jonas from Mayflower'. In the mean time, one witness withdrew his statement, claiming that he was far too drunk that night to properly recall what happened, while another two had totally vanished by the time Swarts first lobbed the docket on to Harry's desk. All this because the first officer on the scene had neglected to take down contact details for the witnesses. The case's rapid degeneration did not come as much of a surprise to Harry, who had seen enough of these investigative flaws during his stint in Murder and Robbery: uniforms screwing up a detective's chances of solving a case, either by forgetting to grab witnesses or by riding roughshod over the crime scene. Investigators were still laughing about the fingers floating in a peanut-butter jar of formaldehyde on a particular techie's windowsill at the Silverton forensics labs. They had been cut off and sent in by a uniform after he had been asked to preserve the fingerprints found at the crime scene.

Point was, three months down the line, without witnesses nor a shred of evidence other than three bodies on ice in the morgue, Harry had walked into Swarts' office ready to admit that the first investigation on which he had acted as primary detective was also his first real stinker in the SVC.

'Ah!' three jovial voices had cried in unison. 'Look who's here!'

Supe Russell Swarts, he recalled, had his feet up on his desk, near a soft-focus portrait photo of his two teenage sons flanking their regal mother. Captain James 'Blondie' Franklin was leaning against one wall, a heel propped up against it. One hand held a skin rag he had been flicking through; the other cupped a pipe stuck in his mouth. Unlike other detectives in the unit, who preferred to carry their weapons discreetly, he wore his holstered pistol as prominently as possible, slung low around his waist. Captain Combrink, known as 'Kommie' to the clan, was seated next to Naidoo in one of the visitors' chairs. They were a stark contrast: Combrink was so pasty-faced white that it looked like he had varicose veins around his eyes, which were magnified by thick plastic-rimmed glasses. Naidoo, on the other hand, was overweight and amorphous, and still lived with his parents, because his mother could not yet find a suitable bride for him. Together these four men formed the core of the Johannesburg Central SVC Unit, and as far as Harry could tell they had more arrests between them than the rest of the entire unit. The Ballies, they were called: the old-timers. It was not so much their age that had acquired them the name, nor was it the length of their experience in the unit; it was more a sign of respect for their dedication to the job.

'Come in.' Franklin had waved impatiently with the end of his pipe. 'We were just talking about old Naidoo here. Seems he was never blooded – what do you make of that?'

Blooded. Harry had not heard that term in a while. Yet around the time when he was recruited, back in '85, it was a commonplace expression within the specialized units, and referred to a rite of passage in which senior officers often encouraged their subordinates to kill a suspect, more often than not black, in order to prove themselves tough enough, *dependable* enough, to belong to the élite. It was a pact in blood that bound together police officers of a certain breed, and if rookies did not handle the pressure well, or if they did not make the kill, their careers in the specialized units were likely over before they even began.

The sudden air of expectation in the room discomforted Harry, so he thought it prudent to focus on Naidoo. 'You've been shot in the line of duty, what, three times?'

The captain looked relieved at this question; it was familiar ground. 'All in one night. .38 Special. Junkie fucked up on angel dust it was – remember that, Russie? Running around naked in Eloff Street with the gun in his hand, he had piss and shit running down his legs like he was a blocked toilet. What was he screaming? Something about the devil coming for him, out of the ground. Kept waving his piece at the tarmac. Remember that, *boet*? I remember a pair of fucking vets trying to dart him with enough ketamine to bring down a rhino, once he started shooting. Isn't that right, Russie?'

Franklin shook his head with a lopsided grin on his face but said nothing. Instead, his eyes stayed fixed on the centrefold he was admiring. To Harry it seemed like a condescending gesture.

Naidoo noticed it too. 'Hey, I don't wish that on anyone, not even you, ugly. That shit *hurt*. Eight months in bed with a colostomy bag strapped to your side, a nurse the size of a hippo wiping your butt like you've just come out of your mother's womb – it screws you up, *boet*. No jokes. I've paid my dues.'

'Sing hallelujah to that,' says Swarts.

'And you're still here? You're not working for some fly-by-night security company?' Harry smiled and shrugged. 'Sounds to me like he earned his badge better than most.'

There was uproarious laughter all round and Harry felt relief that he had sidestepped any talk of rites of passage. Whoever these four guys were, and whichever units they came from to end up here, their reputation for closing cases spoke louder than words, and often hushed up criticism too. He met Swarts' eyes, who gave a slight nod, as if to say he had given the right answer to some test.

Combrink pushed a bent pair of spectacles up his nose with a middle finger. As always, he had a sweaty sheen to his face. It had to do with his glands, Swarts once informed Harry, and it was also why he smelled like a fast-food outlet.

'The idea is to shoot the bastards, not to get shot,' he said in a lumbering Afrikaans accent.

'Sure, shooting is better than getting shot any day.' Swarts raised his voice without taking his eyes off Harry. 'But a man that takes a bullet and sticks to his guns is a better man than the one who's never felt pain in the line of duty.'

Turning back to Franklin, Harry asked, 'Were *you*?'

'Me? What, blooded?' The tip of his pipe stayed firmly clenched between his teeth. 'Hell, Mason, what kind of a question is that?'

He unbuttoned the cuff of his right arm and rolled up the sleeve to his elbow. On his forearm was a faded but unmistakable Airborne tattoo. 'Did all the killing I ever wanted up in Angola before I joined the force, thank you very much.'

The Ballies again roared with laughter, and Harry had to wonder why they were in such high spirits.

'What can I help you with, Bond? You look like you ate something bad.'

Harry had then briefed Swarts and the clan on the ice-cold Mohosh case. When he finished, a brief silence hung in the room.

'Well, gents, what do you think?' Swarts pulled his feet off the desk and looked at each of his crew in turn, an excited glint in his eyes that could not be ignored.

Combrink was the first to speak. 'Sounds like Bond's got a hard nut to crack here.'

'Better to bust his nuts than mine, hey, Kommie?'

Naidoo indicated Harry. 'Why don't *you* take this nut's case and stay off mine?'

'I'm not enough of a nutcase to do that. I take that docket from him, my performance scorecard is likely to be worth less than the paper I wipe my arse with.'

Franklin snorted as he packed his pipe with fresh tobacco.

'Sounds like they got us this time.' Swarts leaned forward and gazed conspiratorially around the room. 'Now, if you arseholes could just shut up one second, I think we should try this . . .'

Harry felt grateful that his commander talked about the Mohosh case as the team's problem and not his own failure, which he had half expected, and as he listened to the superintendent he was taken by how neatly the man dressed the problematic situation up as a minor setback, not the dead-end Harry had thought it was. The Supe's plan was expansive, and likely to stop a lot more killing than just the arrest of two or three who would most likely walk anyway, given the circumstantial evidence. To him, this was not about the Mohosh family's killers any more; whatever group had committed the triple homicide, they had clearly irritated Swarts enough for him to want to go after every single vigilante organization on the Rand, one at a time.

It was proactive policing at its best. For, as Swarts liked to put it, 'a good handyman always keeps his work-shop clean, because if his shit's left lying around, he can only blame himself for when he finally slips in it and takes a fall'.

Swarts continued: 'We know who the perpetrators are most likely affiliated to, so we go after the Abasindisi first.

They duck and dive, we follow them; they want to cause shit with us, we shake them down every time one of them so much as picks his nose in public. We stick to the ones we know by name like flypaper, until they burrow so deep underground they either land up in hell or their bosses decide to cut their losses and throw them to us. If we can't catch the killers and can't prove it was the Abasindisi who ordered the killing, then we blimming well keep bullying them till they make a mistake.'

Franklin struck a match, which caught everybody's attention. 'Sounds like fun. Might even be able to put some time aside for this one. But we need to convince Molethe it's worth it. I'm not doing this operation on a shoestring.'

'Director Molethe will go for it.' The decisive way Swarts said this invited no argument. It was a good strategy, coming from a police officer considered a legend for his work in the now defunct South African Narcotics Bureau. Harry had occasionally wondered why this man who had won the Best Detective Award three times in as many years was still only a senior superintendent, but then he had heard about the time Swarts had been hitting a bottle of Richelieu a little too hard at an awards ceremony held at the new Sheraton Hotel in Pretoria. It was a big affair: the media, the national commissioner, the Minister of Safety and Security were all there. Rumour had it that the commissioner had confronted Swarts about his disgraceful display of public drinking, on which Swarts had shoved him backwards and replied loudly, 'And you, *groot kokkedoor*, have a disgracefully small brain, about as big as my left testicle in fact!'

This comment had made front-page headlines in just about every newspaper from Cape Town to Mussina, and it had got Swarts suspended for six months.

The superintendent was an icon for the shock troops of policing, not one likely to appeal to the top brass and polit- icos who spent their time on endless *lekgotlas* – strategic meetings far removed from the office – where they haggled over crime-prevention policies that took six years to come into effect. The only thing that probably saved Swarts' skin that evening at the Sheraton was the Lifetime Achievement Award he had picked up. At forty-eight, Russell Swarts became the youngest cop ever to receive it.

This, and maybe the fact that his partner was shorn in half by a bomb blast in Cape Town, two weeks prior to the event. The officers had been wrapping up a two-year investigation into a massive shipment of Mandrax destined for Hard Livings territories in the townships when the gang had decided a courtesy call on the two detectives was necessary . . .

Combrink broke into Harry's train of thought. 'They've already proved more slippery than eels, so what makes you think we're going to make their lives any more difficult than this case will make ours?'

'Kommie, in the famous words of Captain Kirk: We make it so.' Swarts stood up and came around his desk to knead Combrink's shoulders. 'Since I trust old Bond here when he claims that our killers are long gone from Diep- sloot, we'll start off with a little chat to the suspected Abasindisi we already have behind bars.'

A sudden thought struck Harry. 'I might have a better idea.'

'Whoa!' Franklin grinned. 'And suddenly he comes up with a cunning new angle, where he couldn't before. Speak up, Bond. We're all ears.'

Harry ignored him. 'Most of the Abasindisi are miners, right?'

'On the money,' said Combrink. He looked strangely sheepish with his perpetually bent spectacles and Swarts' big hands massaging his shoulders.

'I think I know someone who can help us,' said Harry, though he still did not know how he would ever persuade Makhe Motale to do just that.

Last time he had seen the man, back in 2000, his bruisers had Harry's face thrust down in the dirt while two greedy Rottweilers snuffled at his crotch. As Makhe had held a switchblade to Harry's eye, his message had been clear: '*Suka*, pork chop, while you still can. There's no place in Alexandra for a pig like you.'

'Like I said, Mason, we're listening,' said Franklin through a haze of blue pipe smoke, despite the strict rules banning smoking in the building.

And so Harry expanded.

7

Half an hour's walk behind, the scramblers have been left abandoned with all the other vehicles prior to their long march to Tsolo. Looking up from his plodding boots, Harry notices he is trailing right behind the local station commissioner, who had seemed more than willing to play a supportive role to the out-of-town SVC team. To one side the soldiers proceed in an alert group, and only Swarts' Ballies seem to be in high spirits. They are invisible in the fog, but Harry can hear their occasional boisterous laughter as they walk ahead of the column, and it seems Swarts is not the only one carrying a hip-flask.

Like a bunch of bloody punters off to a rugby match, he thinks.

He has worked with a number of cops who took their courage from a bottle. As far as he is concerned, it comes with the territory, and he would rather have a level-headed drunk at his side than a nervous twitch who might gun him down in a flash of panic. Yet the point at which the drunkard becomes the twitch is a question he has never fully considered, until right now.

'Hey, Mason!' Naidoo's bark pierces the nimbus of mist. 'You think this is some kind of Boy Scout outing? Up front, *boet*. The Supe himself commands it.'

'Make it so!' yodels Franklin, who is the only one among them not wearing a bulletproof vest. 'No point in wearing something that turns you into a turtle,' Franklin once explained, just before following a tactical squad into a speed factory run by triads in Westdeen. 'If it's your time, it's your time. A chunk of ceramic isn't going to change that.'

'You really want to let them know we're coming, then go on yelling like that,' Harry responds in a lower tone.

'No point in worrying about that any more,' comes a reply, though the fog makes it difficult to guess who is speaking.

Stopping a moment, Harry adjusts the bulletproof vest which is chafing his armpits raw.

'He said, get up here, Bond!' hollers Franklin, and there is a bite to his voice. 'Aren't you the blimmin' investigating officer?'

The squad of soldiers throw Harry a withering glance as he passes them.

'Captain Mason, do you reckon you can get them to shut the fuck up before we all get caught in an ambush?' asks Lieutenant Moraal.

'Easy now,' is all he can say in reply.

'If I knew we'd be going into this with a bunch of *mamparas*, I'd have—'

Harry loses the rest of the lieutenant's complaint as he quickly regains the lost ground and finds himself up front with Swarts, and an unruly welcome from the rest of the clan. Up close, Harry can see that the Supe's face is flushed red from a combination of brandy, exertion and cold weather.

'Can we lay off the booze a bit there? I don't think this is exactly the time for it.'

Franklin collides heavily against him. 'Fuck's that, Bond?'

His powder-blue eyes appear clearer than crystal, without the alcoholic blur Harry might have expected, and it occurs to him it might all be a bit of an act.

'You trying to patronize us?' calls Naidoo. 'Because, shit, if you are, you'd want to think about it twice.'

Harry flashes Naidoo a scornful look, which causes the man to blink in surprise and turn away.

'Gentlemen.' Swarts hooks his own flask back into his belt and gives it a reassuring pat. They wait for him to say more but, when it seems that nothing else is forthcoming, Harry notices Combrink tuck his flask away too.

Thereafter an abrupt silence falls over the trudging column, so that Harry is reminded of a funeral procession. Without the endless nattering, the dense fog seems to draw in like an ever-tightening noose. Before long he realizes that the yakking might have served a purpose in keeping the gloom at bay.

Suddenly a single rifle shot cracks in the distance. The entire party immediately pulls up short and listens. But the brief sound is quickly gobbled up by the smoky dawn light and leaden silence.

'Where did that come from?' Swarts eventually asks.

'Can't tell for sure,' replies Harry. 'That was a heavy calibre – R1, you think, Franklin?'

The rest of the Ballies draw close.

'R5, I reckon.' Franklin taps his pipe against the butt of his holstered pistol. 'Lighter weapon, that.'

'How do you know?' asks Combrink. 'It was just one shot.'

'I just know.'

'Wasn't anywhere nearby,' remarks Swarts.

'Could be someone out hunting,' adds Naidoo.

'Hunting with an R5? In this weather?' Combrink pulls out a handkerchief and polishes his misty glasses. '*Jirre*, someone get this guy some toilet paper so he can wipe his chin with all the shit he's talking.'

'Hush.' Swarts' expression is distant as he chews over what to do next.

From behind the halted troop, Moqomo appears through a thick swirl of fog, his men trailing him closely. He looks worried.

'Superintendent Moqomo, let me hear from you,' Swarts demands.

'People should have met us by now. The first building, it's up ahead, maybe just two hundred metres.'

'If that was a warning shot to let the village know we're coming, we might as well go home,' says Combrink. 'In this mess, their weapons and *dagga* will be long gone. There's no chance of us tracking them either.'

'Speak for yourself, Kommie,' says Franklin. 'I'll find

31

them for us, Russie – if the boys in the hills don't pick them up first.'

Swarts nods but does not reply. Instead, his hand drifts towards the flask at his belt, but at the last moment it falls short of pulling it out.

'Our men coming in from the north should stop anyone leaving the village in that direction,' calls out the sergeant who was giving Harry a bleak look. He is a stocky African, with black pock marks along his jawline. His eyes now seem to glitter with an enthusiasm that smacks of trigger-happiness.

Swarts laughs. 'Sergeant, I did exactly this kind of thing for four years. Those *plattelandse boytjies* of yours, fresh out of Klipdrift Base, they don't know the first thing about these mountains. The entire village could be running circles around us not fifty metres away, and we won't know it.'

'We can't go back now,' says Harry. 'At least let's go show the bastards we're on to them.'

'Aye,' says Franklin, 'I second that.'

'We'd better go in slowly, then. Announce to them that we're coming.' There is an edge to Combrink's voice, and the familiar sheen of sweat on his face has become downright soggy. 'I don't know about any of you, but I'd rather see them run than get ambushed myself.'

'What?' says Naidoo. 'You *okes* crazy?' He turns to Swarts. 'Russie, we can come back tomorrow for this, man. It's not worth it, you know?'

Harry picks up a stone and throws it deep into the fog. Even the *clop* of it striking the track ahead is muted. 'Fog like this, they can't necessarily see we're police. And Kommie's right, taking into account that for the last six months this bunch has been attacking, or been attacked by, this or that village, if we don't let them know who we are, we're just another group of hostiles in the mist. Whatever's stashed up there, they're more likely to try and smuggle it out if they know we're the police, rather than simply open indiscriminate fire on us.'

'You hope,' Naidoo mutters glumly.

Franklin hawks loudly and spits over to one side. 'Naidoo, I can't remember now, did you get shot in the front or in the back? 'Cause if it was in the back, I don't think it was because someone tried to ambush you.'

'Hey, fuck you, Blondie.'

The twisted grin spreading over Franklin's face is surprisingly cruel, and in that moment Harry does not find it hard to imagine this man running around deep in the Angolan bush as a soldier with his face painted like he is some kind of Captain Willard.

'We could wait it out, see if the fog clears,' says Swarts without conviction.

'We don't know how scared they are,' says Moraal. 'And that makes them unpredictable – and dangerous as hell.'

Swarts scratches his beard a moment, still not quite willing to meet anyone else's eyes. By now the entire task team has gathered tight around him, like footballers swarming around their coach at half-time.

'Lieutenant Moraal, have you been able to contact your *troepies* up north yet?'

'No, sir. This mist has fritzed our communications. But they're under orders to sit tight in their last positions till they hear more from us.'

'Which means they could be anywhere, for all we know.' Swarts claps his hands. 'Right then, here's what's going to happen. We might, we might not, miss grabbing those weapons if we go in now making a racket, but if we go in tomorrow, or even this afternoon, it'll be a certainty they're gone. I'll be honest and tell you all, the bosses back in Jozi will have way too many uncomfortable questions for me to handle about a failed operation that has already overshot its budget. Chief Molethe's certainly not going to dance on a hotplate on my account. So we go in now, and we go in loud, because no one's getting shot on my watch just because we tried to surprise them. Is that all right with you all? Any objections, speak up now.'

There is a rumble of agreement. Franklin strikes a match and puffs again at his pipe.

'Let it be one of you whiteys calling out to them, then.' There is a distinct edge to Moqomo's voice that wasn't there before. 'They won't trust a black man shouting "Police". The ambushes these last few weeks, they have made sure of this. They'll shoot anyone they think may come from one of the other villages.'

Naidoo seems about to say something further, but bites it back at a sharp glance from Franklin. His eyes flick from one to another before he lights a cigarette and stalks off silently.

'Let's go then.' Franklin unclips the strap securing his pistol and heads on up the track. 'I'm getting hungry.'

8

At first Harry had not known anything about the cache of guns buried in Tsolo, or even much about the Phaliso brothers who allegedly ran the Abasindisi organization. That information began to unfold in late February after he drove into Alexandra by himself one overcast day, looking for the man who had threatened to kill him the next time their paths crossed.

So there he was, a single white cop blundering into a black township with a population the size of most small cities, all packed into an area the size of an average uptown neighbourhood. As always, he felt like the one black sheep sticking out in a bleach-white flock, when visiting a place like this.

Every township surrounding Johannesburg has its own character: Soweto is an eclectic mix of rich and poor, vibrant and with a famous history; Thokoza and Kathlehong are little more than rough, brow-beaten mining townships. Then there are the ironically colonial-sounding 'villes': Troyville, Slovoville, Dobsonville ... Leachville near the leaching gold-mine tailings, Payneville near the toxic slimes dams, Sharpeville, where the massacre of 21 March 1960 cut a nation to the quick. Then there is Alexandra.

Down London Road it lies, close to Johannesburg's eastern industrial complex, Wynberg, and the vast garbage heaps on the airport side of the N3 freeway, over which hangs a perpetual cloud of scavenging seagulls that seem to have forgotten how far inland they have flown. Some call it the slum of slums, others call it home because here, as they do elsewhere, children play on the few grassy patches along the River Jukskei – river by African standards but little more than a trickle compared to European waterways. Families live here; teachers educate; friends meet in dusty yards and open spaces to drink and eat and sing songs to the clap of hands, the thumping of feet on the earth, the slightly off-beat sound of ancient big-band instruments handed down from father to son, son to grandson. Here, as elsewhere, the hive of humanity makes itself heard. There is tragedy, there is romance, there are people who call to each other by their first names. Nothing different about that in the end. Nothing strange or exotic. Just people.

This was where Harry went looking for Makhe Motale, whose life he had saved during a blazing riot in the autumn of '87, back when he was still a rookie uniformed policeman of the already collapsing apartheid state.

Parking his police-issue white Mazda on the cemetery side of a collapsed bridge over a treacly stretch of the river, Harry got out and slammed the car door shut behind him. Surveying the Jukskei's banks for the best place to cross into the warren of shacks on the other side, he saw that they were both coated with tons of trash dragged into the township from Johannesburg's centre by the savage annual summer thunderstorms. However, a little way off to the left, a well-worn path led down the eastern bank to a line of cement slabs jutting out of the shallow water, which he hoped he could use to cross to the other side.

It did not take long for a single white police officer, standing by a white car with SAPS stamped in blue on its doors, to attract some attention. Two young heavies eventually appeared on the opposite side of the river, each with an excited Rottweiler straining at its chain-link leash. Down a broken stretch of asphalt they proceeded, towards the edge of the fallen bridge – which many of the residents preferred to see in ruins because it formed a natural fortification against unwanted police vehicle patrols. For a brief moment Harry wondered what he would do if they let those dogs loose, and suddenly the pistol clipped into his faded jeans at his back felt a lot more comforting.

The two men pulled up their hounds at the point where

the ruined carriageway dipped into the water. One of them eventually waved him over. Whether it was an invitation to a palaver or a beating he could not tell, but he accepted the gesture anyway.

9

Ahead, the first shack looms through the cold fog. It has been patched together with a variety of recycled materials, not unlike the buildings back in Alexandra's shantytown. Built on a grassy knoll to the left of the access track, it gives every impression of being a watchtower. Green and red flags, hanging limply from long thin reed-poles, appear and disappear through the mist, while an empty doorway looks like a black maw opening in a silent scream. Harry calls out, first in English then in Afrikaans, but no answer is forthcoming. All he hears is the *clang-clang, clang-clang* of a nearby cow-bell, like a buoy lost far out at sea. After Moqomo follows up the same warning in Xhosa, they wait a full minute before the commander shakes his head.

'Something, she is definitely wrong,' he says. 'Where are the children? After all the noise we have been making, the young men of the village, they should have been here with the elders to meet us.'

'Even if they're dope growers?' asks Harry.

'Yes.'

He silently studies the building. Brownish smoke is pouring from a twisted old paint can on the roof which has been converted into a chimney. 'Someone should at least be tending the fire inside.'

The wind whispers through unseen long grass, sometimes pitching high enough to sound like a whistle, other times dropping low enough to resemble an animal howl, while that lonely cow-bell keeps on clanging.

'That fucking thing's going to drive me mad,' says Swarts.

Harry nods, knowing the Supe's complaint is not so much about the solitary bell as the feeling that they are being watched. 'Settlement like this should have at least a dozen dogs barking at us.'

'You really think they'd try to ambush us?' asks Naidoo.

'Is that a problem for you?'

It is the first time since Harry began working with him that Franklin looks under strain.

'Easy does it,' says Harry. 'This might be an Abasindisi stronghold, but that doesn't mean everyone is an active member. By the looks of the place, they're more likely dope farmers on the verge of starvation.'

'All the more reason for them to be shooting at us, Bond,' says Naidoo.

Swarts pats Naidoo on the shoulder. 'We've been through this before, men. We knew we were likely to be walking into a shitstorm, but we did it anyway. So let's see this through.'

Two more steps up the track abruptly become two steps in the wrong direction. Sudden gunfire rips through the air, immediately followed by a dull *pop* as Moqomo is hit square in the chest. A croak of alarm escapes his lips before he pitches backward, clutching his breastbone.

All around, the men immediately throw themselves into the long grass growing alongside the track. The soldiers meanwhile scatter, instinctively securing point and rear in kneeling positions, their rifles up.

'*Downdowndown!*' Swarts shouts belatedly.

Harry and Franklin grab Moqomo by his armpits and drag him clear of the exposed path, towards where Swarts has ducked behind a large boulder at the base of the steep knoll. By the time the gunfire report has rolled down the hill and silence has returned, the entire task team has positioned itself behind what little cover it can find.

'Where the fuck did that come from!' The 9mm pistol Naidoo is waving towards the mountain's vast expanse looks about as effective as a toothpick. 'Where they coming from, hey? You see 'em? Hey?'

Harry listens to the troops speaking urgently amongst themselves in a language he does not understand, although Lieutenant Moraal seems to follow them well enough.

'They're saying they saw a flash over to the shack's right.'

'Hold all fire!' bellows Swarts.

'What?' shouts Naidoo. 'Are you crazy, wallah?'

Swarts nods towards Moqomo. 'How's he doing?'

Harry and Franklin have already rolled the wounded man over and are desperately probing him. The policeman's eyes are wide open with fear, and there is sweat on his brow and upper lip. His breath comes in ragged hitches, even though his mouth is wide open.

'Where's the entry point!' Franklin fumbles with the zip on the downed man's heavy jacket. 'Christ, can you see it?'

'Nothing!'

Moqomo makes eye contact with Harry and forms a few words through his clenched teeth.

'What was that?' Harry leans over and places his ear to the man's mouth. 'Where do you feel it?'

'Russie, I'm shooting any fuck that shows his face,' yells Naidoo. 'I don't care who it is, I swear.'

'Will you shut up and listen, man!'

'I repeat, hold your fire!' Swarts pats the air with one hand as he peers up at the shack from around the corner of the boulder.

Deep within the nimbus of the fog more gunfire begins to crackle.

'Sir, that might be an engagement with our own troops up to the north.'

'So try get them on the radio again, damn it!'

'Here, what's this?' Franklin fingers a bloodless puncture in Moqomo's windbreaker.

'What is it?' Harry urges Moqomo.

'Chest.' Moqomo's eyes are wild with fear.

Yanking down the zip of the man's windbreaker, Franklin releases a pungent combination of cologne and fresh sweat.

'Well? Is he blimming well going to be all right or not?'

And there, just a centimetre from the rim of ceramic armour plates, is a crumpled 7.62 mm round buried deep in the fabric of the vest.

'Vest stopped it.' Franklin sits back with a sigh of relief. 'Lucky bastard.'

'Time for you to get one, then, isn't it?' Swarts says to him as he shimmies over and slaps the commander's face, with a laugh. To Moqomo he says, 'All right there? Guess that one woke you up a bit, hey?'

Moqomo manages to sit up and shakes his head. '*Hi wena*, it's not funny.'

Swarts turns his eyes back towards the shack, but a fresh bank of mist has now obscured it. 'Damn this fog,' he mumbles under his breath. Then he raises his voice. 'Moraal, can you spot anything from back there?'

'No, sir.'

In the distance the rifle fire escalates. Harry draws his pistol and cocks it. Glancing down the hill, he sees Moraal kneeling next to a trooper, frantically trying to reach the other squads on a bulky military radio.

'I can't see anything,' yells Naidoo. 'We're all going to die if we go on like this.'

'Will you shut up, Sameer!' yells Franklin.

'Lieutenant!' There is relief in the radio operator's voice as he holds the receiver out to Moraal. 'Beta's engaged about two clicks to the north-east. They're pinned down by gunfire from both the south and west.'

'This isn't for us,' says Naidoo in a calmer voice. 'Russie, leave this to the army, man.'

'You *know* we can't do that,' barks Franklin with such sudden vehemence that Harry glances back in alarm, convinced the man is about to assault Naidoo. Franklin seems on the point of adding more, but catches Harry's eye and abruptly swallows his words.

'Fucking coolie arsehole,' he growls and stalks off.

'What did you call me, hey?' Naidoo yells after him. 'I'm talking to you!'

'I said you're a fat piece of shit.'

'Will you two shut up?' roars Swarts. 'Christ, if I knew I was going into the field with a bunch of juveniles, I'd have shot myself and saved these other arseholes the effort.'

Harry double-checks his pistol. To his left Moqomo has loosened his vest to rub at his bruised chest, while two of his team members are bunched around him. He gives Harry a grateful thumbs-up. 'Thank you.'

Harry nods back, knowing that the real deal has not even started yet. 'No problem.'

The hand that claps on Harry's shoulder nearly has

him jump out of his skin. Brandy-reeking breath assaults his nose.

'Easy, *boet*.' Swarts' voice is low and reassuring. 'What do *you* think?'

'What the hell is going on between you four?'

Swarts glances back at Naidoo puffing heavily on a cigarette some way off, while Franklin is in a huddle with Combrink, gesticulating urgently.

'They're just a bit eager,' he says. 'There's a lot riding on this, and you should already know that.'

'Is that all?'

Swarts holds Harry's gaze evenly. 'As far as they are concerned, yes. What else would there be?'

'I don't know. Maybe you tell me.'

'Jesus, Harry, I told you this morning I have your back. Didn't I tell you that?'

Harry probes his superintendent's expression for signs to confirm his own unease, but the bushy features makes it impossible to read what Swarts is thinking.

'I guess so.'

'Good. Now, I meant what do *you* think of the situation?'

Harry turns his gaze to the village ahead, and his mind begins to race through plausible explanations: the single burst fired at them, the army's Beta squad engaged from two different sides further up the mountain, the eerie silence throughout the area. Whichever way he thinks about it he comes up with far too many assumptions and no definite facts to substantiate them. None at all.

'I really don't know. But that wild burst that happened to hit Moqomo was fired by someone who knows nothing about assault rifles, otherwise he could've easily taken him down.'

Swarts shakes his head. 'I don't know either, captain, but my guess is that we would've had a lot more trouble by now if we were the main target. And you're right about the gunman, I reckon. It's probably the village retard, left behind as a diversion while the rest of them head for the hills.'

Moqomo sidles closer. 'If they were thinking the attack, she was coming, the villagers, they would have gone to the caves. Many of those around here.'

'Harry, are you sure your source isn't fucking us over here?'

'Yes, I'm sure.'

'How, though? Who is it, your source?'

He wonders how to tell his commander that the only reason he can be sure is precisely that Makhe Motale hates Harry's guts enough to be honest about this.

'Just trust me,' is all he eventually says.

Franklin gets down next to them on one knee, looking a lot calmer now. A cigarette rather than a pipe plugs his mouth. 'So what do we do now about our sniper?'

'Sir!' Moraal calls out from where he is huddling with his sergeant and the radio operator. 'We still can't reach Alpha, but Beta needs some support.'

'I reckon we let the military guys here go help their own men,' says Harry. 'And then we split up their search quadrants between us.'

'Good idea, Mason.'

'Tactical squad might've been fun, after all.' Swarts shakes his head with regret. 'The helicopter too.'

'This is going to be a long day,' adds Franklin.

Harry feels a fresh kick of adrenalin and grins. 'Come on, Supe,' he says. 'This is old hash for you, surely?'

Superintendent Russell Swarts laughs at Harry's tone,

then slaps his junior about the head. 'And you think these old bones can't do what they used to?'

'Let's see it, old-timer,' replies Harry.

Franklin raises an eyebrow. 'You're a cocky son of a bitch, Mason, I'll give you that.'

Swarts cups a hand to his mouth. 'Lieutenant Moraal, you and yours go after your men. The rest of you, you know the lie of the village, so keep it tight and head for your quadrants. Do *not* engage anyone unless you're fired upon, understood?' Without waiting for any reply he turns to Harry. 'We're sure those weapons are most likely in quads three or four?'

'As sure as I can be.'

'Then let's do it.'

Swarts leaps forward in a half-crouch, nimble as any man ten years his junior. Wordlessly his gang of Ballies falls in behind him, their animosities shed momentarily like water from a raincoat.

Harry, who has opted to stick with Moqomo and his men, watches them go after the sniper with a slight pang of jealousy. There is something about how they move together, as if they are living extensions of each other . . . it makes him miss the days with his Murder and Robbery partner, Jacob Tshabalala.

He turns to the local commander. 'Ready?'

Moqomo smiles jaggedly. '*Yebo.*'

'Then follow me.'

Harry leads the way up the rutted path and breaks east into the village as soon as he can. Within seconds he has lost track of Swarts and his Ballies, and meanwhile the soldiers have disappeared into the fog off to his right. Left alone, the five police officers wander deeper into the collection of abandoned shacks.

10

The side of Harry's head hit the shanty's makeshift corrugated-iron wall hard enough to mash the inside of his cheek against his teeth. Blood welled up inside his mouth as the tallest of Makhe Motale's goons went on twisting his shoulder joint until a groan of pain escaped him. Then he grabbed Harry's hair and yanked his head right back.

'Look at me, *umlungu*,' a voice said quietly.

A man was seated on the bonnet of a rusty Chevrolet's shell, his eyes burning into Harry with the heat of a blast furnace.

'This is a dumb thing to do, Makhe,' said Harry through gritted teeth.

'And just like a stray dog, you seem to come back for one beating after another.' Makhe pulled his crippled legs up on to the car and crossed them by hand. 'You know why we don't eat pork here in Alexandra, English? It's because it smells too much like white man's meat. You fucking *umlungus* all smell like wet watery pork to us. That's why I don't ever leave this place: the constant stench of you in the cities you've built for yourselves would have me gagging all the time.'

'You prefer the smell of that open sewer you call a river, then?' Harry spat blood, which elicited a deep growl from one of the Rottweilers. He glanced at it and saw drool hanging in translucent strands from its black lips. The second heavy – who had patted him down, found his gun and immediately hooked him in the chin – merely grinned. 'Funny, that,' Harry said. 'I see not much has changed here, despite all the hot air.'

His arm was abruptly twisted back and up to a point

where his hand sat right between his shoulderblades. Bright blue sparks fired across his vision, but somehow he managed to bite back a scream.

'You watch what you say to the man.' The heavy's voice carried the weight of a ten-pin bowling ball. 'For us he's done more than you will do in your entire life.'

'Why have you come here?' asked Makhe.

'I need your help,' grunted Harry.

Makhe laughed at that, flashing large, yellowing teeth. The man was in his mid-thirties, his head shaven baby-butt smooth, and he had a powerful build except for his underdeveloped legs, a result of the spina bifida with which he was born. The car wreck he sat on served as his room, its insides all torn out to make space for a single mattress, while the dashboard featured tattered manifestos and a small television set hooked up to a DC battery. Leaning against this makeshift caravan was a battered skateboard, Makhe's preferred mode of transport. Between its axles was stuck a picture of P. W. Botha with the words TOTAL ONSLAUGHT scribbled in red over his bald head. It was the same skateboard he had been using when Harry first encountered him, nearly twenty years ago. At the time they had both been teenagers caught up in a mad world not of their own making; Harry had joined the police force as soon as he was spat out of the school system, in an effort to dodge compulsory military service on the border between two countries he had never even visited, while Motale, barely fourteen, was one of countless angry schoolchildren no longer willing to swallow the indignities heaped upon his people by the apartheid state.

'You need my help?' echoed Makhe in disbelief. 'King, jog his memory, please.'

The muscleman holding Harry pulled him back and

smashed him face-first against the sun-heated iron of the shack. Harry swore out loud as pain and noise shot through his head.

'This has never been a place for whites to come looking for help.' Though Makhe was born and bred in Alexandra, his English was refined to the point where Harry suspected he was educated abroad. 'You've all helped yourselves long enough on the backs of us black people, and I thought I made that clear last time.'

'I reckon you did, too,' replied Harry as he spat out a foamy pink mixture of blood and saliva.

Makhe uttered a short, disbelieving laugh. 'So, you're not only arrogant and stubborn, but stupid too?'

'Might well be.'

'You've got less than a minute to persuade me not to let my dogs have you.'

Harry struggled to find a more comfortable position, without much luck. 'You're bluffing, Makhe. We both know that.'

'I can do whatever I want here,' was the man's offhand reply. 'Just because you dragged me clear of that street when I didn't even need it doesn't mean I owe you.'

'If you can do whatever you want, then why aren't you in government where you could make a real difference to your community, instead of sitting here whinging in the gutter?'

'You already know what I think about those fucking intellectuals who led us into the firing line, only to disappear once the shots rang out.'

Harry grinned despite himself. 'They have absolutely nothing to do with you being stranded here.'

'Who said anything about stranded?' Makhe barked irritably. 'Not everyone strives for your Babylon towers,

English! You better not be here again asking for information on a brother.'

Harry grinned recklessly. 'I want information on a brother, *mfo*.'

The man known as King pulled Harry away from the wall and slammed him back into it. He did this a few times, the corrugated iron creaking with each impact. Eventually he stopped when Harry's legs began to buckle and a signal must have passed between the bruiser and his boss. In the next moment the vice-like grip on his arm loosened, and Harry fell to the ground. The Rottweilers immediately began barking and leaping about, as though they expected him to run.

When he picked himself up out of the dust, Harry fixed his eyes on King. 'If I thought you had more than a peanut for a brain, I'd send you up to Sun City faster than you could shoot up your horse steroids. But as it stands you're probably better off going home to your mother, because in there you'd be nothing more than someone's inflated bitch.'

King looked hesitatingly at Makhe, who merely shook his head.

Choosing a gutted office chair that stood over in one corner of the gritty yard, Harry fell into it and began brushing dust off his clothes. A foul miasma from the nearby outhouse permeated the air. His eyes quickly passed over a giant blackboard fastened to the shack wall, and a mountain of stolen red plastic Coca-Cola crates threatening imminent collapse, and wondered what they were needed for.

'You once told me that the unions would be the lifeblood that saved this country, how the shop stewards would lead the people from the ground up. In fact, you gave me the whole proletariat shebang.'

'If you're going to insult—' began Makhe.

'How about I tell you there are some bastards using your blessed, infallible mining unions to build up networks of assassins around the country, who burn down the People's houses while the Children of the Nation are still inside?'

Makhe's response was not immediate; instead, he called over one of the dogs, which jumped up to rest against the car with its forepaws and began to lick his open hand. 'Assassins? Is that what you call the Abasindisi? The same way we were "terrorists", though we were only fighting for an equal share in this country's freedom?'

'Cut the shite,' said Harry. 'They're busy breaking the laws of a free country and killing indiscriminately.'

'A killing is never indiscriminate, English. There is always purpose in it. The men you speak of as "assassins" have taken the protection of their families into their own hands because the law you speak of is nowhere to be found beyond your leafy white suburbs.'

'The Abasindisi run nothing better than an extortion racket that plays on the public's fear of crime.'

'Like the "legitimate" security services you employ to run a black man off some green lawn when he is momentarily enjoying the shade of a foreign oak tree after a long day's walk back home, because he can't afford a bus ticket?' Makhe allowed a jaundiced smile to spread over his face. 'How can you talk of an extortion racket? Have you ever spoken with some of the people they protect? Wait, I forget, you whites aren't in the habit of speaking to someone of a darker colour than a freshly plucked chicken, *né*, *baas*? The crime in those areas the Abasin-disi patrol has gone down. People now feel safe there, vindicated. You shouldn't be hunting down the same people who are doing something worthwhile for the community.'

'Police statistics don't support that claim.'

Makhe laughed out loud. 'Police statistics? *He banna!* How many people bother to report to the SAPS when they know nothing's ever going to come of it? Police statistics, *my gat!* Are those the same statistics that the ones in power don't allow to be verified independently?'

'Will you hear what I have to say,' asks Harry, 'or are you going to waste my time all day?'

'You see? That's what I'm talking about, always bossing us around, you are. Never talking like one civilized person to another.'

With a sardonic laugh, Makhe slid off the car's bonnet and quickly pulled himself across the exposed earth of the backyard on his knuckles. His faded jeans sported tough leather chaps that had been specially sewed on to protect his clothes from such rough treatment. He disappeared into a shack-like extension that had been grafted on to the side of a cinderblock home. It served as the kitchen so that more family space could be available inside.

A fridge door opened and bottles clanked.

'Beer, English?' Makhe called.

'Are you still running this place off a pirated line to the power grid?'

'Electricity is a basic right, not a privilege.'

'It's illegal, and it's also dangerous.'

'Do you want that beer or not?'

As of old, this revolutionary was only just warming up

to a heated debate with the only white man, as far as Harry could tell, he ever allowed into his inner circle.

Harry shook his head. 'Can't go back home to my daughter stinking like a brewery.'

Makhe laughed again, and this time Harry could hear it was genuine pleasure.

'A daughter, English? Has it really been that long?'

'Yes.'

'How old?'

'Going on eleven.' .

The laughter grew from inside the residence which, the last time Harry had visited, was occupied by Motale's mother, his two sisters and their children. 'You mean you actually found yourself a wife, with that ugly face of yours?'

This comment cut Harry deeply because it reminded him of a time when his wife Amy was still alive, and he had tried to introduce the two of them. But Makhe had been unwilling to leave the township, and his fiancée had been afraid of setting foot in one, so that was the end of it.

'I did,' he said. 'No beer for me, thanks.'

'Your loss, then.'

Makhe put the quarts of beer down on the floor, pulled himself forward a few paces, then reached back for the bottles and handed them to King and his companion before he drank deeply from his own. His hands were covered in a pachyderm-like hide from all his years of dragging and pulling himself everywhere.

'If the Abasindisi are such a blessing, then why are villages now burning again in the Eastern Cape?' asked Harry. 'Why are there rumours that the organization's regional officers threaten innocent people who just want to withdraw their membership and stay out of trouble?'

'These "innocent" people you talk about, English, are as backstabbing as all the ones in government right now. They ask these men to protect them, despite the fact that they have to be away from home to put food on the table. These men, they say fine, we'll do it, give us the *moola* and give us the support we need when we have to use force, and then we'll do it. The community says yes – they'll say anything to stop the *tsotsis* – but the moment they see what real protection means, they get frightened by what's being done in their name.' Makhe points an accusing finger at Harry. 'You tell me who is wrong: the men courageous enough to do the community's dirty work, or the community itself that betrays them halfway through the job?'

'There are limits,' argues Harry. 'Assault, murder, arson – they're not protection, they're crimes. These are people operating outside the framework of a democratic state possessing a constitution and a human-rights charter.'

'Tell me, Harry, why do people listen to a policeman?'

'I'm sure you're going to tell me I'm wrong whatever I say, so enlighten me.'

'It's because you have a uniform, you have a gun. You are a symbol of violence that is state-sanctioned.'

'Yes?'

'So any man that wants to protect his home when the state won't do it has to create that same symbol for himself. He must be feared as a police officer is feared. Perhaps the Abasindisi's methods involve what you might call crimes, but then the threat of violence you cops use to earn respect on the streets might also be considered criminal, only you can hide behind the barricades of laws and bureaucracy. You warp the process of justice to protect each other. No, English, these men, they exist because our state has forgotten us, because you cops only have your own interests at heart, and because not much has changed for us poor, apartheid or not. We are still left to fend for ourselves.'

A sly smile spread over Makhe's face then. Sensing victory, he took another long swig from the beer bottle he gripped by the neck. And what exactly could Harry say in reply to this? As long as crimes occurred throughout this violent country, people would remain unhappy with the police service. It did not matter to the public how much crime was the result of neglected social services, stunted economic conditions and policies: the more insecure people felt, the more justified they would feel in committing crimes themselves to rectify those wrongs committed against them.

Harry sighed in frustration, and at this Makhe's expression brightened considerably.

'You know I'm right, don't you?' he said.

'Look, Makhe, I didn't come here to talk about whose set of morals outranks whose. There's a sixteen-year-old boy lying burned to a crisp in our morgue, alongside both his parents, and chances are there'll be many more like him wherever the Abasindisi operate. I want to track down the men responsible, and your connections in the mining unions are what I need to help me.'

Makhe wiped beer froth from his lips and smiled devilishly. 'You can't be serious, English. You are still asking me, after what I already told you on more than one occasion?'

'Yes, I am.'

'But why?'

'This is important.'

'No good can come of it, ever.'

Harry locked eyes with the man perched on the door-sill. 'If you had given me Ntombini back then when I asked you, things might not have turned out as bad as they did.'

This is it, then. We're right back where it all started.

It was in '98 that Parapara Ntombini had been implicated in the gruesome murder of a heroin addict in Yeoville. Harry had been assigned to a task team made up jointly of Narcotics Bureau and Murder and Robbery detectives, briefed to find the culprit amidst outcries from the neighbourhood's rapidly diminishing Jewish community. Junkie arranging a pick-up or not, they saw the murder of a woman driving alone as the final straw, and wanted police to act swiftly on the further decay of the neighbourhood's main drag, Rocky Street, which had become infested with some of the toughest drugs and prostitution rackets in the city after the clubbing scene exploded in the area. It was how Harry had met Swarts for the first time. Then barely promoted to superintendent, the man had led his newly formed team with that hardened zeal for which he would later become celebrated, and within two weeks they had found a name. Within three weeks, they knew where Ntombini was most likely hiding: in Alexandra.

Yet somewhere down the line the goal of their investigation had become blurry, and a Mexican stand-off ensued between the edgy gangs operating in Yeoville, who were losing thousands with each passing week that the task team kept harassing their customers, and the South African Narcotics Bureau desperately trying to prove its continued existence was essential to a police service that was beginning to favour a decentralized approach to drug enforcement. As the stand-off escalated, the junkie's homicide fell by the wayside, and when Ntombini was found murdered one day, taken down in what looked like a professional hit, the female addict's dossier and all its dead-end leads quickly disappeared into the filing cabinet reserved for unsolved cases, along with her alleged murderer's details. Case closed, by all accounts, and the cold war out on the street blew over within the month. The brass and officers on the beat alike breathed a collective sigh of relief, because no one wanted it to end with a cop getting shot dead.

'I told you he was innocent, but did you do anything to redirect the investigation?' said Makhe. 'No, you didn't. After all, what does a black man know, when the white man has been given his divine authority?'

'The case was clear-cut,' argued Harry. 'All we needed to do was nail him down and drag him to court.'

Makhe shook his head. 'Only clear-cut for a bunch of *boere* who don't ever care about the truth.'

Harry lost his patience then. 'Not everything that happens in this country is about the state trying to exploit you! His fingerprints were found in her car. He was the last person seen with the victim, and her handbag was later found in a vehicle which he'd been driving. Yes, he did it, and the only reason we could not nail him for murder was that he got killed before we could get him to court.'

'It was you lot that killed him!'

'Why the hell would we do that, if all we needed to wrap up the case was him?'

Makhe suddenly hurled his beer bottle across the backyard to smash against the opposite wall. The dogs began barking furiously as foam sprayed in all directions. 'King, give the cunt his gun back. We're finished here.'

Harry ran a hand over the stubble on his cheeks and rose from the office chair. He should've realized: speaking to Makhe about this was like chasing his own tail. 'Don't you feel the slightest obligation to contribute to a wider society than this neighbourhood in which you're hiding?'

'This country, it has no wider community. Not any more.'

'The world isn't your enemy, Makhe. It's about time you realized that.' Harry fished out a business card from his shirt pocket and dropped it in the dust. 'If you're so sure about Ntombini then get me some proof that it was police officers that killed him. I'm still offering you the opportunity, the way I did then. I promise I'll look into it. But for that you give me names for some of the active Abasindisi operatives.'

'Take your deal and shove it up your *gat*, English.'

When he got back to his car, he found it had been stripped of everything portable, from its tyres to the radio and spark plugs. Harry thumped the roof in frustration. Turning, he saw King casually wave to him from the other side of the broken-down bridge. He might just have gone back and wiped the grin off his face, but at that moment a dozen primary-school kids, dressed in grey-and-white uniforms, came running towards the thug and his Rottweiler, encircling them both with loud hoots of glee. Thinking better of it then, Harry got out his phone to call Dispatch.

11

The original plan was to discreetly surround the small village, and peacefully negotiate a door-to-door search of the homes and kraals until the suspected cache of weapons was found. Squads of four policemen or soldiers would take responsibility for searching a handful of quadrants, based on a roughly drawn map of the village, as supplied by Makhe Motale.

Of course, all that flew out of the window the moment the mist crept in over the foothills, and the troops found themselves pinned down.

A steady breeze kicked up as the day warmed, and is now sending fog billowing down the mountain in a south-easterly direction. There is a strong smell of wet hay, manure, and an occasional wisp of cordite in the air, while in the distance intermittent reports of gunfire continue to echo in the hills.

Harry wipes a cold sheen of sweat from his face and looks towards the unseen mountain cliffs. The dense white veil has thinned somewhat, and occasionally it breaks up to reveal clusters of traditional thatch-and-mud huts interspersed with haphazard shanties. Some are little more than lean-tos, others tilt dangerously to one side as if on the brink of collapse. The spaces between them are filled with hard-packed footpaths. Any livestock kraals have had their gates broken open and now stand empty.

To Harry's left, Moqomo cautiously peers into yet another seemingly abandoned home, his pistol gripped tightly in both hands. He is impressed by Moqomo continuing with them, despite the bullet that might have killed him still firmly lodged in his vest.

'This one, clear,' calls out Moqomo.

He can hear but not see the rest of his team of local police officers as they work their way from dwelling to dwelling in the same methodical fashion, searching for someone whom they can question as to what happened here and, more importantly, where the Abasindisi guns may be hidden.

The breeze nudges back the shroud of fog to momentarily reveal the body of a plump woman in her late twenties, lying face-down in a patch of grass beside a chicken coop. A blue fleece blanket is still wrapped tightly around her midriff against the cold. Harry sees that her eyes are half open, while in the stinking pen behind her lie a dozen chickens that have had their necks wrung.

'I've got another one,' he calls to Moqomo. 'That makes five.'

'O, *thixo*!' Moqomo exclaims from inside a shack. 'Then that makes this one here number six. Their attack, it must've come fast. This, man, she was still in bed.'

The team had known what they were in for once they found a couple of combatants only a short way into the village from where Moqomo was shot. The two were lying not six feet apart on a steep bank adjoining the main access track into the settlement. One had been killed by a deep gash to the head from a panga, the other most likely taken down by the zip gun still clasped in the other dead man's hand.

The feeling of having wandered into this nation's heart of darkness will not leave Harry. They came here to conduct a large-scale but uncomplicated search-and-seizure, aimed at putting pressure on any local Abasindisi members, but now this . . . what were they supposed to achieve here in these killing fields?

'This attack on the village, it was the reprisal.' Moqomo's voice floats grimly through the wispy air. 'The thieves, they are not even taking the livestock any more. Killing these people is not enough now. It looks like they want any survivors to starve.'

Harry's gut clenches as the unmistakable boom of a grenade joins the sound of semi-automatic gunfire higher up in the hills.

Are we still in control here? he wonders, and the thought is immediately chased up by another. *Were we ever?*

'Don't forget, this village would probably have done the same to their neighbours, given the chance.'

'*Ja*, I know it.'

Harry kneels next to the woman in the fleece blanket and feels for a pulse. Though her body is still warm with the afterglow of life, he realizes his gesture is nothing more than a formality.

This close to the ground, as he crouches, the fog is not quite so dense, and he can see Moqomo step over the corpse of a well-fed German shepherd, lying in a puddle of soapy kitchen-sink waste. Blankets lie strewn all around the animal, most likely discarded by fleeing villagers, either late at night or just before dawn.

A sudden flicker of movement to Harry's right distracts him. Bare feet. Naked legs.

He jumps up and shouts for whoever it is to stop, then takes a few quick steps in that direction. But, as suddenly as they appeared, the feet have vanished. He stops to listen, but hears nothing more than the gunfire, the wind and still that infernal cow-bell.

'What is it, Harry?' calls Moqomo.

Glancing back towards where his team members

should be, Harry notices he has been engulfed in a fresh white veil of mist. Suddenly the others are no more than detached voices whispering to him.

'I'm not sure,' he mumbles uncertainly.

He takes another confused look around, suddenly feeling very exposed. It isn't just the dead who are lying in wait amongst the buildings.

'Where are you?' Moqomo urges, with some irritation.

'Give me a minute,' Harry calls back.

He drops to one knee so as to peer underneath the worst of the blanket of mist. Behind him he hears Moqomo urgently speaking to the other officers in Xhosa.

Of those ghostly legs in raggedy denim cut-offs, which could not have belonged to anyone older than sixteen, he now sees no trace, and decides to head deeper into the bank of fog.

Come on, kid. Show yourself before you get shot by accident.

He listens carefully, but does not pick up any unusual sound close by.

But you're being watched, aren't you? he tells himself. Harry feels his arms begin to crawl with gooseflesh. *You're being watched, and you know it.*

'Mason!' shouts Moqomo. 'Mason? Get back to the group.'

'I'm right here!' Harry hollers back, suddenly furious with the continued noisy interruptions.

His unexpected bellow flushes out the child hiding behind a large devil's-claw bush nearby. The first thing Harry notices is the battered AK-47 rifle gripped in one skinny hand. Then, for a brief moment, he registers a tear-streaked face before the child bolts.

Harry reflexively brings up his pistol, but drops it

again. The boy is armed, yes, but far from dangerous enough to be shot in the back whilst fleeing. *''Mfana!'* he yells. 'Stop!'

In the moment before the child completely disappears into the fog, the frightened boy throws a wild glance over his shoulder and meets Harry's eyes. The terror in them reminds Harry of the man who directed them here. During the riot in '87, Makhe had been about the same age, and had worn much the same expression as he unsuccessfully tried to drag himself out of harm's way. Left abandoned in the middle of an Alexandra street by his panicking comrades, one arm broken and dangling uselessly by his side, and with live ammunition, rocks and petrol bombs flying in all directions, he had been a sitting duck.

Without thinking of what he could now be running into, Harry gives chase.

12

It was almost exactly a month before this raid on Tsolo that Harry finally received the hoped-for call from Makhe Motale.

Up to that point, the mood in the unit towards him had been declining steadily. Swarts and his Ballies had scented blood the day they had originally discussed the Abasindisi organization in the Supe's office, and had been eager to get moving on the case. But when Harry's lead had petered out pretty much as soon as it was aired, their usual rough-and-tumble banter quickly degenerated into snide comments. Though Swarts kept himself above such sniping, only shrugging silently when Harry reported his failure to secure any further information on the Abasindisi, he sensed the Supe's disappointment with equal discomfiture. Word of his failure got around to the rest of the unit fast, and for the first time Harry had to wonder if this team was as sophisticated as he had first thought. The issue had come to a head one July morning as he sat in a police car with Franklin at the top of a cul de sac on the outskirts of Alexandra. They were staking out the home of the two brothers Phaliso, suspected heads of the Abasindisi organization, and the pair had been riding each other's nerves all morning when Franklin finally spat out what the rest of the old-timers must have been chewing over all along.

'Bond, if you can't deliver, then what the fuck are you doing here?'

'No promises were ever made.' Harry was caught off guard by the vehemence of the comment.

'First case you get handed, and I'm stuck on it, wasting time more often than not. I've got my own shit to worry about.' With that Franklin had stepped out of the car to take a leisurely piss against a neighbouring wall. 'SVC is for detectives who can make every hour count,' he called over his shoulder. 'So if you can't wax it, you might want to go back to General Investigations and rough up teenage shoplifters.'

'English, the information you wanted, I have it.' Makhe had finally come through over the phone.

Harry replied in a tone suggesting he had just discovered dogshit on the sole of his shoe. The endless paperwork and explanations that followed the ransacking of his unattended SVC vehicle in Alexandra had been only one of his recent headaches.

'How is business in the spare-parts industry? Sell any stolen Mazda hubcaps lately?'

As Makhe laughed, the mockery in his voice was enough to tell Harry he knew full well about the stripped police car.

'*Eish!* So sorry to hear about what happened, *baas*. It's unfortunate, but you know, *baas*, you know what they say about the townships, *né*?' His authentic impersonation of a luckless shantytown black was marred only by an aloof cynicism. 'Those are places for the *tsotsis*. *Baas* should have known there is not a single honest man or woman among them.'

The way Harry was feeling that particular day, he could have smashed the receiver against the wall. But even if that made him feel better, it would not get him anywhere with Motale, so he took a deep breath and cut to the chase.

'What information's that, then?' He kept his voice as casual as possible, knowing any hint of eagerness would have Motale walking all over him. 'And why now?'

Makhe laughed with genuine mirth this time. 'I have what you wanted on Ntombini and, would you believe it, I've had a change of heart, English. This thing with the Abasindisi, it didn't sit so easy with me after all, so I stuck my nose into it further.'

Bullshit, you have something up your sleeve, was Harry's first thought.

'Nothing ever sits easy with you, Makhe.'

'I think you and I should meet, to talk it over, English. And trust me, there's a lot to talk about.'

'I don't know. I'm enjoying having the use of a car again. And to have your *fuzies* breathing into my face and your dogs snuffling at my crotch doesn't exactly seem like what I would call a rewarding prospect.'

At this Makhe paused, as if for the first time genuinely surprised by Harry's hostility. When next he spoke, his tone was more serious.

'English, you and I have business to conclude.'

'If you still think some police officer offed Ntombini, take it to the investigating officer, or to the Independent Complaints Directorate. I just don't care any more. Goodbye.'

'Wait!'

'I can hear a bum deal in your voice, Makhe.'

At this the man laughed out loud, and Harry imagined him shaking his head in disbelief. 'You and I, English. *You* know Makhe Motale wouldn't ever kill you, and *I* know that, under all that pig meat, Harry Mason is a very inquisitive cop – and maybe even an honest one, too, so I can't quite give up on your sorry arse, and that gives me a small bit of hope still. You meet me at Winston's – you remember where it is? – at the Corner of Capsicum and Hollyhock Crescent. All those nice—'

Harry finished his sentence for him. 'Nice white street names for bad black townships. Jesus, Makhe, you're a broken record if there ever was one. OK, I'll be there.'

An hour later he was sitting at a picnic table bolted to the concrete floor of a backyard shebeen on the outskirts of Alexandra. Cheap beer and easy access was what made this place appealing to most of its customers – all of them working-class black folk, who eyed Harry warily.

He did not have to wait long till, from the other side of the high wall enclosing the backyard, came the unmistakable sound of a skateboard rolling over gritty tarmac. It was accompanied by the whistling of the old Afrikaner national anthem, 'Die Stem', and for a moment the chatter in the place quietened as people recognized that unwelcome melody. Then uproarious laughter erupted once the patrons realized who was singing. Loud greetings broke out on the street-facing stoop, and then Makhe Motale appeared and began shaking hands with acquaintances at half a dozen tables. The smile he reserved for the other patrons here was radiant, untouched by the anger to which Harry had grown accustomed.

'Harry Mason, what the *fuck* are you doing with that cripple kaffir!' he abruptly remembered a police lieutenant shouting at him over the chasm of nearly two decades. That day chaos had thundered all round him, as he ran to the rescue of the injured demonstrator who had lost both his skateboard and the use of his arm. Harry had later almost faced a disciplinary hearing for that merciful stunt. Going to the aid of a dissident, whether disabled or not, against orders was certainly not in the job description of South African police officers in the late eighties.

'English,' said Makhe simply by way of greeting, and chucked two manila files on the tar-sealed table. At a glance Harry could see at least one of them was crammed with information.

'With Mama Annie Twala dead,' Makhe had once boasted to Harry drunkenly, 'I have become the very heart of Alexandra. Through me flows her blood; she knows me and I know her, the way husband and wife know each other under the sheets.'

Harry did not immediately reach for the folders. 'I notice a few things have changed with you. Your accent sounds like a BBC correspondent's, and you've become quite the celebrity round here.'

'The old Chinese maxim of "Know your enemy" has gone a long way to keeping me alive, pork chop.'

A pretty teenager with her red shirt tied together in a knot over her flat stomach brought over four quarts of beer – compliments of the house, she explained – and plonked them down on the table.

Harry sat back. 'Not for me, thanks. I'm on duty.'

Makhe pulled himself up on to the bench opposite so he was directly facing the police officer. 'Come, English, talking is hard work and I don't like to drink alone.'

The sombre way Makhe regarded him made Harry uneasy. The girl looked him up and down and said something in Tswana to Makhe, at which he burst out laughing.

'What's that she just said?' he asked.

'She says you look like you've swallowed a roach.' Makhe opened two of the beers and placed one in front of Harry, despite his further remonstrations.

'I trust this isn't just another one of your pranks.' Harry gestured to the pair of files.

'I've got some of what you want here, and maybe a little more.' Makhe shrugged. 'But you get nothing at all unless you look into Ntombini's murder.'

'Unsolved narcotics homicides aren't officially in my job description.'

'It was a SANAB detective who killed him.'

'How can you be so sure? Ntombini had become a liability to the entire Yeoville narcotics industry. He had more enemies than he could wish for, just because of that.'

'Were you there when it happened?'

'No.'

'Then you don't know for sure, do you?'

Harry sighed. 'Give me the file, then.'

'You can look at it in your own time. Only promise me you will take it all the way, regardless of what's in it.'

'You know I will.'

Makhe pushed the top file towards Harry. 'I can't ever be sure of that, as much as you can't be sure of what happened the night Ntombini was killed. He was murdered for nothing but pride. Just think about it. Why would he have killed that white woman when she was a regular source of income? No, the evidence you speak of, it was planted. All of it.'

'Could be she owed him money; could be she threatened him. Maybe she cheated on him with some other dealer, I don't know. It wouldn't be the first time that a supplier kills one of his customers, that's for sure.'

'I want you and only you to look into this, understand?'

Harry hesitated before taking the folder. What would he find in there? More importantly, who did Makhe want him to go after? If he took the file he might be obliged to go after a fellow cop. Not even an ordinary uniform, but a detective, and most likely one with whom Harry had worked in the past. And if he did not take it? Well, then it would become Makhe's responsibility to take his evidence to the right people. But what about nailing the Abasindisi?

'I said it before, if you think one of *us* killed him, take it up with the Independent Complaints Directorate. Personally, I don't see one of us risking his job and pension on a shit like Ntombini. What for? These aren't the old days; that stuff just doesn't happen the way it used to.'

Makhe snorted. 'Are you kidding me, English? I don't work for a newspaper, so you don't have to dish up that bullshit. As for the ICD, those idiots couldn't get one of you lot to court if their lives depended on it.'

Makhe leaned forward, the usual anger flaring in his eyes. 'Listen here, English, and listen good. The police force you belong to is more corrupt than you think. Or at least, what you'd like to believe. I have a feeling you *make* yourself think otherwise. How else does a man like you go to work every morning, when you must know that in any place and at any time a dodgy *gata* for a partner has your back? Ntombini might not have been the kind of model citizen you introduce to your mother, but that's no excuse for killing a man in cold blood.'

Harry shook his head at the all too familiar direction this conversation was taking. 'Just give me what I need about the Abasindisi.'

'Impatient, hey?'

'I have work to do, and this toing and froing is getting on my nerves.'

Makhe sat back and chuckled to himself.

'I couldn't find anything about the men who killed Mohosh, your politician. It might not even have been the Abasindisi; after all, it's not like they're the only ones who burn people inside their houses. But I did stumble on to something you'll love.'

Harry raised an eyebrow.

'What if I told you the Abasindisi had over four dozen AK-47s hidden away, with crates of ammunition and some grenades, too? Fifty-four rifles, to be exact.'

'I'd say you're required by law to tell me where they are.' Harry again reached out for the envelope, but Makhe was faster and snatched it away.

'It's all in here, but . . .' As he trailed off his fingers made an unmistakable gesture.

'Are you asking me for money?'

'Yes, I am – and that you look into Ntombini's death for me.'

Harry stared, dumbfounded.

'You're surprised?'

For nearly a decade Makhe Motale had acted the offended friend after Harry asked him for information on a murder suspect, and now he was ready to offer up a group he had readily defended the last time they met. Of course he was surprised, because something smelled like a very dead fish.

'Has it come to this, then, Makhe? Are you turning yourself into a common informant, after all?'

'*Quid pro quo*, as they would say in the Latin fraternity, English.'

'How much are we talking about here?'

'A hundred grand.'

Harry snorted in disbelief.

'This is better information than what you asked for,' said Makhe. 'I guarantee it.'

'How about I arrest you right here and chuck you in jail? Maybe I'll start a rumour that you're a rat, see what happens when the Twenty-Eights get hold of you. I'm sure that would get you talking pretty soon, and for free.'

Makhe made a *tut-tut* sound. 'Harry Mason, my English gentleman, leave that kind of talk for your colleagues, OK? I'll be honest with you: if what I'm proposing goes through, I'm definitely taking my cut. But I'll also tell you this right now, that *moola* isn't going into my pocket.'

'I still don't trust your sudden change of heart.'

Makhe's grin grew even wider. 'It's a straight bargain here. You go after the man who killed Ntombini, and I'll help you. This thing in Tsolo, let's just say that it fell into my lap when I started asking around. Let's call it a bonus for the both of us. A clever man like yourself could probably earn a very big promotion from this.'

'Why do I feel I'm cutting a deal with the devil?'

'Because I'm a black man, born with a tail the doctors had to cut off? I don't know. After we're done here, you and I are finished. I'm buying back my soul as of today, understand? You saved my life once and, as much as I can't stand it, I owe you.'

'I never asked you a thing in—'

'Until you came knocking at my door for favours!' Makhe spat to one side. 'I thought you were different, but you lot are all the same. The day I meet a cop who knows how to give, rather than always take, is the day I'll chew off what's left of my own legs, I swear it.'

The contempt in his eyes made Harry blush. He wished he had paid more attention to fixing his friendship with this man right after the original argument, when there had still been time to do so. But now it was too late, too late by far, he felt.

'Fair enough. If that's how you want it. But for a hundred grand there better be something substantial in there worth reading. A lot of people will need convincing to come up with that sort of cash.'

Makhe laughed again. 'Aye, I know that. And our canary does, too. What I have here is a taster, and I must trust you not to use it unless you can secure the money.'

'I can't guarantee that.'

'You better, my English gentleman, because those guns won't lead you to anyone specific. The Abasindisi have already seen to that. No single person owns them, and they are hidden on communal property. So how do you plan on arresting an entire village, my friend? Whom exactly do you prosecute? Their presence in a certain place only proves the good will of your informant.'

'A bunch of guns won't be good enough, and a list of crimes committed is only hearsay without evidence. Whoever it is will have to testify in court, take us to crime scenes, et cetera.'

Despite Harry's misgivings about what Makhe was throwing him, he could not help but feel excited at the offer.

'I think our bird has been thinking about this for some time. It's asked me to convey to you that it's willing to testify, provided you can give it complete immunity and witness protection. Not the crap you people normally offer, mind you. Our singing bird is thinking of flying north for the winter. Maybe for good.'

It was Harry's turn to laugh. 'This isn't the goddamned United States! A hundred grand will pale in comparison to what an international witness-protection programme will cost us.'

'Aye, English,' said Makhe matter-of-factly, as if this closed the deal. He lifted his beer bottle by its neck. 'And I can see by your face it will be worth all that paper-work you'll be filling in. Let's make a toast to our little bird, then to you, pork-face, and to me. Let's finally be free of each other.'

13

Ahead of Harry Mason, the terrified boy bounds through the dilapidated village of Tsolo, agile as a klipspringer. At one point Harry almost had him with an ankle tap, but the kid turned abruptly and threw the rifle he was carrying at the police officer, forcing him to duck.

Unencumbered now, the boy is fast putting distance between them as he skips nimbly over familiar territory: rusty vegetable fences, heaps of dried cow manure gathered for smearing mud-hut walls, a block for chopping wood. Their surroundings go by in a blur, with Harry noticing only the obstacles between him and the fleeing child. They race across an empty patch of land which, if the cattle bones strewn everywhere are anything to go by, must be used for the slaughtering of livestock.

Bad move, Mason, bad move, grumbles a voice inside his head. It is undoubtedly the rational side of him, which realizes he has left the urgent calls of his team far behind. *What the hell are you running into?*

In the distance the gunfire has dropped off, and anxious voices can be heard calling out to each other in the lifting fog. For the first time this morning, Harry might have felt the warmth of the sun on his shoulders, were he not so intent on catching up with the boy.

The kid disappears into yet another bank of dense fog trapped at the bottom of a steep donga, and Harry's already thundering heart thumps out a few more beats of alarm. But then the lad appears again, scrambling up the far side of the gully, which is overgrown with purple morning glory and devil's claw. Harry is about to slide down the near side of the ditch when he is brought to a halt by the loud crack of wood smashing against something hard. He twists around just in time to hear a strangled hiss escaping someone's lips, and spots a shadowy figure hovering tensely over a large wooden crate.

'Police!' he shouts instinctively. 'Ge—'

The shady figure reacts faster, however. There is an orange flash, closely followed by a loud bang, and a white light sears across Harry's vision. Sound explodes in his ears as his head rocks back violently and his legs buckle simultaneously. Something wet and warm splashes across his cheek. Then he feels his body twitch involuntarily as a hot poker seems to press hard against his belly, just under the bulletproof vest. The warning he wanted to shout a moment ago dies on his lips as he exhales violently in surprise. For a moment he totters, unable to see anything except that bright light, hear anything but a high-pitched ring. Then he feels his arms go limp, his gun drops from his hand and finally his legs give way completely.

Harry falls face-down into the cold wet grass, and knows no more.

TWO

1

Two days later Jacob Tshabalala wakes up to the sound of heavy gusts from a fresh cold front pummelling the neighbourhood's roofs. Flying grit scratches against the bedroom window and his kitchen door rattles in its frame. For a second he imagines a large rat or bird scrabbling across his roof, and was that an owl's hoot? When last did he hear an owl hooting in Soweto?

Jacob's eyes flutter open. Staring up at the darkened ceiling of his modest bedroom, he unsuccessfully tries to calm his thumping heart by taking a few deep breaths. Though he should be reassured by the room's familiarity, by the soft sound of Nomsa sleeping next to him, by the duvet's warm comforting weight, Jacob nevertheless cannot help but feel he is still stuck in an uneasy dream – stranded in a strange place where something has gone seriously wrong.

Relax. It's only the wind.

Yet the confluence of his restless dreams and the eerie weather outside unsettles him even more.

Switching on the bedside light and glancing at the digital alarm clock on his bedside table, he sees it is half-past three in the morning, a full hour before he was intending to get up. Next to him, Nomsa moans softly in her sleep. Jacob brushes her cheek gently with one hand and feels the muscles in her face tighten as she subconsciously smiles.

That feeling of dissociation continues to worry him,

however, until Jacob wonders if it is perhaps some sort of premonition. Is this feeling of unease somehow connected to his sick father, who has been hovering at death's door these last five years, or is it to do with Harry Mason?

The latter thought causes a sharp twinge in his gut, and reminds him of the call he received from Director Molethe the day his ex-partner got shot. Harry had taken a bullet in the abdomen, Molethe informed him, and another one ricocheted off his skull. Now he is lying comatose in an ICU unit in Port Elizabeth, and no one has any idea who the gunman might be. Indeed, from the clipped conversation Jacob gathered that the SVC director himself was still in the dark about much of what happened in Tsolo. Whether Harry's condition has suddenly deteriorated overnight, Jacob cannot know, but he is certain that Harry's mother, who had immediately flown from England to watch over him, would surely have called if there had been any change for the worse. As for his sick father, Jacob is convinced someone would have contacted him the moment the old man announced that his time had finally come. One thing is sure: he is the type of leathery man who wants to dictate to death when he is good and ready to make his exit, and not the other way around.

Jacob rolls over to face Nomsa, inhaling her fresh scent of soap as though she has just stepped out of a hot bath, and he begins to sink gratefully into her sleepy peace.

His recent dreams have been troubling, yes, but nothing as powerful as a premonition of death. They were more like – he thinks back a moment – the experience of *ukuthwasa*, the calling of the ancestors, which he has occasionally felt over the years. It is that deep-seated restlessness and frustration experienced by those who have not dutifully embraced their mystical calling to become holy men or women in tune with the spirit world.

Jacob's smile twitches on the verge of a laugh. *Growing impatient with me again, Grandfather?*

For a moment he can almost touch the ancient healer, so vivid is his sudden memory of the old man: chasing after a young Jacob and his cousins with his walking stick, arms held up high and hollering at them as if he was the blind spirit Lumukanda himself. Jacob brings a hand up to his chest. His fingers brush past the gold crucifix that Nomsa gave him for his thirty-fourth birthday, and find the amulet his grandfather created for him the very day he was born. It is comprised of a leather string to which is attached a rolled-up section of the caul that covered his head at birth. To some this is a sign that he has the gift of prophecy; to others it is a very powerful protection against the evil eye; but to Jacob it is even more than that: a symbol of the continuing bond of affection between him and his now dead ancestor.

'What time is it?' murmurs Nomsa in Zulu.

He reaches out underneath the duvet and finds her warm belly under her vest. 'It's not time yet, baby,' he whispers in her ear. 'I'll wake you up in a little while.'

'With breakfast?'

Familiar enough with the landscape of her face, he finds her eyelids with his lips in the darkness and kisses them lightly. 'With breakfast.'

2

The first thing Jacob sees when he switches on the fluorescent kitchen light is a Murder and Robbery Unit memo lying on the square lino-covered table. It has been signed by both Senior Superintendent Niehaus and Director Visier, and states that regrettably they cannot grant his request for a transfer from Murder and Robbery to Serious Crimes, 'due to that unit receiving an inordinate number of requests at this time'. With yet another restructuring of the police service under way, and all the specialized units except for Organized Crime and Serious and Violent Crimes being reabsorbed by regular station-level policing or General Investigations, Jacob has been worried about getting stuck at the rank of detective inspector for ever, and therefore put in this request for a transfer.

Me and everyone else, by the looks of it.

The kitchen door again rattles violently in its frame, startling Jacob. For a moment it even sounded like the handle was being turned.

Seeing the neatly printed memo renews the disappointment he felt when he first read it yesterday. Ten years in Murder and Robbery, five of those in one of the toughest precincts in the country, Brixton, and commendations from all the seniors who could directly effect his transfer – and still they cannot find a gap for him. He cannot help but feel that he has done something to offend someone very high up, and that somehow he is not good enough for the SVC.

Jacob sighs. He should have known. He should have acted earlier.

Just about everyone in the service below superintendent level is pushing and shoving like a bunch of soccer players in the penalty box to get into either of those two units. OCS and SVC get you places, they open doors. There are extra resources to help close cases faster. They even improve your salary.

Filling the kettle and switching it on, Jacob recalls how Nomsa reacted to the memo.

'They're racists, all of them!' she yelled. 'That Niehaus and Visier, they don't want to see any black man getting a promotion.' When he pointed out to her that it was a black man, Director Molethe, who gave the go-ahead for transfers to SVC, she rather changed her pitch. 'But how do you know they even forwarded your request to him?' He told her he could not be sure, but that he did trust these two men because he had worked closely with them for a number of years. She shook her head in resignation. 'Jacob, baby, I don't know how to say this, but not everyone is like you. You're too nice. You're too trusting. Look out for yourself for once, please?'

Her comments amused and stung him at the same time. Amused him, because her invective was due more to sympathy for him than actual anger, a way of showing her solidarity with him; stung, because she voiced a suspicion which had been nagging him a while now, but on which he preferred not to dwell at length. He did not want to believe that maybe the service had been using him, that maybe he had got himself bogged down in showing diaper detectives the ropes, while neglecting his own career.

Blaming others for what you've done is not going to help anyone, least of all yourself.

The lights of a minibus taxi flash across the kitchen window and draw him out of his reverie. Parting the curtains, he sees a steady stream of blue-collar labourers ambling along the dark street outside: domestics in colourful headscarves and aprons wearing winter jerseys; miners already wearing their overalls and helmets; artisans with their brushes, tile cutters and spirit levels. Some of them shield their eyes against the grit and coal-smoke the wind is gusting through the murky streets.

Behind him, Nomsa clumps into the kitchen in her plastic-soled house slippers and yawns out loud. 'Is that brown dog out there digging in the garbage again?'

Jacob lets the curtain go and turns towards her with a smile. 'No. I think old Tito might have finally caught it, and turned it into a stuffed trophy dog for the mantel.'

'Don't say that!'

Jacob laughs. 'How come you're up, anyway? I remember promising you breakfast in bed, didn't I?'

Nomsa runs a forearm across her still-sleepy eyes. This gesture, along with her rounded face and short, tightly combed hair, make her look fifteen years younger than her actual thirty. She wraps her arms around Jacob's waist and splays her fingers over his buttocks. 'I should be bringing *you* breakfast in bed.'

Jacob kisses her forehead. 'And why is that?'

She lays her cheek against his chest and hugs him tighter. 'The tour. It was so nice of you. I think it's the best gift I've ever been given.'

A surge of satisfaction at her obvious happiness fills him. Their church choir – in which he considers Nomsa to be the best singer by far – has been planning a tour of the Western Cape for months now, but at the last moment it discovered a shortage of funds. In an effort to rescue the trip the committee asked its members to pay their own way. This was a tough blow for Nomsa, seeing that she did not earn enough money working as a cashier in a supermarket. But her bitter disappointment moved Jacob to borrow money from a cousin and his godmother, Mama Hettie Solilo.

'You really didn't have to do that,' she says again. 'You know that, don't you?'

'But you deserve it,' he says gently, though he has no idea how he is going to repay his loans. As things stand, he is only barely managing to cover the monthly instalments on this house and the car. 'Besides, that choir of ours would be pretty useless without you, so I'm sending you along to save them a whole lot of embarrassment.'

'Don't be so nasty!' Nomsa slaps his chest in mock anger.

'I'm not. Just being honest.'

Her hands find his face and pull it closer for a grateful kiss, which soon grows more passionate, till Jacob ends up wishing that every day could be about a moment like this.

3

Riding in the rear of Jacob's compact red pick-up are neighbourhood acquaintances, catching a lift into the city. Inside the vehicle, Nomsa is squashed between Jacob and Tito, sitting up against the passenger window. Swinging the car out on to the Golden Highway, he heads east towards central Johannesburg. Torn grey clouds lour overhead, while yellow curtains of grit kicked up by the wind scour the burned and dried-up landscape.

The ominous weather seems to have affected his passengers, though Jacob himself feels a little better with the promise of rain – even though it is far too late in the year for a thunderstorm. Nomsa's hand creeps over his thigh, seeking assurance.

'What an ugly day it is,' she observes.

'Nonsense,' says Jacob. 'It looks like rain. What can be better than that?'

When he receives no reply from either her or Tito, he lets the comment hang, quelling an urge to open his window and feel the chilly air against his face.

4

The first thing Jacob does when he gets in to work is phone Joan Mason and check on her son's condition. When she informs him that there has been no change, he rings off with a sense of relief, but the earlier feeling of unease refuses to stop tugging at his mind.

What is this? What's got into you?

Clearing the line, he hesitates before dialling his parents' number. He can almost hear his father's grating response if his mother insists on taking the phone through to the bedridden old man: *You don't visit us any more, so why should we call you up when things aren't going well?*

Deciding to hell with his father's comments, he dials their number and, after a moment's static as the line redirects, the phone begins to ring at the other end. And it goes on ringing . . .

A fist begins to tug at his guts. *This is it. He's finally gone.*

Abruptly there is a click, and a sonorous voice answers. 'Tshabalala.'

It's his mother, speaking as if nothing in the world could be wrong.

'Ma,' he says. 'It's me. I'm calling to find out if everything's OK there. We haven't spoken in a while.'

'Jacob? Yes, why?'

'How is Taté?'

'You know how it is with him. He's been looking worse again these last few days, but his eyes, they are still as lively as ever.' Jacob hears the smile spread through her elderly voice. 'He won't let go until you—'

'So he's fine, then?' Jacob interrupts.

'Yes, he is.' Then he hears the nature of his sudden concern dawn on her. 'Jacob, have you seen something?'

Ever since that day he felt strangely ill as a child, and told his mother of the premonition that preceded the arrest of his father and grandfather for their part in the killing of a local witch, his mother has become convinced of his powers of prophecy. In the minds of his parents he is, after all, the first-born son of a long line of respected Zulu *sangomas* – but also the first one not to embrace the call of his lineage.

'No,' he says. 'It's nothing. Just Ndoda acting up again in my dreams, I suppose.'

His mother laughs. 'That man! He spent his old age herding you into bed, and now in his afterlife he throws you *out* of bed.'

'I wish he would leave me alone once in a while,' Jacob agrees.

'Your father would advise you to offer libations.'

'Ndoda is in my heart, Ma, and no spilled beer is going to make him happy.'

She laughs. 'He always *did* prefer his beer in a gourd. Anywhere else, he considered a waste.'

A deep breath, Tshabalala, is all you need, he reassures himself as he rings off.

A note on his desk from Supe Niehaus, scrawled on a yellow Post-it note, catches his eye. Jacob dials the number, and his superior answers on the first ring. While listening to the morning's instructions, Jacob's free hand travels up to the bridge of his nose and he pinches it hard.

'I'm sorry, supe,' he interrupts, 'you want me *where*?'

'*Boet*,' comes the reply through the receiver, 'they dropped this shell on me like a lump of birdshit this morning. They figure the regulars and riot guys need back-up after what happened in Hillbrow last Thursday. This request went out to all departments, not only us. I'm already here, and I know you're one of the few who gets in to work this early in the day, so could you come over, chop-chop? This is a back-up job only. We could be on our way by ten.'

This is a task that has nothing to do with detective work and everything to do with a uniformed cop's daily in-the-trenches routine. Jacob glances at his watch and then at the teetering pile of dockets filling his plastic in-trays.

'Supe, I . . . there's a lot of work waiting for me here.'

'I know, I know. Look, I'll give you the time off later in the week. How's that?'

Jacob grimaces at this empty promise. There is no time for a day off. He has already clocked over six hundred hours of unpaid overtime this year – and got the certificates to prove it. Just pieces of paper that neither pay the bills nor make up the time he loses with Nomsa.

'Jakes, I'm asking you nicely here.'

Jacob could go off the wall about it not being the first time this week he has had to drop everything, urgent or not, how he needs to prepare a dozen files for the state prosecutors and his own court appearance on Friday. He could talk about the drive he needs to take to Pretoria to recover blood and hair samples that have somehow gone missing between the Johannesburg office and the labs, but what does any of that matter when this man who regularly sticks his head out for his staff asks him a favour?

'Sure, supe,' he says eventually. 'Give me about half an hour.'

Replacing the receiver, Jacob recalls what Nomsa said the night before. 'You're too nice.' Not for the first time today he forces that thought out of mind. He just does not want to have to think about it right now.

Twenty minutes later he is heading out to Wynberg in an unmarked white Mazda, similar to the one Harry Mason was driving when it got stripped in Alexandra. The motor sounds like a dozen golf balls are rolling around in the engine block, and Jacob only hopes it will manage to get him where he needs to go.

5

With the police vehicle parked at the top of a road leading into a rundown quarter of the Wynberg industrial complex, west of Alexandra township, Jacob leans against the driver's door and surveys the low-built, grey factory squatting at the end of the cul de sac. It looks every bit like a hulking dung beetle in the morning haze, with a humid miasma steaming from orifices along its sides in the cold air. At its gate, activists from various anti-capitalist and human-rights groups have joined over four hundred squatters behind barricades of burning tyres and slabs of broken pavement. Jacob watches a man on a skateboard, wearing a red shirt printed with a golden hammer and sickle, push off down the hill towards the mob and throw up both his hands in clenched fists as he gathers speed.

'*Amandla awethu*, brothers and sistahs!' He shouts an old apartheid battlecry. 'Power to you! Your battles, they are not over. The state always promises, but it only takes away. You have a right to this roof over your heads. That is what the constitution says, and that's what we are fighting for here today!'

Guttural cries resound from hundreds of angry throats. In the front ranks youthful men toy-toy, all aggressive jerks of the hips and shoulders, waving nailed clubs, pipes and poles over their heads. Two *sangomas*, wearing animal skins over jeans and fleece sweatshirts, streak from one side of the demonstration to the other and incite protesters to hold their ground while offering them concoctions of herbs to induce courage. Behind this line of *impis* – the self-proclaimed warriors of the dispossessed – worried women watch with children slung on their hips and backs or standing at their sides. In their faces glows the last desperate hope that this latest forced removal can somehow still be staved off.

A bellow from behind Jacob draws his attention back up Lees Street. Amongst the police cruisers and riot-control vans another line is readying itself. About a hundred men wearing red construction helmets and overalls, wielding transparent shields and black sjamboks, they look like a small army of exterminators. Dubbed the Army Ants by inner-city slum dwellers, the eviction squad is listening to a rotund African in a cheap chequered khaki suit as he marches up and down the column, barking orders. Two olive-skinned business types in pressed shirts and chinos – the men who probably hired this private security company to effect the sheriff's eviction order – stand nearby with a second suit, a man who looks like he might be north African from his aquiline nose, except his skin is a high yellow. The group looks relaxed, unconcerned with the promise of impending violence or where the mass of squatters they are evicting this morning will sleep tonight.

'What a mess this is becoming,' someone says in Afrikaans.

Niehaus comes stomping along the pavement, clutching a walkie-talkie in one hand. His thinly moustached mouth is fixed in a sardonic smile. 'You missed the best part, Jakes. I guess it's what you call smart negotiations for the twenty-first century: ten minutes of self-righteous bullshit that's as meaningless as a condom stapled with an Aids message. Who's that guy on the skateboard anyway?'

'They couldn't come to an agreement?' Jacob pulls the zip of his blue police windbreaker all the way up to his throat, in the hope of keeping out the chill. Overhead the torn clouds have been gathering into ponderous dark masses filled with rain, while the landscape flickers under their heavy shadows against the bleak yellow sunshine that occasionally breaks through.

'Couldn't?' Niehaus laughs. 'It's more like *wouldn't*. You think those two bloody Greeks are going to pay for a few hundred tents to be erected somewhere else, or that the government will pull some RDP houses out of its arse right here?'

'This is not how it is supposed to be.'

Two weeks before, a similar situation at a condemned building in Joubert Park had escalated into a full-blown riot. Another security company had been tossing on to Noord Street the belongings of a few hundred squatters, and then allegedly barred the evicted from retrieving their possessions. Some of them had even begun helping themselves to the heaped-up loot. The resulting outrage and unrest was barely contained, and had left much of the area surrounding the Johannesburg Art Gallery strewn with the wares of the ghetto hawkers who set up around the train station nearby.

Niehaus grows stern. 'Of course it's not, but these people are breaking the law, Jakes. The sheriff gave them notice seven months ago, and they still haven't vacated. Their time has come.'

'But where will they go?'

He shrugs. 'Isn't our problem beyond the fact that they're currently breaking the law.'

'I would stay here too!' Jacob slams the car door shut. 'If this place has stood empty for four years and I had nowhere to go, *I* would do it.'

'Without protection for private property, where would we all be, hey, Jakes?' Niehaus sighs and scratches his pencil moustache. 'Look, we're just here as back-up. Don't worry too much about it.'

'*Aikona*, Kobus! I get pulled off a full morning's urgent work to stand and watch a forced eviction. I thought those days were over.'

'This is diff—'

'What about their dignity? These people, they . . .' Jacob waves at the air in frustration. 'This is how you treat *dogs*, supe!'

Niehaus sucks at his teeth. 'What's got you wound up like this, hey? Is it what happened to Harry?'

'Yes and no,' replies Jacob in a calmer voice. 'But the thought of all these people sleeping in the bushes along the highway tonight . . . it is so very wrong.'

Niehaus pats Jacob's shoulder. 'The moment he's stabilized, they'll fly him up here. Don't worry, the guy will pull through.'

Orders are shouted along the phalanx of riot police.

Helmet straps are fastened; tear-gas launchers, shotguns and water hoses are checked. News crews inch closer along the perimeter, eager to document the coming action for the late-morning TV bulletins and newspaper editions. Further down the wide street, oily smoke obscures the chanting and dancing and taunting protesters. A young shirtless man runs forward, leaps into the air and screams at the top of his lungs before he falls to the tarmac and pretends to have been mortally wounded. Mothers and grandmothers of all ages are rounding up children and quickly herding them back into the factory, except one particular woman dressed in a pink tracksuit, who merely stands and watches from the factory gate, three little girls huddled around her knees, each one of them dressed in a similar pink outfit.

Turning to his superior, Jacob decides to voice what has been bothering him since yesterday afternoon. 'I received a letter from Director Visier yesterday. Could you not have told me in person?'

Niehaus puts both hands on his hips and nods slowly, his eyes fixed on the pavement. 'I thought you might take it the wrong way, and I was tied up in Bloem the whole of yesterday. I asked his office not to send it down to you before we had a chance to talk it over. But they did it anyway.'

'Between you and the chief, you really couldn't find *anything* for me?'

'The short of it is that ever since the redeployment was announced Chief Molethe has been getting requests for transfers to his unit from some of the best and most experienced detectives left in the country. He's got captains applying who are willing to work for an inspector's salary, for God's sake. They might've accommodated you in an

OC or SVC unit elsewhere in the country, if you weren't so insistent on staying in Johannesburg.'

'You know I can't leave here. I have the house, and my woman has a job here.'

Niehaus lifts his shoulders in a gesture which says *That's my point exactly.*

Aloud he says, 'Then you've got to have a bit more patience.'

The clucking of a nervous woman journalist ('Is here all right? What about there? Can we get a shot here, please, on the action. Mikey, swing that camera around this way, *this* way!') reaches the two cops from just up the road. They both turn to look in her direction, and she briefly makes eye contact with Jacob before her gaze skitters away again. Wearing an open cream-coloured coat, and with an SABC microphone clutched in one hand, she fires questions like a nail gun at one of the property developers. With his hairy arms crossed defiantly over his chest, he answers her with self-assured precision: over six hundred people have been living in squalid conditions in that factory building. They don't have separate cubicles, and the property was never built with human habitation in mind. The floor space is now subdivided into 130 rooms that are simply delineated by blankets strung up on lines in a rough matrix pattern. 'You're asking me about toilets? God no! The mains were cut off when the place was first shut down, four years ago. No, that means no running water. You think about that for a minute,' says the man after a studied pause. 'They don't have electricity,' he goes on. 'It's so filthy in there you can barely breathe. You can't imagine it. And the kids, they're all cooped up twenty-four/seven, not going to school, not eating decent food. How can that be allowed, eh? Besides lacking the most basic necessities,' he adds in a convivial tone that annoys Jacob, 'the warehouse is a firebomb waiting to happen. You must understand, with all those paraffin stoves standing next to beds and under blanket partitions, and with all those *children* . . . Shanie, I don't need to tell you, but that's just *looking* for trouble. We're not only asserting our rights as property owners here today; we're undoubtedly saving lives in the long term.'

Jacob might have been sceptical of the man's measured exposition, except he can see for himself the refuse strewn all around the parking lot – the culmination of a few years' worth of dumping by hundreds of people with no facilities for municipal garbage removal. In fact, he can smell the rot, the stench of human waste, even standing upwind.

When the reporter tries to ask him some inconvenient questions about the forced removal of these destitutes – does he feel guilty about it? What about the ethical implications for the company? What about accusations that this is a new form of forced removal, merely for the sake of making money? – the businessman holds up an immaculate hand with a thick gold bracelet dangling around its wrist. 'This isn't some exercise in apartheid. Please don't try to call it that. Remember, a legitimate court order has been issued. What would you do if three, four, a hundred families decided to move into *your* house simply because it stood empty while you were on holiday?' He waits for her to fumble an appropriate reply then abruptly continues, 'I want you to think about that. What happens to these people now is the government's problem, not ours.'

Niehaus lets out a short, disbelieving laugh. 'Money grubbers, all of them. Wave a handful of cash in front of their noses and they turn into sharks at feeding time. It's the way of this city, Jakes. It's the way of this city.'

Jacob nods towards the two black businessmen standing nearby. 'Aren't those the Phaliso brothers?'

'In all their glory, my friend.'

'I didn't know the Army Ants were owned by the Absindisi.'

'They want to get their greedy little fingers in every security pie they can get their hands on.'

'But surely convicted felons are barred from owning security companies.'

'You're right about that, but these two have never actually been convicted of anything. I don't even know if anyone's ever had the courage to charge them. Show me the bloody squatter who'll finger one of these two in a line-up. No one wants to be seen accusing community heroes – doesn't matter if they just strung your wife up for defaulting on a fifty-rand loan. With the popular backing they have in the townships, they're virtually untouchable.'

A line of riot police step-marches past them down the street, batons battering against perspex shields. Further up the road the Ants have fallen quiet and edgy, as they wait now for the police to deal with the initial phase of the job. At the far end of the road, a number of more reluctant protesters are discreetly retreating from the rear ranks, but those in front, more willing to clash with the law, begin to hurl petrol bombs and bricks at the advancing police.

'If they've been here four years now, what's another year till homes can be found for them?'

Jacob asks this question out of frustration, even though he knows how naïve it sounds, even hopeless. There is no money for the poor in a poor country pretending to be rich. Or, more accurately, no political will.

The Army Ants fall in a good twenty metres behind

the riot police. It will be their job to remove the squatters' belongings from the factory and then guard the property until it is bricked up, or renovations are completed and the building is resold.

'This might have gone a lot better if that hardliner on the skateboard hadn't pitched up. His name's Makhe Motale, or some such.'

A powerful gust of wind sweeps down the street, driving tendrils of golden sand ahead of it, and a silver Nik Naks wrapper. Further down Lees Street, Jacob sees the activist pull himself fearlessly towards the police with powerful tree-stump-thick arms. He is flanked by two young bruisers who look as if they were suckled on testosterone. One of them is already filming the riot squad's advance with a digital camcorder.

'We don't ask for much!' Makhe shouts in English at the advancing cops. 'All we want is to keep a roof over our heads, the heads of our *children*! But even that is too much when it comes to making money on our broken backs.'

'I don't know who he is, but he knows what he's doing.' Jacob unclips a pistol from his belt and holds it out to Niehaus.

The superintendent eyes him up and down. 'What are you doing?'

'Sorry, supe, this is rubbish. I have to go down there and put a stop to this somehow. I'm sure I can talk to this Makhe.'

Niehaus grabs Jacob by the shirt. 'We're hanging back, Jacob. You're not going anywhere near that lot. It's between them and the sheriff's office. They've already made their decisions.'

Just then the dull thud of tear-gas canisters being

launched reaches them. They look up in time to see white tendrils of dense smoke hiss through the air over the advancing column of riot police, and plunge deep into the crowd.

'What the hell are they doing?' cries Niehaus. 'They don't know which direction that shit's going to blow in this damn weather.'

Within seconds protesters are scattering like buckshot, while the more determined ones grab the smoking canisters in oven-gloved hands and hurl them back at the advancing cops. One of the canisters falls near Makhe and rolls back down the street. By now the disabled anarchist has lifted himself off his skateboard and placed himself squarely on the tarmac in the approaching police force's path, his legs folded in his lap, his arms crossed over his chest. He seems unmindful of the tear gas boiling all around him. Jacob is impressed by how much Makhe looks like an angry Messiah in the face of his adversaries.

'Look at them!' cries Ncolela Phaliso, dressed in khaki. 'Scurrying like ants under a magnifying glass, they are. Just look at them!'

The four men in charge of the eviction have retreated further up the hill, but are still watching eagerly. Ncolela Phaliso is stamping his foot in excitement, and has his arms draped over the shoulders of his business partners on either side, both of whom look embarrassed by this close contact. Godun Phaliso, who is a lot skinnier than Jacob first thought, in fact almost emaciated, stands apart by himself, with his arms crossed behind his back.

'Je-sus Christ.' Niehaus lets go of Jacob's shirt and turns towards the unfolding havoc. 'What a cock-up.'

'Please don't blaspheme around me.' Jacob keeps his eyes carefully fixed on the crowd.

'Sorry.' His superintendent takes an abrupt interest in his own shoes.

A good ten metres away from them now, the vanguard of cops and the hired hands bringing up the rear hold their position on the perimeter of the unpredictable tear-gas fug. Shotguns crack. Rubber bullets, buckshot and empty shell casings whistle through the air. A suffocating stench of burnt rubber and gas reaches them as the wind begins to shift. Everywhere protesters scramble to get away from the stinging white clouds, but in places they fall in agony, either hit by projectiles or choking on the worst of the fumes.

Without warning, ten officers break away in unison from either side of the bristling phalanx and streak towards Makhe and his bodyguards. As though they knew what to expect and have rehearsed it, the bodyguard holding the camcorder immediately turns and high-tails it back towards the densest cluster of stubborn protesters, while the remaining brute steps closer to Makhe and braces himself. Police tackles like rushing freight trains crash into him a split-second later, and Makhe is slewed along, no one giving a thought for his frail body.

'Jes – I mean *hell*! Look at him go.' Niehaus laughs as Makhe shoves away one armoured cop so hard that the man is sent sprawling backwards. Simultaneously he reaches up and manages to grab another around the neck in a bearish choke-hold, as the unwitting cop reaches down to him with a pair of handcuffs. Makhe flips the officer over to land on his back with a crunch.

'Ha! A cripple tossing them around like cardboard cut-outs! Man, are they going to have a hard time explaining that one in the locker rooms.'

The humour of it escapes Jacob. As he observes, his

mind returns to the riots of the eighties, which he watched erupt all over the country on television from the safety of Mama Hettie Solilo's living room. This was in the years before Nelson Mandela's release from prison, before Jacob's acceptance into police college. He remembers that time as being frightening in its uncertainty, even though people sang of hope.

'Jacob,' Mama Solilo often said in those days, 'do you want to join all those youngsters dying in the streets? Is that what you want for yourself?'

Sitting on her living-room floor, his knobbly teenage knees pulled up against his chest, he would look over his shoulder at the old herbalist sitting slumped in her green easy chair, a quilt tucked in around her body. Though by day he often joined his schoolfriends in dabbling in the fight for freedom, he always managed to quell the excitement boiling in his chest under her disapproving gaze when at home. She was of the very strong opinion that an education would be of much more benefit to the future generations than his breaking laws that were already crumbling.

'No, *Magogo*,' he would say, 'but it feels wrong, me just sitting here.'

She would nod. 'Good, my boy. It's not that those protesters are wrong, understand, it's that your grandfather, and the ancestors of your tribe, have something better in mind for you. Those people,' she would glance at the television with a mixture of sadness and respect, 'they are the *impis* of the present. Look how destructive they are! But you – you will be someone for the future. You will not tear things down. You'll help build them up instead. It's in your nature, Jacob Tshabalala.'

He shakes his head at this sudden vivid memory, but

it refuses to let go of him. Fixing the future? Here he is twenty years on, and the same rubbish is still happening. This is not why he became a cop. This is not how it was supposed to be.

KHUMBULA!

The sudden thunderous bellow burns through Jacob's head and he staggers backwards as if blinded. Niehaus's excited running commentary instantly fades out, along with the rest of the clamour, and Jacob's skin begins to tingle as though covered by a film of spider webs.

Khumbula, Jacob!

Shaken by this intrusion on his awareness, Jacob throws an anxious glance at his superior, but Niehaus is still consumed by the spectacle, and does not seem to notice his inspector's bewilderment.

Remember!

It is his grandfather's authoritative voice, the way Jacob remembers it from when the old man was still alive. And he sounds angrier than he did the time Jacob and his cousins forgot to close the family's livestock kraal and lost all their three goats. Shaken, he looks around for the source of that voice, because surely this time it is far too loud to be coming from inside his head. He sees nothing but slow-motion clips of Niehaus's constantly moving lips, and the self-satisfied real-estate dealers shaking hands with the Phaliso brothers. Empty shotgun shells spin through the air like tops, while cagey riot police and security men look as if frozen in a Kevin Carter photograph. A short way down the street batons continue to pummel Makhe's aide, now curled up into a tight ball, while at the factory gates a retreating line of determined protesters becomes nothing more than a wavering mirage in the hot air rising off the burning crates and tyres. And above it all the half-dead sunlight continues to flicker through brooding clouds.

There! At the edge of the fracas, to the left of the factory gates, stands a wiry African figure wrapped in leopard and jackal skins and swathed in the beads of a *sangoma*; he grips a white staff in one hand. Jacob begins to smile at this familiar apparition . . . but, as suddenly as he was lifted clear from the pandemonium, he is dumped right back into it. Gone is the figure he thought was his grandfather, and in its stead a flash of pink catches his attention. Horrified, he observes a little girl amid the panicked rush of escapees, wiping at her tear-gas-blinded eyes. Her mother and siblings are nowhere to be seen. Though he cannot hear her over the bedlam, he can see she is screaming at the top of her lungs.

'*Maye babo!*' he exclaims.

'What was that?' asks Niehaus.

But Jacob has already shoved his side-arm into his superintendent's hands, and is off without a reply.

Sprinting as fast as his legs will carry him, he passes the Army Ants swarming down the hill, and angles past the rear line of riot police. He then realizes that a scrawny protester behind the fiery barricades has also noticed the little girl. The man separates from the retreating squatters and bolts for the helpless child, but before he can reach her three officers mark his charge and turn to fire on him. Rubber bullets and buckshot send him reeling, and the last Jacob sees of the would-be saviour he is falling to the ground and clutching at his face, blood seeping between his fingers.

Jacob leaps past three policemen who are still struggling to handcuff Makhe. For a second their eyes meet –

Jacob's wide with adrenalin, Makhe's glaring and hate-filled – but then the anarchist senses a gap in one of his opponents' defence and savagely bites his neck. The officer's surprised scream follows Jacob down the hill. Through the rancid black rubber-smoke and trails of tear gas he streaks, the fumes stinging his eyes and throat, burning his skin. A few steps later the billowing smoke forces him to stop as his throat constricts and he is overcome by great hacking coughs.

'Get out of the way, you!' someone shouts at him from up the hill.

Fighting not to black out, he realizes that the girl's terrified screams have been sounding close for a few seconds now, while from deep inside the chaos the panicked mother, who can hear her child but cannot see her, is calling out to her with mounting despair. Then he spots the disorientated child stumbling about near a stack of burning tyres, the curls of her afro hairstyle already beginning to frizz in the heat.

'*Bekha!*' shouts Jacob as he leaps forward. 'Ntombi, *bekha!*'

His shout must have startled the little girl even more, for in the next moment she takes one last doddering step away from him, and backs straight into the knee-high tower of burning tyres immediately behind her.

6

The girl's hair ignites like bundled straw, and her terrified screams climb several octaves.

He catches her roughly in his arms and yanks her away

from the flames, but is forced to leap awkwardly over the barricade as his momentum slews them forward. He is still anxiously brushing at her smouldering hair when he trips over a slab of broken concrete and topples forward. Instinctively, he rolls with the fall while protectively cupping the girl's head with one hand as he hits the tarmac with his right shoulder. Dazed, he sits up – and the first thing he focuses on is Makhe's lieutenant filming him with the camcorder.

'Go for help!' he yells angrily in Sotho. 'She's badly hurt!'

The camera keeps rolling, however, the man acting as if he is filming a documentary rather than a human tragedy.

Unexpectedly, the girl is wrenched from Jacob's arms and a dozen fists begin to rain down on him, while feet strike his ribs, his face, his back. Sticks and stones find a way to hurt him, even when Jacob laces his hands over his head and curls himself up into a foetal ball against the sudden attack. Within seconds his body is numb from the blows, and he has to struggle to keep hold of his senses.

How much later it is he cannot be sure, but suddenly riot police plough into the crowd assaulting him. Alarm and pain rise up all around him, but he is too disorientated to take advantage of the opportunity created for him. Then rough hands seize him by the collar of his windbreaker and drag him away, back up the hill, while an Afrikaans voice shouts at him, '*Is jy OK? Praat met my, ou!* What's your name?'

The ragged tar rips holes in his jacket, while one of Jacob's cheeks occasionally slaps against the backs of running heels. Exhausted and out of breath, his nose and mouth and eyes burning from the tear gas, he cannot manage more than a croak for a reply. But in his head a mantra has formed.

Thank God, yes, I'm OK.

7

'Fuck, Tshabalala!' An enraged Niehaus yells it so close to his face that Jacob feels a fine spray of spittle on his cheek. 'Are you totally *crazy*? What were you thinking, hey?'

Jacob pays this admonishment little attention as he examines the deep cut above one eye in the side mirror of an ambulance. It is bleeding heavily, but he does not think it will need stitches. Swellings already cover his newly shaven head and his ribs feel like he has been going twelve straight rounds with George Foreman.

'I told you *not* to do it!' bellows Niehaus. 'Which part of that particular order did you not understand?'

A broad sunny smile, eight parts exhilaration, two parts relief, brightens Jacob's face. 'You mean I should have left that little girl to burn, supe?'

The media has crowded around an ambulance parked on the other side of the street, where an emergency crew is now treating the child. Shouting over the toddler's cries of pain is her furious mother, demanding in Sotho the heads of the sheriff, the judge, the real-estate developers, interspersed with a range of expletives that might have put veteran miners to shame. Jacob glimpses the black sound engineers and cameramen grinning amongst themselves as some of the white reporters try desperately to get a translation out of them.

Niehaus interlocks his fingers over his head and seems

to deflate. 'Yes . . . no. *Ag fok*, I don't know. How the hell did you spot her anyway? I couldn't see shit from where we were standing.'

Jacob holds his singed left hand out to a paramedic with carrot-red hair, who begins to apply a greasy ointment and bandages. 'My eyes just fell on her. Maybe I heard her screaming, I don't know.'

Niehaus pulls a bag of peanuts from a blazer pocket, tears it open and upends half the sachet into his mouth with one brisk motion. 'Over that noise?' he says sceptically through a mouthful of nuts. 'Sure. And I'm King Goodwill Zwelithini at your service, you bloody lunatic.'

Preferring not to tell his superior about what had attracted him to the girl's plight in the first place, Jacob remains mum and instead allows his eyes to wander back towards the milling crowd on the other side of the street, where camera crews jostle with media-greedy squatters hoping to feature in tonight's scoop. The injured child's two sisters are clinging to their mother's knees in bewilderment at the crowd surging all around them. With the bandaging of his hand finished, Jacob pushes past Niehaus and heads across the street, angling his route in such a way that he manages to climb aboard the other ambulance unnoticed, via the driver's door. Before long the back door opens, and two hassled medics deliver their terrified patient into the rear. Spotting pen and paper lying on the dashboard, Jacob begins to scribble down a phone number just as the patient's mother and sisters climb aboard. As the doors close behind them the mother's boiling venom evaporates, and she throws herself down on her knees next to her child. Up close the family's bright pink clothing looks soiled, and the mother's wild hairstyle is tangled and grey with filth. The sour smell of destitution fills Jacob's nose.

'My sistah.' Jacob squeezes towards them between the two front seats. 'Is she going to be OK?'

The woman looks up in alarm, and the fire in her eyes flares up again. 'What do you want?'

Before he can reply the driver's door opens behind him, and a paramedic starts in surprise at finding a stranger in his vehicle. Without his torn windbreaker, Jacob is wearing nothing to identify him as a policeman. 'What the hell are you doing in here? Get out immediately.'

Jacob holds up a hand. 'Relax. I'm with the police.'

'The police!' exclaims the woman. 'Get away from us, *gata*! You see what you have done to my daughter? Just look at her!'

'Please calm down, *sisie*.'

'I said what do you want?' she snarled.

Offering her the warmest smile he can muster under the circumstances, Jacob gestures with his bandaged hand for her to ease off. 'I just wanted to see if the little *ntwana* will be fine, and to let you know about a shelter where you could stay.'

'She wouldn't be in this mess if you didn't throw us out of our home in the first place!'

'Hey pal, do you mind?' says the paramedic from behind him.

'Just a second,' replies Jacob.

'That girl needs to get to a hospital quick-quick.'

By the set of the woman's face, Jacob guesses there is no reasoning with her, for the moment at least. He glances at the little girl, quieting down now that the painkillers are taking effect.

'For what it's worth, I agree what happened here today is wrong.' He holds out the number he had scribbled down for her. 'Please take this.'

'You people think *nothing* of us! Do you know what it feels like to be treated like an animal?'

Jacob feels his lips tighten. 'It's the number of a church shelter in Soweto. My own number is—'

The woman hawks noisily, and to Jacob's utter surprise she spits in his face. 'Get away from me, I said! Get away from all of us, *gata*.'

She hisses out the last word as if it were poison, and a mutual sense of revulsion hangs between them like a miasma. Then hot rage takes hold of Jacob. He might have hurled himself at the woman, but for a sudden warning from his grandfather at the back of his mind, and the paramedic grabbing his upper arm. He glances at the two little sisters huddled against the rear doors, one with a thumb stuck in her mouth.

'Have it your way then, *sisie*.' With restrained movements he wipes away what he can of her spittle with a shirt sleeve, and exits the ambulance the way he came. It is only after he crosses the street to where the police vehicles are still parked that he allows his rage to overtake him.

8

Jacob's bruised body is trembling so badly by the time he is driving back to the office that he almost swerves off the blacktop as he turns into Pretoria Main Road.

He leans over to the glove compartment and fishes out yet another of the fast-food serviettes he found stashed there. Wiping at his face until the skin begins to smart hardly helps relieve the sense of disgust at having been spat on by that woman. A thousand furious questions throb in his head, all of them centred on why she should have done that to him, after he had been the one to save her child.

Where was she, anyway, when it happened? Why were her kids there in the first place?

You were on the wrong side, says another, calmer voice in his head. *That's what matters to her.*

I was only helping!

Did it look like that to her? his grandfather's voice chips in.

I am a police officer, for heaven's sake! He thumps the steering wheel with one fist. *No one can do that to me.*

He wonders whether being a police officer still means anything at all to the average person on the street, given the things they feel at liberty to do these days.

It means nothing. A voice much like his own mocks him. *Not any more.*

He never thought the day would arrive when the rabbits out there would believe themselves stronger than the state-employed wolves, but they do now. To them, a cop's just another person who can't get a better job. A cop's nothing better than a redneck who likes to bully people for a bit of *tjôtjô* on the side, like any other hustler on the street, the only difference being that the blue uniform protects him.

When did it get this bad? he wonders. *Where has it all gone so wrong?*

Can't you see I tried to help you? In his mind's eye he is back inside the ambulance again, but this time shouting sense into her, shaking her till the defiance vanishes from her eyes. Why that unrestrained, undifferentiated, savage hatred?

Jacob winds down the window and allows the cold air

to wash over him in an effort to clear his head. It has been getting harder every day, keeping himself under control. The daylight has all but turned into a suffocating early twilight under the sky's weight. He wonders if that woman would have done it to just anyone, spat in their face, given the circumstances.

No, Jakes, it's because you're a police officer, says a voice now sounding like Niehaus. *You should know that by now*.

To that, the mocking voice quickly adds, Mfo, *it's because you're black, and you're a* gata, *a* boer, *a dirty pig in their eyes*.

This thought rings true, whichever way he looks at it. She would not have dared do that to a white cop, he is sure. They still command a kind of grudging respect, despite the handover of political power in this country, and the appalling legacy that white police officers from the apartheid era have left behind. He has experienced it often enough while working with Harry Mason. Have an *umlungu* along with you, goes the saying in the Friday-night off-duty bars, and the scum of this city are less likely to try to buy you, or shoot at you. If there is a badge on your chest and your skin has any real colour, the civvies treat you worse than shit. Knock on a door with a white cop next to you, the person who opens it, doesn't matter if he's black or white, will speak to the *umlungu*, the man with all the power. It wouldn't matter who of the two carries the higher rank, because history lives on, even when most people try to pretend it is dead and buried.

Jacob takes a deep breath and forces his aching shoulders to relax. If he is going to brood continuously on how society reacts to the colour of his skin, he might as well hand in his service pistol and badge right away.

He smiles wryly at the memory of one of Harry Mason's favourite sayings:

'What we do, Jakes, is not so much about fixing things, you've got to realize that. It's about wading into the filthy quagmire of the human condition to fish out a few principles there worth saving. That's what makes it worth it.'

The first drops of the rain that has been threatening all day smack against the windshield, and soon foamy run-off is washing over the highway, slowing the traffic to a crawl.

Rain in August? Jacob stops the car under a bridge and watches the windscreen wipers chase each other back and forth across the windscreen. *Who ever heard of this kind of rain in August?*

9

Back at the police office, Jacob is standing at a washbasin, splashing hot water over his face and scalp as if to wash away the remainder of his rage, when the door to the men's lavatories opens, scraping loudly over the floor. In saunters a tall man in his early forties. His golden hair is neatly trimmed, and his long hands swing at his sides like a cowboy's. Jacob realizes he has met the detective before.

'You're James Franklin, aren't you?' he addresses the man's reflection. 'From SVC?'

The Serious and Violent Crimes detective briefly rolls on to his toes as he unzips his fly and begins to piss into the urinal.

'Suppose I am.'

'Thought so.' Jacob chucks the damp tissue paper into

a wastebasket. 'Harry Mason introduced us about two months ago.'

'Really?' Franklin goes on pissing with a look of almost religious bliss directed straight at the wall. 'I don't remember.'

'No problem. Jacob Tshabalala. I'm with Murder and Robbery.'

'Right.'

Jacob moves over to the third-floor window and peers out at nothing specific. 'Were you there in Tsolo on Monday when Harry got shot?'

'Yes, I was.'

'What happened, exactly?'

Franklin flushes the urinal and takes his time to zip up, then strolls over to the washbasin before answering.

'A raiding party from Qumbu, which lies about five Ks east, ambushed the village an hour before dawn. The fighting was still going on when we reached Tsolo, but they weren't after stock this time. It seems they wanted revenge for the murders of two cattle boys somewhere up in the mountains, the week before. It was all fogged up when we arrived; you couldn't see your own hand in front of your face. One of the guys in the team says Mason must have seen someone, because he shouted something and just ran off. Like we were in a fucking shopping mall. Don't know what he was thinking, pissing off like that into an area that hadn't been secured.' Franklin hitches his thumbs in the front loops of his jeans and shrugs. 'He paid the price, I guess.'

'Any idea who did it?'

Franklin probes at something in his mouth with his tongue. His unblinking gas-flame stare begins to agitate

Jacob. 'No, I don't. But we're looking into that, so don't worry yourself.'

At that moment the door screeches open again. 'Tshabalala, you in there?' calls a gruff voice in Afrikaans.

'Yes.'

'Call for you. Lady says it's urgent.'

'I'm coming.' To Franklin, 'Who found him?'

'The Supe, Russie Swarts. Carried that boy on his back all the way to the nearest open field. He's damn lucky the weather lifted when it did. If it wasn't for the chopper we managed to get in, Mason would've been dead.'

10

'Detective Inspector Tshabalala,' begins a dry British voice weighted with exhaustion. It has always been Mrs Mason's first instinct to address him that way, although he has begged her not to on numerous occasions. 'Jacob, I mean.'

His blood runs cold, since an urgent call from Harry's mother can surely only mean one thing. 'Is everything all right?'

'Under the circumstances, I should say yes. The doctors say he's stable, but it's still too early to move him away from this backwater.'

There is a long pause, during which Jacob hears an urgent announcement being made in the background, and he imagines Joan Mason herself listening acutely to what is being said.

'Yes?' he presses eventually.

'Do you happen to know who Tanya is?'

Tanya? 'No,' he says. 'But can you tell me more?'

'About an hour ago he stirred for a moment and

mumbled that name.' There follows a heavy sigh on the other end of the line, and Jacob wonders whether he has ever heard someone sound so worn out.

Tanya. Try as he might he cannot think of anyone with that name, except . . .

Jacob suddenly recalls an unusual observation he had quickly dismissed from his mind, not six weeks back. He and Nomsa had gone over to the Mason home in Brixton for a Sunday barbecue. As Harry flipped lamb chops and a marinated chicken flatty on the fire, he seemed in a more jocular mood than Jacob had seen him in a while, and yet more distracted than his usual self. He kept checking his phone and sending messages when he thought no one was paying attention. Finally, Jacob could no longer hold in his curiosity and asked, 'What's with you, my friend? Did you win the lottery?'

Harry had glanced at him in surprise, then grinned foolishly. 'No, better.'

When Jacob had probed, his friend smiled and shrugged his questions off. 'I'll tell you soon enough,' he had said. 'Not now, though. Call me the superstitious one for a change, but I'll not risk a jinx on this one.'

Is he finally seeing someone again? wonders Jacob. *Has he finally stopped mourning Amy?*

Tanya?

To Harry's mother he says, 'I haven't met anyone of that name, but have you checked his mobile?'

'It got . . . it was soaked through with his blood and wouldn't work, so I think there might be a good few people who have no idea where he is.'

'I'll try my best to find out who she is and put you in touch with her,' he says. 'How does that sound?'

'If it's someone he loves, I need her down here with

me, Jacob. I really do.' Harry's mother rings off abruptly, but Jacob still picks up the sudden tears in her voice.

11

Later that afternoon Jacob takes the lift up two floors, to the Serious and Violent Crimes Division. The full brunt of his pain and exhaustion beats down on him as he waits for the lift door to open, making him both irritable and restless to head home.

As the doors slide open with a ping, he sees a burly man wearing a dark green birdseye suit block the exit. He looks up from a wad of loose papers resting in his hands. A star-shaped scar puckers one cheek, while the rest of his face has a peculiar mashed look about it – the culmination of years of bare-knuckle fistfights during his younger years in the rawer sections of Soweto.

'*Sawubona, Tshabalala!*' Director Simon Molethe greets him in Zulu and moves aside to allow Jacob to exit the lift. His corpulent belly bulges from underneath his blazer. In English he adds, '*Eish mfo*, long time no see, man. What's happened to your face?'

Jacob smiles at the thought of the director addressing him as an old friend. 'The usual,' he shrugs.

Molethe, who was commander in Murder and Robbery for a number of years before taking a promotion to SVC, shakes his head knowingly. 'Some of you can't stop play-ing rough, like a bunch of children.'

'Do you mind if I take a look at Harry's desk?' replies Jacob in Sotho, the chief's mother tongue. 'I'm looking for a telephone number.'

Molethe's face clouds. 'Whose number, exactly?'

'His mother says he came round for a second and was asking for someone called Tanya.'

Molethe's eyes wander towards the ceiling, then he shakes his head. 'I don't know any Tanya.'

'It might be important, so is it all right if I check?'

'Yes,' agrees Molethe. 'Don't remove anything, though. It all has to be boxed up for analysis.' The surprise evident on Jacob's face spurs him to add, 'Harry was knee-deep into something no one quite understands yet – and, in the end, people got killed.'

'But I thought you recovered the weapons, that it was just some panicked villager who most likely shot him?'

'We didn't quite find what we went looking for, and it's not completely about the gun cache, either.' Molethe glances over his shoulder as two passing detectives greet him, then he grabs Jacob's elbow and pulls him closer to the wall. In a hushed tone he adds, 'Four soldiers were killed out there, one of them an officer, and fifteen locals are dead. The papers are calling it a massacre, Jacob, and by the end of today the Independent Complaints Directorate will be swarming all over my division like flies on a dead horse. I don't quite know what's going on, and that's by far the worst of it.'

The chief lets go of Jacob's arm to wipe his face with a hand the size of a baseball mitt. There are exhausted rings under the man's eyes, as distinctive as the rings on a felled tree. The Independent Complaints Directorate is an institution created for one purpose only: to nail police officers who either break the law or infringe the human rights of civilians. A fair number of police officers do not take this organization – understaffed and with few resources to take complex cases to court – seriously, but nevertheless it sometimes catches dissident cops by surprise.

'Who are they after?' Jacob asks.

Molethe shakes his head. 'Don't worry about it.'

'Chief?'

The director pulls a face like he is fighting to prevent his mouth from speaking, then he sighs heavily. 'There are rumours that the Defence Force is putting together formal complaints of misconduct. ICD's saying Harry and Russell Swarts forced a situation that no one was adequately prepared for.'

'But from what you've told me they didn't really have a choice.'

Molethe does not immediately answer him but fidgets with his papers instead. 'That's how I got it from Swarts.'

'Tell me who they're after, chief, please,' Jacob presses. But it is an unnecessary question. The guilty expression on Molethe's face tells it all.

'Harry *was* the investigative officer,' Molethe says carefully, as if he does not want to insult Jacob.

'But Swarts was his superior!'

'A lot of questions need answering, Jacob.' Molethe lowers his eyes to the floor. 'And nobody is around to do it. Russell is in Port Elizabeth with Harry, and the rest of the men claim they don't know all the particulars. They insist that Harry and Russell ran a tight ship, with Harry's informant at the centre.'

'He's in a coma and they want him to take the fall? What's that all about?'

'Don't be so impatient, Jacob. There's no question of anyone taking any fall. Harry is a good man, and so are the rest of them. Russell has a helluva lot on the line himself. He put his name to this investigation and pulled in some favours from people placed far higher than me in the service. And now that he has little to show for it, they are asking me some very uncomfortable questions about the budget.'

'I don't see why you're so worried about Superintendent Swarts when Harry's the one fighting for his life.'

Perhaps realizing he has already revealed too much, Molethe squares his shoulders. 'A due process has to be followed, Jacob. You know that.'

'You could stall them.'

'I can't afford to be dragged into this!' Molethe looks around to see if anyone has heard him raise his voice, then adds in a softer tone, 'And stall what exactly?'

'Stall them till you at least get Harry's side of the story.'

'Jacob, that will come in good time, but right now anything I do in that direction could be misconstrued as interference, which could do both of them a lot more harm. This has to be treated just like any other investigation.'

Suddenly Jacob is livid. 'You're cutting them loose, chief? Your own men!'

The restlessness he woke up with this morning is back with a bang, and commanding his full attention. *Is this it?* Jacob wonders. *Is it Harry's trouble that you've been on about, Grandfather?* But no answer is now forthcoming, and that aggravates him even more. *Then WHAT is it?!*

'I'm not,' protests Molethe, 'I—'

'Then *what!*' barks Jacob.

Molethe raises his eyebrows as Jacob realizes he has spoken this last word too loud.

When the lift bell pings, they both look up in time to see a tall black woman step out. Her corn-row-braided hair is pulled up into a tight bun, and her navy blue suit screams banker, accountant, broker – anything but police. She looks completely out of place, yet completely at ease with her surroundings. The eyes behind her expensive-looking square glasses drift over Jacob to settle on the chief.

'Director Molethe. I hope I'm not late?' Her voice is silky and deep, her English like refined sugar.

Molethe straightens up and sticks out his hand. 'Detective Mosetsane.' She does not reciprocate the attempt at a handshake; instead, her hands remain stiffly at her sides. Flustered, Molethe wipes at his chest as if to disguise his misfired gesture. 'No, I was on my way to the boardroom myself. Please, follow me.'

As the two turn away, the woman turns her eyes on Jacob once more, and this time they rest on him more leisurely. Though she is attractive enough, and her clear eyes with their chocolate-brown irises are downright gorgeous, that gaze still makes Jacob feel uneasy. It somehow reminds him of a CAT scan he had that required lead to be placed around his genitals. The last thing he notes before she turns away again is the square white visitor's badge pinned above her left breast. ICD it reads across the top, in emerald-green letters: Independent Complaints Directorate.

12

As he pushes open the door to Harry's office, Jacob Tshabalala is still wondering who can move so fast in the police service, or the ICD, as to launch a full inquiry into the Eastern Cape shoot-out barely forty-eight hours after it happened. A man wearing a bent pair of glasses is seated in his absent friend's chair, and is so surprised by the newcomer's arrival that he drops a file and very nearly tips the swivel chair over.

'*Jirre*, but did you give me a fright! You ever hear about knocking?'

A disarming smile spreads over Jacob's face. 'Sorry about that.'

'Who the hell are you, anyway? Wait, it's Tshabalala, isn't it?'

'Yes, Captain Combrink.' They met at Harry's SVC welcoming party, on the same occasion Jacob had met James Franklin and the other Ballies. 'We met through Harry.'

'*Ag*, it's a shame about him.' Combrink stoops behind the desk to pick up the documents he just dropped. The pear-shaped butt and pale plumber's crack now exposed amuse Jacob considerably.

'I remember that party,' the man continues. 'It was a piss-up like none other. What can I do for you?'

'I've come to look for a personal phone number. Do you happen to know a friend of Harry's called Tanya?'

A red-faced Combrink emerges from behind the desk, still stuffing loose pages into a docket, which he jams into one of the new white file boxes resting on Harry's desk. 'Tanya? No, never heard of her. She good-looking?'

Jacob throws his eyes over the room, wondering what it is this man might be looking for in an office that has been technically sealed up for an investigation. He is also wondering where the ICD investigators who should be overseeing the procedure might be.

'I don't know,' Jacob says in answer to the question. 'But I do know a woman from the ICD is here already to discuss Tsolo with Chief Molethe.'

'She is?' Combrink looks unfazed. 'A woman?'

Jacob nods. 'Do you mind? I need to find a telephone number.'

Combrink claps his hands on his thighs. 'Me? Of course not. I was only checking up on a case we're still trying to crack. It's a bloody mess picking up where another detective's left off, especially when he's not around to answer any of your questions.'

'I know all about that.' Jacob smiles. 'Especially when it's one of Harry's.'

'Don't you know it.' Combrink brushes past him, a strong odour of old frying oil following him into the passage. 'Cheers, Tshabalala. I'll see you around.'

Before Jacob can ask him any more about what exactly happened in Tsolo, Combrink is lumbering away down the corridor, his ample arse jiggling like a jelly tart under a washed-out custard-coloured shirt which hangs halfway out the back of his trousers. Jacob shakes his head at the absurd sight, wondering whether the man's wife left him because he was so slovenly, or whether he became so untidy only after she had the signed divorce papers.

13

A pang of jealousy hits Jacob when he re-enters Harry's office and surveys the modern L-shaped desk, the computer so unlike his own stone-age abacus – the sheer *space*. From the window he watches icy sheets of rain wash over the beige edifice of the Civic Theatre poking out from behind a line of trees, just two blocks to the east. The evergreens sway in the breeze, as though dancing at receiving this watery gift so early in the year.

Clearly, landing a job in this kind of unit gets you all the amenities you can wish for, he reflects. It is not quite the National Prosecution Authority's élite Scorpions div-

ision, but it could do well enough for him. Jacob recalls
his first job as a new recruit. That was in a bantustan
building in the old Bophuthatswana homeland, a warren
that housed all the puppet state's administrative blocks.
The buildings were huddled close together for one reason
only: that way they were easier to fence off and protect by
the small contingent of black policemen stranded out there
in the sticks. In those days, neither he nor his colleagues
dared venture too far into the township they were supposed to patrol, for fear of getting necklaced by the local
residents, who saw them as collaborators of the apartheid
state. His first desk was located in the mortuary because
the senior officers got to occupy the only two offices
assigned to the police station, and there were no holding
cells to use for prisoners. The one patrol car they possessed
was broken down more often than not, and he had a
difficult time sleeping in the police barracks situated at the
edge of the compound, on a bunk bed which creaked
louder than a rusty bicycle chain. He is only too glad that
things have finally moved on from those sad early days.

Someone has almost completed packing up the contents of Harry's office: two drawers of the filing cabinet
stand halfway open; computer cables have been unplugged
and wrapped around the keyboard; the white cardboard
boxes sitting on the table are filled with dockets and files.
Jacob assumes this information is destined for Detective
Mosetsane's desk, where, if her gaze is anything to go by,
it will no doubt be dissected as meticulously as a forensic
pathologist picks apart a corpse. But where would he find
information on Tanya?

Jacob recalls that Harry has never owned a Rolodex,
or any other kind of telephone index that makes sense.
His customary method of filing contacts is a tray of scrap

paper on which names and numbers are scribbled. Riffling through these pieces of paper, Jacob comes up with nothing that looks like it relates to a woman called Tanya. Smiling inwardly, he wishes Mosetsane the best of luck finding what she wants in among Harry's chaos.

He is just about to give up his search when he spots a doodled heart with a question mark inside it, on the edge of the coaster underneath Harry's coffee mug. Jacob carefully peels the coffee-stained cardboard off the bottom of the mug, and examines the number along with the name, *Sibiya*.

From the telephone number Jacob guesses this person is located somewhere in Fordsburg, the less affluent Indian quarter of Johannesburg's inner city. He sits down on the edge of Harry's desk and proceeds to dial the telephone number. After a few rings, the voice of an elderly black woman answers.

'Sibiya Kekana,' she says.

This is an unexpectedly curt greeting, and in the background he can hear several children shrieking at play.

Jacob introduces himself in Sotho. 'Ma, do you know Detective Harry Mason?'

'Me?' asks the voice. '*Aikona*. But I've heard all about him.'

'From who?'

'The girl that runs this place, Ms Tanya Fouché.'

'And what place is that?' Jacob asks, happy that he has located his goal so quickly.

'This is the Sibiya Kekana Home for Street Children.'

'In that case, Ma, can I speak with her?'

'She's not here right now.'

'Does she have a cell number?'

'She does, but she's always leaving the bloody thing

behind in the office. She's at a meeting all of today, and won't be back till late.'

'Will you tell her I called, then? It's urgent.'

'Don't you tell me that man's dead. He's not dead, is he?'

'Harry Mason? No, he's not dead. But please ask her to call me. Can you do that for me, Ma?'

'No offence, but I've told her, nothing good can come of her seeing a cop. *Ever*. I was married to one for three years till he started beating me.'

Jacob interrupts her to give his own number, and rings off before she can fill his ears with any further information he can do without.

14

The secret his grandfather has been hinting to him all day finally reveals itself shortly after eight in the evening, not long after Jacob gets home.

Pulling the oyster shape of his gun holster from the small of his back and dropping it on the coffee table, Jacob throws himself on to the living-room couch without even bothering to take off his shoes. His bruised body has turned into an all-encompassing throb, and his mind is rancid with the eventful day's stress. Yet, despite his physical discomfort, he manages to doze off within seconds.

It is only when a tentative finger touches the cut above his eye that he is called back into a drowsy wakefulness, and discovers that Nomsa has been quietly busying herself in the kitchen. One of his favourite tunes, 'Stella by Starlight', fills the room.

Jacob smiles. 'Miles Davis.'

'The one and only.' Nomsa giggles. 'Hope you're not feeling too sore to be hungry?'

He focuses on the concerned-looking, upside-down face peering down at him. 'I could do with a handful of aspirins and about two days of sleep, that's for sure.'

'But first you must eat.' She lets her hand run over his bruised, clean-shaven head and then plants a warm kiss on his forehead. Heading back towards the kitchen, she remarks over her shoulder, 'I don't know how you take it every day, Inspector Tshabalala. I really don't.'

The smell of *putu* and spiced mutton wafts into the living room, and he has to swallow hard as his mouth begins to water. 'Sometimes I don't either,' he murmurs.

He sits up and tries unsuccessfully to stretch the tension out of his neck and shoulders before heading into the kitchen. As he sets the table, Nomsa busies herself at the stove with the mutton and pumpkin mash, excitedly telling him about the other choir members who have already confirmed their places.

'We can just be glad Teddy's replacing Mfumandi as our conductor. He's so much—'

'Teddy?' Jacob interrupts, familiar with that name but not immediately realizing how he should recognize it.

There is a silence from the stove which causes him to look up.

'Yes,' she says, a deep colour rising in her cheeks. 'You know – Teddy. Remember him?'

Jacob raises his eyebrows questioningly. And then it hits him.

'You mean Teddy Bakwena?'

'Yes.' She watches him with carefully contrived neutral interest.

Jacob returns to laying the knives and forks on the

placemats, suddenly very meticulous about where each should go. 'I didn't know *he* was back in the choir.'

'Oh, I didn't tell you? For a while he's been with the His Glorious Presence congregation, but he didn't enjoy himself much there, so he moved back to our church about a month ago?'

Whenever Nomsa grows nervous her sentences begin to end on a raised note, as though she were asking for confirmation. He has always found this nervousness endearing, but right now he feels irritated by it.

'And this happened when?' He still cannot bring himself to look directly at her, because he does not want her to see the jealousy he is trying to bring under control.

Nomsa pauses. 'End of July. I thought you might have seen him around by now.'

'No, I haven't.'

She yelps as mutton fat suddenly spits from the frying pan on to the bare skin of her forearm. She turns away from Jacob for a moment, turning down the heat and moving the pan off the hotplate.

What is wrong with you? he asks himself. *So Teddy Bakwena is back in town. Who cares? It's been years since she dated him, years since the man once offered her father a substantial* lobola *for her hand in marriage. And in the end she declined him, didn't she? Her father had readily accepted her choice, too.* She started seeing Jacob instead, didn't she – and she's still his, isn't she?

Except now she is going on a two-week vacation to the Cape with Teddy Bakwena, while the two of them, she and Jacob, have never been anywhere outside of Johannesburg except his parents' homestead near Hartebeespoort Dam. They have never been able to afford anything else.

A rusty cackle of derision starts up in the back of

Jacob's head. *Your woman you should never leave untended*, says the ancient voice. *If she's in your kraal, you keep a bell around her neck, otherwise she strays.*

Shut up, Ndoda!

'Jacob?' she asks in a timorous voice as she turns back towards him. 'I can still go, can't I?'

He returns his gaze to her, and Nomsa cringes behind the pot lid she holds protectively in front of her like a miniature *ihawu* shield.

'What can I say?' he says in an exasperated voice. 'I don't like it, but I'm not going to forbid you. I trust you.'

'Thank you.' A relieved smile creeps over her face.

Jacob is taken aback by her reply, because he had hoped she would show some concern for him and not go. 'You don't have to thank me. I've already made this trip a gift to you. Don't thank me for not taking it away.'

She responds with a frown. 'What do you mean?'

'I mean: am I the kind of man who would prevent his woman going on a trip because . . . because . . .' Jacob cannot bring himself to say it.

'Because you're jealous?' Nomsa says it with a disarming smile. 'I won't go if you don't want me to.'

'I said you could go.'

'But I won't feel happy about it if I know you'll be sitting here at home wondering if I'm cheating on you.'

There is a hint of annoyance in her voice, and it immediately puts him on the back foot.

'That's not at all what I'm saying,' replies Jacob.

'But it's what you're *thinking*. And how can you?' Her eyes begin to glitter with angry tears. 'This is a *church* trip, for goodness' sake – with people we both know. Teddy is only our conductor, and that's where our relationship ends.'

'I'm not worried about you. I said I trust you, didn't I?'

'Then *do* trust me!'

Jacob's grip on the chair's backrest has intensified so that his knuckles are turning a bright pink. 'I don't trust *him*, though.'

'Oh, come on! I'm a grown woman and I can make my own decisions. Don't talk to me like I can't be responsible for my own behaviour. Either you trust me or you don't. So which is it?'

He shakes his head, exasperated by her reaction and his own at the same time. Later he will wonder why he cannot maintain an even head at home as easily as he can at work. 'Anything can happen on a trip like that.'

'No, Jacob, it *can't*.' Nomsa sucks in air to add more, but her voice falters. She looks everywhere but directly into his face, like so many criminals do when they have been caught out, he reflects. Again she tries to summon a steadier voice, but fails. Finally, she slams the pot lid down on the counter and pushes past him.

Realizing too late he has taken this too far, he grabs for her shoulder. 'Nomsa. I'm sorry. It's been a bad day. I'm not that jealous a person. You must know that.' At least, he feels confident he can control it.

'I *do* trust you,' he says softly. She does not turn around to face him, and Jacob can see her body shaking with emotion. 'Please look at me.'

She takes a long shuddering breath and shakes her head. 'You just poisoned a very beautiful thing, because from this point on, whether I decide to go or not, this argument is going to hang over my head. If I go, you'll think it's to spite you, and you'll go on being suspicious of me. If I don't, well . . .'

'Come on, that's not true.' Yet he knows she is right, and it makes him curse himself.

'Yes it is, Jacob. I'm damned if I do and damned if I don't. If I go, you'll be sitting here and wondering whether I can control myself.' She shakes her head bitterly. 'Teddy and me – that was over seven years ago!'

'You were *engaged*,' he blurts out, and immediately regrets it.

'That's right, Jacob. I *was*,' she says coolly, and walks away from him. 'I'm going to take a bath.'

'Nomsa, I'm sorry!' he calls after her.

He watches her go, because she has every right to walk away from him and, besides, what else is there for him to say that will make things better rather than worse, especially when he is feeling this way? Jacob checks on the food, but soon finds he cannot pay it any attention. His aching head is too full of the day's incessant noise: the anger, the sudden jealousy and self-reproach. They build and build and build until he notices a familiar crawling sensation at the top of his skull – what *sangomas* call the opening of the head – and realizes it is not only the pent-up emotion pressing in on him. Not quite. That feeling of spider webs covering his skin, which he felt this morning, returns, along with the sound of a buzzing nest of hornets and a sharp pain in his temples. Just as it all becomes unbearable, the old-fashioned ring of a dial telephone calls him back to the present. *Chrring-chrring*.

The portentous calm that suddenly settles over him feels like the gentle lapping of water on a beach, and suddenly he knows this is it – this is what he has been expecting all day. Nomsa will not answer the call because it is for him, and only him.

Jacob walks into the living room, where the ringing

phone is illuminated by a gaudy lamp on a small table set against the wall. He sits down on the wooden stool next to it and picks up the receiver.

'Hello?' The hollow sound of his voice surprises him.

'Jacob Tshabalala?' It is a white woman's voice. Tired and frightened.

'Speaking.'

It occurs to him at that moment that he may be going mad – what could, after all, be so sinister about a telephone call? – that he has perhaps been in policing too long, and the stress which has driven so many others to the brink has finally got to him too.

'Mr Tshabalala – I mean Detective. Christ, I don't even know what to call you! This is Tanya Fouché. You left a message that I should call you. I'm sorry it's this late, but I was told it's urgent. Is it about Harry?'

Jacob barely registers her voice as the clamour inside his head begins to pick up again.

What is *it you want to tell me, Grandfather? Out with it!*

'This *is* about Harry, isn't it? Something's happened to him. Don't tell me he's dead. Oh, please don't.'

Jacob loses himself in staring at the pattern of cracks in the plaster of the wall. Dimly he thinks he should have repainted, but how could he possibly afford that?

'Detective, speak to me.'

He clears his throat. 'Tanya Fouché, you say.'

It does not come out as a question, but a flat and unemotional statement.

'Where is he?' Her voice is on the brink of tears. 'Why can't he speak to me himself?'

'He was shot two days ago; he is now in hospital.'

'Oh-my-God!' exclaims the woman. 'I fucking *knew* it.'

Jacob frowns at her profanity, but says nothing. 'His condition is stable, but he is still unconscious.'

'I need to see him.'

'He is in Port Elizabeth.'

'Who's with him?'

'His mother and daughter.'

'How do I get a hold of them?'

He tells her to wait while he searches his mobile for Joan Mason's number. After she has written it down, he hears her physically swallow her own pain.

In a calm voice, she asks, 'Are *you* OK, Jacob?'

The warmth in the question surprises him, and it drags him back from the strange precipice on which he has been standing ever since he woke up this morning. 'Yes, I am good, thank you. Give Mrs Mason a call. She has been trying to find out who you are all day.'

'She has?'

'Yes.'

He rings off with a fumbled goodbye, and cups his smarting head in his hands a moment before the phone rings a second time. Thinking that Tanya Fouché must have remembered to ask him something else, he answers with a simple 'Yes?'

There is a loud sob at the other end of the line. Someone is weeping, and not just from the throat, but from a deep hollow opened up beneath her heart. He has heard that sound before; a son never forgets the way his mother cries.

'Ma?'

'Your father is dead, Jacob. He died half an hour ago, like . . . just like you thought he would.'

THREE

1

Tonight, for one night only, *homza* Ephraim Thekiso is the king of the world; he is in fact, in the infamous words of Idi Amin, the Lord of all the Beasts of the Earth and Fishes of the Sea and Conqueror of this particular woman, 'Room 315'.

In the cold midnight light of a crescent moon impaled upon the blue-lit Hillbrow tower, he may have witnessed the gathering ecstasy in her expression – the slight snarl on her lips – but he just couldn't give a shit. Neither could he care for the dab of blood at the corner of one nostril, glinting like oil in the half-light, or the stout hands with gnawed fingernails pressed flat against the grimy white wall behind her head as she lurches to and fro. No, Ephraim Thekiso is totally blind to these details. His eyes feed only on the delight of her chocolate-pudding dairies rocking to his boogie, the icing-sugar beads of sweat glistening in the cleavage between them. And cheering him on is the sweet rhythmic smacking of his own naked glory pressing against her.

Booyaka!

Ephraim laughs out loud at the incredible sense of his own majesty. A brilliant gem attached to his canine glitters, as do the gaudy fool's-gold rings on his hands and the thick rope-like gold necklaces round his neck. Her eyes open and she laughs back at him, for no other reason, he's convinced, than that she must be agreeing with him wholeheartedly.

A restless whimper escapes a darkened corner of the scruffy studio apartment, but neither of the two lovers hears it, because right now they are in a place that might be called a snow-white cloud nine.

On the upturned crate beside the bed lies a rolled-up ten-rand note alongside a customer loyalty card, a mirror, the powdery remains of a second gram of coke. Sweet Jesus, does he wish he could have a line of *that* just as he shoots his load. Has anyone ever done that before? he wonders. *Eish*, but that's a fantastic idea, *mzitho*!

He grins to himself and wipes away the beads of sweat that have accumulated underneath his eyes.

The whimper in the darkened corner turns into a muffled cry, and this time it manages to draw Ephraim Thekiso's attention. He stops in mid-thrust and glares into the darkness.

'You gon' shut the fuck up over there?' His bogus American accent, culled from a thousand television shows, has been grafted on to that of a lifetime on the streets. 'I hear yas one more time, I might just have to reconsider things, you hear me?'

'No, babe,' says 315. She pulls him back down on top of her by pressing on the back of his neck. 'Don't pay her any attention. Come on. Look at *me*.'

Ephraim kisses her roughly, and the excessive saliva left on her cheek glistens like a snail's trail in the city light.

'You gon' have to make a plan 'bout them,' he says. 'I don't want to be no showman like this all the time, you hear?'

'Sure, babe,' she croons and tightens her thighs around him. 'But right now you mind me. I'm here, needing you.'

'Don't you be calling me, babe. It's E to you.'

Her voice drifts into dreaminess as she relaxes her head back on to the pillow. 'You go on like *that*, E. Just go on.'

He responds by grabbing two fistfuls of her breasts, as if to get more leverage, but decides he actually prefers to watch them jiggle. The woman wipes at her nose with the length of her forearm, but Mr E does not comment on the blood that comes away smeared on it as a long dark streak. All that matters now is that she is his; she belongs to him. He breathes in deeply and allows himself the smell of his victory: the miasma of unwashed sheets, the smell of their sex, the chemical burn of the cocaine clogging his nose. He is glad his guess about her paid off when she first came a-knocking, looking and smelling like a train driver's armpit. He just hopes she doesn't get it into her head that she can now ask favours of him, like new clothes to replace that filthy tracksuit of hers. If she does, he will have to ditch her. Someone else will come along soon anyhow.

You look at this, bro! You done yourself good by this one, for sure.

Yeah, maybe he will get her something better than that for-shit pink thing she has been wearing, just to show her how gracious the E-man can be.

This one's nothing like that limp bitch in 206, he thinks. Now she's a real candy bar, that one, if looking is all it's about, someone he might've seriously gotten a handle on if she wasn't such roadkill in the sack. Almost ain't worth the trouble, he keeps telling himself. Should toss her out, that's what he should do. But he quickly reminds himself a free *kwiep* is a free *kwiep*, and there's no arguing with *punani*. Now, 315 here, she don't look no better than wet dough rolled in chocolate, and she sure ain't the brightest of the litter, but *man*, does she put out!

'You think I can stay here a month?'

'Don't you worry about that right now, girl. You sayin' I ain't giving it to yous good enough, or what? Is that why your mind's driftin'? What you tellin' Daddy E by talking, huh?'

She closes her eyes again and smiles. 'It's nothing like that.'

'Then hush up.' He grinds his hips from side to side and is pleased when she flinches. 'I's right here.'

'Aye,' she floats off again into wasted semi-consciousness. 'I can feel you there. Got your mamba caught right between my legs, E.'

Yeah, this one's a cherry, dun. Sho' is fine.

When Ephraim Thekiso took the job of building manager six months ago, he never thought he would be having this much fun. At first it was just sitting on his arse the whole day, watching Ricki fucking Lake and the Veri-fart channel. Every now and again some brown-nosing tenants would bring him *moola* to pay for their pads. All he had to do was look important when he opened the door, count the dough, and once in a while hang out the window to check that no one was packing up their shit and moving on without first paying their arrears. But then a single mother here, a poor little honey there, they started coming to him – not to them whitey landlords, not to their mong partners with the nicotine-stained fingers and faces, but to him, Ephra-fucking-*im* – and begging for some slack on the month's rent. Being the diesel *homza* he is, he couldn't turn down no pretty bullet. And so it was that life stepped up a few gears, and went from slow-poke wallowing on the fucking couch to countless parties in his pants, twenty-four/seven.

For Ephraim, they are fair trades, these little arrangements he has going. As far as he's concerned, the women in Copacabana Luxury Suites – Sweets as he likes to call the apartment complex he oversees – they his, anyhow. Most of them turn tricks a ways down the road, for sure. Don't mean much to him. One poke-hole fits all, he is fond of saying. He's easy with that; he don't care much as long as he gets what he wants, when he wants it. *And dat*, in the eminent words of Biggy Big, *is dat*.

The only thing that does concern him is keeping his bosses in the dark about the rooms he dishes out for certain conveniences provided. It's a fine balance to run his little gig smoothly. It takes someone with street smarts, someone with a level head like his, to pull this kind of stunt. Too many skanks in the corridors and too little money reaching the bosses, it's likely to draw attention to him – and he don't need none of *dat*.

So far the problems in this building have been with the tenants, never with him, and he likes it that way just fine. Any issues amongst his flock, one phone call to a number on a piece of paper stuck on his fridge sorts it out quick-quick. One of those arrogant mongs will always answer on the first ring in a voice like a buzz-saw. An hour later three of them will be at his door asking who the problem is, and he'll show them, always making sure he hurries away before the screaming and shouting and occasionally the beating starts. *Dat*'s his thing. *Dat*'s their thing. He can dig it. They can dig it. *And dat is dat*.

It never occurred to him when he took the job that it might be a bit strange for a bunch of white-bread property owners to hire a black kid in his late twenties as a building manager, and also a go-between for the mongs, who all looked like they fell out of a B-grade Asia Extreme movie. He also did not find it in any way surprising that no one else more responsible or mature came up for the job. He simply assumed it was the fine English he speaks (which he does, if you are willing to look past the fake Harlem accent), his good looks (moderate) and his own incredibly slick tongue and winning dress sense (a cocaine-induced figment of his imagination) that eventually got him the job.

'*Bee-yaches!*' Ephraim suddenly caws to the woman pinned underneath him like a frayed moth at the end of a thin needle. If she wasn't so high up cloud coke, she might've got a fright. 'Who's da man, huh?'

The woman replies slowly and without opening her eyes. 'You are, babe. You are *eeet*!'

His spine begins to prickle all the way down to what he likes to call his mamba. *This is power, right here*, he thinks. *For da lord of the Sweets they'll say anything, sooner or later*.

Ephraim's breathing gradually turns into loud buffalo grunts, and on impulse he reaches for the remaining coke, intent on coming and snorting at the same time. Can he do it? *Fa shizzle!* he reckons. He can do anything, and *dat is dat!*

There is a brief commotion in the sparse room's one darkened corner, but it immediately falls silent when he directs a vicious glare in that direction.

Annoyed by the shift in his position, 315 opens her eyes. 'What are you doing?'

He almost spills the snow as she moves. '*Hi wena*, easy there!'

'Are you going to give me some more of that?' Her eyes fix on the coke the way they might be glued to a winning lottery ticket. Her hips start a slow gyration, a gentle cock-tease dance she has learned God-knows-where. 'It's nice.'

'Fuck that's good! You keep that shit up, then maybe.' He barely manages to concentrate on bringing the gear up to his nose, because his moving reflection in the mirror confuses his ability to judge the distance between nose and glass. Damn, did that feel good.

You toasted, bra! You bloody cooked off the bone!

'Hey, my Mr E, can I stay here a month, please? You decided yet? I'll give you whatever you want.'

An annoying whininess has penetrated her voice, a sound that reminds him far too much of that ho in 206.

Fuck, what is it with them all?

Still aiming to keep the note in his nostril and the powder lined up on the mirror, Ephraim wonders if he wants the bother of another 206 in this building.

'Please.' She bucks her hips in a way that pushes a wave of pleasure down into his testicles and up his spine.

'You keep going with that shit you doing right there, three-one-five, and I'll tell you if you deserve it or not.'

Her body tenses, and even before she stops thrusting against him, he knows she's about to bust his balls.

'What did you call me?'

'Fuck, woman!' He glares at her over the note pinched between two fingers. 'Don't you mind me right now. Come on, babe, I's right there, man! What you waitin' for? Let's go! Rock 'n' roll, babe.'

She pulls free from him with a wet smack. The slickness between his legs immediately grows cold against his skin in the badly insulated room. Room 315 pushes herself up on to her elbows. 'I said, *what* did you call me?'

'Ma,' peeps a voice from the darkness.

'Not now, babe.'

'What the *fuck*, woman!' Ephraim Thekiso bellows.

Before he knows what is about to happen, she places a rough cracked heel against his chest and shoves him backwards. Though he manages to save himself from falling off the bed, the hand with which he is holding the mirror upends the remainder of his cocaine in a puff of fairy dust.

'Ah *shit*, man!'

'You called me *what*, Ephraim? Say it!'

He ignores her and desperately scrounges around on the dark bed for his cocaine. 'It's all *gone*. Look what you done!'

The woman hugs her knees against the cold and laughs as she watches him scrape together the remainder of his cocaine with one finger.

'It's not funny, bitch!'

'Ma!'

'Not now, babe.'

'But they got guns, Ma.'

'Who?'

'I said shut *up*!'

Ephraim Thekiso takes a frustrated swing at the wall. The punch would have made Mike Tyson proud had it connected with an opponent's face, not plaster. There is a crack as a fingerbone breaks inside his hand, and suddenly the Lord of all the Beasts of the Earth and Fishes of the Sea and Conqueror of the woman he calls 315 is squealing like a five-year-old who just dropped his ice-cream in the dirt.

'Ma, they're coming here!' yells the excited little voice he has been trying to ignore without much success.

The two girls wearing identical pink tracksuits, who

have been messing around in the dark studio apartment when they should have been sitting quietly facing the wall with their hands over their ears, are now standing at the window. The older is pointing outside at the parking lot three floors below. 'I saw them running inside!'

2

Lucidity burns into her like a Jehovah's Witness's scornful eye. Number 315 rolls out of bed and searches for her clothes, but remembers she had dumped them by the front door, where the building manager ordered her to strip as they entered.

'You stink,' he had told her bluntly the minute he unlocked the door. 'Take 'em off. You ain't coming in here like that.'

It had been an offensive thing to say, but she also knew it to be true. She could not remember when she had last felt hot water on her skin, when she had toothpaste on her toothbrush. As she had hesitated, he added, 'We both know why yous came to me for a possie, and I's tell you right here, I's got standards. So take that shit off, now. Lemme have a look at you before yous have a shower. Lemme see if yous worth the water bill.' She had dropped her tracksuit right there underneath this stranger's eyes, and in front of her children too, not because she was easy or even overeager for the shower, but because another winter night was coming, and there was no way she would let her children sleep in another doorway if she could help it.

'Will you look at that?' he had said with a mixture of

lust and disgust, as he closed the door – and she had never felt so humiliated. That is, until he called her a number too, like she was queuing to get with him. *Him!*

'My hand's broke!' yells this … *man* in that stupid accent of which he is so damn proud. For the life of her she can't understand why any Tswana would want to speak English like he has never lived in Africa. 'My fuckin' hand's broke, you hear?'

Ephraim, naked in the dark, is scrawny and unusually hairy for a black man. He looks similar to that cop whose face she had spat in yesterday – same forehead and chin, but not nearly as well built or dignified. She briefly wonders if this one has it in him to attack her and the two girls – she has had that happen before – but decides he is too wasted on his drugs and too much of a coward to be a serious threat to her.

She leaves her clothes where they are and rushes over to join her daughters, in time to snatch a glimpse of a man carrying an AK-47 rifle as he glances over his shoulder before disappearing into the ground-floor foyer. The coked-up tension in her climbs several notches at the thought of what might happen to all the women caught in a building hijacked by a group of armed men.

'Ephraim!' she yells at the man still stomping around the room and clutching at his wrist. 'Will you shut up and come here?'

'Can't you see I'm hurtin'? Look what those damn kids of yours done to my hand.'

Three-one-five, that's what he had called her. *Fucking 315.*

She has seen and heard and felt more than her fair share of abuse over the years, but that stung badly. She might be nothing more than a cash machine on legs for

the cops that regularly shake her down, or a damp hole
for a few johns here and there – but they at least accord
her a name, however filthy it is sometimes.

'I don't care if your cock's caught in the doorjamb.
There really are men coming into the building with guns.
Big ones.'

'So what the hell you want me to do about it?'

He holds his hand up to the light filtering through the
window and carefully studies it, as if he is waiting for her
sympathy. All the while that thing of his – what does he
call it, a fucking mamba? – hangs shrivelled between his
legs like a dried-up earthworm stuck in a bird's nest.
Suddenly she feels nauseous at the sight of this man she
was humping not five minutes ago. She cannot believe
what she was willing to do just for a month's warmth and
a roof over her head. Has it come to this so soon?

'I don't know,' she says. 'Call the *gatas*, maybe?'

His eyes glitter in the blue light as he looks up at her.
Then a high hysterical titter escapes his mouth and sends a
bolt of pain through her wired head.

'Me, call the *boere*, fucked the way I am? You crazy,
bitch? I's not going to jail, man.'

'Ma, I don't want to stay here,' says her oldest.

She glances at her two daughters, the younger clutching
at her older sister for reassurance. The third is still in
Johannesburg General Hospital recovering from the burns
she sustained thanks to those goddamned cops raiding the
factory. It had been a stinking dump, but at least she had
had a warm refuge for her and the kids; at least there were
other single mothers like her, who took turns looking after
the children while they went searching for work. The two
sisters seem incomplete without the third one. They don't
look like her children, but they are – and the only good

things she has left in this life, at that. She glances at the door. It had looked like that man below with his rifle was a rear guard, which means chances are that others are spread throughout the building, many of them. She had seen it once when they overran a building in Jeppestown, cleaned it out. Poor people – with practically nothing to give, just like those here in this building – lost everything they owned.

She does not want her two daughters to see what she herself witnessed on that occasion, not if she can help it.

'Ephraim. What are you gonna do?'

'Do about *what*?'

'The fucking *tsotsis* here in the building, you dumb shit!' she barks with sudden fury. 'They've got AKs, and I don't think they're here to hand out flyers for the Malaika show.'

The look of childish astonishment on his face infuriates her even more.

'AKs?' he says dopily. A foamy pink tongue slips out of his mouth and slicks across his dry lips. 'I'm staying right here, that's what I'm doing.'

'No you're not.'

He yanks the damp sheet off the bed and clutches it to his crotch with a sudden self-conscious glance at her two children. 'Don't you be telling me what I can and cain't do, woman. They don't pay me enough to reason with no robbers.'

'What? One minute you're tough enough to screw a mother in front of her daughters, the next you can't even do your job?' She pushes him towards the door, secretly glad that she is built more powerfully than he is. 'You're a loser, Ephraim. That's what you are.'

'You cain't talk to me like that!' His eyes widen with a sudden realization. 'They're not coming for me, are they?'

'I don't know.' She shoves him harder and is satisfied when he stumbles all the way towards the door, past her crumpled clothes. 'I'm just a room number, remember?'

He tries to straighten up and gather himself together. 'What you doing, woman? This here's my apartment, man!'

'I've earned it, arsehole.'

She fumbles the door open, and with a mighty push she manages to send Ephraim Thekiso stumbling backwards into the freezing cold passageway beyond. It takes another good kick for her to free his uninjured hand from the door handle, but eventually she manages to slam the door shut on him.

'Let me back in!' He thumps a fist against the door. 'Come on, babe, let's talk about this.'

'Only if you start calling me by my name, but you don't remember it, do you?'

'So remind me. I promise I won't forget again.'

She ignores his request and fixes her eyes on the pale blue light streaming through the unfurnished studio apartment from the window. In the half-light she makes out two pairs of frightened eyes watching her intently. Exhausted, she slumps against the rough unpainted wood of the door and gestures to her two daughters. 'Come here, my babies. Come to your ma. She needs you.'

3

The suddenly not-so-majestic Mr E stares at the door to Room 315, not quite sure how he ended up on the landing outside it. A winter wind gusts down the exposed passage-way and sends a chill through his naked body. Gooseflesh breaks out all over his skin and his teeth begin to chatter like a mouthful of typewriters.

'*Heta!* Open up, woman!' Ephraim Thekiso bangs on the door with his uninjured hand. 'It's fucking *cold* out here, girl.'

For the life of him, he cannot remember her name, or whether she even told him it in the first place.

'Get lost!' comes a muffled response through the door.

'My clothes. Damn it, bitch! At least lemme have my clothes.'

A voice at the back of his head is yelling *Shit, dun, there be men around with gatts, and you worried about the* cold? *Didn't you fucking* hear *her?* But the coke and cold, not to mention his embarrassing nudity and broken hand, are all demanding his attention. Glancing down the passageway towards the lifts, Ephraim makes sure no one is around to see him totally exposed before he shakes out the sheet he has been clutching to his crotch and drapes it around his shoulders. Dimly he is aware of a lot of knocking and yelling going on downstairs.

Something rattles through the partly open kitchen window and a bundle of keys drops on to the concrete floor of the walkway.

'Your shit's down in the parking lot, Mr six-oh-six, and I'm keeping the keys for this room awhile,' calls the woman. Then she adds as an afterthought, 'And dat is dat, arsehole.'

'Come on, girl, don't be like that. How long you think you gon' last in there? Fuck's sakes, open up! Open up or yous dead, man! All I needs do is pick up the phone and the *macheana* are on you. That's me! I make one call, man, one call, and that's it for you and your dirty piglets. *Open the door!*'

When he receives no response whatsoever, he stamps his bare foot in frustration; it sounds little more than a wet smack on the concrete. Pulling the makeshift garment tighter around his shoulders, he stomps off down the passageway in the direction of the lifts, looking like an Ethiopian holy man in his bedsheet. As he rounds the corner towards the central lift shaft, he spots two men come up the main staircase next to the lift itself. For a moment they are as surprised to see him as he is them. One's dressed in a cheap purple polyester windbreaker, and is strapped with (*Oh shit, those damn kids weren't lying!*) an AK-47 rifle and a sjambok. The other man is carrying nothing more than a pen and a standard examination pad. Despite his thinness and the seeming innocuousness of the items in his hands, the man unnerves Ephraim. There is something dreadful in his rheumy eyes, the firm set of his mouth, like something lying in wait in the dark.

The man in the windbreaker laughs. 'And then, Superman?' he announces in Sotho. 'But why is your thing hanging out in this cold, eh?'

Ephraim, whose ego has been bruised one too many times over the last twenty minutes, and his judgement nuked by all that coke and a half-jack of cane, sweeps up his stained and crumpled toga as though about to address the full Senate. 'I am da building manager here,' he proclaims. 'And who the fuck are yous?'

For a moment his bold statement hangs in the air like a frozen speech bubble, then Windbreaker Man lets out a rumbling belly-laugh that brings a glint of humour to the other man's eyes, even though the mouth doesn't so much as crinkle. He reaches out and slaps his companion on the shoulder. 'Did you hear that, Godun, eh, my bra?'

All the silent man does is nod his head and smile a thin-lipped reptilian smile.

'Is that right, Superman? You're the man in charge here?'

'Dat's right.' Ephraim shifts uncertainly, unable to take his eyes off the one with the notepad. 'Just happens I'm in a bit of a . . . *situation.*'

Wordlessly, the one called Godun begins to write on his pad, and without knowing why, Ephraim feels his legs begin to turn into porridge.

'Yo, *bizza*, what you writing there, man?' His voice cracks under a sudden sense of impending doom.

'Shut up, Ephraim.' Mr Windbreaker takes a threatening step towards him, and Ephraim begins to retreat, but the pair of them match him step for step. 'A man dressed like that doesn't get to ask questions.'

'How's it you know my name?'

Godun finishes his scribbling by underscoring it with an emphatically drawn line. He shows it to Windbreaker, who takes a quick glance.

'Aye, OK, my *makhonya*. Whatever you say.'

'What's it say, *dun*?' A sudden wild panic seizes Ephraim Thekiso, and he points back towards Room 315. 'I only put this bitch up for one night. She got kids, man. I can't let her walk the streets at night with nowhere to go. She's payin' double end of the month. That's the arrangement, my bra, I swears.'

'Maybe it's for the best, you know.' Mr Windbreaker adjusts his rifle so that it lies more comfortably against his back. Then he tightens his grip on the sjambok.

'It's best, what?' Ephraim Thekiso's voice grows shrill.

Windbreaker Man shakes his head. 'You know, it's rude for you to keep speaking to me in that language. What's the matter, are you ashamed of who you are?'

'No, it's nothing like that,' Ephraim quickly switches to perfectly good Tswana. 'If this is about the *moola*, I got it. I was just helpin' the bitch out, you know. You not gonna fuck up a brother for the sake of some bitch, are—

He tries to make a break for it in mid-sentence, but the other man must have sensed it coming. As Ephraim turns, the first blow of the whip whistles through the air and cuts across his back with a loud wet slap. Ephraim screams at the top of his lungs, in what the whole complex will later agree is a very unmanly manner. Where a moment ago his feet felt like icy cinderblocks weighing him down, his whole body now feels nothing but a brilliant white heat. In quick succession, a second, third, fourth lash strike Ephraim as he desperately ducks and dives to avoid them in the confines of the narrow corridor. Weaving to avoid yet another blow, Ephraim suddenly comes face to face with the one called Godun. The man's face remains as impassive as stone.

'Don't do this,' pleads Ephraim Thekiso, and clutches for the man's hands, but he jerks away from the contact. 'I don't deserve this, *makhonya* – please.'

'It's been a long time coming, friend,' says Mr Windbreaker behind him. 'Did you really think you could go on shaving money off the rent for ever? Did you think the other residents wouldn't mind you keeping all these women shacked up in rooms they couldn't pay for?'

'I've got an explanation, man! Let me speak to Niewoudt. Let me speak to Li. Please, bra,' cries Ephraim Thekiso, thinking the whitebreads and mongs will go easier on him because they know him. 'Let *them* handle this.'

'They *are* handling it, stupid.' Windbreaker raises the sjambok and brings it down again. It whistles through the air, hard and fast and brutal. This time the skin on Ephraim's back splits open like an overripe fruit.

4

Inside number 315 a mother sits on her haunches with her naked back pressed against the thin plywood of the door, not daring to move. Her arms are wrapped around two children, and her tear-streaked face is pressed against their cheeks. Occasionally she mumbles for them to not utter a sound. With every crack of the whip and ensuing scream in the passageway outside, the mother gives a small jerk.

Please, oh please, Jesus. Don't you let them come in here, you hear? I'm asking you for my girls.

As quickly as the assault outside began, it ends. More feet arrive, along with the rough voices of men on the prowl. There are grunts; sneakers squeak over bare concrete; then there is the sound of a giant snake slithering away.

'Everyone on this floor, did you hear that?' shouts the man who had been baiting Ephraim. 'A few of you asked that something be done about this man; it has now been done. Some of you might have been thinking of cheating your landlord like this man has, but let me tell you this will then happen to you, too. If you steal from us, you will be beaten. If you bring your dirty business into this residential block, you will be beaten. If you do not pay your rent, you will be beaten. These are the new rules here.'

Footfalls head nearer to Room 315, and suddenly there is a violent banging at the door. Her heart hits the back of her throat.

'*Magosha!*'

One of her girls cries out in fright, and the mother clutches a hand over her mouth. She whispers to the second child that she better keep quiet, and in vain searches the single-room studio flat for a place to hide.

'Whore, I said open up!' The fist continues to pound at the door, and she imagines the thin wood cracking under its force.

Her options are few. If she does not respond soon, the man will surely grow irritated enough to break down the flimsy barrier between them, and whatever happens then will be played out in front of her innocent two daughters. But if she replies, what then?

'Do not test me, woman.'

'Yes?' she stammers.

'You are off the street, I hear. With children?'

She glances across this new haven at the blue-lit Hillbrow tower outside the window. Will she by some miracle be allowed to stay here after all? Or will she have to move on yet again? The tears in her eyes give the tower a beautiful electric halo. How nice it would be to call this room her own.

'Yes, I am.' Though she would like to add more in her defence, her voice fails her.

'And that's also the only reason why you yourself do not end up like that *nja*. Be glad, woman. Count yourself lucky. But like everyone else here, you will pay for this room at the end of the month.'

'I can't,' she mutters through the door. 'I have nothing.'

'You *will*. If you want this room, you will pay two

months' deposit, like everyone else. Nothing is *pasella*, you hear me? And you will pay the month's rent up front. You may think you are different from the other residents who work hard for their money and pay on time, but you are wrong, do you understand me?'

'Yes.'

'Good. You have till the end of the week, then.'

Footfalls recede towards the lifts, and she is left alone with her children. She lets go of them and curls herself up into a tight ball on the carpet. Where to now? She begins to weep in the darkness, and hardly notices when small restless hands touch her hair, her face, and press on her mouth in an effort to stop the despair from seeping out of her.

FOUR

1

Harry returns the elderly man's level gaze. His eyes are kind but grave, partially hidden under heavy folds of skin, and deep sorrowful wrinkles frame his mouth. He blinks again, this man who watches him, but still he does not say anything.

The man seems oddly familiar to Harry, but he cannot rightly place him. The faded powder-blue shirt, buttoned all the way up to the collar, and the washed-out ink stain on one pocket, seem both known and yet strange; so too does the man's stiff almost military posture, like a soldier presenting arms. But try as he might, the man's identity remains nothing more than a word lost on the tip of Harry's tongue.

And this place? Where exactly is it? He is sure he recognizes these white walls and the white sheets draped over him, the odour of iodine, the steel rails at the foot of an old-fashioned bed. Through the small square window, just to the right of the man's shoulder, is visible a red-brick wall. Again, it feels like he should know it well, but for what reason eludes him. The sensations he suddenly associates with this place are unpleasant.

Why is it that he himself cannot move his head? Why is it that he does not ever seem to blink, while his silent visitor both breathes and blinks, and sways ever so slightly in his soldierly stance?

Harry searches his memory for more information but finds nothing, because his mind is as empty as a salt flat. There is a racket so deafening and painful between his temples that it feels like his head is stuck inside a sawmill.

That's not quite right, though, for he can hear the man's heavy breathing; he can hear it quite clearly over the noise. It is a soft steady whistling through the man's nose that he picks up on, a sound Harry finds strangely comforting.

'Harry, that arsehole had it coming. I know he did it. We all knew he did it. The *neighbourhood* knew he was guilty. Something had to be done about him. He couldn't get away with it.'

Harry frowns. Though he is sure he knows both that face and voice, he is convinced they do not belong to-gether.

'That blimming crack runner was laughing at us, Bond, and he watched us blundering about like a bunch of blind bloody mice. You can't have them do that, Bond. I don't need to tell you, it's not the gun you carry that stops you from getting killed, it's your reputation. Once the ridicule starts, it's only a matter of time before one of them will put a bullet in your back. Ntombini had enough clout out on the streets to sign our death warrants in any of the neighbourhoods we worked.'

'Who are you?' The question comes out as nothing but a cottony mumble. 'And where the hell am I?'

His visitor ignores him and goes on talking. 'You and I, we're dumped into a shitty no man's land, Harry, with nothing more than a shovel, and we're expected to make it smell like roses.'

What is this man talking about? Harry wonders.

'It was poetic justice the way he died: a greater good written in between the lines of an imperfect law that protects the criminals before it does either us or their victims.'

Harry flicks his eyes towards the little window, and is not surprised to see an endless black line of ants now trundling across the wall of the building opposite.

Then abruptly it hits him. It is the whistle in his visitor's nose that does the trick.

The man's face finally breaks into a reticent smile, the kind of benevolent expression a lifelong headmaster adopts on the rare occasions when he purposefully bestows it on an exceptional student. Colin Mason takes one jerky but anxious step towards the bed in which Harry finds himself, and reaches out. With one elongated hand that ends in bulbous fingertips he brushes back his son's hair, the way he once used to do when father and son still touched each other.

How are you, lad? You doing all right there? says his father now, without a trace of that other voice.

A tight knot abruptly forms in Harry's throat, and it nearly chokes him. *What's going on, Dad?*

His father pats his shoulder sympathetically, as though they had just been discussing the latest miserable cricket score at Lord's. That grave twist of the mouth returns. *Quieten down, son, or you'll have your mother in a state. You just get some rest. Remember, the most important thing right now is to see you through this.*

Suddenly Harry feels overwhelmingly claustrophobic. He tries to move but feels completely straitjacketed.

What's happened?

Don't exert yourself, son.

Let me loose! Harry tries to turn his eyes towards the rest of the room, but an unexplained paralysis continues to restrict his field of vision.

You're in a safe place, says his father. *No need to worry.*

Harry turns his head as far as he can manage, suddenly feeling a darkness accumulating beyond his line of sight. Then he flicks his eyes back towards the right side of the bed, but his father is gone. There is only the window now, and the black ants crawling across the red-brick wall. Thousands of them, meandering aimlessly, as though to prove by their movement the absolute meaninglessness of life.

That other voice floats back to him over the grind of the sawmill in his head. 'I had nothing to do with it, Harry, if you're thinking that. You better get that straight. Don't you worry, I'm after the blimming son of a bitch that did this to you. And when we have him, we'll show him that we look after our own, right, Harry? Through thick and thin, isn't that right, Harry? We're the only real family we have, in that way. No one else understands it the way we do.'

It cannot be his father, this person, because his dad never called Harry by that name. But who is it, then? And why does Harry feel so uncomfortable? That bloody saw-mill! And where are the goddamned headache tablets?

'Jesus, Bond, when I said let's hope it's not our funeral, I didn't really mean it, you hear? When you wake up, we'll go after that double-crossing contact of yours, 'cause those rifles weren't there. You hear that? They *weren't* there.'

A pressure on his left hand, which might have been meant to be reassuring, only bewilders Harry more when he cannot see who is pressing it.

'Harry, leave Ntombini alone. It was a long time ago. Do me this one favour, please.'

Dad?

A flash of panic takes hold of him.

I can't fucking REMEMBER! he yells at the top of his voice, but it comes out little more than a croak. *What are you on about?* he then whispers.

Don't forget, Harry, says a voice filled with flowers. *We have to do this. Friday night. Dinner and movies. Do you think she'll like that?*

He has heard that voice before, but who does it belong to? His wife? His *wife*! That's right. He remembers her . . . and a daughter. Amy and Jeanie. Those are their names.

She loves film, Amy. He laughs despite the encroaching terror. *You should know that by now.*

Unexpectedly she is there, sitting on a bedside wooden bench, her mint-green eyes fixed on him, her Grace Kelly lips turned up in a reassuring smile. *Bear,* I *know that, but* she *doesn't.*

What do you mean? How can Jeanie not know what she likes?

Amy shakes her head. A melange of sadness, resignation and longing crosses her face. She gets up from the bench and turns to leave.

Wait. Where are you going? You only just arrived, and I haven't seen you in a while. Where have you been?

She does not answer him as she meticulously straightens her pleated black skirt and embroidered emerald blouse. Harry catches sight of her marble-pale neckline and the protrusions of the collarbones he so loves to caress. *How long will you be?*

When she leans over to kiss him on the cheek, the single diamond pendant he gave her for some past anniversary slips free from her shirt and brushes across his face. *I don't know, Bear,* she says. *But I can't stay at your side any more. There's someone else now, remember?*

At first he is surprised to hear this. Then jealous fury erupts inside him.

Who?

She turns away from him and heads towards the window, where twilight is now throwing a copper light over the floor.

Christ, Amy, answer me! Who is it?

Over her shoulder she says in a voice not her own, *Don't forget Friday. Dinner and movies.*

Then she is gone.

Harry blinks ... except this is not a blink but more like a skip in time. He gathers up all his will to call Amy back, but it is useless. His throat is too dry and swollen.

When he tries to steady his breathing, he finds even that is not under his control any more. Turning his mind inwards, he frantically begins to sift through the wasteland of his memory in an effort to discover more than salt and dust and questions, but to no avail. The panic at not knowing where he is, and what is happening to him, climbs another notch.

'What's wrong with him, doctor?'

It sounds like his mother, that distant voice. There is fear in it. No, not fear, he realizes, but outright terror. What is it that she knows and he doesn't?

'Jeanie, what are you doing in here? Get out! Get out *right* now!'

Jeanie? She's here?

Her name fills his heart with warm chocolate and the sweet scent of fresh apples, yet he somehow cannot put a face to his own daughter. Why can't he see her? Why do they all sound so damn far away?

What seems to be the goddamned problem here, officer? he thinks.

Harry's hands involuntarily close into tight fists that bunch the white sheets covering him, and his back begins to arch upwards, as though pulled towards the ceiling by some unseen hand.

'Ma'am, could you please excuse us?'

'I'm staying right here with my son!'

'For Christ's sake, Mrs Mason, you're getting in the way! If you want me to help your son, just leave – now!'

Harry swallows, and the taste of blood in his throat is warm and thick.

'But you said he's stable!'

What's stuck in his throat? Why can't he move his legs?

'Well, he isn't, is he!'

'Harry, can you hear me?' calls an unfamiliar voice. 'Give me a thumbs-up if you can.'

He tries to respond, but can't. Then it occurs to him what's wrong: he is dying. For some reason he's fucking dying, and he can't even say goodbye to his daughter.

A cool hand abruptly lands on his forearm and presses it gently.

'Give me two cc's of adenosine, quick!'

Hi there, officer, says a soothing voice that is so much closer to him than any of the others. *How are you feeling?*

Harry opens eyes he did not even realize he had closed, and discovers a woman with raven-black hair standing next to the bed. She is wearing a well-worn black leather jacket over a bright orange turtleneck, and her head is tilted to one side in a curious expression. Bewildered, Harry searches his salt-flat memory for the newcomer's name but cannot come up with anything.

Her hand runs down his forearm to his fist, and her fingers close over it.

Relax, she says with a wink, *I'm here now*.

And miraculously, he does. The tension in his entire body seeps away, and his grip on the sheets begins to loosen. The woman sits down on the edge of the bed, pulls his limp hand into her lap and starts kneading it. Gradually, warmth returns to his cold arm and spreads through his body.

You know, I can't wait to see you again, says the stranger.

He swallows and feels his dried-out mouth working hard to form words.

Go on, she encourages him.

Harry Mason manages to roll onto his side and take a better look at this stranger. Somehow time has skipped forward again, and a golden light is already filtering through the window behind her, dust dancing like starlight in the pleasant dawn. There is a smell of spring rain in the air, although he is convinced it should still be winter and dry.

How long have I been lying here?

I don't know, she says. *I don't even know you are here.*

What do you mean?

'Daddy, are you going to be OK?'

The woman looks up at the air as though she heard the same faraway whisper he did.

Is that Jeanie? she asks.

What's your name?

She turns back to him and traces a long nimble finger up a vein on the inside of his arm.

Don't worry, the woman says, as though she did not hear his question. *She'll be fine as long as her daddy pulls through. And Harry?*

He swallows the last of this bloody dryness in his throat. *Yes?*

Don't forget Friday. Dinner and movies? We have to do this.

The sudden realization of who she is sends a bolt of electricity through him. Vivid memories bloom in the desert expanse of his mind, and Harry is jarred into wakefulness. His eyes fly open and he inhales deeply . . . not the air of open spaces but the cloying tang of hospital rooms.

2

The emergency seems to have passed. Joan Mason closes her eyes and breathes a sigh of relief.

'Nan, you're hurting me,' says Jeanie Mason. She pulls herself free from her grandmother's grip on her shoulders, then reaches up to take her hand. 'Sorry,' she says. 'But it's kinda sore.'

'If you have to say it that way, dear, then it's kind *of*,' Joan Mason says reflexively.

She meets her granddaughter's upturned face. Jeanie's green eyes are still glittering with the frightened tears she shed after Joan abruptly yelled for her to leave her father's side. There is an adult's concern in that expression, mixed up with the expectations of a child needing answers to difficult questions she cannot yet fully articulate. Joan is glad to see none of the reproach she half expected.

'I'm sorry I shouted at you like that.'

'That's OK, Nan. You looked really scared.'

I'm still scared, angel – scared to death.

Joan summons a smile for Jeanie, which she hopes is both convincing and reassuring.

'When are they going to let us see Daddy again?' asks Jeanie.

'I don't know.'

'Today still, you think?'

'I hope so.'

Ever since Director Molethe had called her three days ago with the dreadful news of her son's shooting, there has been a knot sitting in Mrs Mason's throat. At Jeanie's last question it unravels again, releasing the tears that have become so familiar these last few days. 'I hope so,' she reiterates.

It has only been half an hour since the alarms on the instruments attached to her son began screaming, yet it feels to Joan that an eternity has passed since the doctor yelled at her to leave, and the nurse unceremoniously shunted her from the room. The nurse had hastily gone on to draw closed the white curtains around Harold's bed so that the doctors could work in peace. Joan then watched helplessly as a second doctor, then a third – much older and more distinguished-looking – ducked through the curtains to join a growing army of medical personnel. She kept listening to the hidden commotion for clues to what was happening, but their jargon gave away nothing enlightening. Finally they began filing out, so many people emerging from such a confined space. Some nodded at her with guarded sympathy, as though they expected her to fly into a rage. This embarrassed her, but she stood her ground, and confronted the senior-looking doctor to ask what had gone wrong. He in turn deferred to Dr Hirson, the cheeky upstart who had earlier scolded her for getting in his way.

She glances back over her shoulder at the waiting room, and sees it still as empty as when she and Jeanie practically took up residence there. To Joan it seems that tragedy does not often come to Port Elizabeth, or at least not to this particular hospital. The only sound comes from a television set placed diagonally on a coffee table in one corner of the room, its volume turned down to a whisper. Near it are two armchairs directly facing each other, with several blankets strewn over them to form Jeanie's little nest away from home.

Joan turns back to the observation window in time to see Dr Hirson flick aside the curtain screening Harold's bed and stride towards the connecting door opening on the waiting room. From the set of his lips she guesses the news is bad, and she notices a thin streak of blood across the midriff of his white overcoat that was not there before. Joan quickly turns away to dab at her eyes with a tissue retrieved from her sleeve.

'Jeanie, why don't you clean up that mess on your chair?'

'No, I want to stay here with you. The doctor's coming.'

A door swings open and Hirson enters the visitors' area. His eyes first meet Jeanie's, and what was probably meant as a reassuring smile comes out as more of a smirk. The doctor then clears his throat and turns to Joan.

'Can she stay and hear what you have to tell me?' Joan's hands quickly find Jeanie's shoulders again, and she unconsciously positions the little girl in front of her, like a human shield.

'Yes, she can.' The doctor nods his head.

Joan breathes a quiet sigh of relief. If Jeanie can stay, it must surely mean good news – or at least not too bad.

Hirson takes a seat in an armchair while the Masons remain standing, and cups his finely chiselled face in both hands, before running his fingers up through sandy-coloured hair.

'Well?' she asks nervously.

'First of all, I want to apologize for shouting at you.' Joan waits to hear if there is more, but clearly this apology is as far as he will go. 'However, if I ask you to leave my ward, I expect you to do so immediately.'

He watches her carefully as a hot flush rises up her neck.

Joan straightens up a little before she answers stiffly, 'I'll try my best, doctor.'

A tired smile eases the lines on his face, and he winks at Jeanie. 'Good. Now, let me tell you about your son. The problem was a sudden increase in his heart rate, which almost led to what we call a ventricular fibrillation.'

Joan stammers, 'You mean a heart attack?'

Jeanie steps backwards, pressing against Joan's legs.

'Not quite but, left unattended, it could have become very serious.'

'And now?'

'We have it under control, and we'll be watching him closely for the rest of the night.'

Joan sinks into a nearby chair, though keeping a tight hold on Jeanie. The little girl climbs on to her lap willingly.

'What brought this on? I thought you said he was stable?'

'We've been keeping him under sedation with Ditropan, so that he's been oblivious to most of the pain. My only explanation for what happened there is that he started to wake up before his next scheduled dose, and he reacted violently to confronting an unknown situation. Chances are Harry doesn't even know that he's in an intensive-care unit. Maybe your son was even re-experiencing his shooting, I don't know. Those are my best guesses at this stage.'

'Is it wise then to keep him this way?'

'Mrs Mason, surgery and medicine are not exact sciences. In cases where there is trauma to the head, this is even more so.' The young doctor gets up and approaches them. He squats near Jeanie, who warily lets him stroke her hair. 'Believe it or not, what just happened may be a good thing.'

'How?'

'If it *was* a dream or memory that sparked this off, it means his brain is still in good shape, and that he might be ready to wake up.'

'Can we go in to see him, then?' asks Jeanie.

Joan touches Jeanie's kinky blonde hair. 'Dear, now is probably not the best time for you to go in.'

'Actually, I don't mind.' The doctor rises. 'If Harry is being such a busybody in his head, then he might be receptive to some company, even if he is still under.'

'Really?' Jeanie turns hopeful eyes on her grandmother. 'Does that mean Daddy will get better if I talk to him?'

Hirson laughs, and Joan decides to upgrade her opinion of him as a brash youngster.

'He might hear you, Jeanie, though he's in a very, very deep sleep. Don't expect your dad to show that he can hear you, OK?'

Jeanie leaps off Joan's lap and pushes past the doctor before her grandmother can restrain her. They both watch her duck into the ICU cubicle before again meeting each other's eyes.

Here it comes, Joan thinks. *The 'but'.*

'She certainly is a cute one,' is all the doctor says, however. 'Where's the mother – or is that prying?'

Joan musters a waxen smile, and touches her forehead where a migraine is threatening. 'She died a few years ago.'

'I see.'

'Is that all, doctor? My son's going to be all right then, is he?'

Hirson checks his watch. 'Mrs Mason. It's ten o' clock at night, and you've been here since before my shift began early this morning. Go home now. I think . . . I'm *sure*, he'll be all right for the rest of the night.'

'Yes, perhaps I *should* get some sleep.' She glances over at Jeanie's nest near the television set and lets out a small laugh. 'Though if I was as compact as that little thing, I'd put one of those beds together for myself.'

Hirson picks up his clipboard and makes to leave the room. 'Have you found out who Tanya is yet?'

Joan gets to her feet with a loud pop from her left knee. 'Yes, Tanya Fouché is her name, and she should be arriving tomorrow.'

'The cavalry is on its way, then?'

Joan smiles. 'I certainly hope so.'

'And Superintendent Swarts isn't here any more?'

She thinks of the lumbering police officer and his gruff manner. 'Having a stranger by your side isn't quite the same, is it?'

'Tanya, come back!' This sudden roar from Harry is followed immediately by a surprised shriek from Jeanie.

3

Joan Mason glances up just in time to see Jeanie stumble away from her father, clutching her arm as if she has been burned.

'What the hell?' mutters Hirson.

He yanks open the door leading into the emergency room, and rubber soles squeak over the linoleum as he is closely followed by a duty nurse from the nearby station.

'What was that?' asks the nurse.

Joan looks over to where her son should be sleeping still in a deep coma. She feels her hackles rise, for Harry's eyes are wide open and staring right through her. Tanya? It's the second time her son has uttered that name. It both bewilders and hurts her. Why is it that he has never confided in her about this person who obviously means so much to him?

For the briefest moment she wonders if this same Tanya might have hexed her son. It is a fleeting thought, fuelled by stress and a touch of jealousy, she will tell herself later, but it still leaves her rattled.

4

By the time Joan enters the room Harry has slumped back into unconsciousness. Hirson and the nurse are both fussing over him without paying any real attention to their patient's distressed child. Joan finds the little girl pressed back against the observation window, about as far away from her father as she can get, and she looks more angry than shocked. Joan gingerly kneels beside her, wincing as her joints pop again.

'What happened? What did you do?'

'I didn't do anything! I was just holding his hand, like the doctor said I could, and then . . . Daddy sat up and looked straight at me and called me someone else!'

'Dear, your father is very ill.' Joan tries to hug her granddaughter, who backs away.

'Jeanie, come here, please.'

'Nan, he doesn't know who I am any more. He's not going to remember me when he wakes up.'

'That's not true. You just got a bad fright. Please, come here.'

She barely manages to grab hold of Jeanie's arm before the child shakes herself free and storms out of the room.

'Jeanie!'

'Mrs Mason,' hisses Hirson. 'There's been enough shouting around here for one day, please.'

With some effort Joan gets to her feet and approaches the bed.

'He's lapsed right back into it.' The doctor shakes his head in bafflement. 'Yet none of the monitors show anything out of the ordinary. All I can say is your son seems very intent on waking. I wonder why.'

Joan says nothing in reply, instead lets her tired eyes rove over her boy's appearance. A reddish four-day stubble roughens his chin; there are bruised rings under his eyes, and a large white bandage covers the wounded right side of his head. That is where a bullet drilled underneath the skin but deflected off the skull before exiting at the back of his head. Various types of tubes run into his nose and exposed arm.

Joan Mason takes up Harry's limp hand. *Oh God,*

Colin, she thinks, in conversation with her deceased husband, *how did our son ever get so old, so bloody and broken?*

The doctor gently lays a hand on her arm. 'You look like you've seen a ghost, Mrs Mason. Go get some rest. You need it as much as he does.'

Joan Mason jerks away at the physical contact, then realizes that the young doctor is only showing concern.

'Yes, my nerves are at an end. Good-night, doctor.'

5

'We need to do this,' Tanya Fouché remembers having said to Harry just a week ago. 'Sooner rather than later.'

Today, she thinks. *I was supposed to be meeting her today. And now I am – except he's not with me. I'm doing it alone.*

During the two-hour flight from Johannesburg to Port Elizabeth the aircraft has been pitching and rolling over a bleak, ochre-coloured winter landscape, only partially visible below the wing. She unglues her eyes from this craggy expanse and lets them run over her fellow passengers, crammed tensely into the discount carrier. Sitting right in front of her, a bald-headed man with a scalp as smooth as a Dutch cheese has barely managed to shut up about how abominable this flight is. The unfortunate geriatric seated next to him looks ready to slash his own wrists with a plastic knife to escape from his neighbour's incessant whining.

Normally, the frequent gut-wrenching lurches experienced between air pockets would not have bothered Tanya unduly. She grew up with nomadic parents, travelling from one remote part of the country to another in pursuit of work opportunities that might provide a few rand to support the family for another month or two. Such lurching and bumping was second nature to her by the time she began helping her father fix motorbikes with her nimble fingers. At the age of seventeen she had taken part in her first rally, finishing up on a pitted track way up north near a town called Louis Trichardt, way back when. Nothing like a single teenage girl riding her own bike amid a horde of brutish males, all with their little trophy birds perched high-up on the backs of their cycles. The way Tanya Fouché figures it, pitching and rolling is all part of the fun – except now when more of it is going on inside her head than outside.

This apprehension did not just start when Detective Jacob Tshabalala eventually tracked her down, for it was two days earlier when she abruptly stopped receiving the usual text messages from Harry Mason. Over the last four months she had got so used to them clogging up her inbox, the moment they suddenly dried up it felt like a betrayal. Gut instinct soon told her something was wrong, but she did not know enough about the demands of police work, so she kept quiet, hoping and waiting, admonishing herself for having grown so dependent on any man's bloody text messages. It was at this point it dawned on her what the wives of police officers must go through on a regular basis, and the future she now risked exposing herself to.

Tanya had desperately wanted to find out if Harry was safe, except she did not know where to start. She was barely acquainted with any of his friends; and the few she had contacted did not even know he was currently off on an operation in the Drakensberg. She badly wanted to call the police station, but could not be certain whether she was meant to know about this special operation in the Eastern Cape. The last thing she wanted was to jeopardize Harry's new appointment by revealing he had discussed things with her that might be classified.

No, she thought ruefully, *this isn't what the wives of cops feel at all. It's worse.* At least they knew exactly whom to call, while all she had was a cup of tea, a cat, a phone and the television news to keep her company. After two days of growing anxiety, she gave herself one more night before she would call the damn commissioner of police himself, if need be, just to find out what was going on. But that turned out to be unnecessary when Jacob Tshabalala found her instead.

What the hell have you got yourself into, darling? she thinks again. *This isn't like you. Not like you at all.*

The last time she had allowed herself to be kept in the dark like this ended with a crystal-meth-head called Jackson Durant sticking the tip of his bowie knife up her nose. It occurred in a cheap motel called Lucille's, somewhere outside Clarens, and he wanted his money – and he wanted it *now*. She had been with him three years by then, and so knew about the drugs – had enjoyed her fair share of them, in truth – but she knew absolutely bugger-all about his bloody money. In the time Jackson Durant shacked up with her, she never saw a cent of the cash for which he was now threatening to kill her. Heck, in her reckoning, he had been living off *her*, not the other way around.

Harry Mason's world-famous disappearing trick. Only he turned up a few days later with two bullets in him, and now she is sitting in an aeroplane heading off to meet his mother and daughter. Neither had seemed to even know she existed, which made her feel like a dirty secret.

How could he do that to her?

6

That's him. Tanya feels sure it is Jacob Tshabalala, if she correctly remembers the old photo she once saw in Harry's study at home.

She is waiting, as agreed, by the news-stand in the bright but compact arrivals hall of the Port Elizabeth airport. The front page of the *Mercury* is headlined POLICE TERRORIZE HOMELESS, while the accompanying photograph shows a police officer – Tshabalala – leaping through the air right above a little black girl dressed in a dirty pink tracksuit. Her frizzy hair is on fire, and her horrified tear-streaked face is turned up towards him. His hands are raised above his head, as though he is about to bring them down violently upon her. Is this terrifying man on the front page the same gentle-voiced police officer she spoke with on the phone yesterday?

'You shouldn't believe everything you read in the papers, miss,' says a gruff voice unexpectedly at her shoulder.

With a start, Tanya turns around to find a tall but heavy-set man with a well-trimmed grey beard smiling at her.

'Russell.' He sticks out a large woodcutter's hand. 'Senior Supe Russie Swarts to my men. And you must be Tanya Fouché? Pleased to meet you, miss.'

She glances around the emptying arrivals hall. Right across from her is a big billboard welcoming travellers to the Windy City.

'How did you know?' She smiles and shakes his hand. 'Not even Mrs Mason knows what I look like.'

'Are you kidding me, little lady?' Russell Swarts eyes

her up and down without a hint of embarrassment at
the directness of his scrutiny. He seems to approve of her
tight-fitting faded jeans, the denim jacket and tan boots.
'You're the only woman around here I can see our Bond
dating.'

Tanya blushes at the compliment, though it is the kind
of line she usually flings right back at any man who acts
too presumptuous.

'Bond?' she asks, bemused.

The cop laughs heartily. 'It's on account of that *rooi-
neck* accent of his.'

'Harry's spoken of you a great deal. All good, I must
add.'

'He has? I hope he didn't ruin my chance to make a
good first impression.'

'No,' she says, 'he admires you, I think.'

Swarts grunts non-committally, grabs the trolley
already holding her luggage and aims it towards the exit
before she can get a chance to tell him she prefers pushing
it herself.

'Thanks,' she says lamely.

She folds the newspaper in her hand and follows
Swarts out into the airport parking lot. A strong breeze
forces her to tie her long hair back with a red rubber band
she otherwise keeps around her wrist. The air tastes salty
but clean; the cloudless sky is an alluring turquoise.

'How is he doing?' she asks anxiously.

'He's getting there.'

She waits for the police officer to say more but he
tramps on briskly, pushing the trolley ahead of him as
though it were a battering ram.

Just look at what you've got yourself into, girl, a voice
at the back of her head pipes up. *He's a cop. They have*

personalities as bland as baking flour. You've got this all wrong, darling!

She wills that voice to quieten down. For now she just wants to watch and learn – only later will she make a final decision.

'The guy in the photo there is Jacob Tshabalala, Harry's ex-partner.' Swarts finally breaks the silence, which has been growing uncomfortable for her. 'Is that why you were staring at it?'

'The face did look familiar, but I haven't even met him yet.'

'Oh?'

'Trust me, I'm not happy about that either.'

'I don't want to interfere between the two of you, but if I had a pretty lady like you around, miss, I wouldn't be hiding her away.'

Tanya feels the angry colour creeping into her cheeks. 'Thank you for the compliment, but I don't normally see myself as just a showpiece.'

Swarts glances at her, an eyebrow raised. He seems to realize that he has offended her, because he very quickly changes the subject.

'If you're going to be with a cop for any length of time, miss, you'll need to know that the press are hardly ever our friends. I mean, does it say anywhere in that article that Tshabalala saved that kid from becoming a human *flambé*?'

She thinks about that for a moment. 'Perhaps it would not have gone this far if the police were a bit more in touch with those homeless people in the first place.'

'Sure, it's easy to blame us for everything, and you know why? Because we're the only ones who have to accept responsibility in any situation that demands a police presence. Take those idiots at the warehouse, for example: where were the men who hijacked that building in the first place, and then rented it out illegally to those squatters? And were those innocent "tenants", as they call themselves, really too stupid to realize something might be wrong about such an arrangement? Did they even care? Of course not. In this country, they take what they want now, and worry about any consequences later.'

Tanya feels herself bristle at this man's condescending tone. 'If the police genuinely want to cultivate an image of serving the community, and not constantly bludgeoning it, a bit more finesse in dealing with the destitute might be in order, don't you think?'

Swarts once more gives her a sidelong glance with eyebrow raised. 'The syndicate that took control of that building packed those blimming squatters in tighter than you'd find sardines in a can. Then they charged them six hundred bucks a head for the privilege of living in conditions the SPCA won't allow a bunch of egg-laying chickens. And when we pitch up, they decide it was the state that had wronged them. Suddenly we were responsible for the shit they willingly stepped right into. Why? Because it's cheaper and easier to point a finger than accept your own shortcomings.'

'That's a bit one-sided, don't you think?'

'It's the truth, and I see it every blimming day.'

She thought the idea was for him to meet her at the airport, then lead the way to the hospital after she had arranged her own hire car. But as they reach a white sedan with the SAPS aloe logo printed boldly on the door, she realizes this cop had different thoughts.

'I was actually thinking of hiring my own car,' she protests. 'It'll be easier to get around that way.'

He stops the trolley. 'I'll take you to the hospital. It's no problem.'

She manages to force a smile. 'Mr Swarts—'

'Russell.'

Tanya pauses. 'Russell, I'm sure it's not a problem and I appreciate the offer, I really do, but I insist on not imposing. I'm sure you're a very busy man and not inclined to acting as anyone's chauffeur.'

Russell Swarts holds her eyes for a long moment that stretches increasingly into what feels like interrogation time. Then he smiles serenely.

'That Harry, I never figured him going for the head-strong type. OK, miss, get your own car, but I'd still like to take you in to—'

'I'll get one here at the airport, thank you.' The fixed smile on her face feels so tightly stretched that Tanya thinks it might snap at any moment.

Swarts clears his throat and she can sense he is annoyed at being interrupted. 'As I was saying, I can take you into town. There's a rental place I know there that's half the price. Just because you step off the plane here doesn't mean you have to pay these Shylocks every blimming penny you brought along with you, does it?'

'Oh.' Tanya feels her colour again deepen, this time in embarrassment. 'Yes, I could definitely do with a bargain, thanks.'

'No problem, miss.' His voice is as frosty as tundra in the bright seaside sun. 'But next time do me the favour of hearing me out first.'

Swarts unlocks the boot and offloads the trolley before he steps round to open the passenger door for her.

'By the way, that man you see in the picture?' He nods at the newspaper in her hand, and it is as though he has been mulling over what she said earlier about the police needing to become a bit more diplomatic. 'He might be a black, but he's come a hell of a lot further than most of the bloody instant cops they squeeze through the system these days. He's got more finesse than the Queen of England when it comes to policing, and he's got guts too. You keep that in mind, miss.'

7

The drive into the city is a short one. Having grown used to Johannesburg's endless sprawl, Port Elizabeth strikes her as more like a large coastal holiday resort than an important city. And, like most of such seasonal places, the main road extending along its golden beachfront is crammed full of restaurants, guesthouses and brightly painted holiday homes, with a scattering of more ponderous buildings among them to give the central business district a veneer of gravitas.

'Can you tell me exactly what happened?' she asks the superintendent, after a protracted silence.

'I can tell you some of it, but I'll do that over a drink, if you don't mind. It's already been a long day, and I'm heading back up into Tsolo the moment you're taken care of.'

'Is it OK for you to drink on duty?'

His answer comes fast and glib, as though he has used it often. 'I'm not on duty during my lunch break.'

Tanya shrugs. 'Well, I'm about to meet the daughter and mother of my boyfriend while he is still lying out cold, so maybe I could do with something strong myself.'

'Right, then. I know a place up here.'

For a second Tanya feels the car slow down, as though Swarts actually believes she wants to head into a pub before she even sees Harry.

'But only after I've seen him.'

The car picks up speed again, as Swarts laughs. 'Fair enough! You've got a deal there, miss.'

'It's Tanya, please. Do I look like I should be wearing a white pioneer's cap and answering only to "miss"?'

Swarts looks her over carefully. 'Suppose not. Tanya it is, then. You really haven't met the mother yet?'

'I only spoke with her on the phone. She sounded pretty . . . strained.'

This time it is a deafening belly laugh, and Tanya begins to think that she might actually grow to like the bastard.

'Strained! I like that. We better make it a double later,' he says. 'In fact, I guarantee you now, you'll probably be needing two of those.'

8

On their arrival at the Abraham Goodman Clinic, an expensive one if the Spanish-terraced façade is anything to go by, Swarts insists on leading the way. He also insists on opening every door for Tanya Fouché, which would have irritated her no end if it had not been for their conversation during the car ride. When she gives him a reprimanding but good-natured look, followed by, 'Russell, God gave me hands to open my own doors,' he only shrugs and winks.

'Little lady, I'm nothing but an old fart from a different generation. The young guys, they know all about expressing their emotions and *cordon bleu* cooking; us older men, we know opening doors is just plain good manners. So bear with me.'

As they are about to head into the intensive-care unit, Tanya feels the fist that has been gripping her insides ever since receiving Jacob's message begin to tug a little harder. Suddenly her legs feel weak and she has to clench her hands to stop them from shaking.

'You OK?' Swarts' deep tone, which she thought so gruff not an hour ago, is now remarkably soothing to her ears. Tanya smiles up at him with as much courage as she can muster.

They find Harry Mason's mother reading to him from a magazine. Her hair is like blow-dried white silk; her skin, despite her age, promises a downy smoothness if Tanya were to dare touch it. Turning her attention to Harry's daughter, she feels an invisible hand push gently against her chest. The girl is still preoccupied with reading her book and does not notice her. Framed by fair curly hair, her face emanates a remarkable beauty, the pale skin and emerald eyes contrasting starkly with the black jeans and navy blue pullover she is wearing. The purple plastic bangles around one wrist gleam bright in the fluorescent light. Tanya has of course seen a dozen pictures of Harry's daughter on the few occasions she visited his house but, here in the flesh, a fierce energy seems to radiate from the child. An abrupt pang of jealousy hits Tanya – that Harry should have such a gorgeous daughter by another woman – but she violently shoves the thought aside as soon as it materializes. He has his past, and she has hers; neither of them can change that, nor should they try to.

When Jeanie suddenly reaches out towards the bed,

Tanya follows her gesture and, for the first time, notices Harry's arm sticking out from underneath the sheet. Coloured hospital bands encircle a wrist that looks like the life has already run out of it. She finds herself wanting to bolt into the room and grab that hand, but the presence of his family, and knowing herself a complete stranger, put the brakes on her. Suddenly she feels self-conscious and embarrassed here.

What do I call her? wonders Tanya, when no one has yet noticed her standing in the doorway with Swarts. *Mrs Mason? Joan?*

Tanya Fouché glances at Swarts for reassurance. He gives it to her in the form of a smile.

OK, girl, you walk in there good and strong.

She nearly balls her fists like a boxer entering the ring, then forces herself to relax. Taking a deep breath, Tanya knocks softly against the doorjamb. 'Mrs Mason?'

Joan Mason stops reading mid-sentence and turns around in her chair. She is clearly a woman exhausted, but her bright blue eyes still blaze keenly with interest. Jeanie looks up from her book and brushes a stray curl of hair from one eye. Tanya has to force her hands not to begin wringing.

'Hello, I'm Tanya Fouché. We spoke on the phone.'

Jeanie gasps and stares at her with a mixture of astonishment and, perhaps, suspicion. Tanya is somewhat taken aback by the intensity of that gaze. Yes, it is definitely suspicion, because she has worked long enough with abandoned children to know what it looks like. But why?

Tanya gives the girl a smile that feels broken on her face before quickly returning her eyes to Joan Mason, who has now laid aside her magazine and stood up. Her expression, too, remains wary and questioning.

'Tanya?'

Tanya takes a few steps forward, her hand held out stiffly. Joan Mason shakes it hesitantly, then abruptly pulls her into a hug.

'Good God, it's so good to finally meet you, dear. I didn't know at all what to expect.'

Tanya returns the embrace, and becomes acutely aware of a body lotion smelling of lilies. Strong emotions seize her, and she has to swallow hard to keep down tears of gratitude and relief. After what seems an age, Joan Mason gently pushes her away. 'There now. Let's have another look at you. '

The older woman scrutinizes her from top to bottom, then finally reaches out and pats her on the shoulder.

'Thank you so much for coming.'

'I would have come sooner, if only I'd known.' She turns to Harry's daughter and waves. 'Hello. You must be Jeanie.'

'Hi.' The child waves back reluctantly, her green eyes remain as probing as her grandmother's.

Tanya goes over to focus on Harry's bandaged head more closely, and a strangled gasp escapes her lips at the sight of him. Tubes enter his nose and a ribbed white pipe exits his mouth. The left side of his face has the mottled colour of an aubergine. Distantly, Tanya hears Joan Mason greet Swarts as he too enters the room.

'Oh Jesus, what have they done to you?' Tanya whispers as unwanted tears well up in her eyes.

Suddenly Joan Mason is at her side and grabbing hold of her trembling form. Faintly she hears Swarts urge her to sit down, as he pulls a chair closer. Tanya cannot seem to find a response for either of them, however hard she tries to explain that she is fine and does not want to sit down right now. All her attention is fixed on this man she has come to love so much in so little time, who now seems to be hovering on the brink of death.

'Jeanie, won't you fetch Tanya a glass of water?' says Joan.

'No, I'm all right, really,' says Tanya a little more confidently. She musters a smile for Harry's mother. 'It's just . . . seeing him like this is a bit of a shock.'

'It's not as bad as it looks,' insists Joan Mason bravely. 'Dr Hirson will be taking him off the sedatives tomorrow morning. With any luck, he'll be wide awake by tomorrow afternoon.'

Tanya has taken Harry's limp hand in her own, when small warm fingers touch her outstretched forearm. She looks up and is surprised to find Jeanie standing right beside her now, those emerald eyes level with her own. All the child's earlier suspicion seems to have evaporated.

'I'll go get you some tea, Tanya.'

She offers the child a smile. 'Thanks.'

Jeanie almost runs from the room, but for a warning from her grandmother.

Harry's hand is cold and waxen in hers. With Joan Mason and Swarts hovering right behind her, she feels uncannily like a widow seated at a graveside. The sensation makes her skin crawl.

What is this shit? I didn't sign up for this, that voice at the back of her head reminds her.

Tanya traces a finger up the inside of Harry's arm.

'I'm here,' she whispers.

An office chair rolls across the floor, and then Joan Mason is sitting next to her.

The older woman leans forward and takes both Tanya's hands firmly. In a voice not to be ignored, she says, 'Now, let's hear why I don't know anything about you. And please, you'd better call me Joan.'

9

Feeling shocked, drained and confused, all at once, Tanya Fouché followed Russell Swarts out of the hospital. When she tried to pin down all her tangled emotions they refuse to stay put, especially with that voice at the back of her mind still grumbling over her predicament. Swarts threw her a concerned glance on the way to the car rental, then hesitantly began to suggest they cancel their drink.

Tanya shut him off with a firm shake of her head. 'My father was a dirt-poor drifter, who could never make the right decisions in life. There wasn't much useful he could teach me, except the one lesson that you always keep a date for a drink.'

'Sounds like a wise man.' Swarts nodded sagely. 'I take it he's now dead?'

'Crushed under a tractor,' Tanya nodded with a distant look on her face. 'He died alone in a broken field, miles away from anyone who could help him.'

She did not tell Swarts they could smell the rum on her dead father before they eventually found him in the tall maize.

The cop clearly respected her matter-of-fact tone. 'It's a good enough way for a hard-working man to go. Men like your dad, they don't have much place left in a country where handouts exist for just about anyone who claim that apartheid made them lazy.'

She glanced at him in an attempt to decipher what that is supposed to mean.

'Or perhaps dying under that tractor says more about the futility of life itself, and has absolutely nothing to do with this country's history.'

On the ground floor of a narrow two-storey building near the railway station, the bar they enter is the kind of nondescript watering hole drifters can sniff out easily in any corner of the world. Blackboards set out on the pavement advertise, in faded white chalk letters, the day's special offers, which seem not to have changed much in over a decade.

'Are you sure you're fine with this place?' Swarts asks her. 'We could go somewhere a bit more . . .'

'Ladylike?' Tanya laughs sardonically. She can see his question is out of politeness only, and feels sure Russell Swarts is the kind of serious drinker who would rather spend his hard-earned pennies in a place where booze rather than ambience is the priority. 'Believe it or not, I've gone into places far worse on my own.' She pushes open the door before Swarts can reach for it.

'S'truth?' he asks, surprised.

Her mind wanders back to the youthful days when she rode with Jackson Durant's gang, the Boksburg chapter of the Hell's Angels. 'Is truth,' she confirms.

The gloomy interior of the bar has a guarded yet homely feel to it, which she finds welcoming in its sheer familiarity. Rickety barstools line the counter and the wide planks bolted as extra table surface along the walls. Untold cigarettes and penknives have taken their toll on the woodwork, while the upholstery in the few available booths is torn and matted with dark unidentifiable gunk. The air itself reeks of stale beer, nicotine and the sour odour of desperate men hiding from an unforgiving world.

Tanya promptly orders drinks at the bar before Swarts can fish out his wallet.

'Hey, no.' He almost shoulders her out of the way. 'I'm paying for this.'

'Old man, remember I'm nothing but a woman from a liberated generation. The old aunties you mix with, they know all about hair curlers and cooking meals for their men; us younger types, we know about paying our fair share – and taking it too. So bear with me, if you can.' She winks at him playfully with a lopsided smile.

Beside the rear door they find a high table at a dirty window. It overlooks a small square lot out back, where a group of feral vervet monkeys are digging in the garbage. When she turns back to Russell Swarts, he is quarter way through his first brandy and Tab, and is already longingly eyeing the bar.

'So tell me exactly what happened out there, Russell. Who shot my man?'

Swarts belches into a fist and apologizes. 'How much do you already know of what took us to Tsolo?'

Her earlier fears resurface, of getting Harry into trouble for disclosing what might be classified information. But sitting here now, with Swarts, she must admit that there is actually very little she knows about the case.

He smiles reassuringly. 'Go on.'

'Harry just told me he was looking into the murder of a small-time ANC politician, and that some members of a vigilante group called the Abasindisi may have been responsible. He said when you guys couldn't crack the murder, you decided to go after the entire association. You were hoping to force their hand, I guess. He mentioned there were a few leads pointing to Tsolo – and that some guns were apparently hidden there.'

Swarts nods thoughtfully. 'That's about right, except we didn't have many leads at all. One moment the case was as cold as frozen steak, the next Harry comes up with a contact willing to sell out the entire gang, whether they were connected to our particular murder or not. Raiding Tsolo was supposed to be a sweetener for the big deal, so to speak.'

'Harry put all that together?' This side of him, largely hidden from her, fascinates Tanya. It is as if she is getting to know him all over again, only this time it is the cop inside him coming out. As much as she has distrusted police officers all her life, and is suspicious of what now lies ahead, it also thrills her to think of Harry in this new light. 'How?' she adds.

'I don't even know who Harry's informant is, though it may be important if we want to catch whoever shot him.' The superintendent offers her a rueful smile. 'In retrospect, it seems the sweetest berries are often the most poisonous, and that sweetener we were offered has got us into a whole lot of trouble.

'The Abasindisi have always been a difficult bunch, especially once they've taken root within a community. They ingratiate themselves with people by getting rid of one or two featherweight crooks, and suddenly they're the great new deal. They've learned how to do the least work in order to reap the most rewards, which usually entails a lot of violence and little respect for human life. It's a barely above-board extortion racket.'

'Are we really talking about the Abasindisi Security Services?'

'The Security Services thing is about the Phaliso brothers turning what they always used to do into a legitimate business. So far it's working for them. Somehow they ousted the old leaders, and turned the tide of negative public opinion that arose against them in the nineties. That was shortly after their organization got implicated in stock-theft syndicates all over the Eastern Cape.'

'So how come you now say "extortion racket"?' Tanya asks.

'I have a suspicion that if they want to win over a neighbourhood to the services they supposedly render, they just bring in the hijackers to steal cars, they bring in the thieves to break into houses. Once the locals have become paranoid enough, a Saviours Security Services salesman wearing a nice suit steps in and offers the whole community their premium services, with a big toothy smile. At least that's how I think they operate in the upper-class neighbourhoods – but so far I haven't been able to prove it.'

'Jesus,' exclaims Tanya. 'What next?'

'It's more complicated than that,' says Swarts. 'Their agents, the ones responsible for the violence, usually roll into town, do their deed, and are out of there almost within the hour. They are never known to the community where these "acts of retribution" are committed – which minimizes the possibility of identification and retaliation. Add to the transient nature of such crimes the mixture of mining *fanakalo* and township *tsotsitaal* the gang members speak, you can imagine the nightmare Central Intelligence Services has in trying to monitor them. Their patois is a natural barrier to infiltration, and these days they can sniff out potential informants easier than a fox terrier can locate drugs in a shipment of Colombian-manufactured teddy bears.'

Tanya thoughtfully sips her whisky. 'I don't understand it. If you know exactly who their leaders are, then why don't you just arrest them?'

Swarts laughs good-naturedly, and throws another longing glance at the bar.

'Tanya, the laws that protect these two bastards don't *allow* me to get what I need out of them. Forty-eight hours maximum is how long I can hold them without charge, and all they'll do is sit in their jail cells with their lawyers and laugh at us. They've made sure to cover up every causal link between what they've ordered and the crimes that are eventually perpetrated. Even if we managed to catch one of their agents red-handed, it'd be impossible for us to trace the crime itself back to them. We've certainly tried, but the lowly operatives can't even tell us who paid them, and they're purposely kept in the dark about the organization's other operations. It's completely decentralized, and orders are passed down through a human network so complex it's a nightmare to unravel in any court of law. Our only hope now is this informant of Harry's, or else for one of their senior lieutenants to cock up an order. But so far that hasn't happened, and they're sharper than razors, those two brothers. One slip-up on our side, and guess who's branded the villain again? We'll instantly be accused of trying to undermine "the one organization that is proving itself more effective than the police service in dealing with crime", to quote one reporter in the *Star*. People like the national commissioner, they don't want to tread anywhere near that basket of eggs.' Swarts shakes his head in exasperation.

'So how are you going to catch these people? I mean, someone has to go down for shooting Harry, right?'

'It's going to be really difficult. My only chance now is to somehow work back through Harry's informant.

'The thing is, it's not just the way they operate that protects them. Their protection and debt-collection services are extremely popular, amongst both the poor and the powerful, because they know the Abasindisi are the only firm guaranteed to speak the black man's language. That means they have some interesting contacts, powerful ones, which makes investigating them very tricky.'

'The black man's language? What do you mean?'

'Lob tear gas at them, shove a gun in their faces, they don't care, some will tell you. They'll go on doing whatever they want to; it's the revolutionary attitude that's become inbred. But have a *black* man beat the shit out of them with a weapon they respect, a traditional weapon like a knobkerrie or a sjambok, only then do they blimming listen.'

'That smacks of racism, don't you think?'

'It's the truth, though. Ask anyone that's been in those situations, they'll tell you the same.' Swarts tilts the leftover ice at the bottom of his glass back into his mouth and chews on it. 'I'm getting myself another one. For you?'

She weighs him up and wonders whether the man sitting in front of her is just an old bull that refuses to learn any new attitudes. Maybe change has always been easier for the young.

'Fine.'

As Swarts lumbers back to the bar, Tanya briefly wonders whether he drinks this eagerly every day, or whether this is his way of dealing with what went wrong for them up in the mountains.

Of course he drinks all day, every day. That ruby glow

in the face doesn't appear overnight – same as your father didn't die simply because he didn't notice the mole tunnel under the tractor.

Tanya watches the balding cop lean against the bar, noticing how, on his own, he seems to sag, as though some internal preoccupation has punctured his self-confidence.

Is that what Harry is going to look like in five years' time? Ten? she wonders. *Goodness, I bloody well hope not.*

Uncomfortable with what she is seeing, she turns her gaze to the filthy monkeys still digging in the trash outside, and her thoughts drift back to her first meeting with Harry's family. All in all she feels it went a lot better than expected, especially the way Jeanie had sidled closer to her while she was speaking with Joan. Though the little girl said very little, she had seemed to gradually accept her. Harry's mother, on the other hand, had treated her almost *too* politely, the way a rich woman might address a shop attendant.

She doesn't like you, says that inner voice she has come to associate with long hours on the open road. *Stuck-up old bitch thinks her son's too good for you.*

'What? You really don't want this any more?'

Tanya snaps out of her reverie to find Swarts offering her a drink, with just the right amount of water.

'Cheers.' She smiles and takes it from him. 'Tell me more about the raid.'

Swarts takes a long swig of his brandy mix.

'Harry's informant drew us a rough map of the target village, marking the most likely places where two crates of spanking new AK-47s were stashed. Our initial plan was to surround the settlement unnoticed, and before any

Saviours members could manage to get the cache out of there. But it all went pear-shaped from the word go. Especially when a fog came down on us, screwing up our communications. At the same time fighting broke out between Tsolo and a neighbouring village, and it was Harry who suggested we go in anyway to retrieve the weapons before they disappeared overnight. In retrospect, that was the wrong call.'

'Why?'

'What he said made sense, of course. It was risky going in so short on men, but we needed to get hold of those weapons before three months of hard work went down the drain and our department's budget was straight out of the window for the next three years.' Swarts shrugs. 'If you must know what happened: people got shot; people died.'

Tanya soaks up this new information. 'But you were the senior officer. Wasn't it your responsibility, rather than Harry's, to make that decision?'

Swarts' lips grow thin, and he downs the rest of his drink in one quick gulp. 'We're both being currently investigated, not just him.'

' "*Investigated*"?'

He nods. 'The Independent Complaints Directorate is bringing charges of misconduct and recklessness.' Then he quickly adds, 'But it's only routine. We'll beat them.'

'What do you mean, "beat them"? That implies they've got some sort of case against you both in the first place, and it's not routine.'

'It's nothing.' The way Swarts looked at the bar earlier convinces her that it's anything but.

'I still don't understand why you went in.'

'I just told you why,' he says, sounding irritated.

'But aren't you obliged to safeguard people's lives first?'

Swarts pushes his empty glass away with a look of mild disgust, and Tanya wonders whether he is finding her persistent questions annoying, or whether he merely hates being the one getting interrogated for once.

'We're policemen,' he says in that patronizing tone he first used when they met at the airport, 'so risk is one of the few certainties we face in our work. Raids are by nature the most dangerous operations, because the reaction of suspects is so unpredictable. In theory the parameters within which the police service and ICD expect detectives to work are fine. The regulations are designed to protect us, as well as the civvies, but in practice, when evidence might get lost, say, those rules are as much bullshit as you can fit into a teacup, if you'll excuse my language. We all knew what might happen there, but we all still agreed to go in anyway. And you know what, why not? We were there to do the job. If no one had got shot, the newspapers would be washing our feet. But it didn't happen that way: instead it got dangerous, and now the ICD is after us because a few soldiers and a bunch of no-good *dagga* farmers got killed in the process. It doesn't seem to matter to them, or to the press either, that we had nothing to do with those deaths. Not a single police officer under my command ever fired his weapon.'

Tanya closely observes him in the silence that falls between them. Where before he carefully held her eyes as he told his story, his eyes now drift out of the window to fix on the monkeys.

'Bullshit, Russell, what are you not telling me?'

His eyes snap back to hers. 'I'm telling it the way it

happened,' he growls. 'Look, I know people who can easily sort out a rap like this shit the ICD is trying to put on us. They'll get us off before Harry even gets back to Jo'burg.'

They stare at each other as Tanya tries to see behind the wall he so quickly threw up when she challenged him. Before long, Tanya feels herself growing cold, a little scared. She is way out of her league here, she realizes, because this man's had a lot more experience in playing cat-and-mouse with giving and receiving information.

'Fine,' she finally says, folding her arms over her chest. 'What happened then?'

Swarts shakes the ice at the bottom of his empty glass. 'We don't know who it was that shot Harry after he got separated from his team – but we may have some fingerprints. We found a rusty AK-47 abandoned near where Harry was lying, and the prints on it were clear enough to be lifted. We're assuming he was chasing someone, who then dumped the rifle and pulled a 9mm on Harry.'

The thought of Harry running after a man with an assault rifle sends a shiver down Tanya's spine – mostly of fear, but with a tingle of excitement and pride too. 'Why would the shooter prefer a handgun over an AK when confronting a police officer?'

Swarts shrugs. 'Might have mistakenly thought the thing was jammed or had run out of ammo. Those peasants aren't exactly well trained in the use of military calibres.'

'And no one saw this happen?'

Swarts' eyes are focused on the icy remains of his drink. 'No. It was much too foggy.'

'Did you at least get what you were looking for? The AKs, I mean?'

'No, they weren't there.' Swarts sighs. 'After everything we went through, they blimming well weren't even there.'

'So Harry got himself shot for nothing?' Tanya feels a fresh flush of anger creep through her.

'Not entirely. We did find a cache, but mostly of small-arms and a few ancient .308 hunting rifles. There were also three or four old AKs being used by the villagers, and plenty of 7.62mm cartridges, but none of those were the brand-new specimens that had been promised to us. What we uncovered was buried in a communal kraal, so unless someone in that village talks, we won't be able to pin the cache on anyone. And the chance of someone talking is about as likely as me setting off for work in a French maid's outfit. An informer risks getting killed, or exiled from his birthplace – and believe me, some of those rural types consider the latter a worse fate than getting neck-laced.'

He eyes her carefully before continuing. 'The weapons are why I have to go back to Tsolo this afternoon; I need to be there for a little PR showboating with the provincial commissioner. We're setting a charge to what we found there, and blowing it up, just to show the locals we're on to them, and convince the media that we're not the monkeys they think we are.'

But Harry is lying in ICU! Something did go wrong, don't you see that? she wants to scream at him. Instead, she turns away as she feels the corners of her mouth turn down.

'What is it?' asks Swarts, noticing the gesture.

'You seem so offhand about all this. Harry got shot and . . . oh fuck, I don't know, Russell. It's like you're talking to me about how you're planning to fix your car this weekend.'

Swarts unexpectedly reaches across the table and grasps her hand. His fingers are muscular and rough. She begins to weep, even though it is the last thing she wants to do. A part of her wants to yank her hand away, but another leaves it secure in his warm palm. God knows, she needs *someone* to comfort her after the last two days of constant worry.

'Tanya, nothing could be further from the truth,' he says in a surprisingly gentle voice. 'I'm not ignoring what's happened, only . . . when you've been a cop as long as I have, you tend to play down such things.'

'Are you being honest with me, Russell? That's all I need to know from you.'

At this Russell Swarts' lips tighten into a thin line. 'I'm telling you all I can at this point, because this is an open investigation and I still have a lot of questions of my own. We've only just met, but you'll have to trust me on that.'

Tanya wipes away tears and gives a small embarrassed laugh. 'I'm sorry if I've offended you. It's not that I doubt you, but I feel so confused right now, I don't know how to deal with this. Shit, when I first found out Harry was a cop I almost ditched him on the spot, but here I am still. All this gung-ho bullshit of yours – I'm a social worker, God damn it!' She laughs through her tears. 'Make peace not war, I used to say. I bloody well fought the law along with the Clash, and I thought I'd won. But here I am, with a bunch of gun-toting cops that get themselves shot at, and bloody well think nothing of it.'

The clouds that have been gathering on Swarts' face seem to deepen. 'Tanya, never assume a cop takes a bullet and doesn't think anything of it. It's the one thing we're all shit-scared of, especially if you've seen a colleague take one. I've seen men get sick through and through with that fear, good police officers, all of them.'

'I—'

'I want to get to the bottom of this as much as you do.'

'I know. I *know*.' She lets go of his hand and wipes at her eyes again with one denim sleeve. 'Is there anything I can do to help?'

'There is.'

'What?' She leans forward, and despite herself feels childish enthusiasm at the opportunity to maybe help Harry. 'Anything I can do to help him get out of this mess, I'll do it.'

The cop's eyes drift towards the bar again, and for a moment Tanya suspects he is about to fetch himself another glass of Richelieu, his third double in less than an hour.

'What I think is someone deliberately bullshitted Harry into a trap. I think his informant set us all up. I say the Abasindisi had enough of us harassing them, and decided to lay an ambush. Those AKs weren't where we hoped to find them, because they were never there at all. I think if the rival Qumbu villagers hadn't happened to launch an attack that morning, *none* of us would have come out of those mountains alive.'

'An ambush?' A chill runs through Tanya. 'Harry was double-crossed?'

'That's what I'm saying. Tanya, I don't want to drag you into this, but did Harry ever mention his informant's name to you?'

She shakes her head hesitantly. 'He hardly talks about his work . . . Except, he did once mention . . .'

Swarts' eyebrows rise in anticipation.

'About a month ago he came across something that upset him a lot. He cancelled our dinner arrangements, and didn't visit me for a week. For a while I thought he was going to dump me.'

At this Swarts sits back and clasps his hands behind his head. His bearded features make it difficult for Tanya to read what he is thinking. 'Anything a bit more specific than that?'

She thinks hard for a while.

'Does the name Makhe mean anything to you?' She frowns, then sounds a little more certain as the memory grows clearer. 'Harry had just visited an old friend in Alexandra round about that time.'

Swarts eyes light up. 'I know he went there for some reason in February. It was there that one of our cars got taken apart, near Hofmeyer Bridge.'

'I don't know anything about a bridge, but it couldn't have been more than a month ago.'

'Makhe . . .' Swarts shakes his head. 'Doesn't ring a bell. Is that a surname?'

'Sounds like a first name to me,' says Tanya. 'I only remember Harry was in a terrible mood when he got home.'

'You sure that's the name he mentioned?'

'Like I said, he hardly talks about work at all. You lot are so bloody secretive – how else does it happen that I only find out about him getting shot *two days* after it happened?'

An embarrassed smile spreads over Swarts' face and he seems to relax a little. 'Don't judge him too harshly. We pick up enough shit at work, we don't want to take it back home, too. And we don't want our homes to give us grief because of our work either. He's a good man, Harry. Trust me.'

Be a good little girl and know your place, is what she hears him say.

'A good cop seems to make for lousy company, then,' Tanya adds glumly.

'Is that right?' Swarts sits back and folds his arms, pretending to be insulted.

She smiles weakly in return.

Swarts reaches out for his empty glass and swizzles the ice inside. 'I guess I don't need to ask you—'

'If I remember anything, please call you?' Tanya laughs. 'Just give me your card, Russell. I've watched enough bloody television.'

Swarts chuckles along with her. 'When Bond – I mean Harry – is on his feet again, you two should come out and visit the farm. It's warm up there in Limpopo this time of year. I'll take Bond hunting with my sons, and you can liven up the house. My Bessie, she tends to get bored when the men are out all day. I think she'll like you.'

'You have a game farm?' laughs Tanya. 'So being a cop's been good to you.'

The sudden transformation in his expression is astonishing. To Tanya it looks like granite has pushed through the soft grandfatherly exterior and suddenly warped it out of proportion. Her blood runs cold.

The words almost hiss between his large square teeth. 'That farm's been in my family since 1856.'

Realizing what she seems to have implied, she stammers. 'Oh no, I—'

Swarts waves away any further apologies and abruptly

grabs his car keys. 'Don't worry about it. Let's hit the road now. I've got a hard drive ahead of me.'

10

With a razor, shaving cream and a bowl of warm water, Tanya settles down on the edge of Harry's bed and runs the palm of her hand over the rough stubble that has transformed his boyishly freckled face into that of a shaggy beatnik. Above the bed a wall-mounted digital clock reads 21:38, yet to Tanya it feels like three in the morning.

She leans over and kisses Harry on the corner of his chapped lips, happy to see that he is now breathing without the aid of pipes and tubes. Switching on the bedside light to banish the sleepy ICU gloom, she commences shaving her man's haggard face.

What am I gonna do with you? Tanya carefully runs the blade down his cheeks, down his neck, and winces for Harry when the razor nicks a fold of skin and a tiny droplet of blood appears. *Am I cut out to be with you?*

After the day's revelations she is no longer sure Harry Mason is the same man who used to send her all those text messages. In her excitement at this new-found love, she had glossed over for herself what he actually was: a cop.

'Besides that,' she says out loud, 'I didn't realize your mother is Margaret bloody Thatcher's twin sister, Mr *Bond*.'

When she eventually made it to her guesthouse that afternoon, she had fallen into a fitful sleep which almost saw her miss her dinner appointment with Joan and Jeanie.

The meal might even have been enjoyable but for Harry's mother. Jeanie had moved her chair closer to Tanya's early on, demanding to know more about the children at the shelter, while Joan Mason, it seemed, was hell-bent on excluding her granddaughter from their conversation. She kept telling the girl to stop annoying Tanya, and wouldn't she come sit next to her grandmother so that Tanya could eat in peace. The child's apparent warmth and interest in what she did actually put her at ease, while Joan Mason's continuous prying discomfited her. Where are you from, Tanya? What did you study? Oh, you didn't study. What did your parents do? Tanya deflected these questions as best she could – she felt horribly self-conscious about her unsettled background in the presence of such a prim matriarch – but the more she evaded them, the more the older woman pursued the subject, perhaps scenting some dirty secret. With Harry around, Tanya is sure the older woman would have shown more restraint, but now she had Tanya all to herself. Swarts had been right: Joan Mason had a knack for interrogation. By the time they bade each other farewell in the windy parking lot, Tanya had anxiously picked the skin of her thumbs raw.

Am I really cut out for you? Tanya stops shaving him and stares into space for a long time.

Jesus, Harry, the way I feel right now, I don't think I am.

FIVE

1

Wally Khuzwayo, who as the sjambok-wielding Wind-breaker Man was briefly acquainted with the building manager Ephraim Thekiso, pulls up to a faded pink building standing on the northern outskirts of Alexandra township. A sheen of green moss is creeping up the walls where moisture has seeped into the masonry, while large flakes of paint have cracked and curled off the gutters in a way that reminds Wally of sun-baked mud. Up above, on a sheltered second-floor balcony, stand a number of the Phaliso brothers' 'gents', who look neither gentle nor in the least sophisticated; in the bare, untended garden, he notes with disgust the piles of dogshit strewn over a yellowing lawn. When four Staffordshire bull terriers belonging to the brothers come sprinting round one side of the house, yapping in a way that always reminds Wally of his wife and her hysterical friends, he yells and kicks out at them in a vain effort to keep them from pissing on his new white-wall tyres. The men upstairs meanwhile watch all this with great hilarity.

'So look who's here!' Ncolela Phaliso has appeared at the front door, holding his arms wide open as though to welcome home a prodigal son. Had Detective Jacob Tshabalala been there, he would have recognized him as the black businessman dressed in khaki on that day of the evictions in Wynberg. 'Just tell me you've got good news, bra Wally.'

The visitor has just enough time to clock the new olive-green Prado 4x4 parked over to the left of the house before the elder Phaliso has enveloped him in a tight bear-hug.

'Of course I do,' says Wally glumly. 'You don't pay *me* to sit around all day like those lazy arseholes upstairs, do you?'

Though he has arrived with the information the Phalisos wanted, he still does not agree with what they have planned for the SVC cops who have been hounding their operations these last few months. But then, who is Wally Khuzwayo to argue with the Phalisos? Did they not remake the Abasindisi when the organization was foundering? Did they not successfully turn a hodge-podge group of angry miners into a powerful organization that has continuously embarrassed the South African Police Service with its effectiveness? He hugs Ncolela back, a man who is roughly two years younger than him but greyer and shorter.

'No, I guess I don't pay you for nothing.' Ncolela chuckles as he steps aside to let Wally Khuzwayo enter the house. 'Tell me, how is your son?'

Wally feels a surge of excited pride at the question. It is not often that someone asks him about the *piccanin*, because most people do not even know he exists. Wally prefers no one even knowing he has a family, as it's safer that way. 'He has finally made it on to the school's football team.'

'*Hi wena*, really?'

Wally beams. 'Centre-forward.'

Ncolela laughs out loud and slaps him across the back. 'Great news that, Wally! Come in, my friend. Let's hear what you have to tell us.'

2

Not many people know the truth about the Phaliso brothers. Though the pair have been prominent businessmen in Alexandra for as long as Wally Khuzwayo has known them, living very public lives, their real story has not travelled as far as it might have. People clearly consider it wise not to whisper about them, especially now that they have established themselves as the new leaders of the Abasindisi. But the few that do know the legend, and are willing to tell it, speak of the Phaliso brothers with a measure of reverence. In any township or ghetto of this violent country there have been men and women, powerful and deadly, who have lived extreme lives by the gun and the knife – Morris Mothibe and Marcos Maepa, Collin Chauke, Big Man Senne, Zorro, Chops Number One, old 'Obelix' Ntuli – yet none of them was quite like the Phalisos, who seem to have struck the perfect balance between their own needs and those of their community.

Hi wena, Wally himself would say when prompted, the Phaliso brothers are amongst the greats not because they've made their money like those other gangsters, but because they understand the very essence of power. They bring light to their own people, and cast darkness upon those who deserve it. How else do you speak of a pair of impoverished street urchins who have ended up running a successful national security firm? They are men of standing now, regularly invited to the annual Johannesburg Chamber of Commerce Gala at the Sunnyside Hotel, which had once been the residence of Lord Milner himself, as Godun once told him – though Wally still has no idea who that particular *umlungu* was.

The Phaliso brothers ... now *there* is a story, and Wally Khuzwayo has no better one to tell, because he knows for a fact that their legend is 100 per cent genuine.

3

He had originally met the brothers when they were all still running around naked in the backyards of their families' tiny shack homes, shitting outside in the dust of the quaintly named Orange Farm township, a good few miles south of Soweto. The Khuzwayos and Phalisos were neighbours, and their fathers were miners on the Carltonville goldfields, over in the direction of Potchefstroom.

'Dirt-poor, playing in the dirt, slaving away *under* the dirt for the filthy rich were both the Phalisos and Khuzwayos,' Wally is fond of quoting Ncolela's words.

As far back as he can remember, the Phaliso brothers were sharper than him, especially when a few bob were to be made. He did not mind being slower-witted, though, for he was wise enough, even back then, to know he could benefit from their friendship, and so while they were growing up he became increasingly their muscle. At that age being older also meant being stronger, and it had its uses. Ncolela always led the way, however, despite his being younger than Wally. He had the slickest mouth and a voracity that was terrifying. His fuse was shorter than the mini-skirts worn by those *magoshas* hovering around the shebeens on Friday nights when the miners had some money to spend. Godun, he was actually the smarter of the two by far, but the quieter. He was also frequently on the receiving end of people's pent-up frustrations. You see, as Wally would point out, he was the black sheep in the family, for his skin was lighter than any of theirs, his nose was Arabic, his eyes so round they might as well have been lidless. In other words, he was so obviously what they called a bushy in the townships: the bastard child of a rape in the lavatories at the taxi ranks near Queen Elizabeth Bridge. Hated and unwanted in his own home, Godun quickly grew up into a nervous child, anxious and overly eager to please his older brother, who sometimes deigned to protect him from the wrath of their parents, and other times inflicted his own cruelties, depending on Ncolela's own mood and whether his fuse had been lit.

Wally remembers the day when the three of them – Wally no older than fourteen, Godun barely ten – chased each other down to the river, a fresh packet of cigarettes, bought with stolen money, in Godun's pocket. But then Godun had tripped over a tree root and gone sprawling. By the time Wally and Ncolela turned around to see what was keeping him, Godun was desperately digging in his trousers for their treasured tobacco, a look of intense foreboding on his face. Any other kid of ten would have been bawling his eyes out at the bloody scrapes on his hands and knees, but not Godun. No, the terror tattooed across his face over the mashed cigarettes in his pocket overshadowed any physical pain he might be experiencing.

'*Hi wena*, Godun!' bellowed Ncolela, even at fourteen his voice deep as an old mineshaft. 'Don't tell me you broke my cigarettes. Don't you fucking tell me that!'

Godun stared down at the crushed packet in his hands, and Wally watched as silent tears began to roll down his cheeks. To this day, it gives him the creeps to see a child crying like an adult: without any sound or any hope. By rights, there should be no reason for an innocent to know that total despair that early in his life.

'Come on, Ncolie, it's fine.' Wally tried to calm him. 'I can get some more money from my mom's tin.'

But it was too late, and he could hear it in Ncolela's voice. Once it reached a certain pitch, there was no turning him back. The storm had to run its course.

As his brother approached, Godun made no effort to get up from where he was kneeling; in fact, he sank back on to his haunches and cupped his dirty hands in his lap, the mashed packet of Winstons dropping to the earth. To Wally he looked like a boy preparing himself for his own execution as Ncolela closed the distance between them at a leisurely pace. Though Wally could not see it from where he was standing, he knew well enough the malicious grin that would be slowly spreading over the older Phaliso brother's face. After all, every once in a while Wally had also been on the receiving end, despite his greater age and strength.

Ncolela glanced left and right, his nose tilted skywards as though sniffing for witnesses. But he need not have worried, for this stretch of the dusty valley – upriver from the rocks where the township women washed clothes and their daughters drew water – was the sole preserve of children, and there was not a single one among them who ever dared interfere with Ncolela. Besides, it was just that little bastard child Godun getting his due; it was his lot.

Ncolela tore into his younger brother that day in a way that terrified Wally. He cracked two of the kid's ribs, broke his nose. At one point Wally tried to intercede but retreated when he got his share too. When Ncolela's temper was finally spent, he forced a whimpered apology out of his kid brother by screwing one arm up viciously behind his back. His rage now totally abated, he pulled Godun on to his back and carried him all the way to the clinic, over five kilometres distant. This took up the rest of the afternoon, but as quickly as his temper had flared, Ncolela's other side had revealed itself: a sympathetic, fiercely protective instinct hardly ever witnessed by anyone besides Wally and Godun.

A few days later the younger Phaliso was discharged and had to walk back home on his own. He got another thrashing from his father when he stepped into the shack, because Ncolela never told his parents why he had disappeared.

The defining moment that dragged the Phaliso brothers into the stuff of legend came in the summer of 1983. By then they were all young men known by their handles, hard won on the street. They had a bit of money and influence after violently appropriating from the infamous Msomi gang a chop-shop, where stolen cars were stripped down in the heart of Alexandra. A 'successful business model' is what Ncolela called their brand of toil: they went after the *tsotsis* and shebeen queens terrorizing communities and eliminated them by whatever means seemed most fitting. They then grabbed the assets as repayment for honourable services rendered to a defenceless, impoverished neighbourhood. Ncolela always liked to joke about 'hostile takeovers' in the ghettos, though Wally did not know what was so funny about the word. It seemed self-explanatory.

Surprisingly, Godun had been politically awakened during that time, and was soon spying on government installations around Johannesburg on behalf of the Azanian People's Liberation Army. It must have been during those missions that he developed some backbone, though he managed to keep this carefully hidden from his half-brother and Wally. It could not have been that difficult for him, because secretiveness had become an essential survival strategy under the tyranny of his older brother. While Godun disappeared for weeks on end, Ncolela ended up marrying a woman he loved dearly, a midnight darling capable of taming his volatile temper. He was also busy cutting deals with resellers of cars and car parts in countries all across southern Africa. You see, Wally would rationalize, continuing a crooked business after the crooks were taken care of, and provided it was not hurting the people in its immediate surroundings, was not really crooked in the least. After all, community heroes had to eat, and they needed capital to continue the good fight. With the cars they were stripping and selling coming mostly from the white oppressor and the well-to-do black neighbourhoods that thought themselves better than anyone else, there were few objections – especially when the money began to spread around Alexandra.

It was a beautiful red Porsche 924 turbo with leather seats and not too much blood on the dashboard that started the trouble. The window was broken, sure, but it was nothing that couldn't be fixed with a minimum of effort. This was the baby that was going to make Ncolela a packet, he told Wally the night he bought it for R2,000 in cash. If the deal he had in mind didn't get screwed up, that is.

But it did go sour. Worse than milk in a lightning storm.

At that time, what with all the trade embargoes, there weren't many red Porsches around; in fact, you could probably count them on one hand, all of them belonging to very, very influential whites. It was too conspicuous a car, Godun and Wally repeatedly warned Ncolela. But would he listen? No. His fuse had been lit in a different way this time: he had big plans, remember. He was going to diversify their operations with that money, build stronger links with family in their distant home town of Tsolo in the Eastern Cape, get into the marijuana rackets that were supplying an increasingly greedy Europe. This, too, was an honourable trade for them, Wally would answer if asked. After all, it was the heritage of untold generations of proud African warriors who had smoked it long before the whites came and declared it illegal, only to enjoy it themselves in secret.

The way Ncolela talked then, he was going to buy the world.

What he did not know was that the car had belonged to a prominent Brotherhood member of the Nationalist Party who was killed in the hijacking – yes, as common a method of wealth redistribution as any these days, to be sure, but back then a hijacking was serious business. And for murder, you could hang.

The same night they got the car ready for shipment to Zimbabwe, the security police came calling. Not the regular *gatas*, oh no, but the bloody counter-insurgency *izinja*. And there were a great many of them, too, armed to the teeth with heavy weapons and grenades. There was a shoot-out. For years afterwards Wally Khuzwayo would bore people to tears with the details, and liken his role in that firefight to Wyatt Earp's at the OK Corral in the Westerns he loves so much, though he never actually killed anyone that night.

I don't like to brag, Wally Khuzwayo would often say, but I must give up the count, for the story's sake, you understand. Eight cops dead. Five of our own gone, murdered by the state. The three of us, we hardly had a scratch, though. Ncolela killed all but three of the *gatas*.

That was *us*! Wally would thump his chest. We beat a bunch of counter-insurgency bastards that were killing comrades on a daily basis, and without even a day's military training between us.

That night their business went up in flames, and a countrywide search for them began. But they were alive, and would make a good many more friends over the next few months, as word spread through the underground about what had happened. The false names and passes Godun managed to arrange for them through the APLA would later save their lives time and again. Resistance fighters managed to smuggle Ncolela's wife Hlubi over the border into Botswana, while the trio was moved from safe house to safe house, stretching from Umtata in the Eastern Cape to the Zambian capital Lusaka.

Wally remembers sitting in a shack near Jan Smuts Airport, as it was then called, a few hours after the raid. It was just before dawn, and he was still shivering from shock and fear. An acquaintance's wife was stitching up an arm that had been grazed by a bullet as he listened to planes roar skyward immediately above them and Ncolela yelling at no one in particular. Occasionally he thumped a fist in frustration against the tiny kitchen's tin wall, until eventually his knuckles began to bleed. He had got off alive and killed a handful of *gatas*, but he only really cared about the business that was lost. And Hlubi. At that time he did not know where she was, and whether she would remain safe from the police.

It was at this point that his brother, nervous little Godun, the bastard boy too meek to ever do anything in his own defence, finally snapped.

'Shut up, Ncolela,' he said. 'It was you who brought this on us, so stop crying about it.'

Wally shot him a horrified glance that said, *Are you fucking insane? Look at him!* and saw that Godun was already regretting his remark.

Ncolela spun around. Coals flared in his eyes.

'WHAT!' he roared. Spittle shimmered in the dull paraffin lamplight.

The woman who had been stitching up Wally Khuzwayo's arm dropped needle and yarn and hurried out into the night.

There is a particular tone of voice that has fresh blood on it, Wally likes to say at this point of the story. That night, Ncolela's voice had black death hanging from it in rotten strings.

'I mean, Ncolie, I . . . we're all tired. Let's – NO!'

Godun's older brother had grabbed a knife from the nearest kitchen shelf and seized him by the throat. Wally watched as Ncolela pinned his brother against a wall the way he might have squashed a tick with his nails.

There was a lot of screaming and cursing as they wrestled, and Wally was surprised by how strong Godun had got in the intervening years.

At this point Wally Khuzwayo likes to say he leaped forward and tried to drag Ncolela off his little brother, but in truth he just stood there, either frozen in fascinated terror or wise enough not to get involved. Spats in the family, after all, are not the business of outsiders, and anyone who sticks his nose in where it doesn't belong is likely to lose it.

Finally Ncolela found a gap in his brother's defence and dug powerful fingers into his cheeks. 'Open your fucking mouth.' Ncolela spoke through clenched teeth. 'Open it!'

Kitchen utensils and containers spilled in all directions

as Godun tried to free himself. Ncolela neatly flipped his brother on to the broken floorboards and knelt on his chest, driving his full weight into Godun's diaphragm. It did the trick. Winded, Godun opened his mouth in a long gasp. Quick as a hunting spider, Ncolela's fingers crawled into it, curled around the bottom teeth and yanked on the lower jaw. There was an audible snap as ligaments tore and his mouth stretched wide open. Godun screamed like Wally had never heard him scream before.

'You don't tell – stick that fucking tongue out, now! You don't tell me I've ruined you – because I *made* you.'

Godun desperately tried to pull himself free from his brother, but Ncolela was not finished with him. The knife flashed in the paraffin light as Ncolela lashed through his little brother's tongue. Wally remembers it squirming, writhing like a worm on the end of a hook. Then Ncolela slashed to the left. Blood hit his face as Godun's screams turned into a wet gargle.

Wally made it to the front door before he stumbled to his knees and threw up.

4

Ncolela stepped over him and casually flicked the offending piece of his brother's anatomy into the darkness, the way you might throw away an apple core. Wally imagines he heard it land somewhere in the grass. When he looked up to see Godun's older brother caught in the orange glow of the doorway, the man was shaking all over, and beads of sweat were collected under his wide eyes. Wally could not be sure whether it was an expression of shock at what he had done, or merely his fury cooling off. The older brother spotted his acquaintance's wife cowering near the outhouse and ordered her back into the shack, this time to sew up his brother's wound.

'Serves him right, always challenging me the way he does,' is all that he said.

Wally Khuzwayo dared not move, dared not speak for a long time, in case that terrible violence was still frothing underneath the surface. His fingers dug into dry soil and grass as he spat out the foul sick still covering his mouth. Tears from the retching blurred the world into an illusion, and he would not have believed what he had just witnessed but for Godun's continuing cries of pain inside the shack.

Years later, when they were alone and impossibly drunk in the empty pink home that Ncolela had built especially for his beloved wife Hlubi, Wally had finally plucked up the courage to ask his old friend if he ever regretted what he did.

At the question Ncolela had sobered up fast. He stared at Wally in a way that suggested his fuse was about to go once more, but the flame of anger blew out as fast as it appeared.

'Knowing what Godie is capable of, some days I'm happy I did it. Other days I think I might have thought it through a little better.'

'What's he capable of?' asked Wally. 'What do you mean?'

Ncolela held his eyes for what seemed like an hour. 'You grew up with us, Wally. You know what I'm talking about.'

At Ncolela's tortured expression, it dawned on him. Wally *did* know what he was talking about. Well, he had *suspected* it, but never knew for certain.

That awful night under the thundering aeroplanes,

Godun stopped talking with them. Obviously he could not speak, but it was like he descended into some dark place where the world did not exist for him. He never made eye contact; he made no hand gestures; he did not even react when touched, talked to or shouted at, which Ncolela did frequently when their dwindling investments needed Godun's knack for numbers. Then he just disappeared one day. Gone. No one knew what had happened to him, though enough people knew *of* him and could easily have identified him wandering about. Though Ncolela would never have admitted to being worried about his bastard half-brother, his fuse became even shorter in those days, so short that even his beloved wife could no longer contain his temper.

Hlubi. Beautiful, voluptuous, ever-laughing Hlubi – what she had ever seen in Ncolela he never knew, because she was of far better stock than the three of them. But she loved that man none the less, and as fiercely as he did her. Perhaps it was precisely because of Ncolela's ferocious obsession with her that she stuck around. I mean, he would often say, what woman would not want a man so utterly consumed with her that he would voluntarily live in a pink house? Ncolela Phaliso married Hlubi Makhura on 21 December 1980, and he buried her on 22 November 1986, barely a year after their secretive return to South Africa. He had come home one night and found two of his guards murdered. The dogs had been killed too, and when he bolted into their bedroom, he found Hlubi spread-eagled on their conjugal bed. Naked from the waist up, her breasts had been severed from her body, and her throat cut so deeply you could see her spine at the back of the wound.

Until Wally Khuzwayo had his talk with Ncolela, he

had assumed it was some group that had struck out in revenge. They had made enough enemies by that time for this to be more than just a possibility. He had even wondered whether the security police had finally tracked them down and settled their old score.

When recounting the story of the Phaliso brothers, he always waits at this point for the inevitable question that must follow: Why do you think it was Godun?

It's simple, Wally would always say. The next morning, while Ncolela was still storming around the house and tearing his hair out in grief, Godun appeared at the front door, looking as serene as an angel.

'*Ja*, but does that prove anything?' Wally's audience would be bound to ask.

'Well, no,' he would always say, after a pause. 'Not by itself, no. But when Ncolela tried to reach his parents to tell them what had happened, he found out that their shack in Orange Farm was razed to the ground the same night, with them still trapped inside. The neighbours, they never heard any commotion. There had only been the night's silence. Who, I ask you, can slip into the shack of two old people without them kicking up some sort of a fuss, and then kill them before setting the place alight? Who can move off through a squatter camp without being seen, as flames erupt and threaten hundreds of homes? I say it's a man who has spied on government installations for years. I say it's a man Ncolela's parents knew like their own son.'

If Wally Khuzwayo is telling this story to someone who has been thinking of double-crossing the Phaliso brothers, or someone who needs a shake-up, he usually adds a punchline sure to get any idiot's attention as he's tied up in a chair or stuffed into a duffel bag and hanging from a tree.

'Knowing now what you do about these two guys, these two *brothers* who'll do that sort of thing to each other, just think what they might do to you. Do you really want to cross them, *mfo*? Think about it very carefully.'

5

The living room in the dirty pink house is sparsely furnished. An oversized television and an unused karaoke machine are set against one wall, and thick brown curtains are permanently drawn across large windows overlooking the driveway and a wasted garden. The room has been painted an ugly orange with the leftover paint a neighbour gave the brothers a few months back, while a single crude coffee table makes up the centrepiece. The two sofas, a two-seater and a three-seater, were picked up at a garage sale in Vereeniging. It has been a long time since Ncolela has furnished this house with something bought from a store; not since 1986, in fact.

Wally Khuzwayo, who might not be as rich as the two brothers but who has finally married and fathered a son, once again observes out loud, 'Ncolela, I've been your friend for, what? Forty-five years? Take it from me, get another woman into this house. It looks like a mining hostel in here, and smells like a long-drop.'

The older Phaliso, who has mellowed considerably with middle-age and business success, chuckles at this, though his eyes remain cheerless. 'Don't make fun of a man's tastes. It's not polite.'

'This isn't taste; it's a fucking dump.'

'Who do you want me to impress? You?'

'It's about self-respect, Ncolie. What do those shitheads up there tell their wives about the great Phaliso brothers when they go home from this place?'

'There is a difference between a house and a home, my friend. They can't compare their homes to this house.'

Wally is about to ask what that is supposed to mean when Godun abruptly appears in the arched kitchen doorway.

'Godun! Didn't know you were there. Wally's brought us some good news.'

Even with the legend of the Phaliso brothers fresh in mind, Wally still finds it difficult to imagine this sinewy man, with the pious expression of a priest, as Hlubi's killer, never mind that of his own parents. But then he remembers the man's vacant gaze at that block of flats in Joubert Park while he, Wally, had beaten the life out of that scumbag Ephraim Thekiso for skimming thousands off the rent for the whores he'd been dicking on the side. It had been a while since Godun had played a part in this physical kind of work, and Wally had forgotten what a blessing it was *not* to have him around.

'I still don't think going after Swarts and his men is such a good idea.'

A scratching sound draws Wally's attention to where Godun has seated himself on the three-person sofa, his back to the kitchen. The younger brother has examination pads and booklets littered all over the house, and it is on one of these that he is now writing. When he has finished his scribbling, he hands it to Wally.

We have a rat. No other way they could've found those weapons.

We can't let anything lead back to us. We have to

'Get rid of them.' Ncolela mysteriously picks up from his mute brother's written sentence as he walks in from the kitchen with three chilled beers in his hand. 'We have an organization to preserve. A lot of people depend on us for their safety, you know.'

Godun cackles at this. It comes out a grotesque mechanical sound: *a-a-a*.

Though Wally does not fully understand what might be so funny, he smiles drily.

How do they do it? he wonders. He has heard that twins sometimes communicate like this, but these two don't even share the same father. It reminds him that, ever since the night of Hlubi's murder, these strange brothers have miraculously grown closer, when by rights they should have grown as far apart as can be. Not for the first time does Wally wish he knew what passed between them in private after that time of bloodshed, whether there had been some reconciliation, or something altogether more sinister. Many of the men who work as muscle for the two brothers often press Wally for more information on the rumours that some black magic now binds them together and, though he is more sceptical than most, this version sometimes makes a lot more sense to him than the idea that the Phalisos had merely called some kind of truce.

'Why are you insisting on changing a recipe that has been working well for us?' asks Wally. 'First you tell me to go sort out some small-timer for the mongs when it could have been handled by one of our usual people, and now you want to get rid of a bunch of *gatas*? Killing them will only attract more of the kind of attention we don't want.'

'I'll clean house as I see fit, my friend.' An edge of Ncolela's old temper creeps into his voice, and his eyes light up with the same greed Wally Khuzwayo has known for years. 'We're moving into our next phase, and we're looking at offices in Newtown, with fucking mirrored windows and air-conditioning. We're hiring accountants and marketers, Wally. We've come a long way, and I'm not having a bunch of cops put the brakes on me. They have to be dealt with.'

'You're getting offices in the *city*?'

Ncolela smiles hungrily. 'Commissioner Street. We're looking at some second-floor offices, aren't we, Godun? It's low down, sure, but we'll work our way up to some penthouse suites, you'll see.'

'Why? Our business is here, among the ordinary people.'

'Look around you! There's no fucking money here in the townships. Do you see any glass towers? Do you see decent cars parked on these streets, people in good suits?'

'But don't we have enough already?'

'What kind of a question is *that*?'

'Ncolela, with all those strangers doing your paper-work, and knowing what we do . . .' Wally Khuzwayo trails off with the sudden realization that he has not been asked his opinion throughout any of the planning the older Phaliso brother is talking about. He looks to Godun for support, thinking that the younger brother might come to his aid as he has done in the past, but finds none.

'They're professionals; and we need them if we want to grow,' says Ncolela.

Wally takes a deep breath and continues. 'The people here believe in what we do. The city, that is not our place. It has its own rules.'

'Listen to you!' the elder Phaliso roars. 'The problem with you is that your mind is still colonized. You think the way the *umlungus* want you to think. *This* is our place? It might be yours, bra, but not mine.'

Godun scribbles on a page again, but this time he hands it straight to his brother who is standing behind him like a sentinel.

'We cut all our ties, and that's final. We'll be fine.'

'But we can't be sure that will solve the problem,' says Wally.

'What isn't safe,' says Ncolela, 'is those cops digging around too long and too hard. The more time they spend sniffing around, the more people are going to get involved. Can't you see that the longer they pressure us, the more likely it is that someone somewhere will make a mistake? They've got our scent and they're not the type to back down soon.'

'Then bribe them,' pleads Wally. 'Just don't try killing them.'

'A black man bribe a *boer* like that Swarts?' Ncolela laughs. 'Have you started smoking *majat* again, my friend?

'We wipe the slate clean now; *tabula rasa*, like old Godie here would say. And if the rumours begin, we respond with our usual statement: "We cannot be held responsible for the actions of the people who demand justice, the behaviour of violent vigilante groups who pretend to be members of the Abasindisi, or individuals from our own dedicated team who are perhaps frustrated and overzealous in their response to the terrible levels of crime in this country." '

This quote he rehearses with one finger raised, the way the Great Crocodile, P. W. Botha, used to address his nation. It is a sentence with which Wally Khuzwayo has become all too familiar these last few years, and he wonders if anyone has actually ever believed it.

'Besides,' continues Ncolela, 'there are more and more cops prepared to turn the other way and allow us to do what needs to be done. There are also plenty more people who will want to defend us publicly, if only to humiliate the government into action. People have had enough. They want someone to take the *gatas* on, and I'll do it, gladly.'

'Ncolela, there are a lot of maybes here.'

'Trust me.'

There had been another occasion when Ncolela spoke like this; it had involved a red Porsche. The only difference now is that this time, from his expression, Godun seems to have bought into his brother's enthusiasm – or greed.

'Wally, with those cops gone, the SVC won't know what to do with us. They'll have to start again from scratch.'

'I don't agree.' Wally leans back with his arms crossed. 'Something this big is going to bring all of them down on us. And right now there are only five to worry about.'

'That's fine, my friend, disagree all you want. But remember, *we've* run this business from the beginning, and we'll go on doing it *our* way.' Ncolela glances at his brother, who nods in agreement without taking his eyes off their lieutenant.

'I don't know . . .'

'That's why it's us who are in charge, *mfo*,' says Ncolela in a self-satisfied voice.

Wally shakes his head but says nothing more to contradict Ncolela. To do so would be to risk the man's wrath, and Wally is getting far too old to deal with that kind of shit. There had once been a time when he enthused about the brothers for ever and a day, to the point that people would get bored in the bar-rooms and walk away. But these days it has become all the same to him, and he just gets on with the job. Wally flicks through the news clippings and notes open in front of him: information about the destruction of a weapons cache in Tsolo, pictures of some provincial commissioner, and Senior Superintendent Swarts gesturing at a smattering of weapons neatly arranged on a groundsheet for the media to conveniently photograph. There are also a good many handwritten notes containing information given to him by Abasindisi members and their families in the area. It took Wally nearly three days to get the full story of what happened in Tsolo, while the police were sniffing around. Lucky for him, the locals he moved amongst probably hated the *gatas* even more than he did.

'Now then,' says Ncolela expectantly, 'are you going to sit there all day and sulk, or are you going to say something useful at some point?'

'We already know Franklin, Naidoo and Combrink from the way they roughed up Courage's *spaza* shop. This one here is Moqomo; that there is Swarts.' Wally hands them a newspaper clipping with Russell Swarts' face circled in blue ink.

Godun and Ncolela sit forward, suddenly eager to see what the man looks like. They have heard a great deal about this Swarts from the circles they move in, legitimate and otherwise. Word of a cop with a reputation like his always gets around quickly.

'Looks like a common farmer, this one,' sneers Ncolela.

Godun laughs in that strange disjointed way of his, and for a moment Wally sees the stump of a long-gone tongue wriggle at the back of his mouth. He looks away quickly in disgust.

'It seems that Swarts, and another *gata* called Harry

Mason, may be up for charges with the ICD for what happened there in Tsolo.' He shows the brothers another newspaper clipping that hints at the ICD's interest in the case.

At this Godun positively coos, though Ncolela frowns. But he nevertheless signals for Wally to continue.

'This is what Mason looks like.' He shows them an additional article in the *Daily Dispatch* that speaks of the SVC cop's shooting. 'They managed to chopper him out of there alive. He might be dead by now, or he might still be breathing, I don't know. No one could tell me, and there hasn't been anything else in the papers.'

'This thing with the ICD,' says Ncolela thoughtfully, 'do you know when the hearings are supposed to start?'

Wally sits back on the sofa. Though it might have been bought at a garage sale, it is still very comfortable. 'No, I don't. Why?'

Ncolela glances at his brother, who has begun writing furiously. 'The ICD investigation could be very bad news. Too many questions will be asked in public, and this could very quickly spiral further out of control. Those two can't be allowed to make it to the hearings.'

'What do you want me to do about that? We don't know anyone in the SVC, or the ICD either. Remember, we work with miners and dope farmers, not the fucking National Intelligence Agency. We make a move against them now, they'll come after us, one way or another.'

'Just. Find. Out!' Ncolela punctuates each word by pounding on the coffee table with a fist. Startled out of his bored reverie, Godun pulls his head in between his shoulders, almost like a turtle. 'Jesus Christ, Wally, what the hell is wrong with you? They're already all over us like ants on a fucking honey jar – and have been for three months now. We need to do something before we lose all our business.'

Wally sighs. 'Yes, Ncolie, fine. You're the boss.'

'And you fucking remember that!'

Godun finishes scribbling on his notepad and shows it to his brother, who takes a few seconds to read the message.

'I agree.' Ncolela Phaliso nods. 'This is what we'll do.'

6

Two hours later, and with a considerable amount of beer in him, Wally Khuzwayo staggers out to his car with the file of information in his hand and a list of directives freshly stored in his mind. When he accidentally drops his car keys, he stoops to pick them up and takes a moment to look back at the dilapidated pink mansion. The Phali-sos' security 'gents' have withdrawn from the balcony and can now be heard roaring over some soccer match on television in the upstairs games room. Nevertheless he sees the building for what it once was: a place of brief happiness for Ncolela, created by the woman who had been allowed into their tight-knit band for a short time. Back then the garden had sported a well-tended lawn and rare clivias. Roses had been planted at regular intervals along the short driveway, while the dogs had names and their shit was still regularly cleaned away. In that time the windows had always stood open in the summer, the curtains drawn back to allow sunlight into the house. But all of that is gone now and, if Wally was still a superstitious boy, he might believe this lifeless place at the end of the road is haunted by ghosts.

He unlocks the car and gets in. There's a sheepskin strip on the dashboard, and an Orlando Pirates bandana dangling from the rear-view mirror. Glancing at his watch he starts the engine in a hurry, realizing he has again run late for his son's soccer match. The wife is going to be furious when she finds out. He will have to ask the boy to keep it a secret, between men.

Wally Khuzwayo switches on the car radio and has to smile, despite himself, when 'I Shot the Sheriff' by Bob Marley kicks in.

7

Ncolela Phaliso watches from behind the heavy brown curtains in the living room as his childhood friend gets into his beaten-up Passat station wagon and drives off. Upstairs his 'gents' are kicking up a fuss over a goal scored in a match between the Kaizer Chiefs and Sundowns.

Godun appears at his side with a scrawled note. *Get rid of him.*

'Why?' Ncolela asks gruffly. The word comes out slurred and his lips feel unusually slack.

I don't trust him any more.

'You've become one paranoid shit, Godie.'

Where else would the cops have found out about those weapons?

'You're crazy enough to go tell them yourself.'

Our people down there would never have given up those guns. They need them far too much to protect their crops.

Ncolela lets go of the curtain and turns his attention on his brother. 'Wally's been with us since the beginning and he's now got two mouths to feed, too. He's never done anything but what we tell him, and there is no reason for that to have changed. How old are we now, God damn it?'

Godun shrugs, and scribbles.

The AKs. The article mentions that only four were confiscated.

Where are the rest?

Ncolela flops back into his favourite corner of the three-seater couch. 'I don't know, Godie. Maybe they used them when they shouldn't have. I just don't know.'

I don't know. It seems there is too much these days over which he has no control any more. There used to be a time when Ncolela knew the workings of his organization the way his tongue knows every corner of his mouth and can detect the smallest changes. But now he has begun to slip. Perhaps it began as far back as that terrible night when Hlubi was taken from him. Or does it go even further back than that? The day he cut Godun's tongue out? This damn self-doubt. When did it creep in?

I don't know!

Godun again scribbles in his booklet.

What could the cops offer him that he doesn't get from us?

'It's not him, God damn you! What are you playing at?'

Godun stares at him with his eyebrows raised. *Then who?* reads that expression, but it can just as easily be a look of mockery. If he had been any younger, Ncolela might have lashed out instinctively at this suggestion of

Wally's betrayal. But for now he fights down the anger threatening to boil over. One hand grips his other till the knuckles grow pink. Ncolela says nothing, yet the gesture gives away his inner turmoil to a bemused brother who knows him all too well.

Eventually he explodes. 'What the hell were you thinking, dragging him out to take care of Ephraim Thekiso last week, anyway? You and I are now affiliated with the Chamber of Commerce! We have no business on the street any more, and neither does he. We have others to do that for us now. I thought we'd agreed on that.'

Dusk has settled outside, and the light through the drawn curtains is a sickly orange, which causes each of Godun's bright round eyes to float unnaturally in a pool of shadow.

'Answer me, brother.'

Upstairs a goal is scored and some of the 'gents' leap up with roars of triumph, while disgruntled Chiefs supporters give way to a series of outraged invectives directed at the referee.

'Shut up, you arseholes!' Ncolela jumps to his feet and shakes a fist at the ceiling, but the racket upstairs renders his words impotent. 'Keep quiet, I said!'

Godun scribbles a short message and casually chucks it in his brother's direction.

That one has been working alone too long. The Chinese, they are new business and wanted a personal touch, to see if we can still deliver on our promises.

'A personal touch?' he says. 'Fine, then. I hope there is at least nothing that ties us to the body?'

Godun lets the mocking light in his eyes spread over his entire face, but he does not bother to write a response.

How did I ever let this little bastard gain the upper hand on me like this? wonders Ncolela. The answer is, he does not know. And this infuriates him.

I thought we should leave it there in plain view, where the gatas can find it.

The elder Phaliso reads the message twice before he glances up at his younger brother in disbelief. Because the message is written, and Godun's expression is as serene as ever, Ncolela cannot tell whether he is being sarcastic or serious. At times like these, he is frustrated to breaking point with the little shit's inability to speak. But at the same time a morbid satisfaction overcomes him that he himself has cut that spiteful tongue out.

'You're crazy, Godun!' snaps Ncolela. 'You hear me? Mad!'

In a huff he throws the booklet back at his younger brother and storms from the room, only to be followed by a rusty *a-a-a-a* laugh – which continues to ring in his ears a long time afterwards.

SIX

1

Seven days after his mother's fateful telephone call, and three days after fishing the badly lacerated corpse of an unknown black male from the Jukskei River, Detective Jacob Tshabalala finds himself alone with the embalmed body of his own father. Though he knows exactly what to do with the death of a stranger, has done so for many years as a detective, he is now faced with one all-important question: what to do with this dead man whom he once called Father, this *sangoma* whom he hardly knew in life, and who will most likely become even more of a stranger to him now in death?

Just before she closed the door on him, Jacob's aged mother, now dressed in white, the traditional Zulu colour of mourning, had whispered, 'Please, Jacob. I know you had your differences, but remember, you are his only son.'

Another three hours till dawn and four till the funeral which will take place just an hour after sunrise, and Jacob has never felt so lonely and unsettled in his life. Half a dozen candles placed around the room illuminate the coffin, which has been placed on top of two sawhorses. Draped over it is the hide of an ox, freshly slaughtered as a sacrifice to the spirits. The animal's soul will now accompany Jacob's father into the netherworld of the *amadlozi* – the family's living ancestors. The room itself is frigid; whether it is the cold of an early-September night or the sepulchral atmosphere that has made it so, Jacob cannot tell. The cot in which his father battled the tuberculosis that should have taken him five years ago has been removed, and the windows to the dead man's room have been smeared with ash. A mirror and family photographs have been turned around to face the wall or else covered with cloth, because the dead should not tarry over memories of their past lives while on their way to the afterlife. On the air lingers the unpleasantly sweet stench of a very old man and the prolonged consumption that finally took him, amid the bloody tang of raw oxhide, reminding Jacob of an abattoir. Underlying these pungent odours of death are the living smells of his immediate family and the visiting holy men and women who have sat in vigil with Jacob – until he asked them to allow him a moment alone with his departed father.

Depar*ting* father, he reminds himself, because Jacob Tshabalala, only child of Bantu Tshabalala, must first complete the necessary rituals that will open the way for the deceased *sangoma* to pass unhindered into his next life as an ancestral spirit – though these are rituals that Jacob himself rejected long ago.

His hand drifts past the gold cross on his chest, towards the leather thong around his neck and the amulet hanging from it, and his mind's eye briefly returns to the day he heard his grandfather being sentenced to death, not only for inciting a community to take its revenge on a witch living in the hills above their village, but also for resisting the will of a state that violently suppressed his 'barbaric' beliefs. In the same incident, his father had been arrested for taking part in what the whites of the time called 'a savage's mob justice', but he had escaped with a five-year prison term, which he subsequently carried as a token of pride.

Perhaps you haven't let go entirely, hmm, my boy?

mutters his grandfather at the back of his head. The old man has become a noisy presence in Jacob's life these last few days, but a comforting one at that. *Can't get away from us as much as you might want to, isn't that true?*

Seated on a worn mattress, legs outstretched and hands folded in his lap, Jacob wears furred leather bands around his biceps, ankles and wrists. Draped over his shoulders is a warm blanket, and underneath it he wears the traditional skins of a Zulu male dressed for official ceremonies. His feet are bare despite the cold, and at his side lies an assegai which he will use during the ritual proceedings. But only if he chooses to submit to the old ways his father was so adamant about preserving – the same traditions that make Jacob, a devout Christian, uncomfortable.

I can't do this for him, Grandfather.

But he is your father!

I just can't.

Would you have done it for the others that watch over you? Would you have done it for me?

Don't ask me that.

If Jacob refuses to grant his father these last rites, there is the danger of his own shade becoming a restless spirit or, worse, his soul may be completely destroyed. These are the beliefs of his line, and they are also the concerns of his anxious family. But not his, not any more. At least he has convinced himself of this until now.

Before returning to his father's homestead, Jacob resolved to have as little to do with these ceremonies as possible. But the time spent with his mother and extended family has quickly eroded the line he had drawn in the sand. Now it is nothing more than a confused blur, much to Nomsa's consternation.

You are rejecting the traditions of your ancestors, boy,

those who have spoken to God on your behalf for untold generations, snaps his grandfather. *Think, boy! Remember your family*. Khumbula!

There is that word again: remember. His grandfather has been hounding him with it ever since that day in Wynberg.

I am not the one to do this for him. Let one of his own apprentices pray for him and throw the spear.

This is not a choice! You were born into this responsibility. He is your father.

Jacob shakes his head at this. Seven days his father has been dead, and still it is only his grandfather he hears. That tells him exactly how weak a guiding force his father has been all his life.

Why do you hesitate?

This is not my place, Mkhulu.

Rubbish! How can you say such a thing, Jacob Tshaba-lala?

I cannot be his saviour. Only God is.

Why do you hide from your responsibilities like this!

'Hiding? No!' His voice snaps like a dry twig in the silence, yet the moment those words are out, here in his father's last sanctum, Jacob feels as though a trapdoor that held his emotions captive has been sprung wide open.

It's because I'm angry *with him*, he admits.

He waits a moment, listening out for his grandfather's voice – or the sound of mourners shuffling closer to eavesdrop – but hears nothing out of the ordinary.

Jacob finally gets up and winces at the pain in his chilled knees. Slowly he approaches his father's coffin, hands firmly clasped behind his back as though he is afraid of touching it.

'Yes,' he eventually whispers. 'I *am* angry with you,

Father, because even in death you would try to force me to live *your* way. You never were one to discuss things, were you? Here you are, telling me – because I cannot argue with you now, can I? – to prepare your way to eternal life. This, when you *beat* me and you *hated* me, and you threw me out of the *house*! All because I did not want those traditions in my life that saw you yourself thrown into prison and Mkhulu hanged? This is you now, lying dead and so calm in your box, while mother and Landi and Ntuli and Aunt Grace, all of them fret over whether I will venerate you properly in death. Revere *you*, after you turned me out to starve on the street? *Aikona!*

'Sixteen years you waited before you ever asked Mother to phone me on your behalf, to tell me you wanted to make peace. I wonder, was it because you saw death approaching and were worried that all of a sudden you would not find a place amongst our ancestors? That without me our family's history would die? Yes, I think that's why. Sixteen years you waited, and then what? I introduce you to the woman I love, the woman with whom I share *my* beliefs, and you tell her what? That *she* is the cause of my disgrace?' Jacob is shivering all over now, but it is not from the cold. 'I would damn you right here, Father. Yes, I would!'

What are you saying, *Jacob!*

He does not know whether it is his grandfather's voice or his own, but it humbles and silences him. Jacob grabs the hide spread over his father's coffin and bunches it in his fists until tufts of ochre fur stick out between his fingers and its bristles tingle in his palms.

'You did not want to be reconciled for so long because you *loved* me, is that right? No, you wanted to ensure that there would be a descendant to pray to you and yours.'

And yours, too! We are yours just as much as we belong to your father, Jacob. Nothing you do will change that, cries his grandfather. *Your father, he understood what it means to live for others.*

Jacob flinches at that. 'He never lived for *me*.'

You threatened what he held most dear, says a woman's voice, much like his mother's. *And are you not justifying all his fears right now, Jacob? Threatening our family's unity?*

And what of forgiveness? He is surprised to hear what sounds like Nomsa's voice in this room, and he actually turns around to see whether she has come in without his noticing. *Is that not what you and I try to live by?*

For a moment he has an irresistible urge to rip away the hide and tip his father's coffin off the sawhorses. He did not ask for this responsibility, nor would his father have given it to him willingly – he is sure of that. Yet here it is, as undeniable as the earth upon which he treads. A frustrated scream rises up in his throat like bile, but at the last moment he turns away from his father's casket and the intense feeling gradually subsides.

He walks over to one ash-smeared window. Outside a landscape that is no longer completely enveloped in darkness is touched by the sun; the earth is slowly waking up to the calls of birds. Watching and waiting, clearing his mind of emotions, Jacob gradually feels his inner turmoil turn into a dull throb.

Will you reject your entire family for your father's mistakes? This time it is Hettie Solilo's voice, the gentle woman who took in a homeless Jacob at the age of fifteen and cared for him as if he was her own. *Is your anger that important to you, my child?*

Jacob closes his eyes and sighs. It seems everyone else

has a point to make, even the father, lying there obstinately silent. None of what is being said brings Jacob any closer to a satisfactory answer though. Eventually he finds the self-control to speak up for himself.

'I *will* bury you, Father, so that your soul may rest.' His back remains turned to the coffin that stands in the middle of the room. 'But that is all I can do for you.'

He picks up the assegai where it has been lying on the floor next to the mattress. Briefly touching a finger to its sharpened edge, he lays it on his father's coffin.

'Beyond that, you have as much place in my home as I had in yours, Father. There cannot be an *unsamo* in my home for you, because Christ is my voice in heaven; he is my saviour and messenger, not you. Your voice . . . it fell quiet when you would not accept me, or my beloved. Goodbye, Father, and may God will it that you rest in peace.'

Giving the spear's shaft a pat, he heads for the exit.

2

Jacob shuts the door on his father and lays his head against its rough wood to think of the sudden deathly quiet in his head. Where a moment ago there was a clamour like a train station, now there is not so much silence as an over-whelming emptiness settling over him.

It has to be this way, he says soundlessly into that void. *I chose my path years ago, and it never crossed his, and his never met mine.*

He listens for a reply, an answer from just about anyone who will speak up, but all he hears is the steady drumbeat of his own deadened heart.

The memory of the waterlogged corpse pulled out of the Jukskei the day he left for his father's funeral now forces its way into his mind's eye. And with it another bygone memory surfaces: the whistle of a rawhide whip through the air as it landed across a young boy's back. At the age of fifteen, the beating he received felt as shocking as the corpse looked when they pulled it from the river that morning of 25 August.

3

The roots of a fallen tree had snagged the body at a point where the Jukskei cut a tight curve through a Buccleuch smallholding, just north of Alexandra township. Though the corpse had been badly mutilated, the gunshot to the back of its head appeared the most obvious cause of death.

Jacob remembers smiling with bitter relief when he received a call from the local police satellite station. This gave him something other than his father's death to think about, never mind all the unfair press coverage he had received after the Wynberg riot. Though Supe Niehaus had told him to take a few days off after that disastrous day, Jacob continued with his work. After all, he had reasoned, what message did it send out to the media if he simply disappeared? A suspension? Unpaid leave with a cover-up under way? There was no telling, these days, and everybody always expects the worst.

'You don't have to do this, you know,' the supe had told Jacob the day after he tried to give him leave.

'Do what?' he asked.

'You'll get your transfer soon enough, Jacob, I can promise you that. We know what you did at Wynberg, and *we* know how hard you work, even if others don't want to acknowledge it. I bloody well saw it with my own eyes, man.'

But that was missing the point entirely. At that point in his life, Jacob could not think of anything worse than to sit at home and mull over the things that had recently occurred. In the days following his mother's call, he realized how little his family had come to mean to him; or, more accurately, what a repellent force his father had grown to be in his life. He wanted to go back home for his mother's sake, knew it was his duty to be there, but he first needed space to get his head around the enormity of the responsibilities lying ahead. It was an uncharacteristic decision to hover around Jo'burg those few days, he knew, and it had concerned Nomsa greatly to see him so agitated. But then, his relationship with his father, or rather the end of it, had been fairly uncharacteristic too.

It was a cold Thursday morning when he had arrived at the smallholding of one Anthony Ladbroke via a short dirt road that branched off Gibson Drive. Jacob barely noticed the bright red security plaque attached to the gate, boldly heralding:

THIS PROPERTY IS PROTECTED BY
THE ABASINDISI SECURITY SERVICES
24 HOURS ARMED RESPONSE
YOUR SAFETY IS OUR FIGHT

At the bottom of the dirt track that cut through neatly trimmed wild grass and led up to a well-maintained cottage set back in a grove of blue-gums, a man sat astride a bay horse, a shotgun broken open in the crook of his elbow. In his jodhpurs and green tracksuit top he looked like a true Texan prison gunbull. That there were at least half a dozen dogs milling around the horse's legs only reinforced the impression. The only things detracting from the look were a pair of Ray-Bans and his age, for the man looked to be in his late sixties.

The rider spotted Jacob's red Nissan and waved him through towards the cottage, where a patrol pick-up was parked next to a Jaguar and a Black Maria clearly from the morgue. As he got out of his vehicle the dogs bristled and began to bark furiously, which reminded him that most such animals in these parts were trained to attack a black man on sight. He slammed the car door behind him and waited for the gunbull lookalike to dismount and silence his dogs. Off his horse, he did not look that impressive. His jodhpurs hung limply around his scrawny buttocks in a way that reminded Jacob of a toddler that had filled its pants.

'So sorry about the noise,' said the man, leading his horse closer. His accent was not quite British, but refined enough to put him in that class of South African that still longed for the return of empire. 'They certainly are a noisy bunch, but they keep the undesirables off our land, if you know what I mean. I take it you are Detective Tshabalala, yes? Anthony Ladbroke. Pleased to meet you.'

They shook hands, Ladbroke's skin rasping unpleasantly against Jacob's palm. The horseman did not seem particularly bothered about finding a dead body on his property.

'This way.' Ladbroke gestured to one side down the gentle roll of a hill, which grew gradually steeper towards the east where a belt of green vegetation betrayed the river's course.

'I want you to understand right away, detective, that I don't know who this man is. I've never set eyes on him

232

before today, and that's God's truth. I might've easily shot first and asked questions later if I'd found a stranger on my land at night, but I don't even know what kind of calibre of gun can do that much damage to a man's head.'

'When did you find him, exactly?'

'About three hours ago. Just after dawn.'

'Did you touch anything at the scene?'

'No, not touch,' Ladbroke replied thoughtfully. 'I guess I should say that I *did* shoot him – in a way, that is.'

Jacob stopped walking and glanced at him quizzically. 'I don't understand you, Mr Ladbroke.'

'It happened like this: I was taking my daily ride down to the river. It's pleasant enough there around dawn. I turned south with the dogs in tow, along the river's course, towards the boundary fence, over that way.' He flapped a hand in the direction of Alexandra's glittering unpainted roofs in the distance. The gesture made it look like he was trying to keep a bad smell at bay. 'I check the fence every morning to see whether any squatters have tried to cut their way through, because you can never tell these days. But this morning I noticed some strays – a lot of mangy creatures wander out of that township, and for the life of me I don't know how they get on to my property. Well, I saw two of them in the water, tearing at a bloody white sheet stuck in the roots of a washed-up tree. I was so horrified by what I saw I immediately fired on them with my shotgun, which I always carry with me. I killed one outright, but the other got away. The police officers that arrived after my call said I'd hit the corpse too. So there you have it.'

Jacob nodded at the shotgun still in the crook of his arm. 'Is that the weapon you used?'

'No, this one's my wife's. They've confiscated mine for

forensic tests. Will it be safe, detective? I hear all sorts of stories about things disappearing from your evidence rooms these days.'

'It should be secure, Mr Ladbroke. Although I'd prefer it if you put that weapon away until the investigation has been concluded.' Jacob smiled politely, but it felt sour on his face. 'You say you've never seen the victim before?'

'That is correct, sir.'

'Are you sure it wasn't there yesterday, or the day before?'

'Not that I know of. Certainly the dogs didn't seem to notice anything unusual.'

Jacob glanced at the hounds following them. They were well-fed brutes to the point of obesity, every one of them, but they still would have heard any intruders a mile away.

They had passed by the stables and away from the garden shrubbery surrounding the cottage before Jacob finally spotted the coroner who, with the help of several police officers and morgue assistants, was busy untangling a gory bedsheet from a snarl of roots that jutted out of the riverbank. The whole team was wearing thick industrial gloves and green fishing waders. And though the Jukskei flowed faster and deeper here than it did in Alexandra itself, Jacob could still smell that stench of blocked drains coming off the water. On the far bank lay the black dog Ladbroke had killed, its long fur wet and matted. The human body was already on the landowner's side of the river, wrapped in a white plastic sheet on a lowered gurney.

'Is the river your farm's eastern boundary?' Jacob asked.

'Yes,' said Ladbroke. 'Everything on the other side

belongs to the university. It's an agricultural research centre. I hardly ever see anyone close to the river, though.'

Jacob greeted the other police officers then stooped to lift the sheeting off the John Doe's face. A smell that reminded him of rotten chicken assaulted his nose.

'You see what I mean, detective? What kind of gun does that to a man's head? It looks like an olive after you've squeezed the pip out, for heaven's sake.'

Jacob had seen that kind of gunshot wound often enough to know it was made by military hardware – pretty common on the streets of urban South Africa, all things considered. Inwardly, he groaned at the extent of the damage to the victim's face. The man having been shot in the back of the head at point-blank range with such a large calibre, and then the dogs having had a go at whatever remained, would make it particularly difficult to positively ID the deceased. There were not even any clothes to give them a clue, and unless he had a criminal record, with fingerprints on file, this JD would likely remain as nameless as a grain of sand.

'Did you find the bullet?' he called out hopefully to the police officers.

'Are you shitting me, detective?' The coroner, a man called Jonny Pretorius, came wading out of the water with a look of revulsion plastered over his face. 'If you can't see that exit wound, then I can recommend a good optician. That bullet is lost, my friend. Same goes for the casing.'

'Any sign of his clothes?'

'Looking at this sheet we just pulled out, I'd say he was severely beaten while wrapped up in it. It's torn in several places where there's a concentration of bloodstains. Also, that body's got abrasions all over it from floating down here, but the worst lacerations must have been received before death. You want my advice, go back to your office and get on with some admin. It'll be more useful than hanging around here.'

'You sure it washed downriver, Jonny?' asked Jacob.

'Yup, all sorts of dreck was accumulated wherever the sheet snagged it going downstream.'

Jacob focuses his attention on the victim's forearms, where the skin was badly lacerated and he must have been struck repeatedly as he tried to protect himself. His chest and face had also been indiscriminately beaten. Taking a pair of latex gloves from his pocket, Jacob grabbed the cadaver by the shoulder and rolled it on to one side. The JD's back looked like it had been scoured by a giant cheese grater, and on the left side he could see a faint pattern where shotgun pellets had punctured the skin. Jacob felt a surge of sympathy for the victim, as he knew exactly what had split his skin like that. The infections following his own beating from his father might have killed him if the healer Mama Hettie Solilo had not taken him in and cared for him properly.

'Why do you say he was beaten, Mr Pretorius?' Ladbroke asked. 'Those look like knife cuts to me.'

'The skin's been split, not cut. There is nothing neat about the wounds.'

Ladbroke's unwavering curiosity reminded Jacob of a dog prancing around its owner's kill, proudly showing off what was not really its own to flaunt. It seemed also as if this aged Jack Russell somehow felt cheated by finding this body on his property but not having been the one to put it there.

'Those are the marks of a sjambok,' explained Jacob.

'Well, that must mean he's some kind of rapist, doesn't it?' Ladbroke again waved towards Alexandra in that perfunctory way of his. 'That's what they do to them over there, isn't it?'

'Maybe it happened there, and maybe it didn't,' said Jacob. 'There are farmers and smallholders who've done the same to people for less.'

Still, Ladbroke's guess was a fair assumption to make about the informal courts operating in some townships. But in Jacob's experience most of the victims killed in retributive acts like these were rarely serious criminals; instead, they were often little more than petty thieves who had been caught in the act, who then carried the heavy burden of a community's frustration with much larger grievances. In the relatively lawless days of apartheid, when official law enforcement hardly ever extended into the townships, the inhabitants had cobbled together their own justice systems, often purposely based on tribal legal customs that had been suppressed by the government, constituting as much a form of passive resistance as a practical solution to the control of crime. Whether some of the more brutal punishments were outdated did not matter; what was important was that they were a source of identity at a time when everything in the state's power was being done to rob blacks of their ability to define themselves. These were court systems that provided swift judgement for communities that had little access to the country's judicial system. Judgements and penalties were passed down by tribal chiefs or political leaders, but there were emotive mobs, too, which dealt out their own arbitrary punishments. Self-defence units and people's courts sometimes meted out a brand of retribution harsher than anything even the apartheid courts might have condoned.

Jacob therefore decided to test the man's reaction to the suspicion that he might have created his own kangaroo court of farm workers. 'Mr Ladbroke, have you had any kind of trouble on your farm lately? Did someone perhaps try to break into your house, or steal livestock?'

This question seemed to confuse him, rather than put Ladbroke on his guard.

'No . . . I don't have any livestock here, except for our three old mares. Certainly I had trouble with a few break-ins until I installed alarms and motion detectors, and a high-voltage electrical inner fence. We've got a CB radio now, too, since they tried to cut our phone lines a few years back. And we have the dogs, of course.'

'And your security company? Have you got an armed guard employed on the premises?'

'No, not on the premises, but our residents' association has hired them to regularly patrol twenty properties throughout the area. A car comes past here every hour or so, and sometimes young Moses – that's our security man's name – stops off to chat during the day. Good lad, he is, and their reaction time is impressive. Took them about five minutes to get here when our alarm went off in the middle of the night for some reason, about three months ago. I'd say I'm very happy with them, truth be told. Expensive but on the ball.'

Jacob thought of what Harry had told him of his own investigations shortly before leaving for the Eastern Cape. 'What else do you know about your security company, Mr Ladbroke? The Abasindisi, I mean.'

At this Ladbroke seemed to grow uncomfortable, and he turned his head as though to hear Jacob better. 'What are you driving at, sir?'

Behind him, the two police officers helping Jonny Pretorius fold up the gory single sheet laughed at some joke the coroner had made.

'I'm talking about the Abasindisi Security Services,' Jacob replied amiably.

'Yes?'

'I'm just wondering aloud whether you hired them because of their reputation for violence, or simply because they have an impressive reaction time.'

Ladbroke puffed out his mouth at this, then let the air go with a soft pop. 'Detective Tshabalala, if you are insinuating that *I* am somehow responsible for this murder, that I instructed my security company to do *this* to a man I don't even know, then you are *very* much mistaken.' His voice rose to a quaver towards the end of this sentence, and to Jacob it sounded like fear dressed up as righteous indignation.

'And yet you told me earlier that you would've gladly killed him yourself if you'd caught him sneaking around your property at night,' said Jacob. Before the man could remonstrate, he added, 'I'm not insinuating anything, sir. It seems a pretty straightforward case here, like the coroner said. I just want you to think about the people in whom you put so much trust, and consider what they're capable of.'

Ladbroke's head jerked nervously from side to side like an owl's, but he held Jacob's gaze steadily enough. 'Our arrangements with a legitimate security company, which we employ jointly as private citizens, have nothing to do with you, detective. We hired the Abasindisi as a residential association of retirees because our own government has left us out in the cold. These people have a good reputation for controlling crime in all the areas they patrol.'

'And how they actually do it doesn't matter to you?'

'Frankly, no. It seems to me only blacks know how

best to control other blacks. And if it's only violence that a black man will respect, then so be it. Whatever the Abasindisi might get up to, it clearly works, and that's all I care about.'

With the tip of his shoe Jacob lifted the plastic sheet clear of what was left of the victim's face. This man's racist rhetoric insulted him, but to get bogged down with childish tit-for-tat statements would not achieve what he was hoping for.

'Take a good look at what's left of this man here. This is the kind of justice you condone. This was done without a trial, and it could just as easily be you on the receiving end tomorrow if you manage to cross the wrong people. If you want *this* alternative to our national constitution, which was voted in by an African majority, sir, you better be ready for it when it also applies to you.'

Why do you bother pursuing this with him? Jacob asked himself. *You know you're never going to change his mind.* But it was important to him, after what had happened to his grandfather. It mattered a great deal.

'That's preposterous, detective. Moses would never do this, and the Phaliso brothers have now mellowed into respectable businessmen, despite their antics in the news some years ago.'

Antics! At this Jacob felt genuine anger stir, but he bit back on it.

'Tshabalala,' Pretorius called. 'You really want me to do an autopsy on this one?' He pulled a glum, discouraging face.

'It has to be done, Jonny. Do me a favour, though. Can you at least try to reconstruct his face for a photo?'

'Do I look like a bloody plastic surgeon?' said Jonny.

'Come on, Tshabalala, you know we're already six months behind schedule, and now you want me to play make-up artist?'

'Please?'

Pretorius sighed exaggeratedly and pulled off the industrial gloves he had been wearing. 'Sorry, but I'm not wasting my time on this. I'll get you some blood samples and check the body for any other identifying features, but that's it.'

Jacob's only options now were to put out a bulletin describing the man's features, whatever remained of them, and hope someone might be looking out for it. Phoning local police stations for news on missing persons was always a laborious experience, and with so many transients constantly moving in and out around the townships, the exercise was more often than not totally fruitless.

'Are you finished here?' Ladbroke interrupted in a voice that clearly meant *Now, will you get off my property?*

Jacob turned to him and smiled. He wouldn't be done with this man for a good while still. 'All I'm trying to say, Mr Ladbroke, is that just because you employ a security company that has popular support locally doesn't mean you know the ways of violent men like the Abasindisi.'

Ladbroke began to protest, but Jacob held up his hand.

'Pretorius!' he called to the departing coroner, 'please ask the Buccleuch guys to give back this man's shotgun. There's no point in us taking it.'

'Can't you do it yourself?' Pretorius yelled back to him.

'Just do it, please.'

Jacob took a few steps towards the house, then turned to raise an eyebrow at Ladbroke, who was mumbling angrily under his breath. 'You can have your shotgun back now, but I'd appreciate a cup of tea while I take your formal statement.'

4

'Jacob,' says a voice behind him.

He suddenly becomes aware of the bare wood of his father's sickroom door still pressing against his head, and turns around quickly. In the paraffin-lamp light he makes out his mother standing in the doorway at the opposite end of the small living room. She looks angelic in her funereal white robe with its gold-embroidered collar and cuffs, and a white flat-topped traditional hat planted firmly on her grey head. In Jacob's mind she has grown unbelievably old, for it seems only yesterday that she was crushing corn with a millstone under the family's giant paperbark tree, and he was sleeping in this very room with a bundle of young cousins. Her wrinkled hands are clasped solemnly before her now, and her skin's fresh fragrance of camphor mingles with the trace odours of the family's many overnight guests who had been sleeping all crammed into this small living space less than two hours ago.

'Don't worry, Mother,' he says. 'He will be given the burial he would have wanted.'

Relief washes over her face like sunshine, and she rushes forward to hug her son. 'Oh, Jacob, thank you. I would not have felt at all comfortable if Sello had to do it.'

Jacob hugs her back in return, but derives very little comfort from the close contact.

Sello should've done it, he thinks. *He was, after all, much closer to him than I ever was.*

Longer than Jacob ever did, his father's principal apprentice has been living here with the Tshabalala family on their little plot of land in the Magalies Mountains, about seventy kilometres north of Johannesburg. Jacob even heard him address the old man as 'Father' the last time he visited.

His mother hugs him tighter, as though firmly claiming him as hers. Indeed, he is now the only immediate family she has left. 'I know this is what he wanted for all of us, Jacob. Even with him being such a stubborn man, he would not have passed easily into the next life without knowing for certain you'd be here too, returned to us.' She smiles up at him and lays a palm on his cheek. 'In and out of my life you've been, like the seasons.'

'Not by choice, Ma.'

'Of course it was by choice, my boy: your own and your father's. But still, thank you for being here with me now.'

A pang of guilt shoots through him. *Don't thank me too soon, Ma.*

He takes his mother by her shoulders and gently pushes her away, to gaze directly into her questioning eyes. For a moment he feels compelled to tell her that he is not the one to look after his father in death, that he cannot himself complete the ceremony required at the end of the month-long mourning period. But he cannot bring himself to do so.

'What is it, Jacob?' His mother grasps his arm and squeezes it. 'I can see something is bothering you.'

He smiles at her – feebly, it feels. 'It's nothing.'

'Are you sure?'

'Yes.' Jacob presses thoughts of his father out of mind and instead now focuses on being reunited with his family. That makes him feel surer of himself. 'Today we will become whole again.'

The funeral ceremony must be led, and he will be the one to do it, if only to please her and his next of kin, and to heal the wounds inside his family. He will act out his role in this all too human drama, and he will bury his father as a dutiful son.

But when the rite of ukubuyisela idlozi – the bringing-home of an ancestor – *must be performed, things will be very different*, he reflects.

On that he cannot compromise himself, and thus risk infuriating Nomsa.

Jacob forces a broader smile on to his face, and when he sees how happy this makes his elderly mother, the warmth of it gathers a momentum of its own.

'Come, Ma, let us go and meet our guests.'

5

After two dozen introductions to family friends and acquaintances now completely unfamiliar to him, Jacob's mind drifts away from the funeral towards the peculiar conversation he had earlier with Captain Sameer Naidoo. That conversation made him uneasy, and got him wondering about what might actually have happened in the Eastern Cape.

It had occurred the same day that Jacob was called out to Ladbroke's property to recover the body. He had knocked off early and gone to Maloney's for a drink alone, and to think about how best to deal with his father's funeral. He had been glad that Nomsa was rehearsing till late with her choir that night, despite having turned down the tour so she could be there for him. Outwardly Jacob had protested against this decision, but he was secretly relieved: it laid to rest his nagging anxiety over her spending time in Cape Town with Teddy. And though Jacob did not like to admit it, he needed her around.

The familiar bar near the Johannesburg High Court was unusually empty that late afternoon as Jacob crossed a virtually empty floor to sit at the new marble-topped counter. Old Hugh Semenya, the wizened day-shift bartender who had been there longer than most of the furnishings, put down a Black Label beer in front of his customer without being asked.

'Detective Tshabalala! So you drinking alone today, *mfo*?' He spoke in a pidgin mix.

'No, I'm drinking with my grandfather,' Jacob had quipped.

'Ha! Now *that's* one for the loners.' Old Hugh leaned heavily on the counter, his hands spread wide. 'Take that one over there, for example. He's been in here every day this week. Comes in before three and doesn't leave till late. Looking a lot worse today than usual. Sammy or Sameer he's called, I think. He's one of yours, right?'

Jacob swivelled around in his stool and glanced across the gloomy interior. In a booth over by the cigarette machine sat a bulky Indian wreathed in a haze of cigarette smoke, his arms draped over the seats' backrest as if he were sitting in a jacuzzi. Though his eyes were fixed on the rerun of a Bafana football match being screened on an elevated television, the long sausage of ash drooping off the end of his cigarette suggested that his mind was

nowhere near the football action. Nowhere near function-
ing either, reckoned Jacob.

'No, he's with SVC,' he explained. 'That's Sammy
Naidoo.'

Hugh Semenya grunted at this. 'That's how they all
start, you know: first they tell me they're in here for some
"quiet time", and sit by themselves the way you're doing
now. And before I know it they're divorced and in here
every day, slowly turning to stone like Sameer over there.
Then one day they stop coming, and you don't hear
nothing till you read how some police officer finally fell in
the deep end and drowned. I've seen it all too often, *mfo*.
So you just watch your drinking now.'

The old codger with the bushy white hair studied
Naidoo with such morbid fascination, it was as if the
bartender expected him to pull out a gun right there, put
it to his chin and pull the trigger. 'He get suspended or
something?'

Jacob shook his head and explained what little he
knew about the raid in Tsolo.

The barman crossed his arms reproachfully. 'A cop
going through a bad patch on his own is like a wounded
lion that's been separated from its pride. You in here to
drown yourself just because of that picture appearing in
the paper?'

'*Yebo*.' Jacob took a short sip of his beer. 'That and a
few other things.'

'Why don't you just watch the game instead?' Semenya
whistled approvingly as he wandered off.

Jacob watched the yeasty bubbles rising from the bottom of his glass, and thought back on this morning's JD.
The body had disturbed him more than it should have,

and his pointless altercation with Ladbroke had only made his disquiet worse. He was getting edgier by the day, and he was honest enough with himself to know it was simply because he did not want to go home and take on responsibilities he might have once welcomed with pride, had things played out differently with his father.

He smiled ruefully at his glass, and then stifled a bitter laugh.

'What you laughing at, hey?'

Jacob glanced up to see Naidoo reflected in the mirror, swaying unsteadily on his feet. There was a sour unwashed odour coming off the man, heavily laced with rum.

He turned around in his seat and offered the man a reassuring smile. 'Captain Naidoo, it's been a while.'

The man said nothing further for a long moment, and Jacob watched him blink drowsily while his mouth hung slack.

Semenya abruptly shouted for joy at the other end of the bar, clapping his hands at some goal that the old man must have already watched a dozen times.

'You OK?' Jacob asked Naidoo.

The SVC captain's eyes flew open, but remained unfocused. '*Ja*, why shouldn't I be?'

Jacob shrugged. 'Just thought I'd ask.'

'Look at this.'

Naidoo yanked his crumpled shirt out of his trousers and pulled it up to reveal a flabby torso. The reek of unwashed skin grew more pronounced and Jacob restrained his breathing. With one finger Naidoo traced a triangle between three puckered bullet wounds.

'I been sho . . . shot three times in the line of duty, you see that?'

Jacob pushed aside his beer and leaned his elbows on the counter, backing as far away from this man as he could.

'I see, Sammy. Do you want to tell me what's wrong, my friend?'

Naidoo ignored him, fascinated by the old scars on his own chest, as though he was seeing them for the very first time. When next he spoke, spittle bubbled at the side of his mouth. 'Doesna count for somethin'?'

'Counts for a lot, Sammy,' Jacob said. 'Are you still bothered by what happened in Tsolo? Is that what this is about?'

'We almost dead . . . died out there, you know? Sitting ducks, that was us.'

At this the man's eyes seemed to grow momentarily clearer, and he lurched forward, found that he was about to topple over and readjusted himself. Slowly he stretched out a hand towards the counter, grabbed it and roughly sat himself down next to Jacob.

'Hugh!' he bellowed. 'Rum 'n' Coke! Make it a quick one, you old *skollie*, hear?'

Without turning away from the football match, the bartender called back, 'You've had enough, Sammy.'

'I'll tell you when I've had enough.'

Jacob patted him on the shoulder. 'Tell me what's up.'

'Who the fuck are you, hey?' Naidoo glanced at Jacob. 'I know you from somewhere. Tshabalala, right?'

Jacob nodded. 'I'm with Murder and Robbery. Same building as yours.'

'Murder and Robbery?' echoed Naidoo.

'Yes.'

'Hey, don't you maybe have an opening over there for a transfer?'

This question surprised Jacob, considering a lot of cops were jostling to get into SVC, including himself. 'Why do you want a transfer?'

'Fuck those cunts I work with. You know – ' Naidoo made a sweeping gesture with one hand – 'they think I haven't proved myself after all these years? With three bullets in me? Screw them! You just ask Russie Swarts. I've been there! You know what I mean, hey? SANAB was hell, till they closed it down. Same as this shit up in the mountains. It never fucking ends.'

'What are you talking about?'

'All of them.' Sammy Naidoo's eyelids drooped. 'They're a bunch of wankers.'

Jacob thought back to what Hugh Semenya had just told him: Naidoo had been coming in here regularly to drink by himself all this last week, which meant he had most likely started hitting the bottle shortly after Tsolo.

'Sammy, what is it that happened in the Eastern Cape?'

Naidoo fixed his eyes on Jacob's chest. Then, surprisingly, he winked and tapped his nose.

'Yes?' Jacob urged him.

But he would not hear more. The door to Maloney's suddenly opened, admitting the growl of late afternoon traffic. They both looked up, and it took a moment for Jacob's eyes to adjust to the bright glare streaming in from the street. But during that time he recognized the pear-shaped silhouette.

'Hey, Kommie!' Naidoo pushed himself into a more upright position. 'Over here, man. Have a shot with us.'

Combrink looked genuinely astonished to see them sitting together. A smile crept over his face as his eyes darted from Jacob to Naidoo. Then he came charging forward so fast that for an instant Jacob thought he might swing a punch at the man next to him. Instead, he grabbed Naidoo by the shoulder, and stuck out his hand towards Jacob for a rough shake.

'Hey, Tshabalala, I hear old Bond is conscious again. Isn't that great news, man?'

It was the first Jacob had heard about it, and he said as much.

'It's true,' confirmed Combrink. 'Listen, I don't want to interrupt your little party, but I've been looking for Sammy here all afternoon. Why he's drinking when he should be working is anyone's guess. Hey, Sammy, what am I going to do with you?'

Naidoo winced as the grip on his shoulder clamped even tighter. Then Combrink released his hold and gave Sameer a one-armed hug around the neck.

'Shit, Sammy, just look at you! You've got me worried, man. Come on. I'll take you home.' He dragged Naidoo off the barstool.

Though he looked extraordinarily glum at the prospect of leaving the bar, Naidoo wordlessly hooked one arm around Combrink's midriff and followed him.

'Don't mind him, Tshabies,' Combrink called over his shoulder. 'His head is just a bit messed up at the moment, you know? Happens from time to time. I suppose he showed you his wounds?'

Jacob merely smiled.

'I thought so.' Combrink laughed. 'See you around.'

With one arm looped around Naidoo's shoulder, Combrink struggled to open the door. When Naidoo eventually did make it through, he stumbled and fell, striking the side of his head against the bumper of a parked car.

'Bloody drunks,' mumbled Semenya. 'They're all the same in the end.'

Jacob glanced back at the old man behind the bar, who was shaking his head in disgust at the sight of Combrink yelling at a bleeding Naidoo to get up. He picked up his own beer for another sip, but then decided against it. His appetite for anything but going home had been doused by the conviction that Combrink had purposefully tripped Naidoo up and rammed his head into the nearest car.

6

Jacob takes a deep breath and forces the memory out of his mind. This is not the kind of thing he wants to be thinking about on the day of his father's burial – nor are his growing suspicions about Combrink. Had the same officer not been surprised in Harry's office, sifting through files that were destined for the ICD? The way he had guiltily started when Jacob walked in on him had somehow stuck in Jacob's thoughts.

Not here, he reminds himself.

What did it mean though?

Not here, please.

He would need a clear head to think these things through, but later, because if he is wrong in his suspicions—

Jacob turns his eyes skyward and takes a deep breath. Feathery clouds streak across the pale blue openness, and he is glad to see the day promises to be clear and warm.

Red-mud adobes box in the Tshabalala compound's courtyard on three sides. Rising from the hard-packed soil of the yard, a great winter-bald paperbark tree spreads its green-budded white-wood branches over nearly two hundred guests. To Jacob it looks as though the land itself is prepared to bless this gathering. There are shouts of joy and peals of loud laughter as old friends are reacquainted, and extended families of extended families meet each other for the first time. Men, women and children are dressed in their Sunday best, which ranges from the threadbare garments of poor farmhands to the expensive suits of visiting urbanites. Many wear more traditional clothes of mourning: white shawls and robes, animal skins, elaborately beaded headdresses. Amongst them glide a handful of chiefs and *indunas*, *sangomas* and *nyangas* from different clans who have come to see their peer and teacher off. Though most of the mourners are black, there is a smattering of white faces too, and Jacob is overjoyed to shake hands with hoary old Oupa Goosen and his family. Now wheelchair-bound and nearly blind with age, the old man still remembers Jacob from when he was nothing more than a 'snot-nosed *laaitie* who stole my blerrie peaches'. It was Oupa Goosen who first befriended Jacob's grandfather and eventually gave the Tshabalala family a sizeable portion of his farm to call their own, at a time when blacks were being uprooted like blackjack weeds in their own country.

When a lull falls in the greetings and condolences, Jacob slips away from the crowd and into the shade of a jacaranda tree rising near an overgrown creek. Cars glitter in the sun where they are parked on one of the family's small fields, now lying fallow. Nearby are also unhitched donkey carts, the animals contentedly grazing on the long grass found in the shade of willow trees. Jacob inhales deeply, and savours the taste of dust and straw carried on the light breeze. Still feeling the weight of the previous night's exhausting vigil, he is relieved by this momentary tranquillity.

For the briefest moment he catches sight of Nomsa

moving through the crowd beside his mother – the older woman's arm hooked into hers – smiling nervously at people to whom she is being introduced. He is pleased at the sight of the two women together. Though Nomsa was supposed to have left on her choir tour last night, she is here with him, and helping comfort a family that has never quite known how to respond to her.

No, that's not true, he tells himself. His mother had always liked Nomsa from the moment they met, five years ago; she just did not know how to express this around her disapproving husband.

An abrupt memory of ICD Detective Mosetsane disrupts his thoughts. How different the two women are, but attractive in their own ways. Jacob clears his throat and scuffs at the loose soil, discomfited by this pleasantly vivid memory of the detective. There had been something exciting about the way she had smiled at him as he entered her temporary office on the SVC floor, set up for the duration of her investigation into the Tsolo affair. She had looked genuinely happy to see him that second time, though he could have sworn he meant nothing more than peeling wallpaper to her the first time they had encountered each other in Molethe's presence. He remembers equally well how that bright smile had vanished as soon as he explained why he wanted to speak with her.

'A good turn-out, isn't it?' A voice from behind interrupts Jacob's thoughts.

He turns to find Sello, his father's chief apprentice, wrapped in the familiar garment of a *sangoma*: a shawl printed with white, red and black images of traditional warriors, with beads of the same colours criss-crossing his chest. A fresh goat's gallbladder has been tied into his combed hair, so have cowrie shells. For all the years that

Sello, a Tswana by origin, has spent learning his trade from Jacob's father, his pronunciation of Zulu still sounds insufficiently inflected and flat.

'Yes.' Jacob goes back to observing the assembled crowd. 'More than I would have thought.'

Inwardly, he feels pride stir at the number of people who have come to honour his father's passing, but the feeling is closely followed by a leaden realization that he himself will never know his father the way these people have. That opportunity was lost a long time ago.

Sello claps a brotherly hand on his shoulder, as though guessing what is going through Jacob's head, and remarks in a gentle voice, 'He was a wise teacher, but also just a man, like we all are when the end comes.'

Which is the only reason I'm here, thinks Jacob, but to Sello he says, '*Yebo*, that's the truth . . . brother.'

Normally the last word would have easily come to him, but knowing that this relative stranger in many ways replaced him as a son in his father's eyes warps the word's intention and makes him feel a twinge of jealousy.

Nomsa spots Jacob among the assembled guests and waves to him. He returns the gesture, and feels fresh gratitude rush through his weary body.

'She seems a good woman,' says Sello as he too waves. There is a sage gentleness to his voice, unlike the harsh rasp Jacob remembers his father affecting.

'I couldn't pray to meet a better one,' Jacob replies.

'Will you marry her?'

'I hope to.'

'But?'

'Her lobola is steep.'

At this Sello surprises him with a good-natured laugh.

'I thought you city coconuts didn't care much about that tradition any more.'

Jacob smiles back. '*We* do, Nomsa and I. What better way for me to show my gratitude to her parents for bringing such a beautiful daughter into the world?'

Sello nods approvingly. 'Aye, I'm glad you think this way, my brother. All too often people forget it's meant to be a gesture of gratitude, not a purchase price.'

A short but comfortable silence falls between the two men, until Sello breaks it.

'I hear you've had some trouble in the city.'

Jacob shrugs. 'Not more than usual.'

'This Makhe Motale who's appeared on TV to accuse the police of brutality, what will you do about him?' With a chuckle he quickly adds, 'I'll put a curse on the coward for you, if you like.'

Jacob regards the *sangoma* more carefully. 'What good would that do? If I act out against him, I'll only justify his claims of police vindictiveness.'

'Turning your cheek is not always the best response, Jacob.'

'Neither is instant retribution whenever you think you've been done wrong. We can't afford to be hasty in these matters.' Jacob takes the *sangoma*'s hand. 'I appreciate that you are concerned about me, my friend, but as long as I am a policeman certain people will still see me as the enemy.'

Sello laughs out loud. 'Are you sure you're a real police officer, Detective Tshabalala? It seems to me you are far too decent!'

Jacob shakes his head. 'Maybe, but I'm more interested in fixing whatever isn't working.'

Sello nods. 'Your police friend Harry, the one you once brought to visit us, how is he now?'

'He is on his feet again, I hear; they are flying him back up this weekend.'

A single voice amidst the crowd breaks into an ululation, and Jacob recognizes it as Mama Hettie Solilo's calling the assembled mourners to gather closer. After a moment, her cry is joined by those of others.

Sello pats Jacob gently on the back. 'Come, brother, let's go see your father off.'

7

Back in the room where his father died the acrid stench of extinguished candles assaults Jacob's eyes and nose. He grasps the first of the three handles lining the right-hand side of the coffin, while Sello takes the opposite side. Apprentices and cousins make up the rest of the pall-bearers.

For now Sello takes over the proceedings, since the dead man's immediate family may not speak at all during these last rites, for fear of provoking the recently departed's spirit. That is just as well, because a cold numbness has settled over Jacob, despite the rapidly warming morning. His tongue feels like a swollen rag stuffed into his mouth; his mind, which has so actively been weighing up all his decisions night and day this last week, now seems to echo like a warehouse. Jacob almost misses Sello's direction for him to lift the coffin, and very nearly lets it tilt forward as two other men pull away the sawhorses and carry them out into the courtyard.

As they file out of the tiny room, Jacob feels as though he is following the others, instead of leading them. Remembering the spear he laid on top of the coffin, he glances to check whether it is still there, but someone must have already removed it.

The moment Jacob steps out into the sunlight and faces the mass of assembled mourners, that overpowering sense of emptiness inside him increases. Dazed, he listens as the ululation subsides into a mournful song led by the *sangomas* and *nyangas*. He negotiates two short steps down to the courtyard without meeting anyone's eyes.

A praise singer from the royal Zulu court in KwaZulu begins a poem about Jacob's father that harmonizes perfectly with the other singing. Despite the strange torpor overwhelming him, Jacob feels his skin prickle when he hears the word 'remember' uttered over and over again.

The sawhorses have reappeared under the paperbark tree, which Jacob's grandfather had planted shortly after receiving the land from Goosen, in thanks for the gift itself and the birth of his first son. With the help of the other pallbearers he places the coffin carefully on top of them. When he feels Sello gently touch his shoulder to guide him away towards Nomsa and his mother, he realizes that he had become completely absorbed in thoughts of the past.

Bare-chested, with animal furs around his loins and a leopardskin headdress decorated with porcupine quills, the praise singer steps into the circle created around the coffin and lays a hand on the rawhide that drapes it. He silently regards the crowd for a moment until he has their full attention, then he launches into a eulogy, first honouring the dead *sangoma*'s lineage, then plunging into his achievements as a true leader of his community despite his being a Zulu in a region almost entirely populated by Tswanas. The singer's beautifully lyrical Zulu entrances the audience, even those who cannot understand his words.

It sounds like French, Harry had once observed to Jacob of his language, *only without the pomp and garlic*.

Jacob drives this jocular thought from his head, and instead tries to summon up the kinds of feelings appropriate here at his family's side: sorrow, loss, bereavement. But he cannot hold on to them for very long, as they vacillate violently in currents of guilt and confusion.

Surveying the mourners packed around the coffin, Jacob realizes that the old man must have meant much more to them than the irascible old *sangoma* who had once chased his son away from home. Incredible as it might seem to Jacob, his father had not only shared love with these people, but he had also won their respect.

As the praise poet launches into a farewell song, other voices joining him, families and individuals step up to the coffin and place letters of compassion on the rawhide covering. Bodies begin to sway to the mournful words, hands clap to the slow rhythm and strong, practised church-choir voices – Nomsa's included – eventually take up the lead. Over to one side lost white faces are respectfully bowed in silence before the unfamiliar language and customs, while beyond them all stirs the hot smell of the dusty veldt awakening to another warm spring day.

The abundance of messages beginning to slip off the coffin are hastily gathered so that the pallbearers can again take it up, this time to carry the deceased to his grave. Jacob and Sello lead the slow procession out of the courtyard and along a narrow footpath winding northward. Through ankle-high grass they walk towards the tiny

Tshabalala graveyard located in the veldt not half a kilometre from the homestead.

By now Sello has added his sonorous voice to the Zulu
chanting. *And what is this?* thinks Jacob, as Christian
songs of mourning now arise spontaneously among the
crowd. And though his father might have resented their
intrusion when he was still alive, to Jacob it feels like they
also belong, for are they not the hymns sung by the son
now burying the father? Jacob glances at his father's senior
apprentice, but the *sangoma* seems untroubled by these
lyrics from another faith. Jacob's heart yearns to add his
own voice, but no, the immediate family of the deceased
must remain silent, lest they distract the dead from their
onward journey.

At the grave itself, which he prepared along with family
members in the days before the funeral, the praise singer
launches into the last of his poems as the coffin is lowered
with ropes into the rectangular hole. Someone – Jacob will
not remember whether it is Sello or one of the other
sangomas – presents him with the assegai the eldest son of
the deceased must throw into the grave to ensure his
father's safe journey into the netherworld.

For the briefest moment Jacob hesitates, and imagines
hearing his mother catch her breath in dismay. Then his
mouth finally opens to break the family's silence. In a clear
voice that surprises him, he asks his father to protect the
surviving family and not bring harm unto them. With
the necessary words expelled, he feels a leaden arm lift
and throw the stabbing spear into the grave, where it
strikes the coffin with a faint metallic *cong* – a knell of
finality. Jacob brushes at his face and steps back. Now it
is done.

Immediately Nomsa's cool fingers find his, while his mother steps forward and throws her dead husband's gourd into the grave, then the blankets of his sickbed, his carved blue-gum walking stick. Tears course down her cheeks as she thanks him for the time they had together.

The throb of singing resumes as the procession turns back to the homestead, sunlight cutting golden shafts through motes of dust still swirling amongst the gnarled Bushveld trees. At one point in his numbness, Jacob looks up to find Sello walking next to him and holding his hand.

Under the paperbark tree's shade, the chairs and blankets, the straw mats and the smells of mutton, beef, corn on the cob, and *putu* offer a welcoming oasis to the mourners. Yet before entering the cool of the courtyard, feet and shoes are first washed clean of the footpath's dust to ensure no graveside soil makes it back to the homestead. The newly dead must have no way of finding their way home, because the afterlife lies in another direction and they must not turn back.

The guests will partake of a sacrificed bull's meat, which Jacob will now have to kill in honour of his father, and they will also drink of the beer which his mother will taste first and he second – but not before the froth is poured on the ground as thanksgiving to the spirits, because today the living will break bread not only with each other but also with the dead.

Not everyone will take part willingly, though, thinks Jacob. Nearby, Nomsa's expression has become impossibly strained, though it still remains polite. *No, you, my dear, are perhaps as headstrong in your beliefs as my father was*.

He smiles at Nomsa to let her know he understands, and that he supports her. She returns the smile nervously, as though she knows exactly what he is thinking.

8

Later, despite not having slept the night before and the long, emotionally wrought day that followed, Jacob cannot get to sleep. All around him guests are rolled up in tight bundles of duvets and blankets on the living-room floor, and a few of them are already snoring blissfully. A smell of burnt pap and sour beer from the day's feast still lingers on the air. He wishes he could have Nomsa here with him, but she is now sleeping in his mother's room, crammed into it with Hettie Solilo and two of her *twasa* students. Jacob rolls on to his side and stares at the pocked door which leads to his father's newly deserted room. It is now closed and locked until the mourning period is over, when it can be inhabited again without offending the dead.

It is not the old man who is causing Jacob's discomfort now, but a conversation he had with Mosetsane on the morning before he drove here. Their discussion has been steadily filtering back into his mind as his concerns with the funeral subside, and it seems, whichever way Jacob now looks at it, that Harry Mason is in deep trouble.

9

An office had been created for ICD Detective Busisiwe Mosetsane on the SVC floor. It was situated at the back of the building, down an ugly lime-hued corridor lit by fluorescent lights. A prefabricated storage area filled with clunky furniture and outdated stationery had been cleared for her and two assistants.

The door stood open when Jacob arrived, and though it was barely seven o'clock in the morning, Mosetsane looked like she had been busy at her laptop for hours. The way her ochre pupils darted from side to side behind her square-rimmed glasses reminded him of dragonflies dipping over water. In a grey-checked suit she looked every bit as businesslike and fresh as the first time he saw her.

He rapped at the doorjamb and half expected her to start at the sudden interruption, but she merely halted her typing mid-sentence and turned that piercing gaze of hers on him over the rim of her glasses.

'Yes?' she asked in English.

'*Dumela*, I'm—' Jacob began in Sotho.

'You're Detective Inspector Jacob Tshabalala, Murder and Robbery. I know.' That smooth-spoken English was like aloe on an open wound. 'Come in, please.'

She plucked the glasses off her nose, and with them she pointed at one of two straight-backed wooden chairs that faced her across the desk.

Jacob took a seat and glanced around the room. It was stacked with records so old they looked like crumpled autumn leaves. 'Is this room all that Director Molethe could come up with for you?'

'I'm not exactly a hot favourite with anyone around here right now, and I wanted something fairly out-of-the-way.'

'It's not right, putting you back here in storage.'

'It's fine by me. I don't intend on being here long, detective, and I'm not here to make friends in SVC, either.'

'I see.'

'Besides, it has a decent-sized safe, which comes in handy when I'm dealing with certain cases.' She said this with a captivating smile still, though by now it seemed a little frosted over.

The cardboard boxes removed from Harry's office sat inside an open safe the size of a closet. 'Does that then mean you have cause for further investigation?'

'Jacob – can I call you Jacob? – no one in this department seems to be taking what happened in Tsolo seriously. That worries me.'

'That's not what I meant. I was just hoping to find out more about what really happened in the Eastern Cape myself. No one seems able to give me a straightforward recounting.'

She looked at him quizzically. 'You should know that I'm not at liberty to discuss the investigation?'

Jacob smiled. 'I thought I might try anyway.'

'Then you didn't think it through properly, detective. But you're welcome to tell me something that'll add value to my work.'

'Harry Mason is a good police officer.' The moment those words left his mouth, they felt like the lamest thing he could say.

'That's good to know, Jacob, but it's unfortunately not very practical information.'

The easy smile on her face made it difficult for Jacob to interpret what she was actually saying to him – if, indeed, there *was* a subtext.

'Whatever you are trying to pin on Harry, you're wrong about him.'

Mosetsane closed her laptop with a sigh and folded her hands on top of it. 'I am not here to "pin" anything on anyone. The ICD was created to protect the public from human-rights abuses by the police service, and that's what I intend to do here.'

'What about *his* right to be heard, though? He's being judged in his absence for something he hasn't done. Whatever that appears to have been.'

'You sound very sure of yourself.'

'I am very sure of Harry.'

'Funny. I have eye-witness reports of the SVC officers from this same office drinking alcohol as they blundered into a hot zone.'

'Harry wouldn't have been one of them.'

'Again you're so sure. Why?'

'Drinking, detective? What's actually going on here? The ICD normally takes months to put together an inquiry, yet here you are, not even a week after the fact. Which tells me something else is up.'

'Detective Mason is a good friend of yours, yes?'

'I'm sure you know the answer to that by now.'

'Then perhaps you can tell me exactly how a task team made up exclusively of high-ranking Johannesburg SVC police officers ended up in Tsolo? And why they were looking for a bunch of automatic rifles that weren't there, at huge expense to the police service? This, when the case could simply have been handed over to the local Eastern Cape SVC units?' The steel that had slipped into her voice was as hard and sharp as a dagger, and at that moment Jacob realized he had severely underestimated her.

'I don't know about you, sistah, but a case like that – well, no one in this or any other office would have handed it over to a bunch of provincials. They would have bungled it, for sure, and then what? Do you know how hard that team worked on getting there?'

'No, I don't, because for a captain, Detective Mason obviously does not know the first thing about maintaining accurate records. He should be disciplined just for the state his dockets are in.'

'But this isn't about the records he kept, either,' Jacob said.

Mosetsane leaned forward in her chair. 'Maybe we could also talk about who the mysterious beneficiary of a hundred-thousand-rand pay-off might have been? And an international witness protection programme, at the government's expense.'

Jacob let his eyes run over the neatly arranged white cardboard boxes in the safe, and recalled how Combrink had been caught looking for some information in them. Did she actually believe Harry was defrauding the police service of informer funds? He might have been conned by his informant, but not that.

'Are you sure you really have all the information you need to make the right decision?'

'No, I don't. For starters, I don't even know who the supposed informer in this case was.' She glances at the boxes in the safe, having noticed him looking in that direction. 'Why? Is there something else I *should* know about?'

Jacob thought about this. He now had his suspicions about Combrink, but they were circumstantial at best. He *thought* he had seen the man deliberately injuring Naidoo, but he could not be sure about that. He had also found Combrink digging around in Harry's office, but the man might have been looking for something legitimate, just as he himself had been looking there for Tanya Fouché's phone number. Come to think of it, Jacob's presence in that office, in the process of it being sealed for further investigation, might be construed as badly as Combrink's activities there. He decided to steer clear of that particular conversation.

'Harry never told me who passed the information on to him,' said Jacob firmly. 'Now will you answer one of *my* questions, detective?'

'You can try me.' Her voice remained neutral, even soothing.

'Is there a political interest in this investigation?'

'Political or not, my job is to investigate this SVC unit's role in a massacre committed in the village of Tsolo.'

'You're not answering a simple question. And why not? How come the ICD moved so unusually fast? It's almost like you were waiting for this. Was it some kind of sting?'

'I like to work fast.' With her hands folded motionlessly on the desk, she held his eyes, but to Jacob it seemed that a flush had crept into her cheeks. Was this anger or embarrassment? he wondered. Or both? And if so, what about?

He shifted forward in his chair and smiled in an attempt to put Mosetsane at ease. The friendly gesture appeared to take her by surprise.

'Look, I can see that you take your work very seriously, and I'm not questioning your motives,' he began. 'I just want to understand a few things about what I see around me. You've now spent a few days looking into the lives of these officers. So tell me that Harry Mason is the kind of man who'll storm into a village drunk and gun people down. Tell me even that Superintendent Swarts is. He might drink like a fish – everyone knows that – but would he ever put his career and the lives of his own men at risk? You know what they call him?'

By now their faces were barely more than two feet apart.

Mosetsane offered him a lopsided smile. 'They call him "the great Super Supe Russie Swarts". But don't ask me to understand why all of you are so obsessed with nicknames.'

'What does it tell you though?' asked Jacob.

'I find it interesting that you're not mentioning any of the others involved. Why is that, detective?'

'I've only met them in passing,' he replied. 'Sistah, a cop like Harry who decides to return to the police service after a long leave of absence isn't exactly doing it for the money, especially when he left the first time around because his wife was killed during one of his investigations. He came back because this is what he loves. I don't think he can do without it. Harry Mason won't compromise what he has here for a bunch of rifles and some lousy informant money. He's proved that.'

'You see only the best in people. How does a Murder and Robbery man do that?' A smile crept over Mosetsane's face, but when Jacob's serious expression remained unchanged, she brought up a hand to hide her lips. 'Sorry, that was callous.'

Jacob allowed himself a smile at the uncomfortable gesture. 'I'm right, am I not? He doesn't fit the profile of the kind of person you're looking for.'

'I have to work with the facts, Jacob,' she said with a hint of regret in her voice. 'Otherwise where would my investigation end up?'

Jacob studied her intently, trying to figure out how he was going to get information out of her. Eventually she sat back and averted her eyes.

'At least tell me if you're dumping Harry into the same basket with the others. Or are you treating their cases strictly separately?'

'I'll ask again, should I know something else, detective?'

Jacob smiled at her slyly and shrugged. 'Oh, I don't know, detective. You know how it is. I also have to work with the facts, and right now I don't have any to offer.'

She made an irritated clucking sound with her tongue, but the way her shoulders moved suggested she had found his comment amusing.

'You're pretty confident your friend did nothing wrong.'

Jacob became earnest. 'He's in an IC unit with two bullets in him. It's a pretty cruel thing to do, surely, investigating him before he's even out of the hospital.'

'That fact doesn't protect him from the complaints my office received.' Mosetsane picked up a silver fountain pen and ran her manicured fingers along its length. 'Like I said, I'm not here to pin anything on him. But, based on the information I have from the national commissioner's office and what I've collected here so far, I'd say it's in your friend's best interest that you help me figure out what the hell has been going on here.'

Jacob blinked. 'The national commissioner's office?'

'I can't tell you more, Jacob, except that your friend has an uphill battle ahead of him. A very steep one.'

SEVEN

1

Across the congested street four men swagger along the pavement. They are much the same age as Wally Khuzwayo and the man sitting next to him in the passenger seat. The oldest amongst them, with a greying beard and balding head, walks slightly ahead of the rest, his shoulders hunched, his eyes downcast as if following the pavement's square patterning. Swarts is the easiest one to recognize.

In the week that he has been following them, this is the first time Wally has seen all four of them together, and he must say to himself that he is not very impressed. They look like a pack of stray dogs on the prowl together, intent on nothing more than survival. The one called Franklin, who has been the cause of most of their trouble, swaggers with his hands tucked into the back pockets of his jeans, looking like God on a field trip of his own creation. The man's head is constantly on the move, his eyes interrogating every pedestrian they pass. Naidoo has a couple of large plasters on his chin and brow, and lags noticeably behind. As Swarts arrives at the door to Maloney's bar, he yanks it open and enters ahead of the others without holding it open for them. Combrink makes a grab for the door and indicates for Franklin to go first. As Naidoo slinks past, Combrink glowers at him over his glasses before letting the door swing closed.

'Is that them?' asks the man in the passenger seat.

'Told you. Like clockwork,' Wally replies in Sotho.

'All I had to do was sit here between five and six and wait for one of them to arrive, predictable as night and day.'

'They look like a bunch of cops to me.' The man's voice is rusty and broken, and Wally has to constantly refrain from offering him a drink.

'They're not,' affirms Wally.

'Whatever your name is, friend, don't think you can screw me around. I've seen enough cops in my time to know how they look, and all those guys have been at it for a while.'

Wally turns to look at this man beside him, whom people call Mokzin: the boxer. Before today they had never met, and he cannot even be sure that Mokzin is his real name. He has the passenger window wide open, and has one arm uplifted outside, his fingers drumming impatiently on the roof. His head is as round as a cannon-ball, his eyes small and hooded. Ever since Wally picked him up near Western Deep mine, two hours' drive in the direction of Potchefstroom, his expression has remained about as informative as that on a chunk of rock.

'Well, they're not *gatas*,' he reiterates. The last thing he needs is for Mokzin to abandon the job at this late stage. This is turning into a rough-shod enough assignment as it is, thanks to the Phaliso brothers' impatience, and he doesn't need any more drawbacks. 'If you want to know, they're just business rivals of my employers. If they have been cops at some stage, they're not any more.'

Mokzin shifts in his seat and farts loudly. 'OK, I don't care if they are cops; the price will just be higher.'

Wally considers getting into a debate about this price hike, but decides he couldn't care less. Once upon a time he might have looked out for the brothers' interests and made an effort to save them a buck or two, but since they are no longer considering his advice on this mess, or anything else for that matter, he will let them deal with this added expenditure themselves.

'Double,' says the man.

'Fine, whatever.'

'Now.'

'Don't be an arsehole. You think I carry four grand around with me? This is Johannesburg, for Christ's sake, not whatever village you're from.'

'Then we go to the bank afterwards.'

'For that price, you better not screw this up.'

'I won't.'

'That's good, because I wouldn't want you looking any uglier than you already are and, trust me, the people I work for just love rearranging faces.'

Mokzin glares at him suspiciously, but Wally ignores it and turns his attention back to Maloney's. A warm glow begins to spread through him at the thought of this idiot's face when he walks in there only to discover the place crammed to the rafters with *gatas* and state prosecutors. He would even pay good money to witness it. He smiles to himself at the thought, despite the rotten mood he has been in all day.

The whole situation has got out of hand faster than a bunch of skunk-drunk teenagers left at home without their parents, thinks Wally, and he's had it. The last time Ncolela took on the *gatas*, it was in a widely broadcast boast that he could do a better job than them in keeping the streets free of thugs. But that time Godun had been there to help Wally pull him off his high horse and out of the public eye. Not now, however, for this time it seems that the younger brother has been dragged into the older one's schemes.

Or perhaps even orchestrated the madness; Wally wouldn't put it past Godun.

This has greatly disconcerted him, not just because of being sidelined, but also because the dynamics between the Phalisos have obviously changed – a bad thing for him. It means Wally no longer knows where he stands with them. Now all bets are off.

With the brothers' changes under way and old age creeping ever closer, Wally Khuzwayo knows that his time for making money is slowly coming to an end.

He reaches out and twists the knob on the car radio. Metro FM comes on with Hugh Masakela's 'Been Such a Long Time', and Wally allows his finger to briefly touch a crumpled photo stuck on the dashboard next to the volume dial. An eight-year-old boy wearing a mud-caked soccer outfit, with a quarter of an orange stuck in his mouth, is making a face at the camera.

'I'll give them some time to settle in,' says Mokzin.

Wally jerks his finger away from the photo, uncomfortable that this stranger might see an aspect of his life that has nothing to do with the business at hand. 'You do whatever you want, just don't take all day.'

Mokzin. Ncolela. Godun. Wally Khuzwayo shudders to think of the night when he was ordered to contract this stinker. The pink house at the end of the road had been standing in complete darkness when he arrived. Lights out and no sign of the Phaliso wise guys; not even one of those stinking mutts came racing around the house to take its usual piss on his car. It reminded him of that terrible night in '86 when Ncolela had phoned him at three in the morning, wailing at the top of his voice about Hlubi. When Wally had pushed open the unlocked front door, he half expected to find that the Phaliso brothers had finally torn each other apart, limb for bloody limb, yet all he found was a motionless Ncolela staring out into the night through a gap in the thick curtains, and holding a nearly empty bottle of Chivas in his hand. The sour stink of kitchen garbage had almost made Wally's eyes water.

'I see you, brother.' When Ncolela still made no move to welcome him, he asked, 'Everything all right?'

Ncolela gave no instant response – not a laugh, not a snide joke, not even a violent reproach, as was his habit. Instead, he only offered Wally a tight-lipped smile, which looked far too much like one of Godun's. The older Phaliso brother indicated for him to sit down, while he himself remained standing by the curtain. When Ncolela eventually spoke, it was in a voice as hollow as a cave. 'She's out there, Wally, watching me. She's looking in from the cold outside, when she should be in here where she always made it warm. And you know what she is saying to me?'

'What?' he asked.

'She's telling me to kill all the rats in the house. She's telling me to drink of my own blood. Can you believe it, Wally? Hlubi saying these things. What do you think it means?'

Under different circumstances Wally might have joked that finally someone was talking some sense into Ncolela about his domestic hygiene, but there was something too freakish about the silence in the house. It made Wally think that her spirit was indeed standing right behind him, whispering threats into his ear.

'It means you're tired, brother. Nothing more,' he said in as calm a voice as he could manage. 'It means it's time for you to put that whisky away and sit down. I have things to tell you.'

'Yes, perhaps.' Ncolela looked at the bottle in his hand. Then his lips curled into a snarl and he threw it across the room, to smash loudly against the opposite wall. In a voice that could barely contain its rage, he added, 'I will sit down with you this one time and hear you out all the way, *mfo*. I owe you that.'

Wally knew what Ncolela meant: he expected an explanation that Wally was not prepared to give. Though he managed to steer that evening's conversation back towards Swarts and his team, the big question that remained afterwards was not *when* to save himself, it was *how*. The way Godun was pushing and pushing him into ever more risky situations made his chances of negotiating his own survival slimmer by the hour, and the terms ever less favourable.

'*He banna*, you falling asleep?'

Wally had completely forgotten about the man sitting next to him.

'Are you kidding me? The stink you're letting loose in my car is likely to kill me.'

'If you drive off without me, I'll find you, *né*?' Mokzin holds up a warning finger as thick as a sausage. 'You hear me?'

'Just get it over with. I don't have all day.'

He doesn't. He has to pick his son up from his grand-mother's at seven.

Mokzin huffs in response and opens the passenger door. Wally throws a nervous glance at the thick plastic shopping bag as the other man lifts it free from the footwell with a grunt. It strains to breaking point with whatever is inside.

'You sure that bag's going to hold?' he calls after Mokzin.

'Leave me alone. I know what I'm doing.' The boxer leans in through the window and holds up both his pinkie and ring finger. 'Double, *né?*'

'Let's see you do the job first.'

'Get the car started. When I come out, I want to see you easing out into traffic. We'll need to get out of here quick-quick.'

'Fine.'

Wally watches the man lumber across the road, looking like any middle-aged office worker hurrying to catch the six o'clock at Doornfontein Station. He waits till Mokzin has the glass door to Maloney's open, then turns the ignition. The car starts first time round.

Now we'll see how you handle yourself in the ring, my boxer, he thinks with a smile.

With the engine running smoothly, he studies his hands on the fur-covered steering wheel of his station wagon. They appear pretty steady to him, considering what is about to happen. The truth is, he has done many things in his life, most of them not exactly above board, but he has so far never killed a cop. Not even in the shoot-out of '83, when those counter-insurgency bastards came down on the Phalisos like God's own shitstorm. He used to consider the very thought of doing so bad luck, yet now that the moment has finally arrived, and the only thing that makes Wally uncomfortable is breaking his own rules. This step is, he decides, not as monumental a leap as he once thought.

The Phalisos are right on one thing: the time has come to act. With all his options blown up in Tsolo, and that fuck Makhe Motale run off with his money, Wally has nothing left but to play this game all the way to the end and then see where it takes him.

Checking all three mirrors, he pops a handful of chewing gum into his mouth and settles back into his seat to wait for Mokzin.

As it turns out, Wally Khuzwayo does not have to wait long.

2

Old Hugh Semenya is polishing the last of the highball glasses, still hot from the dishwasher, before knocking off for the day and letting the nightshift take over when the stranger opens the glass door with MALONEY'S sandblasted across it, and steps into the green-carpeted entrance.

Over the many years he has worked behind the bar, first as a common cleaner, then a barman, Hugh has enjoyed watching the reaction of any newcomers to the place. Their first foot in, they usually freeze; their eyes widen. Sometimes they actually lift their noses, as though scenting the air for danger. Then they cautiously peer around the room beyond. Most, in fact, make an about-turn there and then, when they realize what kind of dive this is, and go drinking someplace else where they will feel more welcome. Others, they are not so easily discouraged: this breed of stranger will usually descend the four steps and cross the floor determinedly towards the bar. They will impatiently order a drink and consume it quickly, while glaring around the room as though it is some kind of endurance test to drink in a place filled with cops. Then there are others who will end up with far too many rounds in them, and decide to test their mettle by becoming belligerent towards the bar staff or, worse, the servicemen.

These latter strangers will cause the kind of trouble they will regret for the rest of their lives, for what cop, after all, will tolerate bullshit in the one place he can consider his shelter from the world outside, even from home? And what cop will arrest another cop for bloodying a civvy in the one haven they share? In that sense Maloney's is not just a bar, Hugh Semenya reckons, but a sanctuary.

To give this stranger credit, he hovers on the doorsill only for a moment. Then he tightens his grip on the obviously heavy plastic shopping bag in his right hand and heads straight towards the bar. Hugh instantly decides to serve this man a beer only if he does not smell of the street. The clientele are usually tolerant of newcomers who blunder into their territory, but anyone that looks like he comes from the other side of the line might just find himself leaving quickly under very unpleasant circumstances.

As the man continues across the busy floor under a press of suspicious eyes, his own gaze remains steadily on Hugh. His expression, however, undertakes a phenomenal transformation in a short space of time. Instead of hesitation or nervousness creeping into that rotund face, each step closer to the bar seems to take him nearer the brink of some incredible pent-up fury inside his powerful frame. By the time he reaches the counter, the stranger's jaw is working like a piston and his fists are clenched hard enough to cord the tendons on his neck.

'*Dumela*, stranger,' says Hugh, when he does not pick up the gutter stink he has come to associate with sordid train stations. 'Can I get you a beer to ease you into the weekend?'

The man leans against the bar and hooks an elbow around an ashtray. The heavy bag he still keeps protectively close to his body.

'Tell me one thing, old man, is this a pub for cops?'

Hugh chuckles at this. 'That's exactly what I was thinking about.'

'What do you mean?'

'I was wondering how long it would take you to figure it out.'

'It's true, then?'

'You could say that, though they won't mind if you have just a drink or two. Soccer's on, if you want to watch. We've got satellite, and its Bafana versus Ghana this evening.'

The stranger seems to ignore everything he says. Instead, he nods over towards his left shoulder. 'That bunch there, are they cops too?'

'I would think so, considering what I've just told you about this place. Now, can I get you that drink?'

Over the stranger's shoulder, he sees Swarts glance up from whatever serious discussion has been taking place at their table. He eyes the newcomer and raises an eyebrow at the old bartender. Hugh responds with a silent nod: *Yes, I can handle this one; I haven't worked here thirty-nine years for nothing.*

'No,' says the stranger. Without another word, he slaps the counter and heads back out the way he came.

3

A woman leading two girls and carrying a third child whose head is heavily bandaged, all of them dressed in similar filthy pink tracksuits, abruptly cuts into the gap between Wally's car and the one parked directly ahead of it. Their eyes meet briefly, and her expression reminds him of his wife's whenever he comes home smelling like a shebeen mop. Then he realizes he has seen this woman before . . . or someone like her. There had been a girl once; he never knew her but distinctly remembers her face – a face like this one's. Tears were at the corners of her eyes, that earlier time. There had been a boy, too, close to initiation age, who had formed the hub of an angry pulsing wheel of people. He had been arrested for her rape, someone had told Wally at the time, but the community had not been happy with this, so they had paid his bail and abducted him the moment he stepped out of the magistrate's court. It was near a railway station in a township that Wally happened upon them, where the boy had been totally stripped of his clothes and already covered in the earth's red dust from his struggles. One lip was bleeding, and his eyes were swollen shut from the beating he had received. He was now blindly pleading for his life.

The crowd had kept jostling around him, and eyes had burned wild, mouths spitting hatred, their hands and feet continually lashing out at him. To them he had become a despicable object and no longer human, despite his prayers for mercy. It had all ended abruptly when the girl's mother thrust herself into the circle brandishing a broken-off bottleneck. Four men had tackled the boy by his legs and lifted him up so that the back of his head cracked hard against the solidly packed earth. They had pulled the dazed youth's knees apart and braced them in their armpits. A cheer went up from the crowd as the boy twisted desperately this way and that without any possibility of escaping his inevitable castration. Whether he survived the ordeal Wally could not say, since he had left before the first blood stained the dust, but for weeks afterward he could not sleep properly.

Without pausing to check either left or right, the mother that now reminds him of that boy's teenage accuser steps straight out into the traffic, seemingly oblivious to what might happen to her or the child carried in her arms.

An olive-green Prado, its windows black-tinted, slams on its brakes and narrowly avoids ploughing into the pink troop. The driver leans on his horn and keeps his hand there a good few seconds. As though she had been hoping for this kind of reaction, the woman starts smacking the car's bonnet, and swears at the driver in language Wally has rarely heard outside the fraternity of miners amongst whom he grew up. Shocked pedestrians meanwhile turn their heads and gape.

'Will you get the fuck out of my way, woman!'

Wally winds down his own window and is about to yell at her to get out of the way when she beckons her daughters and ushers them across the street, taking no further notice of the driver who had been hooting at her. The Prado, however, stays put, and a sudden irrational fear overcomes Wally Khuzwayo; he imagines that the Phaliso brothers are sitting behind those tinted windows, watching and waiting to see whether he can complete the job or not.

'Our operating cells can't ever be linked to us in any way unless one of us three turns out to be the rat,' he remembers Ncolela say.

Before this thought can turn into anything more than an uncomfortable fancy, he dismisses it. No point in dwelling on things that make you nervous at a time when anxiety is the last thing you need.

A Mercedes behind the four-wheel-drive beeps its horn loudly, and the driver blocking Wally's view of the bar shifts into first, releases the handbrake and drives off. The licence plates on the brand-new car are missing, and he cannot remember what the registration on the Phalisos' car was anyway.

Perhaps, thinks Wally as he tightens his grip on the steering wheel, he is not as ready for what is about to happen as he first thought. Everything seems to be giving him the creeps lately, which is never a good sign.

With his view across the road cleared again, his eyes are drawn towards the pink woman and her children, now at a telephone stand in front of an electronics store next door to Maloney's. She is talking animatedly on the phone, while the young attendant eyes her up and down, clearly wondering whether or not she will be able to pay for the service. The three children gathered around her feet give a start when the glass door to Maloney's is abruptly thrown open and Mokzin comes charging out, the heavy plastic bag still in one hand. He storms across the street like an angry buffalo.

'What do you think you're doing?' Wally shouts out of the window once he is sure Mokzin can hear him over the traffic. 'Go the fuck back!'

The man rushes round the front of the car and yanks open the passenger door.

Wally waves him away. 'I'm paying you to do a job, you shit. Go finish it!'

Faster than Wally could anticipate, the man has fallen into the passenger seat and grabbed him by the throat with one very large hand. He might have been a good boxer in his day after all.

'What do you take me for, uh? I'm not just some fool you can screw around.'

Wally tries to push back the hand that's choking him, but it remains as steady as a wrench. 'You agreed to it!' he gurgles.

'I agreed to do four business rivals, not a fucking pigsty filled with cops.'

Wally throws an alarmed glance at the pedestrians passing by, one of whom glances away furtively.

'Easy. You want everyone here . . . to remember us?'

'I don't care, because nothing is happening here today, you hear me!' Mokzin tightens his grip on Wally's throat a moment longer, then shoves him away. He sits back in the passenger seat and folds his arms across his chest. 'We're leaving. Drive.'

'I'd love to, but we can't leave here before the job's done.'

'I said *drive*!'

'Trust me, bra, you don't want to cross my employers.'

'Screw you, and your bosses!'

Wally balls his fists but manages to control an outburst. He can just see what will now happen: Godun will finally have proof that he is not up to the job any more. Indeed, if Wally is right in his guess, Ncolela already suspects him of being the rat in the organization that led the cops to their stash in the mountains.

And he would be right.

But now, with that untrustworthy go-between Makhe Motale gone with his promised down-payment for information already received, he has to try work his way back into the Phaliso fold somehow, and at all costs.

Abruptly he sticks his hand out to Mokzin. 'Give it to me, then, if you can't do it yourself.'

'Are you insane?'

'Give it to me, or I swear your balls will be cut off and

stuffed down your fucking throat before the sun sets tonight.'

At the fury in his voice, Mokzin bites back a quick response like he is swallowing bile.

'But it'll be all over the news. They'll hunt us down.'

'It's not the first time you've done this, so why worry?' Wally gestures impatiently for the bag.

'Who are your bosses?' Mokzin demands in that hoarse voice of his.

'None of your fucking business.'

'I heard of someone who really was fed his own nuts. People said it was the Abasindisi did that.'

'Might have been, but then, maybe not.'

Mokzin's eyes widen. 'Shit. This is for the Phalisos?'

'Give me the fucking bag, you wimp.'

Gingerly, Mokzin lifts the shopping bag out from between his feet and hands it over. Wally feels the bag's weight strain his arm as he opens the door. He will have to carry it as though it is much lighter, otherwise one of the cops might notice and end up asking him difficult questions. He throws a last glance at the man in the passenger seat and laughs mockingly.

'Double? You actually wanted *double*?'

'I don't want anything. Just take it and leave me alone.'

Wally smiles with renewed confidence. 'You better still be here when I come out, *mfo*, otherwise . . .'

He leaves the warning hanging in the air and slams the car door shut. Wally Khuzwayo looks right then left and right again, before casually jogging across Prichard Street, looking like any middle-aged Joe heading for the six o'clock at Doornfontein Station.

4

The time has come for Detective Senior Superintendent Russell Swarts to tell the other Ballies that Harry Mason has something on him, a holdover from the Ntombini murder investigation so many years ago, when they had first met. God only knows where the man found out what had actually happened in Yeoville that night, but now Swarts feels obliged to enlighten his men why Harry Mason's shooting in Tsolo could bring even more trouble down on them than anticipated.

Swarts briefly breaks off his story to keep an eye on the stranger who barged into the bar and abruptly departed again, then goes back to his account of Parapara Ntombini's death. He gives the details as only he and some of the deceased dealer's lieutenants know them. Though some of the Ballies had been on the investigative team tasked with finding the junkie's murderer, which ultimately led them to Ntombini, they had only known an edited story-around-the-barbecue version of the drug dealer's unsolved assassination. They never knew the most important fact behind it, namely that it was he, Russell Swarts, who had killed the bastard.

The long and short of it was that it had not been a reprisal killing from the other gangs, as punishment for the unwanted police attention Ntombini had brought to their neighbourhood, as many had thought at the time – as, indeed, it went down in the case docket. There had been no internal strife either, at least not in the way it eventually appeared in the case file, which Russell Swarts wrote up. For his part, it wasn't a spur-of-the-moment crime, either, heaven forbid. Swarts had mulled over the deteriorating situation on the streets for weeks before arriving at the conclusion that killing Ntombini was a necessary evil. Rather than risk open war between an understaffed narcotics bureau and the drug gangs of Yeoville, which were growing more powerful by the day, he decided he would douse that particular spark before it could turn into a wildfire. It was a tough decision, one of the worst he ever had to make. But that was how one sometimes had to operate in order to prevent a greater loss of life. Zero tolerance, total force – those were the police terms that popped into his mind, even though they sounded like the stuff of bad action films, starring Chuck blimming Norris. If he had learned one thing from the death of his partner the year before the Ntombini investigation, it was to take the battle to them before they could bring it to you. At least that way you were prepared for whatever might follow.

It was a rainy night when he finally found Ntombini, who had crept back to his old haunts in Yeoville after hiding out in Alexandra for while. The narrow streets had been slick with foamy run-off as he waited patiently across the road from a dim staircase leading up to two crummy second-floor flats until most of the kids in the excessively loud nightclub below had cleared out – all looking like a bunch of Satanists, and the girls wearing little more than cheap lingerie and thigh-high whore boots. He didn't have to worry about any of the usual pimps and prossies seeing him, or any of the other dope peddlers in the area either, since they had all wisely called it a night the moment the cats and dogs came pissing down. He got out of his car, the licence plates of which had been swapped, of course, and strolled across the street looking like any old Yeoville wino with a patchwork leather jacket and rolled-up black balaclava on his head. The constant rain and the dark street helped put him more at ease, and so did that blimming music, which was loud enough to camouflage mortarfire.

The hands buried deep in his pockets were covered in leather gloves – not the latex kind from which the techies could lift prints these days – and in one hand he gripped a heavy .38 snub-nose revolver, which would not expel bullet casings when fired.

He took the steps to the terrace flats three at a time, moving more quietly, it seemed, than his body would ever allow to him again. There were only two apartments above the nightclub, but he knew from his sources that Ntombini was hiding in the one situated to the left of the stairwell. These were the same sources that had grown fed up with dwindling profits because of a hunted boss attracting Swarts and his team; the same people who were growing sick of being strip-searched nightly by SANAB teams, ceaselessly looking for a man whom they were hiding. Ntombini's lieutenants finally offered Swarts a sweet deal, in exchange for a bit of breathing space, so that certain lucrative markets could be quickly re-established.

He was fully aware that he was to act as a common assassin for a bunch of smack dealers screwing up kids and entire families from Woodmead to Germiston, and he might have felt like a right arsehole about it too, if it wasn't for the insurance policy this was buying his own team. He didn't want police officers continuously worrying about getting picked off in drive-by shootings. After all, he knew what could happen to police officers that pissed on a gang's territory too hard and too long; he'd experienced it first-hand, not so long ago. It wasn't that he was forging an alliance with these scumbags – he'd never go that far – but he was restoring a balance that was clearly as necessary to the police service as it was to the criminals themselves. So it was arranged that no guards would be around that night.

'That arsehole never saw it coming,' says Swarts to the Ballies sitting at the table with him in Maloney's. 'I don't know who the hell he was expecting at half-past four in the morning, but you can bet it wasn't me.'

'Double-tap to the heart and one to the gut for good measure,' chips in Franklin. 'That's how we found him the next day, if I remember correctly.'

'Shit, Russie, that was you?' Naidoo asks in near-childish wonder. 'Man, we bullied people up and down that entire street for a week, trying to figure out what happened.'

'So who is it that's been talking to Mason?' Kommie Combrink has been carefully polishing his bent glasses with a crumpled handkerchief ever since the story started. 'I mean, how else does he figure this out nearly ten years later? And how much of a threat are they to us?'

'There never was anything left to tie me to that night, even if Bond can come up with witness statements; there is no hard evidence to substantiate any claims that I was there.'

'How does any of this fucking matter?' interrupts Franklin. 'That scumbag would have sold his own mother for a hundred bucks. They bloody well danced in the streets when he was gone, so why not leave it at that? Why this confession bullshit?'

'Obviously not everyone was happy to see him go – if Russie's right and Mason could have witness statements of what happened that night.' To Swarts Kommie says, 'But Blondie's right. If there wasn't an issue, you wouldn't be telling us this. If that crime scene was so clean—'

'It was,' interrupts Naidoo. 'We found bugger-all.'

'It was a bitch,' agrees Franklin.

' – and we can assume no one's going to take Ntombini's associates seriously, so what are the chances that someone can positively place you there that night?'

'That's why I'm telling you this, in case I need to slug this out with Harry.'

Swarts casts an eye around the table. Given that he had just confessed to a murder, they took it pretty well; just like the Ballies he knew, in fact. Only Franklin appears angry about the news, and that was to be expected. Swarts pours the rest of a can of Tab into his brandy. 'Bond is stubborn enough to screw me over, *all* of us for that matter, if he thinks we tried to kill him in Tsolo to cover up that earlier case.'

'Why the hell didn't you tell us about this before?' asks Combrink.

'I was handling it.'

Franklin huffs sarcastically but adds nothing else; instead, he digs ash out of his pipe and starts stuffing it with fresh tobacco.

Combrink shakes his head. 'He never did strike me as a team player, that bloody Pommie.'

'I say he's been waiting for the right time to blackmail you,' suggests Naidoo.

Three pairs of surprised eyes turn on Naidoo, who is already swaying on his high barstool from that afternoon's drinking. Empty plastic shooter glasses are lined up in neat little rows in front of him. 'I mean, you're going to be a very important man soon, you know?'

'Sammy's got a point there,' says Franklin. 'Your position at Interpol is in Mason's hands now, and there's no telling what he'll want from you once you're over in Lyons.'

Swarts has been thinking many things about Harry Mason of late, but blackmail was never on that list. 'He's not the type,' he says eventually. 'I'm sure of it.'

'But you're convinced he might take this further?' asks Combrink.

He thinks back to the morning that Jeanie Mason came sprinting towards the hospital cafeteria where he and Tanya Fouché had been sitting over fresh cups of coffee and discussing the latest turn in Harry's recovery. The girl had kept screaming Tanya's name at the top of her lungs, and something else: 'Daddy's awake!' Despite remaining in Port Elizabeth to watch over Harry, Swarts had felt shame and trepidation at that same moment. Just the idea of speaking with Harry about what would come next filled him with anxiety. Up to that point he had pretended to himself that the Ntombini case no longer cast a shadow over them.

Tanya insisted that he join her right away in Harry's cubicle, and she would not let go of him until he agreed. The injured man had looked up as they walked in, eyes clear and eager on seeing her. But then his glance had fallen on Swarts and the hand Tanya was clutching, and it was in that gaze that Russell Swarts understood something of what was going on in Harry's head. He felt abysmal disappointment and hopelessness at the anger radiating off Harry; they were clearly enemies now, two men on opposite sides of the ring.

'What does he expect from you anyway?' Combrink asks. 'That you just hand yourself over to the ICD?'

'Things have changed between us since Tsolo,' Swarts says. 'He will come after me the moment he can, and I don't know if I can convince him otherwise. Besides, you forget that the ICD are already probing us.'

'Not over this, they aren't,' says Combrink. 'The payments made to Mason's contact followed proper procedure, so on that issue they have nothing on us. And the allegations made over a few sips of brandy, well . . .' Combrink shrugs, not overly concerned. 'I'll tell the judge in open court, it was fucking cold up there.'

Russell Swarts nods. 'If it even comes to that.'

Franklin lights a match and puts it to his pipe. 'This isn't about the drinking, and you know that. If he gets his way you'll be on a murder charge, and then they'll take a closer look at the rest of us, for sure.'

'*That* we don't need right now,' agrees Combrink.

'What are we going to do?' asks Naidoo. 'Hey, you guys, what are we going to do?'

There is an edge of panic to his voice that Swarts does not like. That will have to be taken care of at some point.

'If you knew about all the crap Mason was about to drag you through, why didn't you leave him there to bleed out his sorry life? If you hadn't saved that son of a bitch, we wouldn't be in this mess.'

The empty Tab can in Swarts' fist crumples like paper. Slowly, he turns on Franklin. 'I should deck you for that right here, James. Right-fucking-here! Where everyone can see what a piece of shit you can be.'

Franklin winks at him over the tip of his pipe. 'You try me, Russie.'

'I think—' begins Naidoo.

'The problem is that you don't think enough of anything, Sameer,' growls Swarts without taking his eyes off

Franklin. If he can't control James Franklin any more, he can at least keep the other two in check. 'You're as much a part of this mess as I am, so just sit right there like the blimming piece of furniture you are and shut up.'

'Sorry, Russie, I—'

'I meant it when I said shut up.'

Franklin's teeth show as his smile broadens. Blue smoke drifts slowly out of his mouth and envelops his face.

'When the two of you are finished jerking each other off like a bunch of schoolboys behind the bicycle shed, I suggest we think of something to do about Mason.' Combrink inspects his glasses in the light. Satisfied, he puts them back on. 'I for one don't feel like getting dragged into your shit, Russie. If you had told me about this in the first place, that would have been a different matter. But that you decided to hide this from us, when you knew—'

'What was I supposed to do? Let the bastard run scot-free till he blimming well stuck a gun in the next girl's mouth and pulled the trigger? No sir, not me.'

'I'm not talking about Ntombini.'

'How the hell was I supposed to know Bond would go digging around that episode ten years down the line?'

'Doesn't matter,' says Franklin. 'But the shit we're in now does.'

Swarts runs his hands over his face in an effort to calm himself down. 'Have you two found him yet? Makhe, I mean?'

'Don't change the subject,' says Franklin.

'Why don't you leave those Abasindisi alone for the time being, Russie?' asks Combrink. 'You've got enough on your plate as it is.'

'He's our blimming ticket out of this mess!'

Franklin shakes his head. 'Listen to yourself, Russie. The problem is you, and also it's Mason.'

'I'm getting another drink,' Naidoo says. 'Anyone else?'

When no one answers him, Naidoo scuttles off to the bar, probably as eager to be away from them as Swarts is to have him out of the way.

'The Abasindisi—' he begins.

'Screw them!' Franklin points a finger at him. 'And screw you, Russie!'

'What else do you want from me?' Swarts suddenly slams a fist down on the table so that drinks slosh in all directions. 'I come clean with you so that we can figure this out, and all you can do is shit on my doorstep and talk about what-ifs!'

Combrink ducks as though a gunshot had gone off, while a hundred-odd inquisitive faces turn in their direction. At the same time, Swarts notices the glass door to Maloney's swinging open at the far end of the bar. A second stranger enters, and in one hand he is strangely carrying a plastic bag very similar to that of the first man who had left in such a hurry. There is something familiar about his face, but Swarts is not overly concerned with that right now.

'What we want from you?' Franklin asks through clenched teeth. 'That's easy enough: take care of your problem before it becomes ours.'

'You know how it is, Russie.' Combrink shrugs uncomfortably. 'It shouldn't have turned out this way in the first place. But now that we're here, you need to *do* something.'

Swarts is about to retort when his eyes meet the stranger's. Since Swarts first spotted him, the newcomer has directly moved to the high table immediately behind Franklin and Combrink, without first collecting himself a drink from the bar. The man quickly glances away like a guilty pickpocket. *What exactly is it about him that is so damn familiar?* wonders Swarts. His mind begins to swarm with names and faces as his instincts start sounding alarm bells.

'Hear me, Russie?' Combrink draws his attention back to their conversation. 'It's plain decency for you to make a plan with Harry. Talk to him, threaten him, fucking take him out to the farm and promise him the world, I don't care.'

'You know what?' Swarts hears himself say. 'My problem would have been sorted out easily, if it wasn't for you. That's what the two of you are missing here.'

The stranger's eyes creep back in his direction to check whether he is still watching. And this time, when their eyes meet again, Swarts places him: Wally Khuzwayo, reputedly number three of the Abasindisi. It *must* be.

5

When he turns his eyes back towards Swarts' table and finds the *gata* still staring at him, Wally Khuzwayo knows he has been recognized. His gut clenches and his mind empties, but he manages to cling on to his cool.

Don't look down, he tells himself. *Whatever you do, don't look down now.*

If he does, he is convinced that Swarts will follow his gaze and notice the bag he is pushing under the table with his foot.

Yet to his utter surprise Swarts does nothing that

indicates he has recognized him, and instead turns back to some comment made by Combrink.

'I can't believe that, Kommie! From you?'

'Sorry.' Someone nudges Wally in the back with an elbow. 'If you don't mind, *bru*.'

He steps out of the way, and is surprised to find Naidoo trying to pass him, eyes fixed on the drinks in his hand.

'Cheers,' Naidoo says without looking up.

Wally's eyes flick back to Swarts, but the superintendent is embroiled in some heated argument with the other two *umlungus* over something that is evidently more important than his presence. He feels mildly insulted by this, but relieved, too.

Get going! he yells at himself. *What are you waiting for?*

Though overly conscious of the packet obscured beneath the table, and convinced he has been recognized by Russell Swarts, Wally cannot bring himself to flee. It is not that he is frozen with fear; instead, it is a thought that has just entered his mind that keeps him there. A choice, rather, for aren't these the men he first tried to contact through that idiot Makhe? Isn't one of them the person who agreed to his demands of a substantial reward and witness protection in exchange for information on the two brothers?

She's telling me to kill all the rats in the house: he can still hear Ncolela saying it.

There is no question about it, the brothers are on to him for the mess he created in Tsolo. Can it now be that salvation sits at this table of four? For him and his son? His wife?

Wally makes a quick decision to attract Swarts' attention, because this revelation suddenly feels sure and right, in light of the limbo he has been stuck in ever since he tried to free himself from the brothers.

6

Russell Swarts forces himself not to look at the man standing over there behind Combrink and Franklin, for fear of missing a single word uttered by those two arseholes sitting across from him. Up until today, he would never have thought them capable of what they are proposing. But here it is, all out in the open. It was one thing to eliminate a parasite like Ntombini – but Harry Mason?

'Think about it, Russie, if you can't turn him, what's the alternative?' Though his glasses are spit-polished clean by now, Combrink takes them off once more and re-examines them in the light. 'Do you really want to sit in the *tjoekie* while Bessie has to go back to work so that your boys can finish university? What about your pension? All because you rightly killed a piece of shit, and some idiot thinks otherwise?'

'Either way, you're screwed.' Franklin shoulders in on the conversation. It is as if they had been planning this little dialogue long before they heard the true story behind Ntombini. Perhaps even before Harry was shot in Tsolo.

Is that really Wally Khuzwayo standing there, or are you just seeing what you want to see?

' – dossier on you, you don't have to worry about *la France*. You better start worrying about Baba taking a keen interest in you when you drop that soap bar in the showers at Sun City, my friend.'

He couldn't be dumb enough to come in here, surely. What for?

'Russie, are you listening to us?'

'I don't believe I'm hearing this,' he says at last. 'The man's just come out of hospital, and you're spouting all this bullshit?'

From the corner of his eye, Swarts watches Naidoo push his way past the newcomer without looking up from the drinks pinched between both hands. If Russell Swarts had been more self-examining, it would have struck him that for the first time in nine years his mouth is not watering at the prospect of another drink. In fact, right now it has turned dry as bone.

'He's a fucking liability.'

'He'll come around!'

'Then make bloody well sure of it.'

'Bras, here we go!' Naidoo announces triumphantly and passes the drinks around. 'They're on me.'

Swarts takes advantage of the interruption to take a proper look at the man beyond Combrink, and is astonished to see him nod in greeting. So it must be Wally Khuzwayo. He looks older than Swarts remembers him from the crappy photos Crime Intelligence hold, and his eyes are a lot more sober.

Gutsy bastard, you! I'll give you that.

An involuntary smile creeps over Russell Swarts' lips. The man certainly has balls, more than the three vultures pecking away at him right now. But Khuzwayo does not notice the smile. Without waiting to gauge Swarts' reaction, he heads past the cigarette machine and down the dim corridor leading to the toilets at the rear.

'You still drinking, Russie?' Naidoo holds out a brandy

and Tab to him. 'Take it, wallah. I'm not your bloody butler.'

'The fuck's not even listening.' Franklin slurps foam off the top of his Red Heart and Coke. 'We're trying to save his arse, and the future of his sons, but do you think he's even interested?'

'Easy, Blondie,' says Combrink. 'No need to put it that way; though I would've thought his family deserves some consideration, at least.'

Swarts ignores these snide comments and slides off his barstool.

'Where are you going?'

'Where you belong, Franklin. I'm going to the pisser.' He tucks his shirt back into his pants. 'If I'd known things would turn out like this with you lot, I'd have given Ntombini my gun and asked him to finish me there and then.'

He surveys the three faces fixed on him and shakes his head. 'I've made my mistakes, sure, but there is no way another man is going to pay for them.'

7

Wally Khuzwayo stares at his own image in the mirror. He looks haggard. Mercurial droplets of water are caught in his curly hair and on his eyebrows after he has splashed water on his face. His heart feels like it is about to burst from his chest, and the acrid smell of long-standing piss hits the back of his throat with each hard, fast breath he inhales.

What has he done? Why the hell did he do this?

Under different circumstances he might easily have answered these questions: there is his son's future to think of, the scraps of money he's been earning compared to the brothers he works for. In other words, he might have given all the answers that first brought him to Makhe Motale, but right now they don't come to him. All he feels is the fear of a man who knows he has done wrong in the eyes of a system that can deprive him of his freedom till he's too old to tie his own fucking shoelaces.

Christ, what if he spots the bag tucked underneath the table?

Calm down, mfo.

If Swarts had noticed the bag, he who is Wally Khuzwayo would surely have been arrested by now. He just hopes to God it was Swarts with whom Makhe had been speaking, and not someone else. It must have been, though, or why else did Swarts not arrest him immediately? He must have been the one officer that Makhe trusted.

Wally has time to wonder how long Mokzin will now wait for him before he drives off, or does something worse, when the hydraulic arm of the lavatory door screeches open behind him.

His breath catches. In the reflection, he sees the door has opened to just a few inches. Momentarily, fingers creep around its edge and it is slowly pushed open all the way. One half of Swarts' face appears and cautiously peers inside. When he spots Wally Khuzwayo standing alone by the washbasins, he nimbly steps into the room, closes the door behind him and leans his bulk against it to keep it shut.

Swarts is not as fat as Ncolela, but he stands a good two feet taller and is clearly far more muscular. The look of their eyes, however, make them brothers. In his right hand is one of those fancy serrated flick-knives which Wally so often sees youngsters carry these days, clipped into the corners of their pants pockets.

'You by yourself in here?'

The man speaks in the kind of Afrikaans accent Wally has come to associate with all police officers – harsh and brutal, and nothing like the flighty tones used in the television soapies his wife watches constantly.

'Yes,' Wally answers in English.

'You armed?'

'No.'

'Keep your hands exactly where they are then.'

Wally remains as he is, with his back to Swarts and his hands on the basin rim. The mirror is large enough for him to watch the *gata* without having to turn around, and for the strangest moment he imagines himself entering the room. How many times did he corner someone this same way in a bathroom, to extract money from him or just beat the shit out of him? Far too often, is probably the answer.

'Wally Khuzwayo, isn't it?'

'That is right,' he replies, 'and you are Superintendent Russell Swarts.'

The *gata* grunts in acknowledgement. Obviously Swarts did not believe him when Wally claimed that he is alone here, because he sidles over to the three empty toilet cubicles and pushes the doors open one by one before he is satisfied.

'I want to speak with you,' says Khuzwayo.

'Shut up.'

'It was me that made contact with you through Makhe Motale.'

Their eyes meet in the mirror, and Wally sees no

gratitude in that gaze, no surprise – not even casual interest. Is it because the man hides his thoughts well, he wonders, or is it because he knows nothing of the bargain Wally tried to strike with the SVC? He hopes it is the former rather than the latter.

'Don't you understand English? I said shut the fuck up.'

Swarts grabs a mop kept in the little alcove beside the entrance door and wedges it under the door handle. Throughout all of this, the knife is held comfortably, and the ease with which he carries it leaves no doubt in Wally's mind that Swarts can easily defend himself with it, if it comes to that.

As Swarts tests his makeshift doorstop, Wally turns around to face him.

'The information I pass you, she was right. The weapons, they *were* there. I don't know what happen, but they should have been there. I swear it.'

Though he has his thoughts arranged in a straight line, his tongue refuses to find the English words to properly express them.

Swarts finally turns his full attention on Wally Khuzwayo. A light seems to have switched on in his face, which Wally now takes as a good sign. At least the *gata* appears to know what he is talking about. Even so, the knife remains pointed directly at him, the hand holding it as steady as a barber's wielding a razor.

'And the small army of *dagga* smugglers you had protecting the weapons? Were they supposed to be there too?'

'I make only the deal for the weapons. I tell you where they are, you fetch them. Those people, they not my problem.'

Swarts grunts. 'Convenient, that.'

'I keep my end of the bargain. Now your turn. I don't have my money. I don't have the protection. My son, she needs the school money. What must I do now?'

'What? The Phaliso brothers don't pay you well enough?' sneers Swarts. 'Is that why you're now stabbing them in the back? Why don't you ask your friend Makhe where your money is?'

'I can't.' Wally grimaces at the thought of that particular betrayal. Makhe Motale had come highly recommended as a trustworthy negotiator, and left him high and dry instead. 'I don't know where she is.'

Swarts laughs quietly. 'You're all the same, aren't you? Can't stop screwing each other over? It's genetic, I reckon.'

'Me and you, we are not so different.'

'Ha!'

'We try to make the living with what we have. I make peace in the places you will not go, the same way you keep the peace in the places where I have never lived.' Wally nods at the knife in Swarts' hand. 'With that we do our jobs. The government, she make you a police man. The people, they make me their guardian. If they did not want us, I would not have been so busy.'

The police officer takes a threatening step towards Wally. 'Don't for a second pretend to me that you're some kind of protector of the people. Abasindisi, my arse! If you were trying to make a decent living, you'd be working down a blimming mineshaft like everyone else. You're here because you always did what you blimming well pleased, and now that the game's finally up, when I'm so close on your heels you can smell my sweet rosy breath, you start to shit your pants and turn on the hands that feed you.'

He glares at Wally, then adds, 'You're not getting anything from me, *chommie*, understand that?'

'But you must hold up your end of the bargain!'

If only he could speak to this idiot properly in his own language, Wally knows he could convince him that they have a common goal.

'I must? My end? First of all, I didn't make a deal with you. Second, your first instalment was paid into the account that was passed to us, the whole twenty grand. I co-signed the goddamned order myself because my boss agreed to this senseless idea. But hey, if that's what it took for him to stay with us on this case, then I don't care. Third, I don't have any weapons in hand. Fourth, the Phalisos are not behind bars, and the people who turned Comrade Mohosh into *flambé* are still out there.' The *gata*'s mouth turns up in an ugly sneer. 'But what I *do* have is a whole lot of trouble, and I have you here to take it out on.'

'You got some of the guns. I read the newspaper articles. That is where I know your face from. What you blow up, she is my proof. If you found those, then you should have found the other AKs also. I want the money and I want the protection for my son. I want to leave here, take him where it is safe.'

Swarts shakes his head. 'You don't get it, do you? I'm not offering you or your dirty *piccanin* safety. You can just forget it.'

Wally opens his mouth to protest but Swarts silences him.

'Tell me, there was a fire back in February. A minor ANC politician got cooked in his house in Diepsloot, along with his wife and son. That was you arseholes, wasn't it?'

Wally frowns. 'I don't remember.'

'It *was* your lot! I *know* it was. Mohosh was the guy's name.'

Wally straightens up. 'Could be. So what?'

Swarts shakes his head. 'You burn up a man and his son, maybe because he didn't pay his membership dues, or because he threatened to shut down your bosses, and then you ask me to protect you and yours? But God in heaven, you're an arrogant one, kuzzie.'

'Mohosh, she was stealing the community blind. The people, they take that decision, not us. We only exercise the will of the people.' Wally Khuzwayo allows a smile to spread over his face. 'Why you think no one speak to you? The people, they protect themselves, not us. There is no chance they will tell you we did this thing for them, because they know we will either bring them to you, or take care of them ourselves.'

The police officer rocks back on his heels in sudden delight. 'That there sounds like a confession to me, *chommie*. OK, turn around.'

'Why?' Wally asks defiantly.

Swarts reaches back with his left hand and brings out an old-fashioned pair of steel handcuffs. 'You're under arrest, that's why.'

'Fuck you, Swarts! I'm telling you all this to show you we want the same thing.'

'Let's get one thing straight: you don't even know me, and you certainly don't know what I want.'

The *gata* takes another step closer, and Wally realizes he has overplayed his hand. All his cards are gone – but one.

'You are not arresting me.'

'Don't make me get nasty, Khuzwayo. You don't want to do that, I promise you.'

Wally smiles bitterly. 'You're all the same, aren't you? You think because you have the gun, the uniform, you are the only ones able to make others do what you want? That is rubbish!'

Instead of reacting to the taunt, the cop returns the smile. 'I guess we are all the same, then, us cops. Just like you people are all the same. But the difference is, sooner or later you get to sit up in Sun City with forty fucks just like yourself and one crusty bucket to shit in between all of you, while I get to go home to my wife and a warm dinner every evening.'

Swarts lobs the handcuffs at him and Wally Khuzwayo catches them mid-air. He opens his hand and studies them.

'I know you've never worn a pair of those before, otherwise I would've been on your doorstep long before the first bird ever caught its worm. But I'm sure you know how they work, so put them on.'

Wally glances at Swarts with the realization that he has made all the wrong decisions after all, which is perhaps why it has always been better for the Phalisos to make them in the first place. He should never have tried to sell them out, and he should never have trusted a god-damned *gata* in the first place – or some guy on a skateboard either. Looking at the self-satisfied grin on Swarts' face, and knowing what the Phalisos still suspect him of, Wally decides he would rather take his chances with the brothers. At least those are the devils he knows.

He closes his hand over the handcuffs, pulls back his arm and throws.

8

Wally Khuzwayo's aim is as true as the day he managed to hit a sparrow mid-flight with a stone when he was sixteen years old. The handcuffs streak straight for the *gata*'s face, and even before Swarts' arm comes up to deflect the projectile Wally kicks off from the washbasin cupboard with one leg and propels himself forward.

He slams into the cop and pushes the arm with the knife up high over their heads. Simultaneously he throws his forehead forward as hard as he can, and it connects firmly with the man's cheekbone. Swarts grunts in pain as he stumbles backward into one of the lavatory doors. It flies open and he is firmly dumped on the seat of an open toilet.

Without waiting to see him get up, Wally dives for the exit, yanks the mop out from underneath the door handle and ducks into the short dark passageway beyond. Spotting a fire extinguisher a few paces ahead of him, he yanks the heavy cylinder out of its bracket just as the door to the lavatories crashes open behind him. For a moment it looks like Ncolela's silhouette there in the doorway, but no, it is Swarts.

'Kommie!' roars the towering shadow. 'Blondie! Get this fuck!'

Wally bolts into the bright bar area of Maloney's, with its television sets, green chequered carpet, police-service rugby-team memorabilia, just as a hundred or so cops turn in his direction. Hands freeze in the act of bringing drinks up to thirsty mouths, eyes open wide, conversation hits the floor like a ten-ton weight crashing down twenty storeys of surprise.

Maye babo!

In his flight he had forgotten exactly what he was running into. Barely slowing, though, he ducks to the right, in the direction of the large windows facing on to the street. To his relief he sees no one has yet settled in this faraway corner of the bar so early in the evening. Hefting the heavy fire extinguisher over his head, Wally throws it – and hopes to dear God the window is not made of reinforced glass.

'Hey, that's Wally Khuzwayo!' shouts a voice.

The window replies with a thousand shattered tinkles.

More deftly than he would have believed himself capable of at forty-nine, Wally springs on to the corner booth's stained upholstery, then its scarred wooden table-top, then leaps right through the broken window itself.

But just as he believes himself free, his foot snags on the remains of the frilly curtain that normally hangs at a seated customer's eye level.

9

As Russell Swarts plunges into the bar after the fugitive Khuzwayo, he spots Franklin and half a dozen off-duty cops go for their side-arms. Glass shatters over to his immediate right, and he glances that way in time to see Khuzwayo step up on to a table.

'Stop! You can't shoot in here!' shouts an aged voice that will later be identified as belonging to a judge nearing retirement.

But the warning comes too late. Three shots crack deafeningly in the confines of the bar, just as Wally's left foot becomes entangled. His elegant leap for safety abruptly turns into a floundering fall. A bullet splinters the wooden windowframe above his head, a second punches through a parked car's rear side window. The third hits a gaping woman passer-by in the throat. Wally Khuzwayo disappears outside.

'Jesus, hold your fire!'

'Sammy, up front! Kommie, Blondie, with me!' Swarts streaks for the window, without even considering whether they will back him up or not. To him it is still a certainty that they know exactly what is expected of them as his team members.

He too gets a foot up on the booth cushioning, but the clumsy angle at which it sinks into the padding tilts him to one side. Swarts curses loudly as he is forced to drop his knife and lunge for support before he falls over. Steadying himself, he pulls out his personal side-arm – a Glock the size and weight of a brick – and vaults on to the table. Broken glass crunches everywhere underfoot.

The first thing he sees on the street beyond is a pavement also covered in crushed glass, which is stained pink with blood. Pedestrians lie on their stomachs everywhere, hands covering their heads. The woman who was hit by the stray bullet is kneeling in the gutter, her handbag's contents scattered over the sidewalk. Her frame shakes as she desperately tries to draw her last breaths.

A crunch of glass draws Swarts' attention to the left, where Khuzwayo, his forearms bleeding from landing heavily on the shattered glass, drops a shoe still entangled in the net curtaining and its rod, and runs straight into the path of the traffic. As Swarts brings up his gun, the man starts waving his arms and shouting in a language he does not understand.

Whatever his words are and whoever they are directed

at, they work magic on the prone pedestrians. All around, those who can understand him abruptly jump to their feet and bolt in all directions.

'*Get down!*' yells Swarts.

Two shots ring out to his left, but they narrowly miss Khuzwayo as he slides over the bonnet of a stalled navy BMW. Swarts glances in that direction and spots Naidoo braced against a lamppost, tracking Khuzwayo with his gun.

Franklin shoulders past Swarts and jumps out into the street, while Kommie clambers up on to the booth table behind him.

'*Chips!* Lemme pass.'

'Wait,' mutters Swarts.

Glad to keep this elevated position, Russie Swarts steadies his pistol with both hands and takes careful aim. He breathes in slowly and waits for his own shot.

People flit in all directions like a nest of angry hornets. There is hysterical screaming everywhere, and cars swerve to miss running bystanders and stalled vehicles alike. Drivers and their passengers scatter, while shouts echo down the street from the direction of the High Court. None of this matters to Russell Swarts, however. For him there is only Khuzwayo. No, not even him. Only fleeing prey which he must take down.

On the other side of the road a beaten-up Passat rams a shiny Audi and forces its way into a relatively clear space between the two lanes. Khuzwayo screams some kind of order to the Passat's driver as he bolts past the front of the car, and points in Swarts' direction.

Naidoo fires twice more, but both shots miss.

Swarts's own finger tightens by a hair's breadth on the trigger of the Glock.

A woman in pink, carrying two children and being chased by a third, dashes right across his firing line just as he is about to shoot.

'Take the fucking shot, Russie!' yells Franklin. 'What are you waiting for?'

His breath is still held comfortably, and he can feel his heart rate steady. He knows it will be a good shot once his line of vision clears. He will fire at the apex of his inhalation, the way he was taught, the way he has fired his pistol a thousand times at the shooting range.

'*Russie!*' Naidoo suddenly shouts in horror from the bar's doorway. '*GET—*'

The world clears of everything else as his clean shot finally appears. There is now nothing but the steel trace of the pistol's barrel connecting to Khuzwayo's brow.

Swarts exhales.

10

The pipe bomb that was hidden in a plastic shopping bag left under the table in Maloney's is three times the size of the device that tore Superintendent Russie Swarts' partner in half over a decade ago.

It detonates at the touch of a button in Mokzin's hand.

Four kilograms of tightly packed potassium nitrate rip through reinforced-steel piping. The table under which the bomb was hidden is thrown into the air. Nails, screws, ball-bearings the size of marbles scream in every direction. The wall-length mirror that was bought in '65, hundreds of glasses and dozens of bottles, disintegrate into a maelstrom of glittering shards which strip old Hugh Semenya of skin and life. The corner booth table on which

Senior Superintendent Russell Swarts and Captain Rayno Combrink are standing tips over a split second before the shrapnel rips through Combrink's body.

The last thing Swarts remembers is a thunder louder than the Apocalypse, and a shove from behind so violent that he is lifted right across the pavement and straight into a parked vehicle.

11

Despite the distraction the explosion should have created for the police, bullets punch through the Passat's windshield. Flowers of crushed white glass bloom on the windows and severed shards spray over Wally Khuzwayo. But miraculously he is not hit.

'Where's all this shit coming from?' Mokzin yells.

God, oh God, get me out of this!

Wally is crouching as far down in the passenger seat as he can manage when he realizes most of the gunfire is concentrated on his side of the car. The High Court side.

The High Court!

'Drive! Drive, you fuck!'

'What do you think I'm doing?'

The old Passat engine is already screaming in first gear as Mokzin batters their way through the stalled traffic. Metal screeches against metal as the wing mirrors are sheared off against other vehicles. Doors buckle; the chassis groans like a sinking ship. Then there is a terrific bang from underneath, and suddenly the vehicle is pulling to the left.

'Tyre's burst!' shouts Wally.

'Who's shooting at us? I can't see through this shit!'

'*Gatas!* Who the fuck do you think!'

'Where are they?'

'There!' Wally points at two uniforms weaving through the traffic from the direction of the High Court. 'They're trying to head us off.'

'What now?'

'Turn!'

'Where to?'

The steel rim of the front tyre radial grates on tar, and they both duck when another bullet punctures the windshield and clips the headrest just inches away from the top of Wally's head.

'Fucking turn or we're dead!'

'Use your gun!'

'I don't *have* a gun.'

'You don't?' Incredulous, Mokzin stares in wide-eyed wonder at Wally. 'Did I hear you right?'

'*He banna*, I wasn't exactly planning on taking on the whole Jozi police force when I woke up this morning. That way!' He points at a narrow gap as it opens suddenly between a white delivery van with W.A.R. SECURITY stamped on its side and a vehicle speeding eastwards.

Mokzin yanks the steering wheel hard right and swerves through the gap, right into oncoming traffic. Hardly a hundred metres down the road from where they first started, the congestion is already clearing as other drivers race away from the scene. Cars have to swerve to miss the banged-up Passat; horns beep; tyres screech. One driver shoots straight across their path and mounts the kerb to crash into a shopfront. As Wally is about to tell Mokzin to turn back before he kills both of them, the boxer swings the sluggish vehicle hard left and cuts back into the eastbound lane.

Yelling for joy at the deft manoeuvre, Wally glances back at an unexpected tapping sound on the rear window of the driver's side.

'Shit!' cries Wally and ducks.

There is a deafening roar as glass showers across the front half of the car.

12

'Russie! Wake the hell up, Russie!'

It was not the shouting of his name that brought him around, nor was it the rough slap across his face. The distraught wailing of a grown man did the trick, however, along with cordite stinging Swarts' nose and the back of his throat.

Bomb!

Russell Swarts opened his eyes to find James Franklin hunched over him, a mixture of apprehension and determination writ large on his face.

The man who had been belittling him barely half an hour ago was now grasping Russie's face in two hands. 'You all right? Nod if you're OK.'

His ears rang like school bells, and though he could hardly hear the man speaking to him, he nodded. Confused memories began to flow back: Wally Khuzwayo turning to face him from across the street, then . . .

'Russie, speak to me! Your eyes are rolling again, *boet*!'

Swarts refocused and noticed the gawping strangers clustered around him. He immediately felt claustrophobic and self-conscious lying there on the pavement, exposed and vulnerable to these total strangers. Gingerly, he tested the muscles of his body and found them to be working fine, though they burned and ached all over.

'Let me up,' he croaked.

As he staggered to his feet he heard fresh gunfire break out, but the sound reached him hollowly like a message down a string into a tin can.

'There they are.'

'Who?'

'Here.' Franklin slapped something heavy into his hand and closed his fingers over it. A pistol. Its weight was solid and reassuring. Then Franklin grabbed him by the shoulder and propelled him through the ring of bystanders. 'Let's go while we can still catch them.'

Russell Swarts stumbled the first few steps, but found his balance was coming back fast enough.

'Move it, Russie!' Franklin nudged him as they jogged side by side. 'The old Passat, see it?'

He pointed across the road at a heavily dented car ramming its way down the narrow corridor between two eastbound lanes. Inside were two figures, and he recognized Wally Khuzwayo as one of them.

'I see it. But where are the others?'

Franklin did not even hear him, as he sprinted on ahead. Still gathering speed, Swarts threw a quick glance over his shoulder towards the crowd.

At the centre of a ring of bystanders, Naidoo sat on his haunches in a field of glittering light, and in his arms he cradled Combrink. Besides the copious blood quickly pooling on the pavement, there was a rag-doll look about the man's body which left no doubt in Swarts' mind that the detective would never be polishing his broken glasses again. Then the crowd of civvies shifted, closing the circle and cutting off his view.

Where most people might have faltered or even turned back at the disturbing sight, Russell Swarts barely missed a step. For now there was only one thing to do: get Khuzwayo, at all costs.

Within seconds he was racing past Franklin in their mad dash eastward. His eyes traced the Passat's slow progress through the stalled traffic as he ran, and when one of its tyres burst, he cheered silently and redoubled his efforts. The distance between the car and himself began to close rapidly. Then it suddenly lurched into the oncoming lanes on his side of Prichard Street, and when the driver hit the brakes and swerved to avoid hitting another vehicle, Swarts knew he would have his man.

He dashes into the street and lays a hand on the car's boot for support. Clawing his way up alongside the rear passenger door, he raises his pistol and takes rough aim. The tip of his pistol cracks against the glass of the rear-side window just a split second before he fires.

13

The deafening roar inside the car does not end with just one gunshot. Suddenly there is more blood than when Wally Khuzwayo finally put an AK-47 to the back of Ephraim Thekiso's head and pulled the trigger. Mokzin bucks and jerks in the driver's seat with each shot before he slumps over the steering wheel. The vehicle immediately swerves back into oncoming traffic, and Wally barely has enough time to reach for the steering wheel before the Passat slams into a parked car. What little is left of the windscreen caves inwards and diamonds of glass scatter all over the dashboard and into his lap. He fumbles open the release on his seatbelt, throws open the door.

'Hey, Khuzwayo!'

He looks up just in time to catch sight of two blow-torch eyes, a split second before Franklin's heavy boot connects squarely with his nose. A bright flash goes off behind Wally's eyelids and he falls back against Mokzin's lifeless body.

'China,' he hears through swirls of fuzzy sound. 'You're going to wish you were dead by the time I'm through with you.'

There is a joy in the other man's voice that reminds Wally of the grim delight Ncolela used to take in hurting people. He is still struggling to sit up when he feels two hands encircle his ankles. A sharp tug pulls him from the car, and the back of his head hits the doorsill shortly before it smacks against the blacktop. A cry of pain escapes his lips.

'Get the fuck out of my way!' he hears a familiar voice shout. 'I'm going to put a blimming bullet in his face.'

Run! screams his mind. But how can he, when his legs are butter and there is no strength left in his arms?

'No, Russie!'

Get up, run!

There is a scuffle nearby as Wally rolls on to his stomach and then pushes himself up on all fours. His teary eyes focus on the bright droplets of blood hitting the asphalt.

'Let me at him!' The man sounds like a raging bull. 'The fuck killed Kommie!'

'I said not here, Russie. This is an open street. There are people around. We'll take him to Motale.'

'What are you talking about?'

'I have him, Makhe Motale.'

'Since when?'

'Relax, Russie. You can have him after he tells us where there are more weapons.'

'What the hell are you on about? Kommie's blimming well *dead*!'

'Watch it, here come the High Court boys. You do the talking, Russie. But keep it calm.'

Wally shakes his head in an unsuccessful attempt to clear away the dizziness. Through the tears brimming in his eyes from a broken nose, he sees the two *gatas* looming nearby; Franklin has two fistfuls of Swarts' shirt in his hand and is straining against the other man's greater strength. Somewhere close by a powerful engine is roaring towards them, and Wally remembers that he is lying in the middle of the street, where he could get run over any minute. Whether it signifies more police arriving, or an ambulance, he cannot tell, but he just hopes it is the latter.

Swarts notices him and spits in his direction. 'Don't you blimming well look at me like that, Khuzwayo!'

Suddenly the engine which has been approaching fast drops into a lower gear, and the roar of it climbs several notches.

'Wha—? Shit, Russie!'

There is no time for Wally to peer around the open car door at what they are seeing. He only notices alarm register on their faces, a moment before they scatter. Then an olive-green Prado screeches to a halt over the spot in the street where the two *gatas* had been arguing a moment ago. A cloud of burnt rubber drifts past the vehicle and envelops Wally. He closes his eyes against the blue smoke, but cannot stop himself from inhaling it. He starts coughing uncontrollably, and his world, which has been swimming dazedly the last two minutes, begins to darken.

The high chatter of automatic gunfire shreds the air. Wally hears car doors slam open over the din, and heavy shoes hit the asphalt near his head. He forces back the darkness threatening to overcome him, and gropes for the car door to steady himself. His hand lands not on cold steel, however, but in a warm palm. A vice-like grip closes around his fingers and yanks him to his feet as though he is no more than a toddler that has stumbled.

'Wally,' rumbles a deep voice by his ear, 'your brothers are here, and family always look after their own, don't they?

'Come,' says that same voice. 'You are going home.'

EIGHT

1

Detective Jacob Tshabalala is comparing the faded sign writing on the bare-brick façade of a seven-storey high-rise to a name he hastily scribbled on a scrap of paper – *Copacabana Luxury Suites*, it reads – when thunder echoes through downtown from somewhere to the west. Thinking he might have missed a sudden change in the weather, he glances up at the sky visible above the budding liquid-ambar and jacaranda trees, but finds it still pale blue with no sign of rain. As the echo rolls away it is replaced by whirring car alarms, the barking of backyard dogs and the suspicious silence of sparrows in the trees.

Must be bringing down one of the older buildings in the centre, he thinks.

Studying the array of apartment numbers next to the intercom, Jacob mulls over the conversation he had not half an hour ago, which promptly led him here. The woman speaking on the phone had sounded oddly familiar to him, though when he asked her her name, she gruffly told him it was none of his business and hung up.

Her call had been a godsend. Chasing this lead was better than listening to the hogwash being fed to them at the office, and right before the weekend too: specialized units nationwide are being given assurances that there will be no reintegration into station-level policing after all. Instead, the project is being shelved for the next two years, they are saying, due to the 'reprioritization of resources'. Police officers vying for transfers can therefore rest assured that their current positions and pay will remain intact.

Whatever, he thinks. It is the fourth time this year that the official message has been changed, and a lot of the officers, himself included, are getting fed up with the continuing confusion. He wishes he knew how the politicians expected the men on the street to do their job when they could not be reassured about where they might be in three months' time – retrenched, reassigned, promoted, *de*moted. The mood all around was brooding as he ducked out of the common room to answer the phone call, and it will no doubt be getting worse as the evening wears on in drinking holes like Maloney's.

He is about to press one of the buttons when the gate is buzzed open and a young mother, carrying on her back a child wrapped in a yellow blanket, holds it open for him. He crosses the ground-level parking lot and heads up a broad flight of stairs leading into the apartment building's foyer. Inside it is much warmer, thanks to the bright orange sunlight splashing through large windows on to a garishly patterned mosaic floor. At the rear of the reception area, a gaggle of obvious hookers – all PVC hot-pants and low-cut tank tops – are seated on either the lower step of a stairwell or on bright green plastic footstools. Two of them are braiding the hair of another pair seated in front of them, while the rest are gossiping aloud over some R'n'B star of whom Jacob has never even heard. He greets them as he approaches.

'Sistahs, can you tell me, does anyone live in Room 315?'

Their conversation dies instantly, and uncomfortable glances are passed back and forth between the six of them till one of the braiders, a girl in her late teens with a wad of luminous pink bubblegum in her mouth, eventually answers.

'No one lives there. Why?'

'Has someone been staying there recently?'

'You police?'

'I am, yes. Murder and Robbery.'

Careful not to let her eyes wander from the braiding task at hand, she shrugs. 'Don't know. It's a big building, right, girls?' There is nervous agreement all round. 'Yes, it's very big, and I'm not around much.'

'Is there a building manager?'

'No, he left a few weeks ago. There hasn't been anyone yet to replace him.'

'Was his name Ephraim?'

'Can't remember.'

'You can't even remember the name of the person who collected your rent every month?'

'No.' She stops plaiting and glares at him, and the defiance in that gaze is louder than words. Once she is convinced that he has understood her meaning – that she does not want him to ask any more questions – she resumes her braiding with such vicious energy that the girl benefiting from her attention hisses in sudden pain.

'What about the rest of you?' He tries unsuccessfully to meet their eyes one at a time.

One shrugs. 'Might have been.'

'I know there was a Mister E living here. Thought he had sunshine coming out of his butt. Don't know if that was him, though.'

'Fucking lord 'n' mastah!' cries a particularly rotund young woman in English, her gravelly voice remarkably similar to the late James Brown. 'And had a snake no longer than my pinkie, I tell you.'

Abrupt howls of laughter erupt, and Jacob is left to wonder exactly what he might be missing here.

'Don't!' a sickly girl no older than sixteen shouts.

'So the name does mean something to you?' he interrupts.

'Means nothing to me.'

'Less than dirt.'

'Ephraim?' says another. 'Never heard of him.'

'No, definitely not.'

'Why are you asking? Did you forget to pay your rent?'

'No, sistah, I—'

'This one here can pay his rent to me, that's for sure. By the looks of him, I'll even give him a discount.'

Fresh hoots of mirth explode in the foyer, and an embarrassed smile forces its way on to Jacob's lips. 'Thank you for the compliment, but my rent's already been spoken for.'

When Jacob glances at the frail girl again, he notices that, compared with the rest of the women, she seems incredibly anxious about the direction of the conversation.

'Girl, I don't believe you just said that to a cop.'

'What? All I said was that I have a home for him *and* his money. Can't a girl tell a man she's all his if he treats her right?'

'Stop it!' The frail girl leaps to her feet and throws down the copy of *Heat* magazine she has anxiously wound up tight. 'You're so stupid!'

'Relax, Talitha. Don't get your knickers in a twist: they might just snap your itty-bitty bones in half,' the rotund woman calls after the teen as she storms away up the stairs. 'There's no law against some fun, is there? Not even here!'

The woman who first addressed Jacob loudly pops her

pink bubblegum. 'Why don't you go up to 315 yourself? There's no one living there, promise. I'll hold your hand, if you want. We can even check the bed, see if anyone's hiding under the sheets.'

The last sentence she covers with enough honey and midnight velvet to make Jacob blush and glance away.

'Might be hiding under the bed too,' quips another.

'Maybe inside the cupboard. You ever try that?'

'No, too cramped for me.'

'Kitchen. Could be hiding in the kitchen. That's where I'd do it if it wasn't in my place.'

'Hell, girls, lets *all* help him check the place, what do you say?'

'Otherwise he might be here bothering us all afternoon.'

Jacob quickly steps over to the lift and presses the call button, in the hope of a graceful exit before he is tempted to join in the laughter himself. Their banter has lifted his spirits higher than he has felt in days, what with the death of his father and then Nomsa treating him with an unexplained reserve since the funeral.

'Tell me, detective, are you thinking of staying the night?'

'No.'

'Because the rooms here get quite cold in winter, especially the ones on the third floor, or so they keep telling me. Just let me know if I can bring you a blanket, maybe something else to warm you up.'

'If I get stranded here, I'll ask you about some hot chocolate.'

'I'm hot and I'm coco too, honey,' calls out the rotund woman as she rolls her hips provocatively at him. 'It just depends if you want some cream with it.'

Jacob shakes his head at these comments. If anything, their obvious refusal to discuss Ephraim Thekiso is proof enough that he has not been led astray by the telephone call. When the lift finally arrives, he turns and bows to the five remaining women and thanks them for their hospitality, to a round of applause.

2

The lift wheezes open on the third floor, and Jacob Tshabalala steps out into a cold draught that whistles around the corners of passageways exposed to the elements. Rows of eggshell-coloured doors stretch along the wings of a horseshoe-shaped high-rise complex whose lift and main stairwell occupy one central shaft. Three storeys down, a smattering of cars are parked on the cracked tarmac of the courtyard. There is no pool or garden here, not even a common basketball hoop provided for children. But there seems to be peace, at least. Though the city's hum is audible in the distance, he finds it surprising how quiet this inner-city locale is; he can barely hear the taxis twitter to potential customers on Wolmarans Street, despite the fact that hundreds of people live stacked on top of each other around here.

He glances at a faded plaque signposting the apartment numbers, and heads down the right-hand passageway towards 315, which is situated at the very end of the wing.

'Are you the one who wants to know about that dead guy?' the woman had asked in Sotho the moment he picked up the receiver. She must have been phoning from a phone booth or stall, because in the background he could hear bustling street life. 'The whipped one in the river, with the bedsheet covering him. Like they said on the TV?'

He had purposefully left references to the sjambok lashes out of the *Police Files* television report, and included only the sheet and a rough description of the man's age and build. So when she mentioned the whipping, he immediately paid attention.

'Could you tell me who you are and where you're phoning from, please?' he had asked.

Ignoring him, she said, 'That hyena at least deserves to be buried with a name.'

'Who?' he had asked.

'Ephraim.'

'Why are you so convinced the person I'm looking for is this Ephraim?'

'It happened last week Thursday.'

Give or take a day, that also added up.

'Do you have a surname for me, an address where you last saw him?

'I don't know what his surname was. You go to Copacabana Suites in Joubert Park. Room 315. People there should know.' Her voice moved away from the receiver as though she was about to hang up.

'Wait!' he urged the woman. 'If this person you're talking about was killed, who do you think did it?'

'I don't know who they were, except it was two men. And they had friends, too. I only heard the one speak, though. An older guy.'

'Was there a gunshot?'

'No. I just told you they beat him to death. Aren't you listening? They killed him in the passageway and dragged him away. They wanted people in the building to hear him die.'

'Why?'

'They said he was a thief.'

'What did Ephraim do?'

'He was the landlord.'

'I mean, what did he do wrong?'

'You go speak to the people there. They'll tell you. They must.'

That was when the phone cut off, as if she had run out of airtime.

Room 315. The door looks as unremarkable as all the others, though the narrow kitchen window next to it has not been cleaned in a while, perhaps for years. He throws a quick eye over the bare concrete floor of the passageway, but sees no sign of the brutal death at which the woman had hinted. Further along the passageway is nothing but a brick wall with a rolled-up fire hose.

Jacob knocks firmly on the door and steps away. Somewhere close by a television rumbles, and in the courtyard below a bunch of kids are chasing each other around noisily. In the distance, it sounds like a dozen emergency vehicles are converging on what must have been a major traffic accident in the city bowel, probably caused by someone taking the Joe Slovo Drive turn-off like it was still the freeway.

When no one answers the door he raps on the painted wood again, a lot harder.

'Who's there?' barks a woman's voice from next door.

The front door to 314 opens up and a key rattles in the ornate reinforced-steel security gate barring the entrance. Out steps a woman who is large by all measures – easily over six feet, and looking fit to wrestle an ox to the ground without breaking a sweat. In her arms a podgy baby is contentedly suckling at its bottle of warmed milk.

'What do you want?' she demands.

'*Dumela*, sistah. My name is Jacob Tshabalala, and I am with the police. Is Ephraim Thekiso here, or anyone who knows him?'

'Ephraim? He left two weeks ago.'

'Do you happen to know where he went?'

'No, I don't,' she says firmly.

'Did you see him go?'

'He just left. Now will you stop making such a racket? You're going to wake up the other kids.'

'Who's there?' a rough male voice hollers over the din of a television inside the woman's apartment. With the door open, Jacob can hear an American wrestling show on the box.

'The *gatas*,' she calls back over her shoulder. 'They're looking for that shit Ephraim.'

'Tell them he's gone.'

The child in the woman's arms grows restless, and she begins to bounce it up and down to sooth its uncomfortable squirming. 'You heard my husband. Ephraim, he just packed up one night and left.'

'Are you sure?'

'Are you saying I'm a liar?'

'Why are they still there?' yells the man from inside the apartment.

'I don't know!' the woman shouts back. 'Why don't you get off the couch for once and ask him yourself?'

From back down the concrete passageway Jacob hears an angry shout, shortly before a group of about a dozen people appear, headed up by the same emaciated teenage girl who had been sitting downstairs, and also by a stocky man as angular as an anvil.

'And this?' Jacob nods at the approaching crowd.

The woman has already turned around to see what the gathering ruckus is about, and once she sees the approaching group, she tightens her hold on the baby and hurries back into her apartment.

'Jovial!' she yells.

'What!'

'Get out here, quickly.'

A man wearing only a pair of unbuttoned jeans revealing yellowed white jocks appears at the door to number 314, with a can of cider in one hand. He glances curiously at the approaching crowd, then turns his eyes on Jacob.

'Tell him to leave.' The woman flattens the man against the wall as she presses past him. 'I don't want more trouble around the kids.'

'She told you that Ephraim isn't here,' says Jovial. 'And nothing happened next door either, because we would have known.'

Jacob faces him squarely. 'I don't remember saying that anything happened here?'

The blocky little man leading his column like a cadre draws up next to the neighbour, and indicates for his followers to quieten down.

'You a police officer?' he asks Jacob.

'Yes, Murder and Robbery. And you? What can I call you by?'

The man ignores the question. 'These days anyone can say they're Murder and Robbery and pretend they're a police officer. I hear the police even rent out their uniforms and guns, so why should we believe you?'

'I have identification,' says Jacob.

'Let's see it then.'

He pulls out his wallet and holds up an ID card for the man to study. As he does this, Jacob makes eye contact with the squeamish teenager and is surprised to find her staring right back at him without any of the anxiety she showed earlier. His gaze wanders over the rest of the group, and finds their reaction towards him as hostile as hers.

The man heading the group steps forward and grabs Jacob's ID card.

'Well?' asks a woman's voice from the back. 'Is he for real?'

'If he is one, he has a lot to answer for.'

'Doesn't look like a policeman to me,' says another voice.

'You mean you've actually seen one to know what it looks like?' The woman's voice drips with sarcasm.

'Now hang on,' Jacob holds up his hands, 'is there something I can help you people with?'

'Help? You?' An elderly woman with a blossom-patterned *doek* over her head pushes forward. 'There's no help that's ever come from you lot. What do you want here, hey?'

'Detective Inspector Jacob Tshabalala.' The stocky man looks up from the card in his hand. 'That's what it says here, and looks like you, too. '

'I would like to speak with Ephraim Thekiso, who I understand was a manager here till two weeks ago.' Jacob holds out his hand for the identification card, but the man shows no inclination to return it. 'And I'll have that back, please,' he adds.

The man taps the card on his thumb a few times before holding it up. 'This?'

A few whistles and uncomfortable laughs ripple through the group.

'Yes, that.'

'Here you go, detective.' The man flips the card back to Jacob. 'There is no need to take that tone of voice with me, though. You can talk to me like you talk to your family – with some respect.'

Jacob stuffs the card back into his wallet, and tries his best not to show his growing anxiety about this unexpected hostility. 'Now, about Thekiso . . . ?'

'That filth!' The elderly woman with the *doek* shakes her gnarled fist at him. 'Why do you care about him when there are real people suffering here?'

'*Magogo*, why is it that you call him filth?'

'We had to pay rent when sluts like that Gladys screwed him instead.'

'And where has he gone now?'

'Who cares? Away.'

'At least now we know our rent isn't going to be wasted on drugs.'

Jacob looks the group over and tries to gauge exactly what he needs to do to turn their mood. 'People, please, I need you to tell me, one by one, what happened here. If there's a problem here, I'll hear it the moment I know a little more about what happened.'

'Yes, we always come last, *né*?'

To tell people in this mood to calm down is like putting a match to dry hay, so Jacob folds his arms across his chest, sets his feet further apart and raises his voice. 'That is not true, and we can talk about why it's not true later. Right now, though, I need to know more about Ephraim Thekiso. And for that I need to get into this apartment. Who do I speak to about taking a look inside?'

'There is no one in charge here any more.'

'No?'

'Who is it that told you Ephraim Thekiso disappeared anyway from here?' the stocky man demands.

'That's none of your business,' says Jacob.

'We have a right to know who is gossiping behind our backs.' The man raises his voice. '*Hé?*'

The group surrounding him agrees in loud unison.

The spokesman nods sagely at their answer, and turns his eyes back on Jacob, as if to confirm whether he understands in which direction they are going. 'Who has accused us?'

'No one's accused you. I just want a look around.'

'And where is your search warrant, Mr Policeman?'

Jacob surveys the hostile faces and rethinks his response. This kindling has already been lit, and he will not be the one to fuel it further. There is no doubt in his mind that something here is being covered up, and people have been threatened in order to leave the issue alone.

'I don't think he even has one.' A cruel smile spreads over the short man's face. 'What did you think you'd do once you got inside? Plant evidence against us?'

Jacob is being cornered by this smart-arse's words, and he feels assured that whatever he says now will be turned against him. There are a number of ways of dealing with a hostile crowd like this, but none involves being cornered in a dead-end by himself. Which means the time has come for him to leave.

'You're right,' Jacob concedes. 'I don't have a warrant. I just thought we might help each other, the way it should be. I thought it might be in everyone's interest if I took a look at what happened here as quickly as possible. But it seems you'd prefer me to go through the bureaucracy.'

The frail teenage girl steps forward and grabs Jacob's

wrist with a remarkable strength, her hand seems uncomfortably hot against his skin. 'Tell me, was she Zulu like you?'

'Who?' He pulls his arm free, and has to resist wiping it on his trousers.

'The one who told you something happened here.'

'No. Now let me through. If no one here is going to help me, I'll have to get back to work.'

'Suddenly he is not even interested in Thekiso any more?' says the stocky man.

'He is covering up for Gladys.' The girl crows to the crowd. 'He is, isn't he? Can't you hear it in his voice?'

'Yes, I hear it,' cries the woman wearing the *doek*. 'I knew that whore was going to be trouble.'

'It *was* Gladys!'

More cries go up, and none of them bode well for him or for this Gladys, whoever she is.

'I don't know anyone by that name.' With that Jacob wades into the group, eager to be away. 'And maybe it's also better for all of you to stop making such careless accusations.'

Halfway through the mass of residents, a hand snags his shirt and pulls him back. He reacts by balling his fist to throw a punch. But a large hand lands on his upper arm and crushes the controlling muscle. As if this were a signal, more hands grope at him, and before he can reach for his pistol it is unclipped by a deft hand and plucked from its holster. When he tries to call for help, an arm as thick as a boa snakes around his throat and constricts. Jeers and whistles and hungry faces invade his senses – and drown out his awareness of everything else.

'Stop this!' he wheezes. 'What do you think you are doing?'

The stocky man appears in Jacob's limited line of vision, with an easy smile on his lips and stone in his dark eyes.

'See this?' He holds up Jacob's service pistol and releases the ammunition clip. 'There it goes.'

He lobs the clip over the railing, to disbelieving cheers and laughter from the crowd. The rest of the pistol follows shortly. Then the man turns back to Jacob, his hands splayed wide and a triumphant light in his eyes.

'Now that your gun is gone, who exactly are you?'

'He's a no one!' comes a shout.

'Look, it's Ephraim Thekiso,' shouts another voice. 'It's him!'

'Solly,' the stocky man says to whoever is holding Jacob, and nods at the railing.

The arm around Jacob's throat clamps tighter, completely cutting off his voice. Bright wild sparks go off behind his eyes as Jacob tries to breathe, while at the same time desperately flailing about to stop himself from being thrown over the edge.

When he manages to get one foot up and brace it against a balustrade, the emaciated girl leaps forward and hooks two arms under his knee. A loud *caw* erupts from her lips as she strains to lift his leg up and then over the railing. With all his capacity for resistance gone, he abruptly slips forward.

Grandfather! Jacob shouts instinctively inside his head. But there is no answer. *Help me, Father!* No answer is forthcoming from that quarter either.

The older woman with the *doek* shuffles forward to help the struggling girl uproot his second leg, just as the steel-mill man holding Jacob heaves him over the railing.

'Don't do this!' He clings to the unyielding arm around

his throat as the cracked tarmac down below comes into clearer relief. 'It doesn't need to be this way,' he pleads.

But no one seems to hear him. No one seems to want to listen.

Then he is held completely over the edge, and there is nothing below him but empty air.

3

Hopelessly Jacob kicks out at the vacuum to find a hold for his flailing feet, while the strangers all around him bay for him to be dropped.

'You see, you are nothing more than what we are now, police-*man*,' says the stocky man in a bored tone. 'Not God. Not the Law. Just a man.'

'Stop your struggling, *gata*!' a strained voice huffs in his ear. 'Or I'll drop you right now, I swear.'

'You feel that?' asks the stocky man. 'Is that fear you now feel? It's what we live with every day, Detective Tshabalala.'

Jacob finally manages to brace his feet against the vertical parapet by painfully arching his back. The strain on his spine makes his breathing even harder. Next to him, the angular little man crosses his arms on the railing and stares out across the rest of the neighbourhood – while down below children are laughing and hooting at the spectacle above them.

'Do you live in the city, police-man?'

The grip on his neck slips and for a second Jacob thinks this is it for him. But the steel-mill workhorse has only loosened his hold marginally, to allow him to respond. The crowd quietens down as though anticipating the next part of a joke. From inside Room 314 a baby howls over the television's din.

'What does that have to do with Ephraim Thekiso?' Jacob chokes.

'If you lived here, you'd understand why we are suspicious of outsiders like you, any people we don't meet in the lift or on the staircase every day. Even *gatas*.'

'I don't see your point.' The blood trapped in his head sings so loud in his ears that it is difficult for Jacob to hear anything but the racing thud of his heart.

'You move to the city looking for a better place to live, for a new life, thinking that maybe you will sleep better now that you've left the squatter camps outside the city. And the first week you do. Then you start awake at the sound of gunshots one night. Maybe you stare at the window a few minutes as your ears try to pick out more signs of trouble: feet running, voices shouting – but often it's just the one or two shots, and then the silence afterwards, which is always worse. You might fall asleep again, eventually. You might then forget. It was just a bad dream, you might tell yourself. After a while those shots become regular background noise, like a car driving by, or people walking past. That sound of death becomes part of your daily routine again, like buying fucking milk and a packet of cigarettes.

'But then, say, the power cuts out one night, and the whole neighbourhood goes dark. It's not five minutes before you hear doors crack and buckle as they force their way into apartments. You hear arguments. You hear the glass break. You hear more gunshots chasing each other up and down the streets, like it's a game with firecrackers. The screaming starts. That kind of sound, *mfo*, is the last thing you want to hear when you can't find a candle in the dark, let me tell you. Maybe you even hear some woman running down a passageway someplace, yelling incoherently with her fear of the dark, the men chasing her through the night.

'Eventually, you hear police sirens the way you can right now – you hear them? Yes, they're always there, aren't they? It's that background noise I'm telling you about – you hear them, except they're never quite coming your way when you need them most. Why must we live like this, I ask you? Is this really what you promised us?'

'Me?' Jacob gulps for air.

'The government!' yells a woman's voice. 'You lied to us!'

'I . . . am . . . working to fix it. That's all I can do. And it is not as bad as you say.'

Cries of disapproval go up from the gathered crowd, and the man holding him wrenches his head right back.

'It's not that *bad*, inspector? Where we live, you hear *everything* the way you hear floorboards creak when you're all alone in bed at night. Police-man, one purse stolen is not just one purse stolen. A man shot dead is not just a man shot dead. Every time I hear about that purse, it's *my* wallet; every time I hear about that man with a bullet in his chest, it's my father; it's me; it's my fucking *son*! These people, it's their wives and sons and husbands. It's not that *bad*? Your statistics, they have nothing to do with being scared shitless day in and day out. What do your statistics know about the word "fear"?'

'I can't do anything more than I already am,' says Jacob.

'You *can*!' shouts one of the residents. 'You must!'

Anvil Man shakes his head in disappointment, as though Jacob were his dullest student giving the worst possible answer. 'How can you say that?'

'I-am-not-God,' chokes Jacob. 'I'm just a police officer.'

'That's right.' The stocky man brightens considerably. 'Just a police-man.'

'Let him fall, this one!' an impatient voice cries.

'He must pay!' yells another.

'Kill him,' shouts a third.

Jacob braces himself as the arm around his neck begins to loosen its grip. It has begun to shake, has grown slick with sweat.

'Leave him alone!' shouts a familiar voice from the direction of the lifts.

Jacob senses the crowd's attention shift in that direction as sneakers come pounding down the corridor towards them, and then a young voice is shouting incoherently. All he can make out is that it belongs to the girl with the bright pink bubblegum, and that it's something about a court. The High Court?

'Do I drop this idiot or what?' interjects the man holding Jacob. His voice now quivers as badly as his arm, and the police officer tightens his hold on the man's forearm.

'She's the one! It's her that told this cop about Ephraim!' the emaciated girl yells on seeing the newcomer. 'Throw her over too.'

'I can't hold him up any longer,' says the big man dangling Jacob over the edge. 'I'm pulling him back up if you can't make up your minds.'

Just like that? The thought flashes through Jacob's dazed mind. *One minute you'll kill me, the next you save me?* What exactly is he to them, he wonders angrily, despite his fear.

So he is dragged back from the abyss and unceremoniously dumped on the concrete floor. Arguments instantly erupt all round him, but where the voices were shrill and angry till only moments ago, they are fearful now, astonished and uncertain. Jacob clutches at his bruised throat and gulps fresh air down into his oxygen-starved lungs. He is grateful that, for the moment at least, they seem to have forgotten him. But this feeling does not last, because he finally catches up with what is being said.

'Someone's blown up the High Court! It was on the radio, I'm telling you,' cries the newcomer, apparently called Gladys.

'What do you mean?' asks the man who had been holding Jacob over the railing.

'The fucking High Court on Prichard Street, it's gone!'

A voice yells, 'Good!' but this time the spark does not catch fire.

'But that can't be,' the stocky man stammers. 'No one can just blow up the High Court. We're not at war, are we?'

'What will happen now?' asks a squeaky voice nervously.

For all the bravado these people exhibited a few seconds ago, suddenly it seems they have nothing to hold on to. They stand there cowed and directionless, and Jacob seizes the moment to make a break for it. He bolts for the stairs and safety, half expecting to be followed by the lynch mob. But he need not even have run, as no one bothers to give chase.

4

When Jacob reaches the ground floor, he takes time to collect the scattered parts of his service pistol from the parking lot, where the laughing children were already playing with it. Hurrying back to his car, which he had left parked on the nearby kerb, he checks the weapon carefully. A few bullets have sprung from the clip, and the grip panels have broken free, but otherwise it appears undamaged by the long drop to the tarmac.

All the time Jacob's mind is racing around one urgent thought: *The High Court?*

He throws open the car door and lunges for the chattering police radio. Repeated unsuccessful attempts to cut into the garble leave him convinced that something very big has happened, and that it might indeed be true: the High Court is gone?

'And?' asks an anxious voice behind him.

He turns around to find the same young woman – the one the other residents called Gladys – coming up to him. Jacob returns the radio to its bracket and reaches for his mobile.

'I can't get through.'

'You didn't answer Kagiso's question. Why?'

'Is that his name? The short one who led that bunch?'

She ignores his question and presses for an answer. 'Who would bomb the High Court? Was it those whites, do you think? The Boeremag?'

'Was it him that killed Ephraim Thekiso?'

'No.' She is clearly annoyed by his refusal to answer her question first. 'What's going to happen now?'

'Then who did?'

'I don't know. They came in the night collecting debts. They made us pay, and those that couldn't, they were beaten and thrown out. Now will you answer me, please.'

'What do you care?'

At this she appears hurt, but he ignores her. He has had more than enough of this building and its people.

The call Jacob placed disconnects: **Network Busy**, says the mobile's screen.

'It scares me as much as anyone else. That's why.'

'It scares you that the High Court's gone? I thought that might make you happy, you and the others in there.'

The words are out before he realized what he was saying, and they transform her inquisitive face.

'Don't you talk to me like that! A minute ago you were hanging over the edge of a fucking balcony. They would have dropped you if it wasn't for me.'

A second call fails to connect, and Jacob throws the phone on to the passenger seat.

'Get off the street, Gladys. Turning tricks is only going to get you killed, especially if you stay here.'

'It's so easy for you to say that, you bastard!'

'I'm not going to argue with you.'

'I can't believe you, dickhead! I should've just left them to do with you what they wanted.'

He throws a quick glance up at the third-floor corridor, now barely visible through the tree branches, and searches for the one she called Kagiso. But besides the burly wife and her husband watching them from the railing, he cannot see any of the others who were so intent on killing him a couple of minutes ago. Did they scatter for fear that he would come back with reinforcements, or was his life, and what they were prepared to do to end it, as easily forgotten as a conversation with a stranger in a lift? The latter thought infuriates him even more.

'You tell those idiots up there I'm coming after every single one of them,' whispers Jacob. 'Because I've had enough now.'

He gets into the vehicle, starts the engine and reverses into the street with a wide arc that nearly hits an approaching car in the opposite lane. As he is about to drop the transmission into first, he cranks open the window.

'I mean it, Gladys, stay off the street. And get out of that building.'

'You've no right to tell me what to do!'

'Maybe I don't, but I'm not ordering you. I'm giving you some healthy advice.'

He is accelerating in the direction of the city centre when a rock bounces off the roof of the car and a voice chases after him: 'You ungrateful piece of shit! I wish they'd dropped you.'

5

He guns the patrol vehicle south down Claim Street, weaving effortlessly through a snarl of traffic that glitters in the afternoon light and reeks of black smoke and frustration. As he swings into Jeppe Street, a coherent voice over the police radio finally answers the question that has been driving out all his other thoughts: it was not the High Court that was bombed, as the radio station had mistakenly claimed, but Maloney's Bar across the road.

He does not know how to take this news, whether he should feel relieved or even more dismayed. It is the first

Friday afternoon after pay day, and how many does he know who go to Maloney's at the end of a hard week, especially after this hogwash about job security that was being served to the department just as he left? Who might have been drinking there when the bomb went off? The answer is, just about anyone from his department, and a good many more from other police units. Didn't Chief Molethe himself tell Jacob that he was going for a drink after work? And what about Ndoda Semenya? Was he still serving behind the bar when it happened?

Jacob's mind turns to who the perpetrators might have been, and the only groups he can think of with sufficient audacity are the far-right extremists. The White Wolves? The Boeremag? Maybe some other new group which has now played its opening hand?

At Von Wielligh he takes the corner too fast and nearly ploughs into a crowd that has coagulated around the hastily erected traffic barriers. He leaps out of the Golf and pushes his way through a mass of people smelling of old sweat, cheap perfume and the sour stench of fear. The faces he looks into are not filled with concern but with greed. The voices he hears do not express sympathy but bay for bad news. These rubbernecks first irritate then anger him. By the time he nears the barrier, he finds himself violently shoving bodies aside and yelling at them despite their indignant protests.

He could not care less about such complaints, though, for they mean nothing to him any more: these civvies who despise the very men that keep them safe, who prefer to bundle police officers into the same basket as the criminals they hold at bay. Cops and robbers. Robbers and cops. They always go together, don't they? Enough so that some of them would toss him over a railing like a bag of refuse.

Screw you all, thinks Jacob angrily.

'Hey, you can't come through here! Get the fuck back.' A young metro cop with a crewcut like Astro Turf tries to push Jacob away from the trellis barricade, but he resists forcefully and steps over it.

'Murder and Robbery, with Senior Superintendent Kobus Niehaus's unit. Is he here?'

'China, I know fuck-all about what's going on here right now, except that the cunts who did this, they're going to get it, big-time.'

'Any idea at all who it was?'

The traffic cop shakes his head.

Passing the front line of officers, Jacob is taken aback by the eerie emptiness of the normally busy street, silent except for a police helicopter circling above and sirens echoing up and down the shopfronts. An occasional emergency vehicle swerves into view further along the street or shoots across an empty intersection. Jacob has to wonder how many city blocks they have already closed off. A Tactical Squad officer rounds the corner from Prichard Street, heading in Jacob's direction, then stops abruptly and starts pounding the wall with one fist before burying his face in his elbow.

'It's the end, china,' says the metro cop standing next to Jacob. 'I'm telling you.'

Jacob hurries along the last block towards Prichard, his steps quickening till he breaks into a run. Before long his feet are flickering over the litter-strewn tarmac as fast as he can propel them. He cannot remember a time when he has ever seen this street so empty before sunset.

He runs on down the cracked pavement, racing past the tactical officer, who has now been pinned to the wall by a concerned colleague. He passes three bodies lying on the tarmac, nylon stockings pulled away from their dead faces, and AK-47s with the stocks removed still clasped in their hands. Spent rifle and pistol shells glitter like a thousand coins strewn over the empty street. The ornate wall fronting the High Court, and its thin strip of yellowed-green lawn, slips by him till, a hundred metres down the road, he can see a throng of police officers and emergency workers loitering amid the emergency vehicles parked in front of the bar where he himself had been drinking alone not a week ago.

When he finally reaches the main crowd of police officers, he searches frantically among them for familiar faces. Inside a large square space that has been cordoned off in front of the bar there is blood on the sidewalk, glass fragments, tattered cloth that might have once been curtains or clothes. He asks for Chief Molethe, he asks for Kobus Niehaus – has anyone seen them? He even asks for Harry Mason, before he realizes the man is barely standing and still on a plane back to Johannesburg, safely thousands of feet above this chaos. No one seems able to give him a straight answer till a passing paramedic directs him over to the injured victims being treated on ambulance gurneys, and the dead lying in orderly lines down the middle of the street. Jacob rushes over to the plastic-covered bundles waiting for removal by the Black Marias and starts pulling back the sheets draped over their dead faces, one by one.

After the third, he comes upon Ndoda Hugh Semenya, and Captain Kommie Combrink with the fifth. There are more faces he recognizes from Maloney's bar-room floor, from office corridors and crime scenes, past investigations. Still sunk on his haunches, Jacob lets the last plastic sheet fall from his hand and drops his own face into his palms as grief overcomes him.

Oh God, what now? he wonders. *Where will this end?*
'Jacob? *He banna*, Tshabalala!'

He stands up and turns around in time to see Simon Molethe burst out from the crowd. His tie is gone and dark bloodstains are evident on his rolled-up shirt sleeves.

'Chief! What happened here?'

Jacob's words are cut off as the SVC director seizes him by the shoulders and gruffly pulls him into a tight bear hug that smells of English Blazer aftershave and fresh sweat.

6

It has been three hours since he tried to help out at the scene of the bombing, along with every other police officer from Midrand to Alberton. The effort quickly degenerated into an uncontrolled scrum as uncoordinated officers began impromptu searches for evidence and suspects, harshly interrogating witnesses and even the wounded. Distress had turned into a pit-bull restlessness by the time the area commissioner arrived to take charge of the scene. It was only then that some semblance of order was established, after which the bomb-disposal unit took over official command of the area. The rest were sent home to get some sleep or to await further orders at their respective offices, amid rumours that a major manhunt would begin sometime before dawn. Reports were emerging from surviving police officers that a man called Wally Khuzwayo was involved, and that he belonged to the Phaliso brothers – the Abasindisi.

The whereabouts of Superintendent Swarts and his Ballies, the team that could easily answer so many of these questions, remained a mystery to all concerned, even their director, Chief Molethe. Not a single one of them could be reached to provide desperately needed information, despite eyewitness accounts that Swarts and Franklin had been involved in a running gun battle with Khuzwayo.

As Jacob eases on to Soweto Highway and heads into Orlando East, the night-time world beyond the windshield appears to him like a film projection. Smiling people jostle past each other over on the road's shoulder, glad to be getting home from work. In the driveways, sons are washing their fathers' cars for the weekend while daughters are fetching in clothes from the washing line. Everywhere he looks, small groups of friends have settled down in fold-up camping chairs out on the pavements, happy to enjoy together one of the first warm days of spring. What he sees here is a world at peace with itself, so utterly different from the turmoil of his own life that he finds it difficult to reconcile the two realities.

Reaching the top of the crescent in which he lives, he turns into his driveway to find an unfamiliar shiny black Daimler-Chrysler parked in front of the single garage. Jacob fishes out his house keys and heads for the front door, throwing another curious glance at their visitor's car. The moment he turns the handle and enters his home, he can hear a playful womanly giggle from the living room, echoed by a confident baritone chuckle.

He enters the room to find Nomsa and an older-looking Teddy Bakwena seated close together on the couch. The man's hair has greyed somewhat at the temples, giving him a rather distinguished look, which is emphasized by the goatee beard. Jacob cannot help but notice that one of Bakwena's hands is resting lightly on Nomsa's bare knee. Jacob's first instinct is to apologize for interrupting them, but then he remembers exactly where he is.

Nomsa's smile vanishes from her lips when she sees Jacob's expression. She leaps up, and Jacob notes how Bakwena's hand drops automatically to the indent in the cushion where she had been sitting.

'Jacob, there you are!' Nomsa cries out in Zulu. 'What's happened? Tell me.'

She quickly crosses the room and takes his face in her hands. He feels pressure in that touch, as though she would turn his gaze away from the stranger in his house. He does not know whether she expects a kiss, or whether she simply wants to avert his eyes from Teddy Bakwena, but he cannot look away from that other man who once came so close to marrying her, and who, it so happens, had his hand resting intimately on her knee just a moment ago.

'Tshabalala, good to see you, man,' says Teddy in Sotho as he gets up, buttons his blazer and offers Jacob a car salesman's smile. 'I hear you're a detective now. Not bad for someone who was little more than a street urchin once. You must be proud of yourself.'

He approaches with a self-assured gait and sticks out a meaty hand.

You covetous son of a bitch, thinks Jacob. *Couldn't you find someone else's woman to pursue?*

The anger boiling over inside is as unyielding as tar.

'Jacob, are you OK?' The anxiety in Nomsa's voice is matched by the uncomfortable smile on Teddy Bakwena's face. 'How bad was it? Tell me.'

'What is he doing here?' Jacob demands.

Teddy Bakwena stops short and withdraws the outstretched hand. Nomsa finally forces Jacob's head around towards her, and their eyes meet. Her large dark eyes show more than a trace of apprehension. To him this merely smacks of a guilty conscience.

'Jacob, listen to me,' she enunciates carefully. 'Teddy just brought me home after choir practice; that's all. Remember how I told you I'd make other arrangements while you were busy in town?'

'You said you'd get someone to drop you off, not that you'd be inviting *him* into my house.'

'I was worried sick, so I asked Teddy to wait with me. I didn't want to sit here all by myself till you got home.'

'It didn't look like that to me.'

Teddy Bakwena clears his throat. 'Tshabalala, this is uncalled for. Nomsa is telling you the truth.'

'Shut up, you!'

'Leave him alone, Jacob.'

'Nomsa,' interjects Teddy, 'I'm sorry if I've caused you any trouble. I'll go now.'

'That's right. You will, and *now*.'

One of Nomsa's hands slips from Jacob's face as she gestures to delay Teddy from leaving.

'No, Teddy. Please don't go. I want to sort this out, once and for all.'

The man looks Jacob up and down, cool and angry now, as though *he* is the one who has been insulted by the other man's presence. A sneer curls the corners of his lips and he shakes his head. 'No, Nomsa, I couldn't ever expect a Zulu man to show courtesy when necessary, much less a *gata*.'

'Jacob, NO!'

By the time the two files Jacob was carrying hit the floor, spilling documents everywhere, he has sidestepped Nomsa and taken two short jabs at Teddy Bakwena, one to his stomach, the other to his face. But the sight of the winded man stumbling helplessly backwards into the living room is not enough, and Jacob grabs him by the lapel of his suit and shoves him against the wall. Drawing the gun from the holster he had clipped to his trousers, he grinds its tip into the man's cheek.

'Yes, Bakwena, I *am* a *gata*. And I *am* a Zulu. But unlike you, I do have manners. I don't go slithering into another man's house, to seduce away the woman I didn't have the balls to marry in the first place. Unlike you, I know what commitment is, and I know when a woman is spoken for.'

A soft hand gently lands on his shoulder, but he shrugs it off.

'Baby, please put the gun away,' says a soothing voice, 'in God's name.'

He hears her but refuses to listen. Instead, he studies Bakwena as if the entire world's evil is concentrated in this one detestable creature, who has entered his house unbidden. The man is now unusually quiet, and keeps his eyes carefully averted, but beads of sweat have broken out on his wide forehead and a muscle in his cheek is twitching uncontrollably.

Jacob nudges him with the tip of the gun barrel. 'Admit it, Bakwena.'

The man clears his throat and in a placatory but fearless voice asks, 'What is it that you want me to say?'

'This is so humiliating, Jacob.' Nomsa begins to weep. 'God, what's got into you?'

'Admit it, it wasn't just a coincidence that you rejoined the choir. Let's be honest here, Teddy Ba-kwe-na. Tell me to my face how you don't respect me because I am a cop, while you are a moneyman who always gets his own way.'

'Jacob, how can you discuss me like I'm not here? We already spoke about this. I don't belong to you like some piece of furniture!'

'Is this the first time you've visited my house while I've been working late?'

'You can ask *me* that, Jacob!' Her voice is rising, and a hand tugs at his shoulder in an attempt to distract him, but he pulls away and presses the gun deeper into Teddy Bakwena's cheek. 'Why don't you answer me, *inyoka*? Look me in the eye and tell me what you really think: that you're better than me, that she is still yours.'

'I won't do that.'

'Why not?'

'I won't condone your behaviour by playing along with it. You're shaming not only God but your father too.'

At this, Jacob loses whatever little control he still retained over the fury built up inside him. Before he realizes what he is about to do he steps back, cocking the pistol in his hand, and pulls the trigger.

7

There is nothing but a soft click from the trigger mechanism. The hammer does not even budge, but the sound might as well have been a thunderclap for the silence that immediately follows.

Teddy and Jacob stare breathlessly at each other, and between them passes the full gravity of the moment and its consequences. Then Teddy utters a low wail and sinks to his knees, and Jacob is free to stare down at the heavy pistol in his hand.

It misfired. The three-storey drop had broken something after all.

'Teddy!' Nomsa shoves Jacob aside and falls to her knees beside the man he would have killed.

'Jacob, how could you!' she yells at him over her shoulder, but he hardly hears her due to the jumble of thoughts surging through his mind.

Meeting her eyes, he finds them burning with a fury he has never seen there before; he never thought her capable of evincing such hatred towards him – towards anyone, for that matter. The Murder and Robbery service pistol, which he has carried regularly for the last nine years and drawn only a few times in the line of duty, slips from his hands and drops to the thick carpet at his feet. Against the woolly beige fabric it looks innocuous, nothing more than a toy.

Is it that easy, then?

Nomsa draws the shattered man up against her bosom and hugs him tightly, and Jacob realizes the anger that led to his drawing the gun is not yet entirely evaporated.

He had meant to kill this man. He had as good as *done* it, but for God's intervention. Horrified, he realizes he is no longer standing inside his home but at a crime scene.

Then Jacob is out of the door, running, past the Daimler-Chrysler and towards his patrol car. A woman's voice calls to him from inside the house, but he does not want to hear it. All he wants now is to get away from here.

He wrenches the door open and falls into the driver's seat and, as he shuts himself in, it strikes him how the rapidly cooling engine sounds like a ticking time bomb.

8

Jacob bangs his palm down on the door lock, and checks that all the others are locked too. Suddenly it feels safer: that by locking himself away, he might also shut out what he has just done. Wide, almost unrecognizable eyes meet his when he checks the mirror; the gaze of a fugitive is reflected in them. Glancing back towards the house, he notices the front door still wide open, and he has to resist an urge to get out and close it too.

What now? he thinks.

He repeats this question over and over again, till he hears Teddy Bakwena finally regain his composure and begin arguing loudly with Nomsa.

Abruptly the voice of a dead man fills his head – a man whose face he recognized this afternoon in a line of bloody corpses laid out in front of Maloney's.

Then one day they stop coming, and you don't hear nothing, till you read how this or that officer finally fell in the deep end and drowned. I've seen it all too often, mfo, and I don't care for it at all.

Old Hugh Semenya, was it really just a week ago that he was giving Jacob that lecture? Did he really see the old-timer wrapped up in a body bag only a few hours ago?

He becomes aware of a beeping sound growing steadily louder, until he realizes it is his mobile phone which he had left in the car by mistake. Thinking that it might be his office calling about the bombing, he finally finds it wedged between the seat and passenger door.

'Yes?' he mumbles.

A high-pitched racket in the background at first makes

it impossible for him to hear what some distraught woman is saying to him.

'What was that?' he demands, then realizes that the background noise is a young girl screaming at the top of her lungs. He pulls the phone away from his ear and checks the caller ID. **Harry Mason Home**, reads the display.

It can only be Jeanie Mason screaming like that, but the desperate voice in the foreground is not Harry's mother, so it must be Tanya Fouché.

His own concerns momentarily forgotten, Jacob sits bolt upright. 'Tanya, what's wrong with Jeanie?'

'They've taken him, Jacob.'

A bucket of ice slithers down his spine at those words. 'Who?'

'Harry, man!'

'I mean, who took him?'

'Russell Swarts and that arsehole Franklin. Naidoo was with them too.'

'Why?'

'I think they're going after the Phalisos – alone.'

'Do you know where they're heading?'

'No, but they were talking about some friend of Harry's, a guy called Makhe Motale. Do you know him? Please tell me you know who I'm talking about.'

Makhe Motale? wonders Jacob. *That idiot from the evacuated factory? The one on the skateboard?*

'Did you hear me, Jacob?'

A dozen confused questions demand answers all at once. 'Where do I find him?' he presses.

'I don't know; I don't even know if the man's still alive. Harry went out to a place called Hofmeyer Bridge to find him a few weeks back. Jesus, Jacob, tell me you know where that is, because I don't.'

He certainly knows the fallen-down bridge in Alexandra, but tracing someone in that section of squatter camp, built on the river's floodplain, will be something altogether different. 'Yes, I know where it is.'

'You get him back to me, Jacob. You hear me? Get him back in one piece.'

Jacob drops the phone on the passenger seat and reaches for the ignition. Just then he sees movement out of the corner of his eye, and looks up to find Nomsa standing at the car window. The resentment burning in her eyes a few minutes ago has been replaced with worry. Her lips move, and her hand makes a cranking motion: *Open up.*

A fresh surge of remorse overcomes him, and his ears begin burning with shame. How beautiful she is for standing here after what he has just done, and how precious she is for the concern now written all over her tear-streaked round face.

How can he ever get her to trust him again, he wonders.

She wipes at her eyes and makes that cranking gesture again, more urgently this time.

What does he say to her? How can he expect her forgiveness?

'Damn it, Jacob! Open the window,' Nomsa yells loud enough for him to hear. There is fear in her voice now, as if she suspects him of contemplating something reckless.

He twists the key in the ignition and the car's engine roars to life.

Nomsa starts banging at the window, but he just shakes his head.

'Jacob, open the window *now*! You're scaring me!'

'I have to go,' he calls out.

Without checking to see whether she understood him,

he drops the transmission into first and swings the patrol car out into the road, accelerating so hard it momentarily dovetails. Then he floors it in the direction of the city, without a clue yet of what he can do for Harry Mason. But by the time he hits the intersection at the end of the road, Jacob has ICD Detective Busisiwe Mosetsane's number fully dialled on his mobile phone.

NINE

1

Before the knock at the kitchen door, before the cosy life she was imagining for herself was run over by a speeding truck out of hell, Tanya Fouché thought it strange how happy it made her feel to be running her first sink of dishwater in her boyfriend's kitchen. It was a stupid, even childish, feeling, and certainly not very liberated, but she revelled in it none the less.

Boyfriend! She nearly laughed aloud. *The man is nearly forty!*

A smile crept over Tanya's face at her own sentimentality. She was not used to indulging in nostalgia, but she allowed it this time nevertheless, because she felt grateful for the emotions it evoked.

While Massive Attack's 'Dissolved Girl' kept her company on the iPod tucked into her pocket, two other exhausted travellers were sleeping off a two-hour flight in a couple of bedrooms at the rear of the modest Brixton house. One was a ten-year-old girl, the other a severely wounded cop who still looked like Lazarus resurrected, even two weeks after the shooting incident.

'You OK there, Bond?' she had asked him as they all stepped off the plane from Port Elizabeth, just before sunset. During the flight she had noticed him gulping down painkillers like they were gumdrops, and every now and again he would run a hand over the large bandage under his shirt, as if to ascertain whether he was feeling seeping blood or merely perspiration. 'You look pretty pale.'

He offered her an exhausted smile. 'Do you have to call me that?'

'It's the name you go by on the job, isn't it, officer?' She poked him in the shoulder with one finger.

'Very funny.'

He had to call Jeanie back when the child raced ahead of them towards the waiting terminal bus. After finding a row of empty chairs at the rear of the bus, they sat down and Tanya instinctively tugged at his shirt sleeve.

'Yeah?' he asked when she did not explain the gesture.

God, it's good to have you back! she was thinking. 'Nothing.' She leaned over and kissed him lightly on the lips. 'Just wanted to give you one of those, that's all.'

He had smiled and pressed his forehead against hers, inhaling the scent of her skin.

'I don't think I've ever been this happy to get home, or so desperate to lie down.'

'Don't worry, old man.' She had stroked the back of his neck. 'It'll just be another half hour.'

There was a hiss of air from hydraulic brakes, and the driver took off at a smooth pace. Jeanie hummed contentedly to herself, lost in her own thoughts.

'Tanya,' Harry began softly.

'Mmm?'

'Thanks.'

She turned to him. 'What for?'

'The last few days. For everything.'

'It's nothing.'

He pulled away from her and stared deep into her eyes with an intensity she found discomfiting. 'It was good to wake up and have you there beside me.'

She patted his knee. 'You can take me somewhere fancy for dinner when you're up and about again.'

He had chuckled. 'Consider it done!'

'Can I come too?' Jeanie had caught the last sentence.

'No, honey.' Harry winked at his daughter. 'I think Tanya here deserves to be spoiled all on her own.'

Jeanie Mason was a sweet kid. Those last few days in Port Elizabeth, Tanya had often watched Harry's child when no one else could see her looking. Though she herself has worked with children for many years, in one orphanage or another, none of them had affected her like this one. Jeanie fascinated her because of the range of feelings she inspired in her. These she found deeply unsettling: jealousy because she was not the mother of Harry's joy; apprehension because the little girl was the axis on which her relationship with Harry would be balanced; even curiosity, because she herself hoped against her better judgement to one day become for Jeanie what the little girl no longer possessed – a mother. When this last thought first surfaced in Tanya's mind, the fiercely independent side of her had baulked mightily, although the other part of her seemed generally pleased at the thought. It was probably a naïve thing to hope for, she kept telling herself, but feelings and rational thought have never been easy bedfellows.

A stranger's dishes in a stranger's kitchen sink, and three sets of them at that. She had never thought she would end up dating a man with a daughter from a previous marriage, but then she supposed she was entering that age when single unmarried men without disastrous hang-ups were becoming an increasingly rare prospect. At least that lug now slumped out in his creaky single bed appeared to be on a pretty even keel. When he had finally opened those grey eyes and smiled up at her, when he had reached out a hand to her from his hospital bed, she knew instantly she had made the right decision in sticking around.

Tanya yanked the plug out and watched water and suds spiral away. It had been a very strange moment when Harry woke up. Russell Swarts, who had turned out a pretty decent guy despite the chauvinism, had stayed at his wounded captain's side for almost the entire two weeks. He was there alongside her when the news arrived that Harry was finally conscious. But by the time she had finished hogging the patient's attention, and turned to summon Russell closer, the senior cop had disappeared without saying a word.

She was still thinking of what would come next for Harry when an insistent noise broke through the music in her ears. She pulled out her earphones to hear a loud knocking at the kitchen door. Through the opaque glass she could now see three tall figures illuminated by the light above the doorway.

'Harry? Tanya?' comes a familiar voice that sounds oddly frayed. 'It's Russell Swarts. Open up, please.'

'Russell?' she responds in surprise.

She chucks the dishtowel over the plate rack next to the sink and hurries over to the door, a smile at this unexpected surprise already blooming on her lips.

2

Despite his exhaustion, and the countless painkillers he had swallowed on the return flight to Johannesburg, Harry could not get to sleep when he lay down after their early supper. Now discharged from hospital, and back in his home town, the same burning questions that haunted him nightly when no one else was around to distract him again urged him to come up with answers. The loudest of these worries was who had shot him out there in Tsolo, closely followed by what his next move should be now that he was back in the ring. In light of what Tanya had told him about the ICD coming after him, and his own suspicions that it might have been Russie Swarts who tried to kill him, he feared his options were running out.

Agitated by these thoughts, Harry had finally rolled out of bed and wandered down the passage towards the kitchen. He stopped short in the doorway and watched Tanya busy herself with the dishes, white earphones plugged into her ears. Though he had known her for barely four months, she was already so much a part of his life, and he had not fully understood how important she had become to him until he opened his eyes in the hospital and found her sitting by his side, so many miles away from home. The feeling of joy then had been overwhelming.

Her long black hair was now tied back with a red rubber band like a high-school girl's ponytail, and she had kicked off her boots in favour of bare feet, which she preferred indoors, even in winter. He was content for the moment to simply watch her, noticing how every now and again she would stop and gaze at the wall straight ahead of her, obviously caught up in her own private thoughts. But when she suddenly giggled to herself, it snapped him out of his reverie. She was not quite the reason he had got up.

Harry turned back down the corridor and entered his cramped study quietly, trying not to disturb Jeanie asleep in the room next door.

3

This whole mess had of course started with the files Makhe Motale had given him. Supplying him with vital information on the Abasindisi in exchange for a promise to investigate the death of that drug dealer Parapara Ntombini – a murder for which Harry's commander Supe Russie Swarts was more than likely responsible – had produced a double-bind situation of which any skilful police interrogator would have been proud. Harry was sure Makhe Motale had set it up this way on purpose. It was a trademark strategy for which he should have been prepared.

Harry now remembered the day he had walked into Swarts' office after a week of unsuccessfully trawling Yeoville for independent corroboration on what had happened that night Ntombini was killed, so he could then compare what he knew about the case from the original file – which had been signed off by Swarts – and what Makhe had given him. But there were no results to be had; after a seven-year lapse it came as no surprise. The demographics of that neighbourhood had completely changed during the intervening years. The old Jewish quarter there no longer existed, and the first wave of black inhabitants arriving from the townships had also moved on as the area gradually turned into a slum, filled mostly with Mozambican and Zimbabwean immigrants, so dirt-poor and desperate that even the church mice had packed up their begging tins and shuffled off in search of greener pastures. The people who had been so willing to tell Makhe what he wanted to hear clammed up instantly when an *umlungu* appeared asking the same questions.

So Harry had decided to bluff it hard and fast with Swarts and see if he blinked. This would be his only chance to get a hint of the truth, he figured.

He had purposefully shoved open the door to the Supe's office so hard that it bounced off the wall. This startled the man who had been pecking away at a report on the computer with his index fingers.

'What exactly happened between you and Ntombini in '98?' Harry began immediately.

'Excuse me?'

'I've come across at least two witnesses who say you gunned him down without provocation. Is that true?'

The moment Swarts jumped up and hastily pulled Harry further into the office before closing the door, he realized the allegation might be true. *Makhe Motale 1: SVC 0.* His old acquaintance had made Harry a willing accomplice in sowing doubt among the detectives of the SVC. One way or the other, he would now be dancing to someone else's tune: either playing Motale's game or conniving with Swarts in hushing up a murder. He knew it, hated it, and could do nothing about it except see it through to the end as best he could.

'You checked who these people are, did you?' Swarts had sidestepped his verbal assault.

'What happened that night?'

'Sit, Harry.'

'I think I'll stand.'

Swarts placed his palms together as if in prayer. 'I thought you were supposed to be investigating the Mohosh murder, and building a case against the Abasindisi?'

'It's my job to look into any homicide that comes across my desk, even those committed by fellow police officers.'

'Will you keep your blimming voice down?'

'What's the story, superintendent? I was involved in that case. After all, it's how we bloody well met. Now I have to be told that a drug killing was in fact a cop assassination.'

'That story is about as old as Noah and his blimming Ark, and it was started by Ntombini's lieutenants, that's who. Every time things heat up for them, that's the first card they try to play.'

Swarts pulled one of two visitors' chairs away from his desk and offered it to his captain. 'Harry, please sit down. I'm asking you nicely.'

'I'll stand, I said.'

'Be glad he went down.'

'Glad?'

'He was a security risk to us all, and we can be happy the gangs thought the same thing.'

'So you shot him.'

'I don't know what you're talking about,' says Swarts. 'The first time I realized he was dead was when Brixton Station rang us to come take a look at what they found the next morning.'

'Bullshit!'

'Jesus, Harry, whose side are you on? I got you in here with us because I thought you understood that this job can get rougher than General Investigations, even rougher than Murder and Robbery. You survive on resolve, not facts, in this job.'

'What's that supposed to mean?'

'There's a blimming albino Nigie running loose out there, whose gang killed your wife and nearly ground your little daughter into bonemeal, tell me you wouldn't put a bullet in his face the moment you spot him out on the street. Tell me he's not still out there somewhere, doing the same things to other children because you couldn't manage to arrest him when you might have shot him dead. Those are the choices you face in this business, Harry!'

This was the closest he got to a full confession from his supe, but for Harry it was enough.

He remembered bunching a fist, as if to take a swing at his superintendent, but he managed to hold back his rage. 'My past has nothing to do with what *you* did.'

'It makes my point as clear as fucking day, Harry. If this were the States or Europe, don't you think we'd all be happy to follow proper procedure? Don't you think we could play the game like civilized people, follow all the rules? We're alone, Harry. A fine fucking line between anarchy and civilization, that's what we are. A blue line thinner than the hair on my blimming head. You and me, Harry – that's us!'

'I'm not buying this for a second, Supe.'

Swarts laughed. 'You want to arrest me for the shooting of a smack-dealing shit like Ntombini? On what grounds? Blimming well go ahead then, but know this: without me there is no SVC, and you can go back to some shit-for-brains station-level job, drinking lukewarm tea out of a tin cup in the dead of night, maybe somewhere on the West Rand.'

'You're not in charge here. Molethe is.'

'No? Why do you think the commissioner would love to shove this pretty face of mine into a meat grinder? Hey? I screwed his chances of becoming Minister of Safety and Security. That was me! I trumped his blimming arse in Parliament, just so that the specialized units could go on doing their jobs.'

Harry did not have a clue what he was talking about

now, and did not want to go into it either. Whatever Swarts' political machinations were, it was the Ntombini case he was solely interested in.

'And that somehow excuses you?'

'Whoever popped Ntombini has my blessing, because the world became a safer place. Murder went down a good twenty-five per cent in that neighbourhood after he kicked the bucket.'

'I can't believe I'm hearing this from you, Supe.'

'You're hearing it, and you're going to have to deal with it, captain.'

Harry remembered how they had then glared at each other – him wanting to tell his commander that the file he had in his possession would be on an ICD desk by nightfall, and Swarts probably knowing any paper Harry had would end up in a shredder before the clock struck midnight. Super Supe Russie Swarts had blinked at his bluff, yes, but he had quickly recovered, and matched him too.

Harry had turned for the door. 'This isn't over, Supe.'

'Harry, I can't let you run around recklessly mouthing off that I killed someone. There's absolutely no evidence to substantiate your accusations. You start talking about what you think happened, you're going to do all of us a lot of damage – and for what? Your pride?'

Harry had faced him. 'What would your wife think of this? Your boys?'

'They're happy there's one less scumbag in this world to worry about whenever they stop at a red light at night. They're blimming well sleeping that much better, because they know he won't be coming through the window with a knife in one hand and his dick in the other. Jesus, Mason, think! There's a lot more at stake here than the truth. Can't you see that? Just let it rest.'

'No. I can't.' He turned and walked out.

That was pretty much the last conversation they had on the subject before the Tsolo raid kicked into high gear. Though he had threatened his commander with the file on Ntombini, the truth was he did not want to take it any further at that stage, even though he had promised Makhe Motale he would, for deep down he felt sympathetic towards Swarts. Men like Ntombini, they were in and out of interrogation rooms and jails like they had revolving doors attached to them, and he also knew how anyone in the force could crack and go too far under the right provocation. There wasn't a single officer in the police service who didn't have the capacity in him. Ntombini's type, they got under your skin after they made enough threats, and if they got off on enough charges sufficient times, you got to feel hopeless about your work and due legal process, too.

There was that to consider, and the obvious question of whether the streets were better off with a man like Ntombini left to run things instead of Swarts. And did he really want to be the one to send Super Supe Swarts to jail, where he'd have to be kept in isolation so that the bastards he put away in all his years of service didn't gang-rape him and then carve their initials all over his skin before stringing him up by his neck? Harry had already been in half a mind to just let the issue peter out, but that changed in Tsolo. What happened there had totally shifted the balance of his sympathy.

With Swarts thinking of moving over to Interpol and France, Harry wondered whether his commander had become desperate enough to try killing him after the cajoling did not work. Or at least have him killed to protect his own future. After his first killing, how far would a man like that go?

Remember who has your back, Harry.

Isn't that what the Supe told him that same morning when he was shot? It had sounded conciliatory at the time, and he had responded in kind. But who, indeed, had whose back?

Lying awake alone in a hospital bed night after night gave him plenty of time to replay what happened that day in Tsolo, and the more he thought about it, the more unclear and confused he became. Why had the Ballies, veterans all of them, been so jittery that morning that they had to drink themselves into a near-stupor on the way to the target village? What did the Xhosa cops he was with whisper about so urgently as they went searching from door to door? Could they have been on the Phalisos' payroll in order to protect the dope growers? And who had been that figure in the fog who had fired on him? Was it feasible that Swarts had put his mates up to the job? When he asked his doctors what had happened to the bullet embedded in his guts, they told him Russell Swarts had taken it away as evidence. Did that mean the superintendent was once again covering his tracks, the way he did in the Ntombini case? But why then did he bother to run nearly a kilometre carrying Harry on his back in order to find level ground where the helicopter with a paramedic could touch down? Wouldn't it have been easier to simply let him bleed to death in that village?

Who had whose back? And who the hell could he now trust to tell him what exactly was going on?

If only Makhe Motale could have kept his stinking manila envelopes to himself.

4

In the minutes before a heavy knocking at the kitchen door fundamentally changed Tanya Fouché's life, Harry listened carefully for sounds of her activity at the front part of the house. Satisfied that she was still busy there, he knelt down next to his chair, grunting as a sharp pain flared up in his gut and blood rushed to his injured head. He found Motale's files still safely taped to the underside of his desktop and pulled them free.

Makhe Motale 2: Harry Mason 0, he thought as he shuffled the two files.

The first had succeeded in driving a wedge between him and his commander; the second, according to news from Tanya, had sent him on a wild-goose chase across half the country looking for weapons that did not exist – a chase that would eventually get him shot.

'Is it justice you're after,' he recalled Makhe Motale asking him once, way back when he was still a frequent visitor in Alexandra, 'or retribution?'

It was a good question, and one he had frequently thought about.

'You can't deny it, Mason, shooting a man who fucks you over is every man's wet dream.' This was what Franklin had once told him, shortly after he walked in on the Ballies talking about blooding. 'Sex is about shooting your load, and shooting your pistol is about revenge. The two acts can't be separated from their most essential element: lust.'

'Then what's justice?' Harry had asked him.

Franklin did not hesitate with his answer. 'It's for limp-dicked liberals, too shit-scared of standing up for themselves, so fucking scared of taking ownership of what they really want to do. I mean, who else thinks of a bird with her eyes gouged out and holding a pair of scales in her hand as a symbol for *justice*? She's for men that feel too guilty about their own inherent ability to manifest power.' It was a rare thing to hear Franklin laugh, but that he did, and it gave Harry the creeps. 'Shit, the shrinks must love the symbolism in that – a mutilated woman called Justice!'

Harry fingered the edge of the file containing the information Motale had given him on Tsolo. The weapons he had been promised there were still missing, according to what Tanya had learned from Russell Swarts, and now so was a whole lot of money supposedly paid to Motale as an advance for the information on Tsolo. Harry briefly wondered whether it was over this that the ICD was after him, or something else. Whatever the case might be, if he could not figure out what Motale was playing at, his career as a police officer might soon be over.

Motale or Swarts? Swarts or Motale? Heads or tails?

The sudden knock at the kitchen door snaps Harry out of such thoughts. He did not hear the front gate open and close, nor did the front doorbell ring. Who would normally head straight for the kitchen door? The knock comes louder this time, and Harry wonders why Tanya does not answer it, till he remembers she is plugged into her music.

'Harry?' It is the voice of Russell Swarts.

Shit, he's the last person Harry wants to speak to right now.

'Tanya? It's Russell. Open up. I've got James and Sammy here with me. We need to speak to Harry.'

There is something feral and desperate in the man's voice, and it makes Harry reach for the key taped to his computer monitor. Quietly, he reaches down and unlocks the gun safe concealed in the lowest drawer of his desk.

5

Tanya Fouché throws open the outer door, a smile already on her lips at this unexpected surprise. 'What happened to you on Wednesday? You just disappeared on us.'

Russell is leaning with one arm against the doorframe while a wiry man with a smoker's papyrus skin stands behind him and stares at her with startling blue eyes. An Indian has his back turned to her and is looking down the concrete driveway towards the front gate. Russell Swarts and two of his famous Ballies, she figures. Though she wanted to hustle them inside and offer them a Friday-night welcome-home-Harry drink, something about Russell Swarts' red eyes and heavy frown make Tanya swallow her words of invitation. The joviality she had come to associate with him in Port Elizabeth is gone, replaced by that same air of ferocity she first felt in his presence.

'Evening, Tanya.' His voice seems as empty as an open grave. 'Is he around?'

With one massive hand, Russell Swarts pushes the kitchen door wide open and proceeds into the house. It is only under the fluorescent kitchen light that she notices the scrapes and bruises on his arms, the spray of dried blood on his shirt, a shard of glass still lodged in his beard.

'You've got blood all over you,' she remarks. 'What happened?'

When he does not immediately answer her, Tanya has to resist an irrational urge to run towards the bedrooms of the house, after locking the connecting security door between kitchen and corridor.

'Harry?' calls Swarts. 'Would you join us in the kitchen, please?'

She still refuses to completely believe that something is drastically wrong about this situation, even though all her natural instincts are telling her otherwise. These are just Harry's colleagues come to see how he is, she reminds herself. This unfriendliness of theirs, it's just the way cops are when they're going through a rough time, right?

'I'm going to check the front.' The tall one with the blue eyes impatiently shoulders his way past Swarts. 'Watch the gate, Sammy,' he calls over his shoulder.

'What do you think I'm already doing, wallah?'

'Check the study too,' Swarts tells Franklin. 'I saw a light on in there as we came in.'

The hairs on the nape of her neck rise as the one with the ice-cube eyes circles past her and lets his gaze linger on her breasts like she is nothing more than a hooker. The sleeves of his shirt have been rolled up to reveal some sort of military tattoos on both forearms. She wonders whether this one is Franklin or Combrink.

It's Franklin, she tells herself. *Harry always said you could smell the other one downwind from a pig farm.*

'Is he sleeping?'

'Yes.'

Swarts nods. 'Must be tired after the flight.'

The man she once mistook for a drunken Father Christmas suddenly grimaces as though he has either been hit by some unseen force or is suffering from a strange form of Parkinson's disease. Even with nearly four feet between her and Russell Swarts, she can smell the reek of stale brandy on him. Tanya listens for Franklin moving around in the living room, but she does not register anything. Any sound he made ceased the moment the connecting door swung shut behind him. She hopes that, whatever these men want from Harry, they'll leave quickly without waking Jeanie.

With every slow step that Russell Swarts now takes in her direction, Tanya retreats accordingly, until she feels herself bump against the kitchen table. She is about to tell him to back the hell off when he quickly steps to the right and neatly positions himself between her and the open door to the corridor, effectively blocking off any escape towards the bedrooms.

'How was your flight?' he asks casually.

'Cut the fucking chit-chat, Russell, and tell me why you're piss-drunk and covered in blood?'

He smiles sadly. 'You didn't hear then?'

'Hear what? I just got off a fucking plane with a man who was injured under your command.'

'They've started a war.'

'Who?'

'The Abasindisi. They bombed Maloney's, the bar where we all drink.'

Swarts runs a weathered hand over his face, and bares his teeth.

'Jesus, Russell.' She makes a move in his direction.

'Don't!' He holds up a hand, while the other actually drops to the unclipped gun that is holstered at his side. She pulls up short. 'Just don't touch me,' he orders.

A faint squeak of floorboards from behind Russell Swarts causes them both to turn in that direction. Harry, with his head still bandaged, steps into the light of the kitchen from the dark corridor beyond. There is a revolver in his hand and an unmistakable click as he pulls back the hammer.

'Evening, superintendent.'

'Good to see you're up and about, Bond.' Russell Swarts' voice is raised, and Tanya can tell this is to alert Franklin to Harry's presence in the kitchen.

'Is there any particular reason why you've invited yourself into my house?'

Swarts shrugs and smiles. 'Just came by to welcome one of my boys home. A man can still do that, can't he?'

'What did you say about a bombing?' Tanya asks.

Swarts briefly glances back towards her, but does not respond to her question. She is astonished by his transformation. This brutal man in front of her has nothing in common with the joker to whom she had first warmed in that dingy pub in Port Elizabeth.

'Come on, Russie,' she says in a placatory voice. 'Whatever this is about, I'm sure there's another way to discuss it?'

Harry nods in the direction of the closed door leading to the living room in the front of the house, then glances spuriously over his shoulder into the dark corridor behind him. The corridor is not the only way to reach the bedrooms; they can also be reached via a modest foyer in the front of the house, connected to the living room.

'Franklin,' Harry says to Swarts. 'Call him back.'

Though Harry's face is ashen grey, his eyes have a gleam in them that provokes a deep unease in Tanya. His voice reminds her of the man who once stuck a knife up her nose and promised her a cutting-edge makeover. She briefly thinks about moving over to his side of the kitchen, but suddenly finds this thought almost as uncomfortable as having Russell Swarts standing between them. With the two men glowering at each other like a pair of pitbulls, she hazards a guess that any sudden move on her part might just set one or both of them off.

And still not a peep from Franklin.

Christ, where is that pervert? She glances at the door to the living room.

'I said, call him back.'

Russie Swarts appears unfazed, however. 'I'm sorry, Bond, but you need to come with us. There's work to be done.'

'He's not going anywhere, Russell. He's got two bullet holes in him.'

'Tanya?'

'Yes?'

'I like you a lot, but right now is not a good time to yak my ear off.'

Hot blood rushes to her face at the insult, and she is about to reply sharply when Harry gives a near-imperceptible shake of his head. Then he positions his back to the kitchen side wall so that he can simultaneously watch the passageway leading to the rest of the house and also the living-room door.

'Franklin!' he yells. 'If I so much as hear a cockroach fart, I'm pulling the trigger. I want to see my living room door open slowly, then a hand come out holding your gun by its barrel.'

'Christ, Harry, what makes you think he's got a gun out?' she asks.

He gives her a look so stern that it embarrasses her, making her feel like a naive country girl.

'The Abasindisi stuck a pipe bomb in Maloney's, Harry,' says Swarts. 'They killed Kommie. Last time I checked in, it was ten dead. Put the gun away, and let's talk about how we're going to take them down.'

'How do you know it was the Phaliso brothers?'

'It was Wally Khuzwayo who brought in the bomb personally, a special delivery just to let us know how little they respect us.'

'And I suppose you're sure about that?'

'I was *there*, you shit! The fuck had the balls to tell me he was our contact in the organization before he sent the whole place to kingdom come. He screwed Makhe Motale, and he screwed you too. What did I tell you from the beginning? Don't ever trust a blimming rat, didn't I say that? Don't ever pay them money, I said. And what did you go and do? You based our entire investigation on information that came from not one but two bullshitters. Christ, Harry, whatever were you thinking?'

Tanya sees Harry blanch at the sound of Makhe Motale's name, and she instantly regrets ever having mentioned it to Swarts.

'How do you know his name?' he asks Swarts.

'It doesn't matter. What does is that you are now going after them with us.'

'I asked you a simple question. *How* do you know his name?'

Swarts glances over his shoulder at Tanya and lets his eyes rest on her long enough for realization to dawn on Harry's face. At that moment she might have stabbed Swarts in the kidneys, if something suitably sharp had been within reach.

'I'm sorry, Harry,' she stammers. 'I thought it would help you.'

He gives her a slight nod and lets his eyes drift away from her, without Tanya understanding what the gesture is supposed to mean. Did he accept her apology, or was it anger and disappointment at her? Did he simply not care?

'Where is Makhe now?' asks Harry.

A self-satisfied grin spreads over Swarts' face. 'That I don't think you have to worry about.'

'Damn it, Russell!' yells Harry. 'What's happened to you?'

'What is it you want to hear from me, Harry? That I've been at this job longer than you've been alive, and that I have ended up with nothing to show for it? Twenty-eight years and enough Extra Mile Awards to wipe my arse with until I die of old age? Boo-hoo, where's my promotion, then? The fucking *real* recognition? My skin's not the right colour to get higher than supe? I don't have the right party card? No, I'm loyal to the force – that's all that happened. To the men I serve with. Where the hell are *your* priorities?'

'I joined the service to uphold justice, not some lunatic crusade like yours.'

Russell Swarts chuckles. 'You did? So explain to me why you have a gun in my face? You want to shoot me because you think I had something to do with you getting shot, isn't that what's been on your mind?'

'It's crossed my mind.'

'I want to know, Harry, is it right for you to compile files on your superior, when you should be going after the killers of the Mohosh family? Is it right to be holding over my head an incident that happened seven years ago, when Kommie is now lying in a fucking morgue refrigerator? Conventional justice only goes so far, Harry, and if that's as far as you're willing to go, then shit, man, the other side will always have an edge on you.'

'What's wrong with a proper investigation now? If

you're so sure it's Khuzwayo who is responsible, then where's the rest of the department?'

'*Fuck* investigation, Harry! Having chunks of your friend splattered all over you does *not* call for an investigation. It calls for retaliation, and you're going to be a part of it.'

'Harry!' Tanya yells in alarm.

Without anyone noticing, Franklin has emerged from the gloom of the corridor. Harry brings his revolver around to bear on him, and freezes when he sees something else.

With one hand wrapped around Jeanie's mouth and the other holding a silenced pistol to her head, Franklin hustles the little girl into the kitchen. In all her years of childcare, Tanya has never seen one look so frightened and confused.

'I thought this might get your attention.' Franklin smiles. 'Russie, he talks too much; it's his biggest fucking problem.' He points the silenced pistol at Harry. 'Put the gun on the floor and kick it over this way.'

'Russell, please tell him to let go of her,' begs Tanya in the most reassuring voice she can muster. 'There's no need for this. I don't care what the three of you are trying to sort out between you, but it doesn't have to involve her.'

'Blondie, this is going a bit far, isn't it?' Swarts remonstrates with his partner.

'By the time you're finally done talking here, Wally Khuzwayo and the Phalisos are safe in custody and then we're fucked. Have you thought of that?'

'Enough.' Harry lays his revolver on the floor and steps away from it. 'There. Now let her go.'

For a second it looks like Franklin won't do so. A cruel thin-lipped smile crosses his face and he yanks Jeanie's head upward and to the side, as if to break her neck. She grunts in pain behind his palm.

'It's as easy as that, Mason. Remember that.'

'Let her go!' cries Tanya.

But the man has already pushed the girl away from himself, and immediately brings his second hand up to steady the weapon already pointing at Harry.

Jeanie runs to her father's open arms, and he embraces her tightly. The way he whispers to her, and squeezes his eyes shut at her touch, brings a hard knot into Tanya's throat.

'Let's go now, Harry,' Swarts says leadenly. 'If all goes well, you'll be back with your family before twelve, and we can forget all about this. That's if some other people can keep quiet.' Swarts glances meaningfully at Tanya, and the threat in his voice is naked.

As if deciding he has gone far enough, Tanya lunges for his sleeve. 'Please don't do this, Russell. I know you're a better person than this. You're a father too, for Christ's sake! How can you do this to her?'

Russell Swarts reacts by tearing his arm loose from her grasp and backhanding her across the face with such force that she stumbles hard against the kitchen sink before collapsing to the floor. For a moment her world is nothing but swimming colours, then she hears Harry cry out in pain and Jeanie begin screaming at the top of her lungs.

They've shot him! is her first thought. *They've shot him, and I didn't even hear the gun go off.*

Tanya's vision clears in time to see Harry fall to his knees and clutch at his head; Franklin has his gun raised, ready to take another swipe at him. Swarts is hunched over and clutching at his stomach, as though Harry had landed a good punch there before going down himself.

'Get up!' Franklin yanks Harry up by his shirt collar and shoves him towards the door. A couple of buttons tear loose and fall on the lino. 'Let's go!'

By now Swarts has grabbed Jeanie and is trying to calm her screaming, even telling her that her daddy will be home soon. She writhes against his embrace and beats at his giant chest with her fists.

'Leave her alone, you fuck!' Tanya cries out and begins to weep uncontrollably, partly in pain but mostly with an incredible sense of betrayal. 'Jeanie, come here, baby.'

'Tell them to give my daddy back!'

'They won't listen to me, baby. Come here, *please*.'

Jeanie pushes herself free from Russell Swarts and takes the few short steps towards Tanya, where she buries herself deep in a waiting embrace.

'Tanya,' comes a soft reconciliatory tone.

'Just get way from us! Just go!'

She tries to stare him down then, to show him exactly how much she detests him, but Russell Swarts is barely more than a blur through the tears swimming in her eyes. She hastily brushes them aside, in time to see him give a resigned nod.

'Call anyone else and you'll force us to do something drastic to Harry. Then we'll have to come for the little one and you, too. And don't for a second think I couldn't erase tonight without trace, if you force me. I've been at this game a long time, girlie, and I always come out on top.'

He turns on his heel and stomps out of the kitchen door after Harry and Franklin. When she hears the gate scrape open and a vehicle rev its engine, she slides down against the kitchen cupboards and pulls Harry's daughter into a tighter embrace.

TEN

1

Stirring underneath the layers of newspaper and sheets of plastic that cover her, the first thing she becomes aware of is the intense pain in her lower back from sleeping on hard concrete, with nothing but a few thin sheets of cardboard to protect her from the cold ground. The rash she has developed on the back of both knees immediately begins to itch, and she reaches down to scratch. The movement dislodges her makeshift blankets and lets in the freezing night air. With the abrupt chill, she is pulled right back into wakefulness and a god-awful stench that she finds bewildering.

That can't be from me, can it?

She takes another sniff and almost retches. The stink brings into stark recall where she is bedded down for the night and why the smell. She had wedged herself and her children into the space between a brick wall and a dumpster located behind the petrol station where she tried briefly to beg for money. After all hell broke loose in the city centre, she thought it safer to find shelter in Alexandra, away from the danger of bombs and police, but by the time she arrived on the township's outskirts night had caught her out of doors yet again, and so, instead of wandering aimlessly around the township after dark, she had opted for the obscurity of this loading bay.

She reaches out for her youngest, whose burns have looked like they are turning infected, but her groping hand only touches gravel and a few old deep-fried chips.

Alarmed, she reaches around behind her, but not one of the three sisters is where she should be.

The mother slings aside the newspapers and calls for her children in an urgent whisper. She does not want to raise her voice too much since it is a Friday night and there is no telling who is out there in the darkness and in what state of drunkenness.

Again she calls, more urgently this time, then listens carefully. All she can hear though is a handful of car engines running in the petrol-station forecourt around the corner, a few gruff voices shouting, and some terrible music blaring endlessly over the distorted speakers. She gets up on her knees and peers around the corner of the dumpster at a section of the loading yard that is visible to her in the dark, thinking they might have gone for a wee in the darkness, but still there is no sign of them.

Panicking, she scrambles out into the open on all fours and surveys her surroundings more clearly.

'*Dumela, sisie.*' A man's deep voice reaches out to her. She shrinks back instinctively. Alone on the street, there is absolutely nothing she can do if cornered here, with three young children in tow.

When her eyes eventually adjust, she notices a car parked over in the darkness, one of those fancy 4x4s the *umlungus* love to drive, but she never even heard it coming in. Then her eyes alight on her children clustered around the figure of a man, and each is busily eating something clasped in her hands.

'Get away from him!' she shouts. 'Girls, you come here right now!'

They obediently come running, happy grins on their faces and grease smeared all over their chins, and she gathers them around her knees. Close up, the spicy smell of samosas makes her stomach rumble, despite the half-pint of whisky she drank earlier to just fall asleep and forget.

'What did I tell you about talking to strangers?' she admonishes her kids.

'They looked so hungry, I bought them some food.'

That deep voice addressing her from the darkness sounds warm and sympathetic, like in those Barry White songs she used to listen to on the radio. It reminds her of how long it has been since someone adopted a sincere tone towards her, and this immediately makes whoever is speaking seem less of a threat. A second man, who had been kneeling amidst her children, stands up at the sound of their voices, and brushes crumbs from his hands. He stares at her as though he is trying to place her, with little success, though she has never seen him before in her life, she is sure. His face looks battered and bruised, his nose appearing freshly broken, and his forearms have a rash of nasty cuts on them. She becomes aware of yet another man who paces restlessly atop the ledge of the loading bay itself. He is little more than a noiseless shadow, a ghost, but though she finds it difficult to focus on him, he makes her feel uncomfortable and tense.

'Wait, *sisie*; don't be afraid of us.'

The first man, the one with the warm voice, steps into an angle of orange light and she sees now that he is in his forties and heftily built. On his lips is a disarming smile which she can't bring herself to completely trust, despite the soothing lull in his tone.

'You must be cold,' he says.

She shrinks back as he approaches, and draws her children back with her. She wonders whether she will be able to herd them all through the narrow gap between wall and dumpster before he can make a grab for her, or whether she should just shout for them to scatter and run, and hope for the best.

'It's a cold night, yes, *ndoda*.' The man who has been beaten up keeps on looking at her, a slight frown on his face.

'And you are hungry, too?'

'It's been difficult.'

'I can see that. No mother should be forced to sleep in the garbage.'

The other men do not seem to make a move in her direction, which she finds encouraging. The third one jumps off the loading ledge, and in the orange light the face she catches sight of forces a gasp from her. It is long and thin, yet the vacant eyes are so round they appear to have no eyelids.

'Godun, just stay out of the light, will you?' The bigger man's voice has moved instantly from gentle to irritable. 'Can't you see you're scaring her?'

Godun? That is an unusual name, and she's thinking that she has heard it somewhere before.

Godun eyes her up and down with open distaste, but for some strange reason he does not reply to the other man. Instead, he obediently steps back and seems to dissolve into the night, as though he is naturally a part of the shadows.

'*Sisie*—' the big man begins again, but she cuts him short.

'I'm not screwing any of you, if that's what you want.'

'What?' He seems genuinely surprised.

'If you want to give me food, then give it to me, but I'd rather have money. I'm not fucking you, though. And you can't have my daughters either.'

He seems visibly taken aback and glances at the others

in surprise, leaving her to speculate whether he is just a smooth operator or someone who is genuinely well-meaning. Maybe this lot are from a church, she wonders.

A tiny kernel of hope begins to irritate her heart at the thought.

The burly man shakes his head. 'No, that's not what I was going to ask you.'

'What do you want from me then? You can see I have nothing.'

He takes another step closer, and this time she feels the semicircle of her children shrink against her legs. If this man is a church-going do-gooder, what would she not do for a decent meal, some warm clothes, and medicine for her daughter's wounds?

'What can *I* do for *you* should be the question, *sisie*.'

He moves closer with an upturned palm held out to her, as though attempting to befriend a dog. The will to escape leeches out of her limbs, not because of any strange power he is exerting over her, but simply because she is too tired to run any further. That irritating kernel in her heart has grown into a tight knot of desperate hope that clamps up her throat.

'*Ndoda* . . .' A sudden violent sob forces its way out of her mouth. 'I can't remember when last I ate a hot meal. And I am so cold, *ndoda*.'

His hand finally touches her head, and she feels herself crumble under that benign gesture.

'Are you a churchman?' she asks in a last attempt to establish his intentions. 'Please, tell me that.'

'No, I'm not with any church, *sisie*.' Both his hands drop on to her shoulders and she tenses, expecting pain to follow. 'But I am your guardian for as long as you will help me.'

'Me help you?' She shakes her head. 'But I have nothing to give.'

For some reason she feels no shame in telling him this – that she has fallen so low, she is simply an animal begging for food.

'Will we live through each other then, *sisie*? That is what I want to know from you.'

Warm tears spill down her cheeks and she is surprised that she can still weep. 'Yes, of course, *ndoda*. If only I can have something warm to eat.'

'Then come with me.'

He helps her up and leads her around the corner into the bright fluorescence of the station forecourt, where the smell of doughnuts and roasted chicken mingles with that of petrol and spilled oil. And when this time the attendants do not chase her away as she enters the shop with this stranger, she knows she is one of the living again, that soon others will speak to her and even touch her again as though she still has some human worth.

For this gift she also knows she will return the favour, whatever it may cost.

2

In the guest bathroom of the Phaliso brothers' home, Wally Khuzwayo is studying his broken nose and swollen face in the mirror. He finds it strange and mildly humorous that he should again be looking himself in the eye, barely four hours after he escaped from the men's room at Maloney's. Only this time he is faced with a different problem than Swarts, namely what to do now that Godun and Ncolela have him back. Though they appear to all be in the same boat again, he has the distinct impression that he is not only still under suspicion but an unwanted passenger as well. Unwanted, but somehow still necessary.

They have worked quickly since his rescue outside of the High Court, and it reminded him of the old days when they were genuinely three, not just two with a third man on the side. The moment they had parked their bullet-ridden Prado behind the petrol station, Ncolela went to work on some of the locals he knew and some he did not know, even contacting some of the runners they used back when they were still only a small Alexandra outfit, and the nationwide Abasindisi Security Services was still but a fanciful dream.

While Ncolela concentrated on the first vagrant he happened to come across, Wally had phoned an old associate and told him where to find the car. He would have it cut down to size before the sun rose next morning, and would keep the weapons hidden in the boot as a bonus for doing a rush job. After this call, Wally smashed the cellphone against the delivery ledge and hurled its pieces up on to the roof of the building.

What exactly Ncolela now had in mind Wally could not guess, but it encouraged him greatly that the man should think they could actually evade the *gatas* after what had happened at Maloney's. Even though they had worked as a tightly knit group up to that point, and it felt good doing so again, it also seemed little more than the bizarre re-enactment of an old ritual.

Do the Phalisos really think they can go on pretending that the Abasindisi had nothing to do with the bomb at Maloney's, now that I have been identified? Fresh on the heels of that thought, Wally Khuzwayo has to wonder what is delaying Swarts and his men, and why the entire city's *gatas* are not yet on their doorstep.

'Brothers always look after their own,' Ncolela had said as he dragged Wally up from where he lay in the street. To Wally those same words rang with an air of finality, especially when they arrived back at the pink house at the far end of the dead-end street, and Godun set about dousing it with diesel and petrol taken from the garage. He grew even more nervous when he tried to call his wife on the house phone and Ncolela intercepted him by yanking the line out of the wall. His voice had dropped then, and Wally recognized that a familiar fuse was burning in his eyes.

'We are your family, and always have been. There is no one else, Wally Phaliso. Not any more.'

It was at that moment that Wally began to severely doubt whether he would survive this night with the brothers. The time to save himself had come and gone, he realized, and he could only hope that these two were interested in him alone, and that they had not already visited his wife and son before coming after him. After all, that was the kind of thing Godun loved doing.

Why oh why did he think the brothers might treat him any differently from the way Swarts and his gang might have done? For an instant he wishes the cops had captured him instead, but this thought is immediately followed by a hot burst of anger.

Hi wena, Khuzwayo! You want this, you want that! Is it any wonder that you've never been able to get away from these two, hey?

Looking at himself the way he appears now – beaten up and desperate like so many other faces he has left in the dust during the course of his life – it dawns on him that perhaps he has not been the wise adviser to the Phalisos he always considered himself; that instead he has been a lapdog yapping around their feet as they strode on towards their destinies. He smiles bitterly at this. With the bruising on his face illuminated by the dull lightbulb above him, his reflection twists into a gruesome death mask which he barely recognizes. It is not the first time this thought has intruded upon him, but it is certainly the first time that it crosses his mind with a measure of acceptance rather than resentment. He is, indeed, nothing more than a fucking *nja*.

In the distance tyres screech as a car takes a corner at speed and races down the long hill of Marlboro Drive. Wally's ears immediately prick up, expecting to hear a hundred more engines following in its wake. He glances up at the small window above the toilet, convinced that he can see blue lights flashing across the white ceramic tiles. But the sound of the car eventually disappears in the direction of the N3, and he is left only with the unexciting silence of a poor suburban neighbourhood located on the edge of a rowdy township called Alexandra.

3

It did not matter how he explained it to himself, that smelly woman from behind the dumpster reminded Ncolela of his dead wife Hlubi. Sure, it might have just been the pink tracksuit – anything pink reminds him of Hlubi these days – but it could just has easily have been the defiance in her eyes as she stood her ground while surrounded by three strong men.

Hlubi come back, to remind him to be humble? It was just like her.

Fuck humble, he thought. *In this day and age who has the time for it?*

Staring out of the darkened window of his living room into the garden lying under the pale moon usually has a calming effect on Ncolela Phaliso, but not tonight. Sometimes he is sure he can still see her out there, moving in and out of the deep shadows on the fringes of his property; other times he is convinced he can hear Hlubi's voice on the wind. People have asked him why he has not sold this house, or at least redecorated it, but how can he sell the place when it is only here that he can still sense her? How can he renovate it when no amount of effort would return her warmth to this cold shell?

He senses rather than hears Godun impatiently pacing around upstairs, sloshing a gallon can over anything that will burn. Ncolela has always known that sooner or later the time would come for him to be rid of this place, and when Hlubi had finally told him to burn out the rats in her home, he realized the moment had arrived. Perhaps he had Wally to thank for hurrying things along, perhaps not. All he knows for certain is that rescuing that idiot from police custody has been his riskiest ploy yet – and it won't be his last gamble before dawn.

A toilet flushes in the guest bathroom and, when the door opens, a sharp light falls across the open-plan living room behind him. The sudden light and noise further irritate Ncolela, and so does the man who is the cause of it all.

'I said, all lights are to be kept off. Didn't I fucking say that?'

Wally takes a step backward to throw the bathroom switch, and the house is immediately plunged into complete darkness once more.

'If we're going to burn this place down and go into hiding, isn't it about time we should be leaving?' asks Wally.

Ncolela feels his hand begin to shake against the curtain, and he has to clamp it around the material to remain calm. The arrogance of the man! If it was not for himself and Godun, he would be in police custody by now, and no doubt singing like a bird. But then, if Godun *was* right in believing that Wally had betrayed the location of their weapons cache to the police, he would then be exactly where he wanted to be, safe amongst the *gatas*.

'We're not leaving,' he says in a measured tone. 'At least not right now.'

'What are you looking out for?'

The man's nasal voice is cautious and uncertain, surely the mark of someone who is hiding something. How did Godun spot it before he himself did?

'Is it the *gatas*?'

Ncolela closes his eyes. 'I'm not looking. I'm listening.'

'Is it her you're hearing?'

'No, Hlubi is finished with us. She has made her point and gone back where she belongs.'

'Ncolela, I need to know that you'll look after my son and my wife if something goes wrong.'

If something goes *wrong*! 'You don't have a son or a wife now.'

'What's that supposed to mean?'

Ncolela lets go of the curtain, and what little light still filtered into the house from the moon and distant streetlights disappears. The entire room is plunged into a velvety darkness that is filled only with the cloying stench of petrol and the other man's fear.

'You only have your two brothers now, to whom you owe all your loyalty.'

'*Banna*, I want a straight answer for once.'

Wally bumps against the couch facing the window as he retreats in the direction of the front door.

Ncolela follows. Slowly.

'You are a Phaliso. If you had married, I would have known, because I am your older brother.'

'What are you talking about? My name is Wally *Khuzwayo* and I'm two years older than you. Let's stop with this shit and put the lights back on.'

'That can't be your name,' he says. 'Khuzwayo is dead because he betrayed his people.'

'I betrayed no one, and I am right here with you, am I not? The way it's always been.'

There is a yelp in the darkness, and something glass hits the tiled floor with a crash.

'Get away from me!' Wally shouts in another direction.

Godun must have crept into the room without either one of them noticing. Who else is that quiet?

'The one called Wally Khuzwayo ran to the police and tried to buy himself an early retirement.'

'I didn't run to the *gatas*!' Wally's voice grows shrill. 'Isn't it enough that I bombed that shithole for you?'

'That one, he sold us out! He has to die, along with his wife and child. The slate has to be wiped clean. That's how we've always worked.'

He listens to Wally change direction and shuffle deeper into the house. Fingers brush along unseen walls, desperately looking for light switches. They eventually find some, but suddenly there is no power. Godun's doing? Of course it is.

'Please, Ncolela.'

Panic is settling into the man's voice. Good.

'What?'

'Tell me you will leave them alone.'

'Who?'

'*My fucking family!*'

'They're right here, brother,' he says in a deliberate monotone. 'Wally Phaliso, he always did what he was ordered to do. The man I know, he'll still get rid of the people threatening his family. He'll risk his life for his brothers, as they did the same for him.'

'What are you talking about?'

'I'm giving you two options here,' he says. 'So choose.'

'Choose *what*?' Wally yells back.

'Are you a Phaliso or a Khuzwayo, Wally?' Ncolela roars into the darkness. 'Is there a traitor in this house, in this family?'

There is a strangled gasp from the back of the corridor, then frightened staccato breathing. Without actually being able to see what has happened, or completely understanding what he heard, Ncolela knows his little brother has got a knife to Wally's throat. A low mewling reaches him and confirms his suspicions.

'Godun says you better answer quickly.' He feels his way around the couch and heads down the passageway in the direction of that terrified breathing. 'Decide, Wally. I won't ask again.'

His outstretched hand brushes across Wally's face, and he feels the man flinch at his touch.

'Are they still alive?' whispers Wally. 'Just tell me that.'

There is a cry of pain from the darkness, and Ncolela

imagines that Godun has tightened whatever hold he has on Wally – perhaps even cut him a little. He finds both of Wally's eye sockets with his thumbs and gently presses against the eyelids. The man's breath catches in anticipation of pain.

'Only Khuzwayo would ask that question,' growls Ncolela. 'Wally Phaliso, he does not know the woman that lives in Graceland Towers, number one-oh-five-nine. He does not even know the boy that lives there either. They mean nothing to him, because he has never met them.'

He begins to press harder on those hidden eyes.

'You're right!' Wally cries abruptly in a shrill voice that makes Ncolela wince. He never thought his old friend capable of such desperation, but then he never thought him capable of betrayal either. 'That one, he is now dead,' mumbles Wally. 'He died in Maloney's with the *gatas*. I was there. I saw it myself . . . brother.'

As much as Ncolela would love to blind this Judas here, now, he lets go of the man's face and asks his brother to release him. There is a short scuffle in the darkness and then Wally is on his knees, weeping like a child.

'Little brother, you did well at Maloney's. What you did makes me proud. It took courage, that. But the *gatas* – every one of them now knows who you are.'

Wally makes an effort to bring his voice under control. 'They do,' he admits.

'And the bomb you planted, it had nothing to do with the Abasindisi, did it?'

'No,' he says.

Ncolela is satisfied by the new tone in Wally's voice. It is resigned, yes, but determined too, as though he has implicitly understood what needs to be done next. He has always been slow on the uptake, thinks Ncolela, but once the message got through, it would take over completely. Wally Khuzwayo will not prove to be a complete waste to him, not even now.

'It was just you acting in your own interests, wasn't it?' says Ncolela. 'You were running a criminal faction within the organization, which has brought shame on us.'

'That's right.'

'But we'll deliver you up, won't we?'

Wally says nothing in reply, which immediately brings Ncolela's blood to the boil. *If this doesn't fucking work. . .*

But then Wally interrupts his boss's train of thought. 'You will give me up, and I understand what must be done.'

ELEVEN

1

The petrol station on the outskirts of Alexandra where he arranged to meet Detective Busisiwe Mosetsane now comes up on the right side of Marlboro Drive. Jacob Tshabalala cuts across the darkened road, which heads down a long steep hill, and pulls into one of the many empty parking bays lined up in front of the station's brightly lit convenience store. It took him nearly an hour to cross the city, time which he spent listening out for any breaking news on what had happened at Maloney's. Though he has learned nothing new, the endless stream of repetitive quarter-hourly news has kept his mind off what he did back home.

A loud rap at his car window draws his attention. He turns to find Mosetsane smiling at him, looking a lot more outgoing a personality when not dressed in her power suit. Despite his fragile mood, he appreciates how good she looks in a baby-blue turtleneck and dark blue windbreaker.

He cranks open the window. '*Dumela*, detective.'

'I told you on the phone, it's Busi.' Again she answers him in English, and he has to wonder why she keeps refusing to address him in one of the African languages.

He nods at the passenger door. 'Get in. There is not much time.'

He leans over to unlock it for her, while taking stock of the empty petrol station. Even the counter inside the shop appears to be unmanned.

No one wants to be outside tonight, is his first thought. *Not after the trouble in the city.*

The people from this neighbourhood probably have every reason to be scared, too, as every police officer on the road tonight will be wound up tighter than a watch-spring. He has already passed through two roadblocks and has no doubt that many more will be set up around the townships by morning.

'So what did you drag me out for on this chilly night?' Mosetsane settles into the passenger seat and clasps her hands for warmth in between her thighs. 'You said this was about Tsolo.'

He again becomes aware of her feminine scent, and he wonders whether it might have been a mistake to call her. But he needs Mosetsane with him, because he needs as much information about Swarts and his Ballies as she has.

'You told me the national commissioner had a special interest in the SVC team that went down to Tsolo. Why is that?'

She glances down at her hands. Even before she opens her mouth, he knows she will try to evade his question, so he persists.

'Busi, Swarts and his men grabbed Harry Mason from his house a little over half an hour ago. They said something about going after the Abasindisi, and I need to know where they're heading before Harry is dragged into something bad.'

'I thought your friend was still in hospital.'

'He'd just got back from PE when they took him.'

She peers out of the window at the eerily empty petrol station. 'Are we going somewhere?'

'We're looking for a man called Makhe Motale. There's a good chance he was Harry's informant in the Tsolo case.'

'The same guy that landed you in hot water?'

'How do you know about that?'

She smiles at him. It is warm and teasing at the same time. 'I keep my ear to the ground, especially when it's about people I need to know more about.' She holds his gaze with that intense curiosity of hers. When he does not immediately react to what she said, she nods towards the road ahead. 'Drive on then, and I'll tell you what I know.'

2

'I lied to you last time,' says Mosetsane, 'or at least I didn't tell you the whole truth.'

Jacob offers her a dry smile. 'I could tell at the time.'

'What exactly do you know of Senior Superintendent Russell Swarts and Captain James T. Franklin?'

He shrugs. 'I've only ever spoken with Swarts a few times. He's a lot like the other older white guys still left in the service: he sticks to his own kind, but he is very good at what he does. At least that's the impression I've had up to now. Franklin I've hardly ever spoken with, but I don't think he is someone I would ever invite home for dinner.'

She nods. 'There have been plans for some time now within the ICD to bring them to book on a number of charges regarding human-rights violations.'

'I've heard they can be rough.'

'Four deaths while in custody, on separate occasions, and all of them linked to the Ballies, as they like to call themselves, is hardly what I would call "rough", Jacob. It's murder.'

'Four?'

'Two this year alone. Then there have been nearly 150 complaints levelled at Swarts, Naidoo, Franklin and

Combrink combined, most of them unresolved or with-drawn when the investigation process took too long. Of those that did eventually go to court, not a single one has stuck.'

Jacob is not surprised. Crime scenes are easily thrown into disarray by complicit cops in order to create reason-able doubt. If you know what the courts will look for, the evidence is even easier to disassemble. When it was still Murder and Robbery that investigated police-involved cases, detectives spent less time trying to figure out what happened than writing up the report so that the officer under investigation seemed justified in his actions, however extreme, because a guilty verdict would not only reflect badly on those police officers involved, but would also bring negative pressure down on the entire service. And if the service itself got under pressure, the investigating officer's life amongst his peers was sure to turn into a slow-burning hell. This obvious lack of impartiality in the process was one of the reasons why the ICD was first created, but even the ICD itself did not want to step on too many police-service toes. After all, they more often than not needed the co-operation of police officers to solve their investigations, and anyway many of the ICD investi-gators used to be in the police service themselves so therefore still had friends wearing blues.

'At least you won't have to worry about Combrink any more,' says Jacob. 'He was killed in Maloney's.'

'You were there when it happened?'

'Got there just afterwards.'

Though he keeps his eyes on the road, he can sense her studying him, as if she is trying to gauge whether to take the subject further.

'It's horrible what they did,' is all she says then, 'and I

hope they arrest every single one of the culprits.' After a pause, she continues, 'Some of the complaints against Swarts were laid barely a month after the ICD was created, back in '97.'

'So what's taken you so long to go after him?'

A laugh escapes her lips and Jacob turns to look at her in surprise.

'First I move too fast for you, and now too slow?' asks Mosetsane. 'You're the demanding type, aren't you?'

Beyond the windshield the terrain has grown darker, with fewer streetlights spaced out along the road winding into the poorer areas of Alexandra, where squatters continuously rebuild their shacks on the floodplain of the Jukskei River after the summer's flash floods have dragged them away. Though the breeze has grown into a driving wind by now, the perpetual coal-fire smog from thousands of homes without electricity still hangs as thick as cotton over the valley, and gives the sparse light thrown on the road a copper colour.

'That was a joke, Jacob.'

He glances at her and smiles, but the act of doing so feels like two meat-hooks pulling at the corners of his mouth. 'Sorry, it's not been the best of days for me.'

'You didn't lose anyone close to you in the bombing, did you?'

Jacob weighs up her words. He did not have to count Hugh Semenya or even Combrink as friends to feel their loss, did he?

'No,' he says. 'Go on, tell me the rest.'

'Swarts might be just a senior superintendent, but he has managed to establish himself in such a powerful position that he has remained untouched. Certain directors at the ICD have been extremely hesitant to pursue him, or any of his men for that matter, because his reputation for delivering results is unmatched, both in the police service and in the public eye. He has undoubtedly earned himself some powerful allies that way.'

'So what's changed? Something big must have happened for you to go ahead with an investigation like this so quickly. What's so important about Tsolo?'

'It was towards the end of last year that the National Intelligence Agency approached the national commissioner with some damning evidence. You may not know this, but there's been bad blood between the commissioner himself and Swarts ever since a gala event in Pretoria in '97.'

'Everybody knows about that. It's a story that's made the rounds at police college.'

'When the commissioner listened to what they had to tell him, I think he must have jumped for joy. Here finally was his perfect chance to nail Swarts. The next morning he was on the phone to my bosses, pressuring them to make all our enquiries into Swarts an absolute priority.'

'What was it about, though?'

Before she can answer him, however, Jacob notices something happening to the south and slams on the brakes, hard enough for their seatbelts to pull tight across their chests.

'What is it?' Mosetsane asks.

'Trouble.'

He turns to look back through the rear window and reverses a short way along the sandy shoulder of the road. Stopping the car, he points.

'Down there. See that?'

About half a kilometre beyond an overgrown thicket a large gathering of people is backlit by flames which seem to have been lit at the entrance to a long, dead-end road.

'Looks like a protest gathering,' suggests Mosetsane.

'On a Friday night?'

'Then what is it?'

Staring into the deep shadows beyond the sparse street-lights, it now appears to him that there may be more figures moving about in the blacked-out gardens fronting the street. He gets the impression that they are all waiting for something to happen.

'I don't know,' he eventually says with a feeling of trepidation. 'But it doesn't look good.'

'Should we call it in?'

At the touch of her warm breath on his cheek, Jacob glances back at Mosetsane, and finds her plum-coloured lips near his ear as she strains at her seatbelt to get a better look over his shoulder. Up close, her scent is irresistible, and the curve of her smooth cheek is suddenly so demanding of his attention that all he needs to do is lean over the shortest of distances and place a kiss upon it to find out how it feels. Their eyes meet close up, but her head nods to one side as though she has asked him a question and is expecting an answer. When the lips that have become so mesmerizing to him part slightly, he feels himself both pulled and pushed towards her.

And why not? he thinks. After what he had seen in his own home, and when his trust has been violated, why is he not a free man, to do what he pleases?

Jacob swallows, then a bit too quickly he reaches for the microphone to radio Dispatch with the information. After repeatedly trying to reach one of the bored graveyard-shift voices at the other end, he eventually gets his answer.

'Detective, with a bunch of cop-killing bombers tearing up the city, do you really expect me to send a patrol out into the sticks just to warn off a bunch of idiots playing with matches in the street?'

'It might be important.'

'It's pissing cats and dogs over here right now, and it'll be doing the same over there in about ten minutes. Screw them. The weather will soon take better care of them than a patrol car will.'

Jacob shakes his head as he replaces the microphone. 'Goodnight to you too,' he mutters.

Mosetsane laughs. 'Alexandra Station, then? They're just around the corner.' She speaks as though the moment Jacob had experienced had not passed between them at all. Did he just imagine it?

Jacob shakes his head in response to her suggestion. 'They only have two patrol cars to cover the entire township, and no one will go near that crowd without some serious back-up.'

'I hope it's not where we're headed.'

'No, I don't think so.'

Jacob releases the handbrake and eases the patrol car back on to the blacktop. Soon they are winding down a narrow southerly lane, past land freshly cleared for more housing projects, and into the heartland of Alexandra itself, a place he has only ever been able to describe as a pocket of people stuffed so full, it is bursting at the seams.

Further to the south-west, he now sees the storm Dispatch was talking about flash over the city high-rises.

'So what did the NIA tell the commissioner about Swarts that finally got you moving?'

'They caught him on tape negotiating the sale of arms to a Zimbabwean group they had been monitoring for about nine months, and wanted to know if a covert operation had been authorized by the police service. It hadn't.'

Jacob feels anger stir in him at this revelation, and instinctive resentment directed at Mosetsane herself. There could be a million reasons why Swarts was caught on that videotape, is his first thought. Why automatically assume that the man is corrupt? But then he checks himself: isn't he now instinctively leaping to a fellow police officer's defence, while assuming that she has the attitude that every cop is bent? And didn't the superintendent just kidnap Harry Mason from his own home?

'What kind of arms?'

'Handguns, mostly. We think they were lifted from evidence rooms and shake-downs when no one was looking. Criminals won't exactly come to us and complain about the SVC confiscating their unregistered firearms, will they?'

Jacob slows as the road becomes narrower and increasingly rutted. 'Is it just Swarts himself you're looking at?'

'They're *all* implicated – the Ballies, I mean. That's why I was initially suspicious of your friend Mason. He worked as close to them as anyone.'

'But why now? Swarts has just resigned because he's moving over to Interpol, hasn't he?'

'I'm thinking that's exactly why the commissioner is driving this issue. If some of Swarts' old allies have expressed their dissatisfaction with his leaving the country, then it might be a good time for the Commissioner to make an example of him, through an ICD investigation. That would lend him credibility as a leader who is willing to crack down on corruption, and it also gives my bosses a chance to shine at a time when the ICD is desperate for a bit of spit and polish. Besides, how embarrassing will it be for the SAPS if all this comes out after his transferral to Lyons?'

Now it is Jacob's turn to smile, but it tastes bitter. 'Didn't you once tell me your investigation had no political agenda?'

He feels the embarrassment coming off her like heat from a radiator. 'I didn't know about all this at first.'

'But once you figured it out, you went along with it?'

She draws herself up, eager to justify herself. 'If that's what it takes for me to get my job done, then I don't care about their power-plays. We've been waiting long enough to get at Swarts.'

'And you're sure it's him?'

She nods. 'I've seen the videotape. Franklin was with him that day, and his profile fits that of a classic arms dealer, even better than Swarts'. He has a military background and there are indications he once ran arms for Savimbi's rebels in Angola.'

'He was a soldier?'

'Discharged honourably from the paratroopers in 1986, with a handful of medals for bravery under fire. For the life of me I don't know how he ended up in the SVC. Why he hasn't since moved up through the ranks is anyone's guess.'

What could have gone so wrong for these two highly decorated professionals to fall so low? Jacob wonders. Was it simply greed or was there more to it? Were they always like this, or was it their work that changed them? Jacob thinks back on one of Harry's more cynical comments, that police work is more about wading into the filthy quagmire of the human condition than enforcing any clear-cut laws. There is no doubt in his mind that some of that muck inevitably rubs off on any police officer, but how much of it came off on Swarts and Franklin? Enough set out to try kill Harry Mason?

And if a man like Swarts can't manage to stay clean after so many years in the service, then what lies ahead for Jacob himself? Is what he did to Teddy Bakwena the first sign of his own slide into who-knows-what?

He is glad when the shattered bridge finally comes up on their right and he has to lay these uncomfortable thoughts to rest. 'We're here.'

They left the copper halos of streetlight behind about a kilometre back, and now there is nothing but moonlight, the car's dull headlights, and distant glimpses of paraffin lamps, candles and occasional electrical lightbulbs illuminating the otherwise dark-grey landscape. Above the horizon he can see the lightning storm gathering pace, as it can only do on the highveld.

Jacob cuts the engine and lets the vehicle coast to a halt on the road's narrow shoulder. To their left, a cemetery stretches away to the east, with a few project houses clinging up against its enclosing walls. Their lit-up windows stare wide-eyed into the night, as though frightened by the surrounding darkness. On the other side of the road, above the trash-encrusted riverbanks, the shantytown sprawl of lower Alexandra climbs up a hill towards the west. The warm fog coming off the effluvial river and the smoke from countless makeshift chimneys collude to give Jacob the impression of a dank sepulchral marshland, rather than a human settlement on a scraggy patch of grassland.

He opens the car door and steps out into the cold night. Behind him is the constant drone of the N3 freeway; climbing up a hill, south-west towards the city centre, is a crackling hive of human activity that reminds him of a thousand termites gathering dry grass in the winter. The wind has an even stronger bite down here in the valley, and the coal-smoke in the air stings his eyes.

Mosetsane's door opens and then closes. 'So where does he live?'

Jacob zips up the windbreaker to right under his chin and shrugs. 'All I was told is that he lives near Hofmeyer Bridge.'

Mosetsane comes around the car to stand close to him, her breath rising like a ghostly plume in the night. 'That's an awful lot of doors to knock on, Jacob. And why is it so quiet here on a Friday night?'

'I wish I knew,' he says grimly.

'Has it got anything to do with the activity we saw coming in, do you think?'

Jacob glances to the north-west, in the direction from which they have come, but sees nothing more than a bright orange glow over the shanties. Whether it is simply coming from the traffic on the M1 on the other side of the hill, or from the flames rising in that dead-end street, is difficult to tell.

'I hope not,' he replies.

Jacob is about to cross the street and head for the eroded footpath leading towards a makeshift walkway through the shallow river when a light abruptly blinks on behind them and a warning is shouted.

3

A screen door squeaks open on rusty hinges, and an elderly man as rickety as his own home totters down the few steps of his porch and shakes his walking stick at them.

'*Hi wena*, if I told you once I told you twice, this isn't Lovers' Lane! What are you parking there for? Go make out someplace else. That's a cemetery next door. Have some respect for the dead, will you?'

He comes to a stop halfway to his gate and glowers at them suspiciously. His mouth is constantly on the move, working uncomfortably around false teeth.

'Did you hear me?' he barks in Sotho. 'Bugger off!'

A laugh escapes Jacob's lips as he hails the old man. '*Dumela, ndoda*, we are not here for what you think. We only want to find a way across the river.'

'What for? It's after nine. You should be indoors like any God-fearing person.'

'*Ndoda*,' calls Mosetsane, 'we are looking for a man called Makhe Motale. Do you know him?'

Her clear and perfect Sotho takes Jacob by surprise, and she follows it up with a mischievous wink at him.

'Why? Who are you?'

'We are with the police service.'

'What was that?' The old-timer dodders the few remaining steps to his gate and cups a hand behind one ear. 'You're with who?'

'I am Detective Inspector Jacob Tshabalala and this is Detective Mosetsane.'

'*Poyisa!*' The man spits out the word as though it were something rotten he had bitten into. 'Aren't you people finished with him yet?'

'What do you mean?' asks Mosetsane.

'He's gone. Haven't seen or heard from him in five days. We don't think he's coming back.'

'What do you mean?' asks Jacob.

'What are you asking me for? You took him away!'

Thinking the man is referring to Motale's activities at

Wynberg, Jacob asks, 'Wasn't he released on bail after the protest?'

'What are you talking about, boy?' The elderly man is so indignant that his entire frame shakes. 'They sniffed around here a few days, two *umlungus* and a *koelie* from what I hear, till someone must have sold him out. The youngsters, they'll do that for a pair of sneakers these days. Heard the shots myself when they killed the boy's dogs. Who does that, I ask you? He grew up with them, and they were as good as family to him. Best-looking animals you ever did see. I swear, if I was any younger, I'd have gone and done something, but all I could do was sit on this godforsaken *stoep* and listen to what was happening there across the river.'

Police officers, two whites and an Indian. Jacob did not need much imagination to figure out who they might have been. But why go after Motale this way, especially if he was already their informant?

Mosetsane throws Jacob a glance, and the light of vindication in her eyes fills Jacob with shame. It was embarrassing to have this old man and her, two civvies, tell him how crooked some cops can become.

'Can you at least tell us where Makhe lives?' he asks.

'At his mother's house. Has been there all his life. She's now moved to her sister's, though. I don't see her holding out very long without her son. I'm not going to tell you where that is, either, because we've just about had it with you lot.'

'*Ndoda*, we're here to make things right,' says Jacob in a placatory tone.

'Make it right? This whole bloody neighbourhood is ready to burn down Alexandra Police Station!' The old man huffs as he nervously moves his eyes between Jacob and Busi Mosetsane. He makes to turn away and head back to his house, but then he throws a last glance back at them.

'There's no point in you two leaving the car out there to be robbed. Pull it into the driveway, while I go explain to my wife why I'm letting a bunch of cops on to our property, heaven knows.'

'God bless you, *ndoda*,' says Jacob.

'Let Him go worry about the rest of the world. It's tricky crossing the river at night if you haven't lived here, so I'll lend you a torch.'

Mosetsane is about to add her thanks when the old man cuts her off.

'Enough, daughter. Just bring that boy back to his family. We need him.'

TWELVE

1

'Here, cut the son of a bitch down with this.'

Franklin lobs a pocket knife at Harry, but he does nothing to catch it, so it falls in the loose dust at his feet.

A heavy gust of wind smelling of rain and earth scissors through the grove of towering blue-gums in which they are standing. A creaking sound above him draws his attention back to the thick rope looped around a sturdy lower branch, and to the large yellow canvas bag swinging over a livestock-water reservoir. Thin tendrils of vapour come off the cold black water.

'Let's go, Harry, we don't have all night.' Franklin takes a step towards him and lazily aims a silenced pistol at his knee. 'And unless you want to go back to your daughter a cripple like that fucking monkey in the tree there, I suggest you get going.'

At first Harry had thought they would head directly to the Phaliso brothers' house on the outskirts of Alexandra, to continue whatever these men planned. They knew where the two brothers lived, from all the intelligence painstakingly gathered over the last few months, but just never had enough evidence to secure an arrest warrant. They had hit the N1 and followed it north towards the Buccleuch interchange, driving in silence all the way, but before they hit the off-ramp Harry expected them to take, Franklin turned the minibus on to a farm track branching away near a brightly lit golf driving range. Within minutes, the city's lights had disappeared behind the dark hills, and finally, when Sameer Naidoo jumped out to open a disused farm gate, Harry had felt compelled to ask where they were going.

'You'll see soon enough,' was the only response he got.

It had briefly occurred to Harry that they might want to kill him out here, after all – that they had lied to get him away from Tanya and his daughter, only to be shot and buried in a place no one would ever find. But then they had parked the minibus in a grove of trees, and Franklin ushered him out, saying, 'Let's go check out your buddy, Mason.'

'Smile, *boet*,' a voice calls him back to the present, and when he turns in Naidoo's direction there is a bright flash that shoots pain through his aching skull.

Franklin grabs a nearby ladder they must have left standing here after they rigged a 'submarine', a torture method commonly used in a bygone but recent era, and stares meaningfully at him through a haze of blue pipe smoke. He wonders what Makhe Motale might have already told them as they dipped him into the freezing water time and again – what he might have *thought* just before he eventually drowned, too exhausted to hold his breath until the next time they hauled him up.

Franklin shakes the ladder. 'Come on, Mason, up you go.'

Harry stoops to pick up the pocket knife at his feet, then glances back up at the sack and wills it to show some sign of life, and give him a better reason to cut it down. Not a shiver, not a shake, however. The thought of a friend reduced to nothing more than clammy meat in a canvas bag that has outdated cattle-feed information printed on it in faded black letters sparks a cold fury in him that makes his hands shake uncontrollably. He stills them before opening the blade and clasping the handle between his teeth. Then he grabs hold of the ladder and begins to climb.

'Don't take it so hard, Mason,' Franklin calls after him. 'It's nothing personal. If the arsehole had just talked, it might never have gone this far.' The man gives a rusty laugh that turns into a cough.

'It became personal for me in Tsolo the moment one of you tried to kill me.' Harry leans across to grab the rope and starts hacking away at it. Another flash from Naidoo's camera blinds.

'Why are you so convinced it was one of us?' Swarts approaches from where he has been leaning up against the minibus and nursing a bottle of Richelieu brandy.

Before Harry can answer, the fraying rope suddenly snaps. The canvas bag drops into the water as heavy as an anchor.

'There she goes!'

Ignoring the stitches in his gut, Harry leaps off the ladder, takes the two steps towards the reservoir and hauls himself up on to its rim as the sack bobs to the surface. He lunges for it and drags it halfway up the concrete lip. Frantically he begins to tug the noose tied around one end.

'Leave it, Mason!' Franklin bellows.

'Bugger off!'

'I said, stop wasting my fucking time!' The man storms right up to Harry and aims the pistol at him with a hand shaking in fury. 'You get right off that ledge or I'll put a bullet in your face. Then what happens with that pretty girl of yours, hey? Fucking orphan on the street, selling her tits and arse, is that what you want?' A savage sneer spreads over his face. 'Well, then, I'll be looking out for her on the street after you're gone, you can bet on it.'

'That's *enough*!' yells Swarts. 'Jesus, Blondie, but sometimes you go too far.'

Naidoo merely watches in silence, nervously fidgeting
with the digital camera in his hand.

Franklin drags his eyes away from Harry and throws a
lazy glance over his shoulder towards his colleague.

'You're dead, Franklin.' The words cut the knot in
Harry's throat like a broken razor.

Franklin turns back to him and cups a palm to his ear.
'I didn't hear that, what?'

'You heard me. None of the old rules apply any more.
Before tonight's finished it's you and me.'

'Hard talk, from a man who can't stop bleating over a
shit like Ntombini.'

Harry drags the bag all the way out of the water, his
hands instantly running over the stiff misshapen body
inside as litres of cold dark liquid drain from a dozen
perforations and seep into his clothing.

Swarts stuffs the brandy bottle into the waistband of
his trousers. 'Here, let me help you with that.'

'Get the hell away from me.'

Harry hugs the sopping wet load to his chest and
braces himself for the pain that is bound to follow when
he jumps off the edge of the reservoir.

'Don't be stupid, Bond. You've just come out of the
blimming hospital.'

'It wasn't him that screwed you around, and you
know it.'

Ignoring Swarts' warning, Harry slides off the reservoir's high rim. The moment his feet hit the ground he
feels something tearing inside him. The sensation of barbed
hooks ripping at the flesh inside his belly is enough to
force a scream from his mouth. He involuntarily drops

Makhe Motale's body and collapses beside it, writhing in pain.

Franklin strolls up and prods the motionless sack with the tip of one boot, as if to check whether Motale is actually dead. 'You dumb shit. You'd do that to yourself for a drowned rat?'

Naidoo grabs the canvas sack and hefts it on to one shoulder with a grunt. Then he offers Harry his free hand. 'Let me help you up, *boet*.'

The pain increases until he is clutching at tufts of dry grass in his agony.

'Harry.' Naidoo is still holding out his hand.

Smeared with dust and black muck from the water, Harry eventually manages to sit up with his back against the reservoir rim, and tries to catch his breath.

'You can quit holding out your hand to me, Naidoo,' he rasps. 'There's no chance in hell I'll ever accept anything from you again.'

The man uncertainly retracts his hand, and adjusts the dead weight on his shoulder. Then he glances in the direction that Swarts and Franklin are already moving, heading back towards the vehicle. 'Take my hand, Harry, please.'

'Shove it.' Harry reaches out and starts to claw his way up the reservoir wall, one slimy brick at a time, masonry crumbling away in lumps under his nails. When he is finally standing on unsteady feet, one hand pressed over his side, he finds Naidoo still staring at him.

'You once took three bullets in the line of duty, didn't you?' Harry asks.

Naidoo appears to flinch under his gaze. 'Listen to me, Harry. Don't be so fucking stubborn. You want to go back to your family, don't you?'

'The bullets you took, Naidoo, remember them? Remember what it felt like?'

'You know I took them. Why are you asking?'

'You better hope your luck hasn't run out, because after what you lot did at my house tonight, I hope to see you take a dozen more. That's if I'm not putting them in you myself.'

The man's eyes open wide in surprise. 'Don't talk to me like that, man. I'm trying to help you here. Can't you see that?'

'I can't – and I don't think I will.'

They stare at each other a moment longer, and to Harry it seems the other man wants to say more. But then his eyes shift away, and find Swarts upending the rest of the bottle of brandy into his mouth.

'Fuck you, Harry,' Naidoo says and turns away.

'That's right, you coward,' he roars after Naidoo, 'run after them. You've always been a brown-nosing son of a bitch, who can't even tie his own shoelaces without someone's help. No amount of bullet wounds will ever change that.'

Naidoo stops, and in the half-light Harry sees his shoulders slump. For a second it looks like he might turn around, but all he does is shift Makhe Motale's body to the other shoulder before proceeding to the waiting vehicle.

Harry takes a few deep breaths in an attempt to still his shaking hands, quell the blood thundering in his ears, but that helps little. He wipes the worst of the muck from his face, and when he dabs his fingers at the bandage under his shirt, they come away discoloured with blood in the darkness. All around him leaves rustle and whisper, and a smell of compost fills his nose. When he looks up into the branches of the tree above him, they look like white bones rearing in the starlight.

Let's see this through, then, you bastards.

2

They drive in ominous silence, Swarts and Franklin up front in the minibus, Naidoo occupying the entire first row of seats, Harry and Motale's body relegated to the back. He places a hand on the canvas sack, the way a father might touch a sleeping child, as it occasionally bumps against his leg with the roll of the vehicle, and tries not to imagine the corpse inside, a grown man balled up in the foetal position, his lungs filled with nothing more than white foam and his drowned cries for help.

Harry's guts are burning hot, even though he himself is cold from the icy reservoir water, and he knows something has gone very wrong behind the patch and staples holding him together. The question is, how bad is it and how long can he keep going?

Don't go there right now, he tells himself. *Keep your head screwed on straight.*

When they swing back on to the highway towards Alexandra, the lights of the golf range come back into view, glowing like an airport on their left. He tries to ignore the intense pain in his gut by concentrating on the dragon tail of orange dust kicked up by the wind, the churning leaves, the frayed plastic bags chasing each other over the manicured green grass lit up under a spotlight glare. Above it all, a velvety tide of blackness slowly devours the dull stars stretching away to the north towards Pretoria.

An unmistakeable ratchet and click at the front of the vehicle draws Harry's attention away from the landscape. The three remaining Ballies have meanwhile put on rolled-up balaclavas, after Swarts and Franklin had smeared their faces with black paint so that only the bloodshot whites of their eyes bear any resemblance to their old selves.

'Catch.'

Harry barely manages to get his hands up in time to catch the object Swarts lobs at him. A .380 automatic, with an attached silencer.

'There's one bullet in there.' Swarts' blackened face is lit up by the sickly green neon from the displays on the dashboard, and every few seconds halogen orange street-lights flash across his grim features. 'If you're so blimming sure it was one of us that shot you, take your pick. Shoot the fuck that did it, Bond. Get it over and done with.'

Sameer Naidoo turns to stare at Harry over his shoulder. His expression is vacant, like his mind is turned inwards to wrestle with whatever demons have nested inside him. A grunt of humour escapes Franklin's lips, but he keeps his eyes on the road.

'No way, Russie. The fuck doesn't have it in him.'

'Everyone does,' Swarts says to Franklin. 'Especially when he's so convinced that he's got it right, hey, Bond?'

Harry turns the chromed weapon over in his hands, barely able to hear anything beyond the blood pounding in his ears. It is cold to the touch, covered in a thin sheen of fresh gun oil, and inside is chambered a bullet. It is therefore impregnated with one single possibility, and that is suddenly very, very appealing.

'Make your decision, Bond. Judgemental fellow like you, that shouldn't be too difficult.'

Harry's fingers run over the faint grooves cut into the

handle of the weapon, the ridge of the magazine slotted into the bottom, and after what seems an eternity they find the safety. A thumb clicks it off without his even having to think about it.

All the while Swarts stares evenly at him through the flash-flash of oncoming streetlights. The reddish-brown beard that once graced an older man's face now looks like ripe moss against the dead features of a blackened corpse.

'The question is, if you're wrong, could you live with yourself?'

Makhe Motale's body nearly slips off the seat as Franklin abruptly brakes and changes lanes, and Harry has to quickly haul it back. Then he raises the weapon and levels it at Senior Superintendent Russell Swarts.

'I knew you were a hard-nosed bastard, but I never thought you would be so fickle with human life.'

A smile filled with contempt spreads over Swarts' face. 'It *is* me then, you reckon. You could be using that thing for some good tonight, but instead all you can think about is your revenge.'

'I don't see how it could have worked out any other way,' says Harry slowly.

Swarts sighs, seeming not overly concerned by his captain's choice. 'All right then. Let's have it out, if you're going to be so blimming adamant about it. I did kill Ntombini. Shot him as he pissed himself in a pair of satin boxer shorts. There's the truth. Is that enough for you?'

Harry thinks about this a moment; his mind is surprisingly clear, all things considered. 'Not any more, no.'

'Thought not. You see, I can live with what I did to Ntombini, but I somehow can't see you doing the same if you shoot one of us.'

'I'll cross that bridge when I come to it.'

'I'm not saying it was right what I did, but I did what was necessary, and *that* is the most important decision every police officer must make at some point. Sometimes we have to carry that burden, Bond. It was the lesser of two evils, shooting him, because that I saved lives; I know it. The same goes for what I'm about to do tonight. But what would you be shooting me for? A suspicion or a conviction?' He huffs sardonically.

Harry could shoot Swarts right here, but Naidoo and Franklin would be left to do with him whatever they wanted. And when they were finished? Could he trust them to leave it at that, and not go after his family – especially Franklin? No, is the immediate answer, there are no guarantees.

Harry tightens his grip on the pistol and feels the grooves of the grip chew into his palm.

'You see that, Russie? The fuck doesn't even believe you saved his arse.' Franklin's voice seems unaffected by the tension around him. 'I told you he's an ungrateful shit.'

Though he can only see Franklin's stark eyes staring back at him in the rear-view mirror, Harry can sense the mockery playing over the man's mouth and he has to wonder if it may have been Franklin who shot him, by his own choice, in an effort to protect Swarts.

'It was *you*, then?'

Franklin shrugs. 'What does it matter? Russie's right. If you've made up your mind, then it's made up. You need to understand this, Mason: sometimes it's not about what you know, but what you decide on. So stop jerking us all off and get on with it. But if you can't do it, you owe it to Russie to help us clean up shop.'

'The bullet that was lodged inside me, what's happened to it?'

'It's with forensics. Where else?'

'Is that right?'

'Think what you will.'

Harry glances at the sack lying next to him, and for a moment the flashing streetlights make it look like the corpse is moving.

'And Motale here? Did you kill him because he wouldn't talk – or was that the plan all along?'

'Can't have someone like him running to the ICD to complain that he was tortured, now, can we?' says Franklin. 'He was enough of a shit stirrer as it is.'

'I never liked rats anyway, especially ones with a hefty price tag that then lay ambushes,' adds Swarts.

Franklin lets out a laugh, but does not elaborate except to say, 'Ah, Russie, round and around we go.'

'If you're so happy to go straight after the Phaliso brothers without following proper procedure, then why bother with Motale in the first place?' Harry asks. 'What did he have that you still needed?'

Swarts says nothing but glances at Franklin, who snarls, 'You're not listening to me. No one sets us up. Not even your friend there.'

'There was no set-up and you know it. You were after something else, weren't you?'

'You talk too much, Mason.' Franklin appears to be expertly catching all the green lights, making sure that they stay on the move. 'I can see why Russie might like you. Fucking motor-mouth twins is what you both are, except one's a Pom and the other a *boer seun*. Go figure.'

From the moment he woke up in that goddamned hospital bed, Harry has been certain it was Swarts who engineered the shooting. He knows he should not have been making assumptions, but his mind would not leave that idea alone: it had to be Swarts. If it had been the Abasindisi, the Ballies would never have been so evasive afterwards. The fact is, knowing what he does now, they would probably have been waiting with the gunman's head on a silver platter for the moment Harry woke up.

But it could just as easily have been Franklin, for no other reason than that he did not like Harry and he could easily have done it as a favour to Swarts, with or without his senior colleague's consent. That is, if he already knew about the Ntombini case and how it could wreck the superintendent's career.

Harry knows he is now being cornered, and they're doing it so easily because he is missing something vital. What are they using against him? he wonders. That they're baiting him is certain; even a frame-up isn't out of the question any more. But why? Surely the Ntombini case can't be so important if Swarts is confident that no incriminating evidence exists after all these years? Are they sowing doubt on purpose so as to exonerate Swarts, or have they got something else up their sleeves? Whatever their reasons are, he can't let them have their way with him. He can't back down.

Outside the van now, a roadblock on the old Pretoria road flashes past, on the other side of a palisade fence, with metropolitan police officers shielding their eyes against the grit kicked up by the strong wind. A line of industrial estates melts into office parks, into cramped, high-walled, barbed-wire-shrouded properties, into a river valley choked with small houses and gardens that gradually deteriorate into nothing more than lean-tos the closer you get to the river. Bright sheet lightning strobes over the south-westerly neon skyline of Ponte City, the Hillbrow

Tower, the Oppenheimer Library which juts up from the edge of a hill above the five-star Westcliff Hotel.

'Come on, Mason,' Franklin says to the mirror. 'The anticipation's killing me here. Who's it going to be? Contestant number one or two? What about number three over there, hey? He's awfully quiet, the fat fuck.'

'You shut up,' growls Naidoo. 'I'm in no mood for your shit tonight.'

'Here's your answer.' Harry releases the hammer on the pistol, pulls back the slide and ejects the single hollow-point from the breach into his waiting hand. Unscrewing the silencer and releasing the magazine, he is careful to wipe down the gun with his sweater, in case of finger-prints the Ballies may want to use, before chucking it, one piece at a time, into the front of the minibus. 'There it is.'

'Ha! I knew the fuck didn't have it in him.'

Swarts nods. 'Suit yourself, Bond, but when the shit hits the fan and you're standing in front, don't come crying to me.'

The minibus slows, and Franklin douses the headlights as they finally come up to the turn that will take them into the lengthy cul de sac at the end of which the brothers Phaliso last lived. To Harry it feels like an eternity since he and Franklin sat in an unmarked car on this very spot, arguing about whose fault it was for their slow progress in the Abasindisi case.

'Who's to say they're even here?' asks Harry.

Franklin is quick on the draw. 'Where would you have us start the search, then, hotshot?'

'What's this?' asks Swarts as they come to a halt.

Three large fires have been lit down the middle of the

roadway, and thick plumes of rubber- and wood-smoke stain the air. With every fresh gust of wind, bright sparks and flames are sent roaring into the sky, yet not a single human being can be seen.

'I don't know,' says Franklin, 'but I don't think it's a birthday party.'

3

Russell Swarts starts digging in a sports bag at his feet and brings out extra clips of ammunition and two hand-fuls of grenades. By the look of them, they are not police-issue stunners or flash, but either high explosive or fragmentation.

'Where did you get those?' Harry nods at the military hardware Swarts is dishing out: two for Franklin, two for himself.

'Doesn't concern you.'

'What about me, hey?' asks Naidoo.

'There are only four,' says Swarts.

'So?'

'They're going to us, and that's that,' says Franklin.

Naidoo's nose flares and his lips tighten against his teeth until they appear like narrow lines. Then he glances abruptly out of the window, like nothing awkward has passed between them.

'Who do you think lit all those?' Naidoo asks. 'Couldn't have been just one person, right?'

The possibility of unexpected extra company finally gets through to Swarts and Franklin, and they both take a closer look at the dead-end street. Not a light glows in any of the small houses along either side of it, and the entire neighbourhood has been plunged into darkness except for the rapidly dwindling flames.

'Doesn't matter,' Swarts eventually says. 'All it means is that old Bond here is going to have a bigger audience than we could have hoped for. I can already see the headlines, "Wounded cop goes berserk – pictures". Not too hard to imagine, is it? Harry Mason loses the plot when he catches up with the people that ambushed him.'

'For a police officer so used to killing people while covering his own arse, you haven't thought this through very far, have you?' Harry asks. 'Don't you think the entire police service will know it was you that took out the Phalisos? That people are going to wonder what's happened to me and my family, if we disappear tonight? You can parade me around in front of your camera and shove a gun in my hand in the hope of getting me to kill folks the way you do. But you forget one thing. I'm not like you, and I will never be like you.'

'No one in the service is going to care about those two after what they did at Maloney's. Not a cop, not a prosecutor, not a damn judge. Even the ICD dicks will look the other way.'

'There will be far too many questions, even for someone like you to deal with,' says Harry. 'There's only one way this story can end, Russell, and that's badly. Can't you see that? For you *and* your family.'

'Leave them out of this!'

'Who the fuck's that coming now?' asks Naidoo.

'The way you left *mine* out of it?' Harry asks, suddenly incensed. 'Jesus, listen to yourself for a second, will you?'

'I *have* to do this. Don't you fucking understand that? They killed Kommie! It's an eye for an eye in this city. Always has been, always will be.'

'Someone's coming,' Naidoo says in agitation.

'Shut up, you two.' The usual mockery in Franklin's voice is gone, replaced by a new tone of caution Harry has not heard before. It immediately catches his attention.

A lone figure approaches out of the darkness far down the hill, from beyond the light of the three evenly spaced street fires. The woman is of an indeterminable age and dressed in a tracksuit at the very end of its use. A man's sizeable heavy leather jacket covers her shoulders, and in her arms she carries a pile of wood. As they watch, she places two fresh-cut logs on each of the pyres, while her eyes remain suspiciously fixed on the minibus parked at the very top of the road. There is a disturbing grace in the way she moves on the balls of her bare feet, between the flames, like a dancer who is an elemental spirit amongst the flames. After feeding the fire closest to the minibus, she finally turns to face them head-on. As the last of the logs has been tossed on the coals, thousands of sparks fly up all around her, only to be sucked away by the growing force of the wind. Close up, Harry can see the thin-set line of her lips, the jet-black eyes shimmering with an orange glow, the wild black hair standing on end like she has shoved a finger into an electrical socket.

'What the hell is she doing, hey?' Naidoo's tone is awed.

Swarts points a short distance down the road they are in, towards a group of minibus taxis parked under a single streetlight. 'Franklin, take the van down that way.'

'It's just a bloody *oussie*, man. What are you worried about?'

'They know we're coming for them, and they've decided to meet us head-on.'

'You think?' asks Naidoo.

Swarts ignores the question. 'Harry, you're getting out with me here. Franklin, park the van then go on foot round the back of those houses over on the right. Head across the veldt behind them, and then over the back wall at the Phaliso house. We'll meet you down there.'

'And me?' asks Naidoo. 'This time I'm not hanging around looking after the fucking car like some pointsman, understand?'

'You're with Franklin.'

'That's just fucking great, then.' Franklin digs about in the glovebox for his pipe, then chooses a cigarette from a crumpled packet instead. 'I should've known I'd get stuck with the walrus.'

'Screw you, Blondie. I might have more meat on me than you do, but that's muscle. And I don't smoke the way you do, so I'll be ahead of you all the way. You just watch me.'

'I'm sure.' Franklin lights the cigarette in his mouth, though his eyes stay fixed on the woman still staring back at them. He exhales smoke through his nose. 'We still want to do this, Russie?'

'If life ever was about what we want to do, I'd do nothing every day but sit on the *stoep* of my farmhouse and drink a toast to the setting sun.'

Russell Swarts throws open the passenger door and steps out into the cold night. He tugs the balaclava tighter around his ears, then turns on Harry.

'Let's go.'

Fresh pain shoots through Harry's gut as he leans over and pulls back the sliding door at the rear of the vehicle. Naidoo yanks it shut behind him with a dull clang, and the mini-van begins to coast silently down the hill towards the houses nearer to the river. Swarts waves a silenced gun at Harry.

'You lead the way, Bond. And look a bit more lively, please. You know what they say about dogs that scent weakness.'

Harry surveys the long narrow street, the empty houses on either side and, above all, the woman watching them like she is hungry for fresh meat. Everything is wrong about this scene. It is the kind of situation they teach you in police college never to walk into, and yet Swarts is forcing the issue.

'This is the stupidest thing I've ever seen anyone try to do,' says Harry.

'Not stupid, Harry. Just inevitable.'

'Bullshit, Russell! You can still turn this around. No one's forcing you to do this.'

'No?' Swarts grunts. 'Funny you say that. Last time I checked, these bastards had outwitted us at every turn, and now they've even put a few of us in the morgue.' He nudges Harry slightly to the right. 'Steer clear of that one; she looks like she might have rabies.'

Harry puts the first of the fires between himself and the woman, while carefully eyeing the darkness around them. With the streetlights out and wind shaking the garden plants all around, the shadows seemed alive and mobile. The fires spit and roar in the wind, and behind him Swarts' boots clomp heavily on the tarmac. The woman circles left, seemingly all too happy to have the fire between them.

'That's it, *squeeza*,' Swarts growls at her. 'Be a good girl and back the fuck off.'

'What information is it you wanted from Motale you couldn't get from me?' asks Harry. 'And why is it Franklin reckons you're screwed if the rest of the department catches up with the Phalisos before you're done with them?'

'Leave it alone, Harry. The less you know, the more likely you are to walk out of this business with your life.'

He is about to ask more when Swarts stops and grabs him by the shoulder. 'Hush.'

Where before he only heard leaves rustling, the roaring wind and fire, Harry now hears stifled laughter and a sharp hiss of caution. And it is not just that. Now that his eyes have adjusted to the darkened street, he can see figures hidden behind shrubs, pressed up against porch pillars and crouching beyond low walls.

Abasindisi: guardians come to guard their masters.

The woman laughs out loud and shouts something to them. Harry can tell it is something vulgar by her crude tone, but neither he nor Swarts can understand her.

The Supe levels his pistol at her. 'What's going on here, hey?'

Instead of being intimidated, the woman stoops to lift a long burning branch out of the fire and thrusts it out towards him, as if to meet his challenge. More taunts leave her lips, more unrecognizable obscenities, while she slowly circles round to their backs. Swarts tracks her with his gun, while Harry tries to gauge how many other people there might be in the shadows. Ten? Twenty? A hundred?

Pack them like a can of pilchards into those houses, you could have an army waiting nearby.

The real question is, how many of them are here in Alexandra? And how many of *those* would not be impartial to disposing of a handful of white cops who have decided to take the law into their own hands, on Abasindisi turf?

Jesus, thinks Harry. *How the hell did I end up here, again?*

'Senior Superintendent Swarts!'

The booming voice drags their attention much further down the road, and from the darkness at the foot of the slope lumbers an overweight man, dressed casually in a chequered sports jacket, jeans and expensive white trainers. Harry immediately recognizes Ncolela Phaliso, and behind him his gangly younger brother, prancing around like a mad spook that refuses to walk in a straight line. A third man with his head bowed, his hands held folded before him as though handcuffed, brings up the rear. His face is puffed up like pastry left in the oven too long, and it takes Harry a while to realize this is Wally Khuzwayo. It takes him even longer to figure out that the man isn't actually shackled, just beaten down and humiliated like he's already walking into Sun City or Leeuwkop prison to serve a few life terms.

'Ncolela Phaliso, you old fuck,' says Swarts as though they have been friends for ever and a day. 'And there I thought you'd make my life difficult by disappearing like the blimming chicken-shit bomb-planting coward you are. That was one helluva fight you put up in the street today, rescuing your man. I'll give you that.'

'That was me?' The older Phaliso smiles broadly, his teeth gleaming in the firelight. 'How do you know it was me?'

'That puke-ugly car of yours, I could spot it anywhere.'

'It was stolen last night. I filed my statement at the Alexandra Police Station this morning. You're welcome to check.'

'You're not ducking this one, *boetie*. Not in a million years.'

'You've got it all wrong, *umlungu*. But then, by the look of things, you're not here on police business anyway, are you? This is more like business used to be, *né*?'

Swarts offers a grunt in response. 'I've got something for you.'

An abrupt shove from behind has Harry stumbling forward a few paces, and this time, when lightning carves up the sky somewhere over Highlands North, it finally brings with it a low roll of thunder.

By the time Harry has righted himself from the searing stitch in his gut, people – nameless, threatening faces – are bleeding into view over walls, through garden gates, out of front doors.

Ten? Twenty? A hundred? Harry thinks again. *Christ, they're pouring out of the goddamned houses by the dozen.*

THIRTEEN

1

Jacob is running as fast as he can, dodging this way and that in the narrow alleys between shacks, as he tries to mimic the bouncy alacrity of Makhe's henchman, who's leading him and Mosetsane ever deeper into the densely packed shantytown. The old man's directions were vague, but at least they helped Jacob find someone who knew Harry Mason and where he might be.

The man with the mashed-up face and pubescent high-school voice stops a few metres ahead of them, in front of a *spaza* shop with its single sales window firmly bolted shut for the night. A beige rat the size of a small dog scurries into the thin glow of a high floodlight, and briefly looks up at Jacob as if to say, *Mind your own damn business*. Then it is gone.

'Hurry!' shouts the man ahead of him, and though he casts a worried eye up at the darkening sky above them, Jacob knows this urgency has nothing to do with the coming thunderstorm and everything to do with an appeal that went out from the Phalisos a few hours ago. 'The *gatas*, they are coming,' was the word. 'They are coming to let blood.'

He turns to see whether Mosetsane is keeping up, and is somewhat chastened to find her right behind him, even looking at him as if he is holding her up.

'This way.' The man ducks right and squeezes through a very narrow gap between two incomplete government-sponsored cinder-block houses already crumbling into disrepair. As Jacob sidles between the two walls, he can hear a couple rutting loudly on one side, and on the other an old-timer ranting about the goddamned racket next door, over the crackle of his ancient transistor radio. In the arse end of Alexandra, the lines of property and privacy blur: one man's porch is another's backyard; one family's living room is another's bedroom; even your bed could be yours by night, but a nightshift worker's by day while you are out slaving away for five bucks an hour or carting your crumpled handwritten CV door to door.

The large youngster, who introduced himself as King, shimmies left yet again, this time leaping over the pegs of a four-man tent that doubles as a hairdresser's salon by day. Then he is pushing his way through a young crowd partying it up in a backyard surrounded by ruined walls – livestock crowd its furthest corner, terrified of the garrulous group and the music pounding out of a boombox. The smell of burning meat and bone, the smell of pap and samp and braai-mix spices, are hot and steamy in the night air, and there seems no concern whatsoever for the oncoming rain.

The streets leading into the township may be empty, but here at its centre the weekend has arrived like any other, and if the man leading them ever deeper into these warrens decides to suddenly abandon them, it will take Jacob and Busisiwe Mosetsane a long time to find their way back to the car. By which time it might be far too late for Harry Mason.

2

They had crossed the river by leaping from one broken slab of concrete jutting out of stinking black water to the next, with nothing but the old man's weak torch and some sketchy directions to guide them. All around them, the water seemed agitated with the promise of a flash flood that could engulf them any minute, but when Jacob turned the torchlight upriver, all he could see were insignificant swirls around the junk and rubble mid-stream.

They had crept up the opposite bank and into the shantytown. Once off the beaten track, it did not take them ten minutes to get lost in the densely packed warren, despite the old man's directions, and if it was not for the flickering light shining through cracks in high wooden boards that formed a makeshift wall to one side of them, the sudden loud laughter of children accompanying some cartoon character's wisecrack, they might never have stumbled upon the home of Mahke Motale.

Busi Mosetsane was getting as anxious about where they were as Jacob was; they were losing too much time trying to find Harry's informant when they should have been looking for Harry. Jacob decided to duck through a low hole smashed into the wooden boards, and abruptly found himself in a large dusty backyard filled with people.

At the far end of this enclosed area, roughly the size of half a basketball court, was the wreck of an ancient rust-bucket Chevrolet, its innards torn out to make a living space for someone. Along one wooden-board wall stood a line of unusually quiet adults with beers, cigarettes and joints in their hands, attentive smiles on their faces as they watched the grainy film being projected on to the corrugated-iron wall of a shack. They were as unmindful of the cold and enthralled by the gritty 8 mm film, rippling and indistinct against the uneven background, as dozens of children sat huddled together on upturned red crates, with colourful fleece blankets drawn tight around their shoulders.

Before he could even make eye contact with one of the adults and request further help, there was a rusty squeak from the darkness as a man the size of a harbour crane launched himself out of an office chair and grabbed Jacob by the throat. Lifting him clear of the ground, this heavy, his face all stitched up and swollen, his front teeth nothing but broken stumps plugging a raw hole for a mouth, shoved Jacob up against the wall through which he had just climbed.

'Who are you?' he asked in a strangely effeminate voice.

It was at this point that Mosetsane clambered through the opening. 'Let go of him!' she cried.

The bruiser reacted by tugging a gun from his sweat-pants and pointing it at her. 'Stay right where you are, bitch. I'm not kidding.'

Her eyes went as large as dinner plates and she carefully raised her hands.

Jacob, who was for the second time today dangling from someone's hold on his neck, squeezed a few words out of an already bruised windpipe. 'We're here to help. We're looking for Makhe . . . and Harry Mason.'

The man, not a day older than twenty, glanced back at the kids and parents and found all eyes now pinned on him instead of the film. Embarrassed by this attention, he pocketed the gun, let go of Jacob and nodded towards a thick black blanket draped across the entrance to a shack.

'Let's talk inside.'

It was remarkably spacious for what looked like such a compact hovel from the outside, because the shack itself was just the kitchen annexe to a larger brick house. An old-fashioned fridge and a chest freezer took up considerable space, while a single paraffin lantern on the tiny kitchen table kept the darkness at bay. The youngster indicated for Jacob and Mosetsane to take the two chairs. In the light his face looked open and vulnerable, more like that of a child seeking direction than a bruiser's well used to the streets. He was nothing like as sinister a figure as Jacob remembered from the eviction, even though there was no doubt in his mind that this was the one who had filmed the riot on his camcorder, and even released the misleading images of Jacob to the media the very next day.

'We've met already,' said Jacob as more youthful laughter broke out in the yard outside. 'Two weeks ago, in Wynberg.'

Instead of taking a chair, Jacob circled around to stand by the fridge door, which was covered with old crumpled photographs and ancient pictures drawn on yellowed paper by some child. The heavy crossed his arms as he hovered in the narrow doorway leading into the house proper.

'We have?'

'You filmed me grabbing that little girl out of the fire. I shouted for you to go for help, but you just went on filming.' Jacob nodded towards the outer kitchen door. 'You have all those kids there in the backyard but couldn't care less for a child getting hurt in a riot?'

'You had her.' The breaker shrugged. 'What did you expect me to do? Run across to your side and shout for help? Your bunch would have shot me like they did all the others.'

Jacob took a closer look at the photographs on the fridge door. They showed Makhe Motale at various stages of his life, always near his skateboard, most of them taken in backyards similar to this one. The joker he saw in them was nothing like the street agitator Jacob remembered from the riot. Then he spotted another photograph down near the fridge handle, and plucked it off the door.

'Is this Detective Harry Mason?'

'That's him.'

Jacob looked at it again, astonished to find it there. Harry was leaning against the same wrecked Chevrolet in the yard outside, a broad smile on his face, his legs and arms crossed casually in front of him. Mahke Motale sat on the car bonnet next to him, and toasted the photographer with a beer held high, while his other arm was thrown affectionately over Harry's shoulders. Jacob's ex-partner looked about the age he was when they first met in the early nineties, back when he still had a horseshoe moustache like every other bloody *umlungu* in the police force.

Will wonders ever cease? Jacob thought. He stuck the photo back up where it belonged.

'We have to know whether Makhe was Harry's informant,' Mosetsane demanded in that businesslike voice of hers.

'He might have been,' replied the youngster, and from his discomfort Jacob could tell Makhe most certainly had been.

'Did he try to double-cross Harry's team?'

'No.'

'We need to know the absolute truth,' said Mosetsane.

'He didn't. And why would he?'

Jacob could think of a few reasons why. He had worked with enough informants in his time to know that some of them were even seedier than the criminals the police service used them to rope in.

'Who did that to you?' Mosetsane was staring at the young man's injuries.

The youngster put a self-conscious hand to his face and averted his eyes. Stitches ribbed one eyebrow, and one cheek looked like he had a wad of cotton wool bunched in his mouth. 'The *boere*,' he muttered.

'Do you know exactly who they were?'

'Sure, they left certified copies of their fucking ID books with me.'

Jacob smiled grimly, then described each of the Ballies in turn as best he could.

'That's them. The curry muncher and the *umlungu* with the glasses, they knocked on the door a few times, doing door-to-doors, but Makhe's mother convinced them she didn't even know who he was. Until one day they just came crashing through the front door here. The one with the fucking pipe, he was waiting for us at the hole in the back fence. It was him that shot Cujo and Nenne; it was him that did this to me.'

Mosetsane reached out and touched the youngster's elbow. 'King, can you tell us more about the Phaliso brothers, the people Makhe Motale was talking to Harry about? Where they live?'

'The Phalisos?' His eyes might have narrowed at her question, but the messy swelling of his face made it hard to tell. 'I thought you said you were going after those goddamned cops?'

'We are,' she said, 'but we need to get to the Phalisos first.'

'Bra,' said Jacob, 'the people who grabbed Makhe, they took Harry as well, and all we know is that they're going after the Phalisos too. Where do we find them?'

King glanced from Jacob to Mosetsane and back again. Then he licked his scabbed lips and said, 'Where are the rest of you?'

'It's only us,' Mosetsane chipped in.

A light seemed to go on in the broken house that was the youngster's head. 'Shit, man, is that why word went out?'

'What word was that?'

'Yo, just about everyone that's ever owed the Abasindisi a favour has gone on over there.'

3

If someone had asked Jacob to find his way home at this point, he would have to reply that he could hardly locate the back of his own hand in the darkness, let alone the car. Their dash through the back alleys and footpaths of Alexandra, so cramped and narrow they might as well have been underground catacombs, has not only completely thrown his sense of direction but all sense of time as well.

He catches up with King at the latest crossing of footpaths that could lead them in any direction. Here there are no maps, no street names nor landmarks beyond the immediate structures crowding them in; there is no compass for a stranger in these parts. And the only person who knows what he is doing is a bruiser currently bent over his knees and huffing like a steam engine run out of coal.

Doesn't look like you thought this one through, says that voice Jacob would prefer to ignore. *Like so many other things.*

'Where are you taking us, bra?' he asks Makhe's man, more than mildly irritated by this sudden delay. 'I need to get to the Phalisos, quick-quick.'

'Almost there,' King splutters.

'You said that ten minutes ago.'

'Five.'

Mosetsane bounds around the last corner, looking as angry as a cat trapped in a bag.

'What is this,' she breathes, 'the Alex by Night Tour?'

'Yo, why do you keep talking to me in English anyway?' King asks in a mixture of Tswana and township pidgin. 'You a coconut from the suburbs, or what?'

'None of your business,' she hisses through ragged breaths.

The way she says it, and the way King's face falls at her reply, convinces Jacob that the kid has not only unsuspectingly whacked that particular nail right on the head, but hit every single finger too. It makes him glad that he never got the chance to ask the question himself. Raised white – black on the outside, white on the inside, a coconut – she probably grew up in the plush northern suburbs, maybe even abroad, in exile. He does his best to suppress a laugh at King's mortified expression.

Lightning rips across the small patch of leaden sky visible above them, and is followed shortly by deafening thunder so loud that children safely tucked away behind closed doors scream in terror. Suddenly the whole world around them is filled with the howling and baying of dogs.

Here and there people run for the shelter of their own homes, while corrugated-iron roofs held down by stones and assorted junk clatter and rattle against their restraints, eager to join the wind in its dance across the sky. Occasional raindrops the size of bullets pound down on flimsy structures, harbingers of what is sure to become a deluge, while the last dry gusts of blinding dust and coal-smoke bring with them the smell of a thirsty earth stretching its expectant tongue towards the sky.

'How far?' Jacob yells insistently over the racket.

More thunder sounds, and a mangy dog nearby starts yelping as it desperately tries to chew through a metre-long chain which restricts it to a two-by-two-foot exposed front yard.

'I said, how far?' he repeats.

King shakes his head as if to clear his mind and waves in a general direction. 'Not long now.'

Jacob grabs King by the shirt and pulls him up. 'Let's go, King!'

With a visible effort the youngster lumbers off in what appears to Jacob yet another random direction. As he glances back at Mosetsane, she rolls her eyes. *What else is there to do?* the gesture seems to say.

Their guide's waist seems to slosh from side to side in his loose sweatpants as he runs. His black trainers are soon spattered with mud and with gunk from the run-off of untold kitchen sinks and backyard water tubs. He cuts left. Right. Straight on. Right again. He keeps having to duck so as not to gash his head on the unexpectedly low roof-ends jutting out over the footpaths. Then he dodges through yet another narrow gap, and suddenly they are racing down a narrow alley between two walled-in sub-urban houses. At the furthest end of the passage, King leaps on to lower ground and sprints across a two-lane carriageway. He ducks through a rusted fence on the other side and stops in open veldt, hunched over again and trying to catch his breath.

Without breaking his stride, Jacob is about to make the same leap when King turns around, and his alarmed expression is simultaneously lit up by bright orange headlights.

'Wait!' he shouts.

Jacob tries to pull up short, but his momentum is too much and carries him forward. He reaches out for the walls on either side to stop himself from overshooting the edge, but his hands find no purchase. Blinding light flashes into his eyes from directly to his left, accompanied by the screech of tyres.

4

A hand knots itself into Jacob's windbreaker from behind and yanks him back from the precipice just as a vehicle skids over the spot where Jacob would undoubtedly have landed. Then Busisiwe Mosetsane has him pinned against one of the walls of the alley, a hand against his chest, her warm breath in his face.

'You're a bit old not to be checking the street before you cross it, aren't you?' An impish grin twists her lips. 'Look right, left, right again?'

'Never had the chance to learn that little trick.' Jacob smiles back. 'Thanks anyway.'

She pats his chest. 'No problem.'

Then she herself takes a few powerful steps and jumps high and far, to land deftly in the further lane. Meeting up with King on the other side she glances back Jacob's way, her chin upturned, as though daring him to better her feat.

Jacob walks over to the edge and looks carefully for oncoming traffic this time.

As a fresh sequence of thunder and lightning blasts its way across the sky and brings the first real wash of rain, Jacob scans the veldt, towards a long line of middle-class homes just a few hundred yards away from his current position. The destitute and the so-so rich separated merely by an expanse of grass that might once have been a soccer pitch. At the very end of a long darkened cul de sac a two-storey structure is belching heavy smoke, and flames lick out of broken second-floor windows. Further along, several fires have been lit down the middle of the street. This is the same scene they had noticed almost an hour ago, as they were coming down Marlboro Drive further north.

He scrambles down and jogs across the potholed avenue to where Mosetsane and King are waiting for him.

'A bit out of breath there, inspector?' Mosetsane asks.

With a sinking feeling about what they might find in that burning house, Jacob points to it. 'Tell me that's not where we're going.'

King squints through the rain that is growing heavier by the second. When sheet lightning slashes across the sky, the pink house is lit up as if it were daylight. The crash of thunder that immediately follows has Mosetsane instinctively cupping her hands over her ears.

'That's it.' King has to yell over the deluge to make himself heard. 'You can't mistake it; looks like a—' He throws an embarrassed glance at Mosetsane and, when he finds her glaring at him, his eyes suddenly find the tips of his shoes extremely interesting. 'The colour is just ugly, that's all,' he mutters.

Jacob tries in vain to pinch his windbreaker closed at the neckline. 'Are the streetlights in that road usually out?'

'They were still working last night.'

A horrible vision enters Jacob's mind, of a car crammed with police officers – a few of them bent, misguided, angry to the core, he can only guess at what drove them this far, but cops still – coasting down that dark hill towards the property which lies at the very bottom, when suddenly automatic gunfire opens up from the buildings on either side. With 7.62mm rounds fired from an AK-47 rifle, powerful enough to pierce light armour, anyone caught in the crossfire would not have a fighting chance.

You've screwed up, mfana. *You're too late.*

As if to validate that thought, there is a sudden bright white flash between two of the unlit houses. A few seconds later there is a dull thud that could be a grenade explosion. Mosetsane is about to ask him a question when gunfire starts rattling off like a thousand ball-bearings shaken around in an empty coffee can.

FOURTEEN

1

Ncolela Phaliso's self-satisfied grin hit the pavement the moment Swarts pushed Harry away and took aim at the Abasindisi leader with a silenced gun that was neither his nor the service's, and would disappear the moment the job was finished, along with all the shell casings. That expression alone, thought Swarts with a smile, would be worth every moment of the investigation that was sure to come after tonight.

Boo, arsehole, he thought. *Didn't think we'd bring the war to you this way, did you?*

It was not just about cleaning up a few loose ends, the way Franklin insisted. This was for Kommie too, he kept telling himself.

He knew full well that their chances of getting away with this little stunt were slim from the beginning. The question now was, how much did all these people believe the police would actually investigate fellow officers over this particular incident? How much did these folk have faith that their witness statements would make a difference to what happened after tonight?

He could just hear it in the interrogation rooms: *Gunfire?* they'd echo in response to an investigator. *No, that was just the rain and thunder. You sleep under a tin roof in a thunderstorm like that, you can't even hear yourself think.*

Swarts believed these commoners would not care to share their version of events with the police or any other investigators. They would not want to get themselves involved in any official process, because anyone making a statement would have to come back here and live amongst others who'd have their own agendas, including those who might become the next Abasindisi leaders, because another two would surely take the Phalisos' places tomorrow, no questions asked. His biggest problem, then, was not whether this bunch was going to spill the beans to the ICD or any other police authority about the Ballies' involvement in whatever transpired here tonight. It was how hard and fast they would come at him once the first shots were fired.

'Don't you blimming wish you had that pistol now, Bond?' Swarts asked.

But Harry did not answer him.

Russell Swarts' index finger tightened on the trigger just as a smile pulled at his lips. He was going to enjoy this one. He never had such satisfaction with Ntombini, because, truth be told, he was scared shitless after what he did, and for months he was looking over his shoulder, sure that someone in Murder and Robbery was going to nail him to the wall when whoever had sold out Ntombini decided to sell out Swarts as well.

But this now, it was just too perfect to foul up.

'Russell,' began Harry in a placatory tone, perhaps sensing what the man's next move was going to be.

'One more blimming word out of you about law and order, Harry, and you become a very big part of the problem.'

'Superintendent Swarts, I am not armed.' Ncolela carefully lifted his jacket up, then his shirt, turning a slow circle. 'See?'

'Shut up!'

'Before you shoot me, let me tell you that this man, Wally Khuzwayo, he was acting on his own. The Abasindisi—'

'I said shut up, Ncolela! Christ, I've heard this blimming bullshit from you a million times before. I didn't believe it then and I don't believe it now. You killed a lot of police officers tonight, and for that you're dying right here.'

'I didn't pull a trigger. I didn't press any buttons. I wasn't even anywhere near that bomb they are talking about.'

Lightning sliced open a pregnant sky, and raindrops began a slow tap-dance over the tarmac. The fires began hissing angrily with steam.

The older Phaliso scanned the crowd, which must have completely encircled Swarts and Harry by now, where they stood near one of the fires in the middle of the street. The feigned innocence of his expression would have given the devil dressed up as Sinatra a run for his money.

'But I'm innocent,' he sang to the crowd. 'And so is my brother.'

The comment brought an involuntary laugh to Swarts' lips.

The next flash of lightning drew Swarts' attention to the house at the very end of the road, burning brighter by the second. Much closer to the action, he also caught sight of Franklin as he vaulted unnoticed over a low wall and dropped out of sight into a yard, not too far behind where the Phaliso brothers were standing. A fresh swell in the ice-cold rain abruptly turned into a roar of water, causing the three low-burning fires to splutter and spit feebly.

Ncolela gestured to Wally Khuzwayo. 'Come forward. Tell him what you told me.'

'Hey, Wally, here we are again, hey *boet*?' Swarts yelled. 'Only this time there's no place to run. What do you say to that?'

Wally Khuzwayo came shuffling forward, and a thought rammed its way through the brandy sloshing around in Swarts' head, amid the handful of Myprodols and Norflexes he had gobbled to keep his muscle pains at bay, to keep going until this job was finished. The thought was simply that whatever this thing coming towards him was, it was certainly not the Wally Khuzwayo he knew.

It looked like him, sure – hell, the guy even had the same wounds as when they had lost the bastard to his rescuers – but something was dreadfully wrong. It, *he*, was out of whack. He had somehow *changed* in the few intervening hours

'Harry,' Swarts said, slightly unnerved by Khuzwayo, but not taking his eyes off that shuffling zombie, 'what's the *squeeza* doing back there?'

'She's just staring at us.'

'And the other fucks?'

'They're watching too.'

The downpour made it harder to see by the second, and what little light there had been from the nearby fires was fast failing, which meant Swarts did not have more than a minute or so to get this party over and done with. If he missed his chance, whatever it might be, the Phalisos would soon have him for dinner, honoured members of the Johannesburg Chamber of Commerce or not.

For some reason the rain did not quite soak through Wally Khuzwayo's shirt as he shuffled towards Swarts, and it only beaded on his arms, face and hair.

Then the broken man's mouth opened, and a tortured voice emerged. 'Superintendent, you know it was me that put the bomb,' the apparition said in its broken English. 'Ncolela and Godun, they know nothing, I tell you. And the guns, they mine, too.'

'What the fuck is this?' shouted Swarts.

'I wanted to take the Abasindisi away from them. It was me, for sure.'

Ncolela pulled his jacket over his head, and allowed a glimpse of that grin to return to his face. 'You see? There is your confession.'

Suddenly Swarts felt stone-cold sober. Suddenly unsure, he took a step back. 'Get away!'

'*A-a-a-a*' Godun Phaliso croaked; Swarts had completely forgotten about this weird-looking mute.

'We caught him for you, superintendent,' Ncolela shouted over the drumming rain. 'Here's our public serv—' Words were lost as fresh thunder cracked overhead. '. . . been responsible for most of the lies that have been spread about my brother and me. And a respectable organization.'

Ncolela turned to the massed crowd, points at Wally Khuzwayo and triumphantly proclaimed to them something utterly incomprehensible to Swarts.

'In English, you blimming arsehole!' he shouted, unnerved by the possibility that he was fast losing control of this situation.

Ncolela turned back to him and smiled. It was a look perfectly pitched, to tell Swarts he had walked into shit so deep and so thick there was no getting out, and when the Phaliso flicked his head slightly sideways and gave a small nod to someone behind him, Swarts knew he should have shot the bastard the moment he laid eyes on him.

'Russell!' Harry yelled a warning just as a woman's scream cut through the rain.

Swarts would have turned and fired, imagining that rabid creature pouncing on his back, her teeth bared, but for the thing that used to be Wally Khuzwayo. It suddenly leaped to life and ran straight towards him. The eyes were vacant and wild, the hands thrown wide open as though beseeching God for some last mercy. But just as Swarts was about to squeeze off a bullet – hell, an entire magazine, if that was needed, to stop the damn creature from touching him – the crowd seethed forward, wielding guns, staves and plumbing pipes, wheel-spanners and crowbars, sharpened branches and any number of knives.

They didn't go for him; they didn't go for Harry; instead they all went for Wally Khuzwayo, the man who had betrayed his leaders, the man who had led men like Russell Swarts into their midst. They clubbed him, they punched, they kicked. They tore, they spat or merely shouted insults. They saved their valuable bullets for a more worthwhile adversary. Then the madwoman was amongst them, waving the remnants of her spluttering torch. When Wally Khuzwayo fell to his knees under this torrent of blows, she brought it down hard on his head. At that moment Russell Swarts understood why the raindrops only beaded on Wally Khuzwayo's clothes and skin, why he looked like he had been rubbed all over with grease. It was some sort of accelerator – diesel, paraffin, propane jelly for all he knew – because in the next moment the man erupted in flames.

Then Wally Khuzwayo was up, stumbling this way and that, as if he was desperately trying to find his bearings. Then he swung around and came straight for Swarts, cutting a flaming path through his attackers.

Raising his pistol, Swarts depressed the trigger once. The weapon bucked in his hands, and a black hole appeared above Wally Khuzwayo's eye. He let go another silenced round, this one shattering the bridge of the man's nose. But still he kept coming.

Swarts lowered his aim, waited to make sure of the next shot, and then put a bullet into the man's kneecap just as he reached out to him with one burning hand.

It did the trick. As Swarts sidestepped Wally Khuzwayo's ongoing charge, the man wobbled, lost his balance and fell.

He had barely looked up from where the burning body collapsed when Franklin reappeared, closer now but still hidden behind one of the low garden walls fronting the street. Fresh lightning caught him in a perfect bowler's pose, and picked out something small and black heading straight their way.

'Grenade!' Swarts grabbed Harry and dropped to the ground.

2

In the moments before Russell Swarts shouted his warning, Harry spotted Naidoo carefully peering over the top of a low wall, two houses up from where Franklin was about to launch an attack. When lightning revealed the gun he had braced against the rim of the wall, Harry realized what was about to happen. Instead of ambushing only the two Phalisos, the other Ballies were reckless enough to take on the entire crowd.

Harry covers his head with his hands as the grenade explodes nearby. His gut screams at this new physical abuse, but it is little more than a distraction compared to the shrapnel suddenly zipping by overhead. There are screams of pain and angry shouting, wild gunshots tearing loose in all directions.

Get the hell up and run!

He tries to pick himself up, but the leg under the wound in his abdomen is slow to respond, and he is forced to duck again when fresh bullets strafe over him, shards of road surfacing scratching across the backs of his hands. Forehead pressed flat against the wet tarmac, he is soaked through in seconds by the icy sheets of rainwater sliding down the hill.

If Harry were not so preoccupied with preventing street muck from trickling into his mouth, if his chin were not tucked so deep into his chest and his hands not so tightly braced over the wound to his scalp, he would see shoes new and worn running in every direction, discarded weapons scattering everywhere, desperate men hurdling over garden walls, wounded humans collapsing as people blindly fire handguns over their shoulders in their retreat.

When this panic-induced spate of gunfire eventually subsides, Harry cautiously turns his head to take a peek back down the slope. Half blocking his view to the left is the blackened corpse of Wally Khuzwayo. A little further down the road lies prone a heavy-set figure which can only belong to Russell Swarts. More than that, Harry cannot tell for sure in the darkness, despite the flickering light from the still-burning house further down the street.

'Supe!' he whispers as loudly as he dare.

Though the rainfall is still intense, the thunder and lightning, having expended their worst over Alexandra, are chasing each other further north.

Eyes are watching the narrow road intently. He is convinced that he can feel them boring into the bodies littered on the street, waiting for someone to make a move in the darkness and thus offer himself as a fresh target. Superintendent Swarts' form remains still, with no suggestion that he has heard Harry calling. Whether this is because he has also realized the danger of their current exposed position, or because something worse has happened to him, Harry cannot tell, but the sudden thought of being the only one from Swarts' group left alive unsettles him. How long before they come out of the woodwork to count the dead and check who is left alive, he wonders.

'Russell, answer me!' he hisses.

Lightning decides to throw a departing barrage across the sky, and for a few seconds reveals the roadway with stark clarity. He registers the still-burning Phaliso house, and three piles of soaked grey ash spreading like sludge all over the street. Then there is Russell Swarts gazing in his direction, and blinking rainwater out of his eyes. He is lying on his back, his legs twisted sideways, while the pistol gripped in one hand is aimed in Harry's direction. Then the light flickers out, turning into a dull peal of thunder, but not before Harry notices the man's mouth gaping open and his chest shuddering with each breath.

'Jesus, Russell!'

'Don't worry, Bond,' comes a calm response from the darkness. 'It's just a blimming scratch. Cunts wouldn't even know how to shoot a fat fish like me in a barrel.'

Careful that more lightning flashes might reveal his movements, Harry slowly crawls on his elbows towards that voice. It suddenly sounded so weak, so goddamned *foreign* to the man he still knows as his supe. Whatever happened between them is instantly out of the window; all that matters is sharing with Russell Swarts that one moment no cop ever wants to share with another: dying in the rain with fear writ large in his eyes.

Harry shakes off a wave of nausea and dizziness when he reaches his superintendent. ' "Scratch" my arse, Russell. Where you've been hit?'

Russell Swarts laughs despite his agony, and it is an ugly sound, like a rusty engine choking out its last revolutions. 'Scratch your arse, Harry? Did I hear you right? What kind of a favour is that to ask at a time like this?'

For a second Harry is stumped. Then he lets his head drop on to his forearms and joins in the laughter.

'What a blimming mess, hey, Bond?'

'You're an idiot, that's what you are!'

'Not stupid, Bond. Just a misplaced old bastard.'

Russell Swarts sounds exhausted, like he is dozing off.

'Keeping talking, Russie, or you'll go into shock, and then who's going to carry your fat arse out of here?'

'I've put it in my will. It's you and only you who's responsible for that.'

'I wouldn't touch your fat arse with a stick.'

'Then kiss it, captain.'

Harry starts probing his superintendent's clothes, then realizes that he will not be able to see any wounds anyway. Everything is too wet for him to distinguish between rain and blood.

'Where?' he starts, but realizes this is an exercise in futility. There is no hope of a speedy extraction to a hospital, not with all that liquid gargling already in Swarts's breath.

A cold podgy hand reaches out and brushes across Harry's face. 'Play your cards right, captain, and you'll still have a job by close of business Monday afternoon. Blame me, blame us, blame the fucking Phalisos, I don't fucking care, but just make it work.'

'Why did you go down this road, Russell?'

'What do you mean?'

'Who the fuck shot me? Which one of you was it? Franklin?'

'It was one of the herders. The Abasindisi.'

His voice fades and, as another flash of lightning rips across the sky, Harry sees Russell Swarts' eyes begin to roll.

'Bullshit!' He shakes Russell hard. 'Stay with me, you son of a bitch. What the fuck did you try kill me for? How could protecting yourself be so important to you? I didn't . . . fuck, Russie, I didn't *have* anything on you.'

Swarts takes a deep gurgling breath and forces out the words. 'Why the fuck won't you believe me, Harry? Hey, just leave it alone.'

'If it had been one of their herders, you would've come clean with me a long time ago. You wouldn't have done a runner when you saw me coming to in that hospital room.'

'Harry . . .' Russell Swarts tries to sit up, then slumps back on the tarmac. 'Fuck, this isn't working.' He stares up at the sky, and coughs as he tries to catch a breath. 'Don't ask me that, please. I told you I had your back, and I did.'

'Then who are you covering up for?'

Harry waits for an answer, but the gurgle in Swarts' throat becomes a long drawn-out splutter. Harry sits up, unmindful of any would-be snipers, and violently shakes his commanding officer by the shoulder. 'Tell me! What the hell does it matter to you now? JUST FUCKING TELL ME!'

But all the tension in Russell Swarts' muscles is gone, and his head rolls loosely against Harry's knees. Suddenly there is nothing left to ask or say between them, only the reality of someone he knew lying dead in his arms.

There is a scuff of a heavy boot as a dim silhouette unsteadily approaches Harry from further down the hill. There is a click as the hammer of a gun is pulled back.

'Franklin?'

Harry is still peering into the darkness, trying to discern who it is stumbling towards him, when he registers other footsteps closing in from behind his back. Remembering the silenced weapon still clasped in Swarts' hand, Harry fumbles for it, but discovers the slide and breach are jammed up so tight he can't budge them.

Three gunshots sounding from behind the houses over to his left draw instant attention – one followed by a pause, then two in quick succession. He holds his breath and listens out for more – or anything that will give him a clue as to what has happened – but there is now just that slow scraping sound over tarmac, as someone heavy drags an injured leg towards him.

Last of the boere *standing*, thinks Harry wryly, then chucks away the jammed weapon. *With nothing but a cheap Czech handgun to keep me company, at that.*

His superintendent bought his ticket along with the rest of the Ballies, and it now seems Harry has been left all alone to foot the bill.

Harry finally makes out a silhouette with Swarts' bulky build.

'I take it you are the *gata* that got shot up in the mountains?' says Ncolela Phaliso. 'What's your name again?'

'Let me guess,' replies Harry. 'You were going to ask me about my health.'

Something sharp jabs Harry in the back and, when he glances over his shoulder, he sees two young black men glaring down at him as they exchange several incomprehensible words with Ncolela. Harry looks from one, who seems to be holding a crude spear, to the other, resting a two-foot plumbing pipe on his shoulder.

'You go on like that and you'll end up like that shit you're holding in your lap.'

'Put the gun down, Ncolela. It's over.'

Though he can barely see the man in the dim light of the burning house at the bottom of the hill, he can sense two eyes studying him. Ncolela is breathing like an asthmatic, and Harry guesses the man must have sustained his own injuries.

'Are you talking like that to me, *gata*? Out here, where the nearest ears all belong to *me*?'

'All of them? Are you sure about that? How long do you think before someone else makes a play for the Abasindisi throne? You're screwed, my friend. Maybe it's already started, I don't know. I don't see your brother about.'

Ncolela Phaliso raises the gun to backhand him across the face. Harry shuts his eyes and braces himself for the blow. But when it does not land, he opens one eye to find Ncolela Phaliso glancing around like a caged animal trying to find a way out. Then Harry notices another thing: the distant wail of police sirens, and a faint flash of blue light approaching through the darkness?

Sweet Jesus, he thinks. *Just let the cavalry be coming this way.*

'It all means only one thing, Ncolela,' he says boldly. 'In the greater scheme of things, you're just another street hustler.'

'Shut up.' This time Ncolela Phaliso does pistol-whip

him. The butt connects squarely with Harry's jaw, and the explosion of pain is worse even than what he remembers of his shooting in Tsolo. Harry keels over like a felled tree.

'I'm a fucking businessman, you hear me? With money. With *respect*!'

Harry barely hears him as the world around him recedes into a sickening haze.

One of the young men behind him shifts nervously and asks Ncolela an urgent question. Even though Harry is fighting to stay conscious, and cannot understand a word anyway, he knows what the question must be: 'What do we do now?'

Ncolela's reaction is a string of invectives and next Harry hears a weapon being dropped near him, and departing feet slapping along the wet road.

His mind oscillates between oblivion and consciousness, but Harry nevertheless tries his best to focus on the one thing that matters right now: survival. Those damn sirens better be coming this way, but at moments they sound like they are on top of him, other times as if they are not even there and it is only the ringing aftermath in his ears of the grenade explosion.

Harry eventually unfolds from the painful foetal ball he has been curled up in, and reaches for the .38 abandoned by Ncolela. Then he takes a good look around. Not a living soul is visible on the street, and of the sirens there is now no sound. They were not destined to save him after all, but heading off some other way.

He slumps back down to the roadway and starts laughing at his present situation: he is going to now die of hypothermia or a bleeding two-week-old gut-shot – whichever gets him first. When this hysteria finally becomes too painful, he raises himself up on his hands and knees. With another effort, which makes him feel like he is splitting open right down the middle, he at last staggers to his feet.

A hundred steep yards uphill will take him to the top of the road, from where it will be another hundred yards or so back down towards the river, to where Franklin parked the minibus van amongst a row of taxis. But with no car keys, and every black face in the neighbourhood no doubt marking him as an enemy, he does not expect to find salvation anywhere in this neighbourhood, for sure. Down at the dead-end of the cul de sac, however, there is a dying fire. And the warmth it could give him . . .

He turns to look for a brief moment and sees distant silhouettes passing in front of the gates to what is left of the Phaliso house. This hint of further trouble in that direction is enough to drive him back up the hill.

FIFTEEN

1

Jacob sprinted flat out through the downpour even as a single thought kept pumping through his head: his father's voice was right: he was too late. There was no saving Harry the moment that grenade went off and the chatter of guns erupted. Now the only things left to do were to bear witness to a friend's death, and to looking that friend's daughter in the eye and convince her the world was still a decent place.

The sheeting rain stung his eyes as he bounded across the field. Knolls of soggy grass and mud pulled and sucked at his feet. He had with him an automatic pistol borrowed from the youth called King. Somewhere close behind him, Busi Mosetsane was sure to be following, even though he had urged her to go with King and find some protection from the weather, and then phone both the chief and Superintendent Niehaus on their private numbers.

'I'm coming with you,' she had argued.

'To do what?' said Jacob as he ejected the clip in the pistol to satisfy himself that it contained a full magazine, then rammed it back in.

The way she glared at him just then, she might easily have slugged him with a wheel spanner if there had been one to hand.

'What I meant is that you're not even armed.'

'But you need someone to watch your back.'

'Go make the call, Busi. That's what we need right now more than anything.' He turned his gaze first to the burning house, then towards the street leading down to it, and imagined seeing tiny cigarette-tip flashes of distant gunfire. 'And maybe a miracle too,' he had murmured.

Thunder cracks close by as his feet splash through ever-widening puddles. In the momentary light he sees people leap over perimeter walls and spill out through backyard gates to head off into the veldt, but he still cannot tell what exactly they are fleeing from.

Then they are flying past him: first a young woman, barely in her twenties, looking over a shoulder in abject terror, followed by a man with a bloodied white safari shirt missing its buttons. Twenty feet away, another woman is screaming that she can't live like this any more, before she stumbles and pitches headlong into the long grass. Another figure turns back to help her to her feet, then pushes her ahead of him. Others crouch under garden walls, waiting for the gunshots to clear, not yet willing to risk making a break across open ground for the safety of the shantytown lying just to the south. They are ordinary people, these, folk like any other he grew up with in the townships, and now they are overcome with fear.

Jacob slams into a low wall and crouches below its rim to keep his head well out of sight. By now he is soaked through and he cannot stop shivering with cold, despite the hot blood thundering in his ears.

He peers over towards the smouldering remains of the pink house, visible above the only electrified fence in the neighbourhood, and notices a small group hurrying across the veldt beyond it, carrying a wounded man in their arms. For a moment he hopes it might be Harry, then realizes how unlikely that would be.

Seeing no immediate route through to the street beyond the line of properties, he starts to move to the left. An open stretch of overgrown land runs all the way up the hill behind these last houses in the row, and Jacob guesses this must constitute the Jukskei River's floodplain. About two hundred yards further to the north is a thicket of trees that obscures a road running east to west, feeding a last set of houses built on a high knoll nearer to the river. Through the web of bare branches he makes out a line of taxis parked under the halo of a single streetlight, where people are now milling around one particular minibus van.

Nearby, one of the backyard gates is unlocked and wide open, and slowly he creeps towards it, making sure to keep his head down low. As he approaches, he sees the gate itself is a home-made affair of steel and barbed wire. Rain gurgles along the wall beside it and clatters loudly in a gutter. Even though now the gunfire has mostly subsided, an ominous air of expectation pervades the night.

Jacob shifts his grip on the wet pistol, not quite as confident with it as he might be with a police-issue 9mm. It feels too heavy and bulky, and what is he supposed to do with it anyway? If he comes across Swarts or one of his Ballies, will he simply announce to them that they are under arrest? They are cops, after all. It makes him uncomfortable to think that he might have to point a weapon at a fellow serviceman.

They would certainly not go quietly if they have already come this far to protect themselves. At least not if confronted with Jacob all on his own.

Jacob stops, an odd prickling sensation suddenly running over his skin. It is as though he can feel a kind of heat pressing through to him from the other side of this garden wall. He listens carefully, trying to figure out if it was some noise that put him on his guard, or whether it is just the uncertainty which has recently blanketed his thoughts.

He waits a few moments more to try to understand this sensation, then has to dismiss it as nothing more than paranoia.

At the gate Jacob hunkers down for a moment to wipe the rain from his face. Then he steps into its gaping mouth, angling himself in such a way that he has at least one blind angle covered with his weapon.

At the same time he hears the faintest squelching sound as a shadow springs out from behind the wall.

2

His cheek is set on fire as something slices through his skin. Jacob Tshabalala is still falling when another lightning flash turns the shadow into a sinewy human form with a long face, high cheekbones and round unblinking eyes. Godun Phaliso is brandishing a large hunting knife, known on the streets as a Seven Star on account of the jail time you can get for carrying one in public. In the hands of a competent fighter, the thing can cause more damage within a six-foot radius than any gun.

Jacob lands hard on his back, his skull thudding against sun-baked earth still as hard as concrete despite the rain, and a sharp piece of rock jabs deep into one kidney so that an involuntary scream is forced from his lips. By the time he has rolled aside from it and has the automatic up and ready, his target has become nothing but splashing feet disappearing into the night.

Hoping to catch sight of him again at the next lightning flash, he flips over on to his stomach and props himself up on his elbows. Abruptly two dark figures come flying through the gateway, right into his firing line, and then race up the slope after Phaliso, before Jacob can even can make out who they are. He tries to get up, but a painful cramp shoots up his back from the bruised kidney and he doubles over, barely able to breathe.

Get up, mfo! He hits the earth with a fist in frustration. *Now!*

A faint popping sound has him looking up, a split second before a heavy gunshot goes off. Lightning brightens the sky to reveal two figures, one lean, the other squat, hovering over a third that crouches in the mud on all fours. As Jacob watches, the lean figure boots the downed man in the face before raising a silenced gun and firing off another two rounds at point-blank range, seemingly just for good measure. The second man then also fires twice at the prone body without a silencer.

'Police!' Jacob yells instinctively. 'Naidoo! Franklin! Drop your weapons!'

Darkness descends on the scene again, and suddenly pricks of white and orange light begin flashing in Jacob's direction. He drops face-down in the mud as bullets sing overhead. Bracing his arms, he returns fire at what now looks like a pair of fleeing figures. Two short controlled bursts buck in his hands, and on the second shot he hears a yelp of pain and a splash, like a tree falling over in marshland. Lying still a few more seconds, he inhales the stink of cordite over the smell of wet grass and fresh mud. The only sound is the wheeze of his own dry throat. Then suddenly, in the distance, approaching sirens can be heard.

Jacob scrambles to his feet and prepares to give chase.

SIXTEEN

1

The rain has nearly stopped. Harry pushes himself away from the garden wall and starts to edge slowly towards the taxis parked under the streetlight, towards the crowd looting the Ballies' mini-van. His sluggardly, unresponsive feet make him feel like an extra in one of those living-dead movies. When he presses a hand to his abdomen it feels hard and distended, though the blood seepage from underneath the massive bandage has seemingly stopped.

When he first spotted this mob at the top of the hill, he had briefly thought about turning back and trying to find a phone in one of the abandoned houses. But a single glance back down the slope, still littered with bodies, decided him against that.

Closer now, the crowd still looks fairly ferocious. There is a lot of yelling and arguing going on, pointing fingers stabbing at faces and chests, and not for the first time Harry regrets not learning one of the indigenous languages of this vast country. Despite the risk that, in their rage, they will tear him apart the moment they see him, he heads straight along the middle of the road, almost eager for them to notice him coming. Sometimes it is just better to try your luck than do nothing at all.

Harry is about ten yards away from the crowd, and still unnoticed, when he hears the back door of the minibus slide open. Abruptly wails go up from a cluster of women as a misshapen object is lifted high over the heads of the men, then passed further along the line until it appears under the streetlight. He now remembers Makhe's body, in the canvas sack, being dumped on the back seat of the minibus.

The bag containing Makhe Motale is quickly stripped away from the body, and more cries of grief resound through the damp night air at the sight of their hero's limbs frozen by rigor mortis into a grotesque imitation of a curled-up baby. Harry stops dead in his tracks at the sight. It was one thing to imagine Makhe Motale was inside that bag, but something else to see him borne over the heads of so many strangers yelling phrases that are completely incoherent to him.

It is at that point that Harry is spotted by a young man with a lightning bolt shaved into his short-cropped hair. A warning is shouted to the others and, in unison, multiple faces turn in his direction. They are faces filled with fear and anger and hatred. The voices fall silent, and Makhe's corpse disappears into their midst.

With a pained grunt, Harry raises his hands high above his head, though he keeps a tight grip on the pistol which he picked up earlier. He is about to shout out to them that he is a police officer in need of support, but decides that will not go down too well here at all. He tries to think of something else to say, but in his head it all suddenly sounds so absurd and so unjustified that he remains quiet. Ask them for help when it will most assuredly be assumed that he is one of the notorious Ballies?

The two sides glower at each other, until Harry stumbles with the effort of holding his arms above his head. The pain in his abdomen forces him to double over and take some of the strain off the muscles and organs under pressure from the blood welling up inside him. Angry voices immediately spark up in the crowd, and the young man with the lightning bolt in his hair takes a purposeful step in his direction.

'Wait!' Harry shouts as loudly as he can, and takes a few steps forward. 'My name's Harry Mason. I was his friend . . .' He runs out of breath and the world starts to spin. 'Makhe and I . . . His mother's name is Letia, his sister . . .'

Harry's words peter out into a whisper, and he staggers again, this time coming dangerously close to keeling over.

'You're dead, *gata*!' someone shouts. 'That's what you are.'

When he looks up at the crowd, it has already begun to surge in his direction.

Oh boy, Harry thinks.

He looks at the pistol in his hand and recalls something Swarts had been fond of saying: it wasn't the gun that kept you alive in a bad situation, it was your reputation. But out here, with nothing and no one to back him up, with a mob of frustrated civvies blinded by an intrusion threatening their safety and by the death of a leader, what is this reputation worth? Isn't it precisely that reputation that is now going to get him killed? And exactly how cool is he supposed to play it when he can barely focus on the approaching crowd?

In other words, how much more screwed up can things possibly get?

Abruptly there is a commotion among the mob's stragglers, then a loud crash from the undergrowth bordering the open field behind the houses. A moment later, a figure bursts headlong out of the brush and straight into the light, brambles and broken sticks clinging to arms held protectively in front of a white face. Franklin spins around under his own momentum and stares back the way he came, completely focused on any would-be pursuers, unaware of the scenario he has run into. His breathing comes hard, like bellows firing up a furnace, and his bright eyes shine with a light all of their own. In one hand he is still holding a silenced pistol, while one of his jeans pockets bulges with the last of his grenades. A triumphant smile crosses his face on realizing he has reached the team's minibus, before he finally turns around.

The crowd had swivelled in unison at this weird interruption, and since remained silent in surprise. But now it seems to lean forward collectively, like a drunkard getting ready for a bar-room brawl.

Franklin stops dead in his tracks, his jaw dropping wide open at the sight of nearly fifty people gathered not ten metres away from him, all murderously glaring at him. His chest swells with one long wheezing breath.

'Fuck,' he expels it.

And with no hesitation whatsoever, born of whatever madness or lust for violence the man has nurtured during all his years as a soldier, a cop, and whatever else he may have been in his spare time to twist his thinking into that air of superiority he throws around in the office, he brings his weapon up to start firing indiscriminately.

'Franklin!' Harry levels the pistol in his own hand.

The man pauses, looks over in Harry's direction, then his eyebrows arch in surprise. 'Mason, you look like shit. Where's Russie?'

'He's dead.'

Franklin barely blinks at this news. 'Oh.'

'That's enough, James,' says Harry. 'It ends here.'

Franklin briefly glances at the crowd before settling his eyes back on Harry. A familiar tight-lipped smile spreads over his face, like something toxic bleeding through the cracks in concrete. 'The hell it does.'

He then dives to his right, and in the weeks that follow Harry will wonder whether he managed to fire first because he was going to do it anyway, or because Franklin never intended to shoot and was ducking in the hope of getting the crowd into Harry's firing line, so that he himself could get away.

Whatever his reasons for moving, Harry's first shot catches him in the shoulder. The second splinters his collarbone. People in the crowd scatter to the four winds as Harry, overcome with a sudden grim fury, advances on Franklin, the pain in his abdomen now utterly forgotten.

Maddening thoughts surge through his mind, cresting on a flood of rage such as he has never felt before. Memories play out in those few seconds and feed his anger the way benzine flares in a bonfire: the memory of this man pretending to break Jeanie's neck, of him promising that he would have his way with her after he had killed Harry. The way he had treated Makhe's body like it was nothing more than a sack of shit. These emotions, thick and raw and amorphous, ride roughshod over all reason and logic and restraint. Though the man is down and his weapon has skidded from his hand, Harry squeezes off three more rounds at close range. The first two catch Franklin in his diaphragm, the third one drills straight into his liver.

Harry comes to a stop a metre away, the weapon now steaming in the cold air as he grips it so tight it feels as if he might crush it. Franklin tries to say something, but the words die in his throat, and nothing escapes his mouth but a long string of saliva and blood.

The trigger in Harry's hand begins to tighten again, as

if of its own volition, and he might have emptied the entire magazine into the ex-soldier but for some further rustling in the thicket. He raises the weapon in that direction just as Jacob Tshabalala, covered in mud and bleeding from a gash across the face, ploughs through the dense undergrowth. Harry's ex-partner pulls up short when their eyes meet. His breath comes in wild gasps; his teeth are bared with effort. Then that high forehead furrows as his eyes travel between Harry and Franklin, the gun in his friend's hand that is still levelled at his chest.

'Harry, what are you doing?' He lowers his own weapon, and presses a hand to the small of his back. A pained grimace crosses his face. 'Point that thing somewhere else.'

Harry stares at Jacob, unable to think, unable to speak. He can feel his molars grinding in his turmoil, and the pistol's grip is slick in his shaking hand. A pearl of sweat trickles down the side of his face, and he can smell blood, hot and metallic, everywhere around him.

Franklin slumps back on to the wet tarmac with a final wheeze. The sound draws Harry's attention back to the man who had threatened to one day rape his daughter, and the pistol in his hand starts creeping again in that direction.

'I said, lower the gun, Harry.' Jacob's tone hardens into steel. 'He's gone.'

Harry blinks. Franklin's eyes are still open, but his gaze is now turned towards the coal-black sky that is just breaking open to reveal pinpricks of twinkling diamonds. A few final drops of rain patter on to his exposed skin under the orange light. His chest looks like it has been splashed with a bucket of red paint, and the grenade in his pocket looks like an obscene erection.

Yes, he is dead. But is he dead enough?

'He . . .' Harry begins, but further words refuse to come. His throat is suddenly as dry as a bone. His eyes creep down the length of his own arm till they rest on the weapon clutched in a hand that is not his own any more.

'It's all right, *mfana*.' Jacob's voice is soothing, but for some reason Harry cannot bring himself to trust it. 'Everything is fine now. Hear that sound? It's the chief. That's our team coming right now.'

The spell finally snaps, like a dry twig in the night, and he feels the tension in his arm drain away.

'Yes,' says Harry. 'That's us.'

He drops to his knees, as all around them termites with glistening wings of gold flutter into the halo of orange light, only to be scooped up by the flitting shadows of bats silently dive-bombing out of a freshly washed darkness.

SEVENTEEN

1

They found Ncolela Phaliso after the shoot-out in Alexandra. He had died of blood loss, from severe shrapnel trauma to the right side of his body, caused by the grenade thrown by Franklin. Apparently the paramedics found him lying in the middle of the dead-end road leading up to his gutted house, his hand outstretched towards something, his eyes still open and focused on his fingertips. What he had seen at that moment of death was anyone's guess, Jacob later told Harry, but apparently he looked more serene than he deserved to be.

As for Harry Mason, who was the last person to see the older Phaliso alive, he got to spend another week in hospital, this time in Johannesburg General, where there is a pervasive smell of urine in the air and clanging sounds echo through the halls like they would in a dark cave. The doctor tells him if he had played it any rougher, he would have ended up with a colostomy bag resting on his hip until the day he died.

In that time he has only a few visitors: mostly Tanya and Jeanie and Jacob, and occasionally his mother, who can't seem to leave alone the fact that he had been kidnapped by his own commander. There are also a few old friends from his days in Murder and Robbery. Hardly anyone from the SVC, however. Word has got around like wildfire that he shot one of their own, and that Super Swarts had died in his arms. At about the same time news got around that the SVC Unit would be disbanded and specialized detectives, who had spent years honing their skills, were now to be lumped into General Investigations, along with all the other Joes who couldn't cut it, all in the name of skills transference. The buzz has it that Harry Mason is a man with an albatross strung around his neck.

One day he receives a box of dogshit made up as a present, on the next a vase of dead roses, on another sheaves of police-department stationery tucked into envelopes but with nothing actually written on them – presumably sent along just to let him know someone in the department is still thinking of him. He tries not to get bothered by all this, justifying these threats with the theory that whoever was sending them will have known Swarts and the Ballies for years, while Harry, the upstart in the department, has no proven record to exonerate him from blame for their deaths. This, at least, is what he tells Tanya when her face turns ashen at the sight of the dead roses. But at night, when the lights go out in his ward and the nurses retreat to their brightly lit stations, he lies awake and listens carefully for every footstep crossing the lino in the hallway outside, every stranger's voice that might just be asking his whereabouts. The truth is, after what Jacob has told him about Franklin's arms-dealing, Harry does not know how many cops are involved in evidence-room gun-smuggling and might now believe him a threat – or how many gunrunners might think to rid themselves of one more interfering *gata*.

The silent threats are not the worst of it, though. The dreams are. Makhe Motale starts to visit him nightly after the skateboard man's distraught mother shows up at the hospital one day with the youthful giant King in tow. While outside it keeps raining in sheets, she tells him how glad she is that her two 'boys' met up again. She tells him she does not blame him for what happened, that her son could make his own decisions. He thanks her for her kind words but, in the witching hours, Makhe Motale is there, now nothing more than a clammy corpse drip-dripping in a recess of Harry's mind, and repeatedly demanding to know why the hell he had ever dragged him into the Abasindisi case.

Harry dreams of Franklin, too: always falling, falling, falling backward on to rain-swept tarmac, endlessly jerking this way and that as round after round strike him from an oversized gun, and blood flows like a river down the slope of the road. This repetitive dream is so vivid that when Harry wakes, all damp with sweat, under an unfamiliar bedsheet, he can still see the blood and the rain, smell the cordite and gun-oil lingering on his hands.

He knows that eventually he will be able to live with the killing of Captain James T. Franklin. Whether he will ever stop wondering if the man had indeed intended to fire the pistol in his hand is another question. But Harry had to make that call, and he did. Returning fire when his life was in danger is not the problem for him; it is the way that he did so, pulling the trigger again and again and again until the barrel grew so hot it could have singed him. Harry had lost his cool; he had gone too far. He had made himself one of the Ballies.

He has to count himself grateful for the fact that no one seems particularly interested in grilling him for the killing of Franklin. The ICD is not pressing any charges after all, and the department is not overly keen to target him during the inquiry, preferring this shitstorm to blow over as quickly as possible. As far as they are concerned, Harry acted in self-defence and, besides, he had been under the kind of emotional stress that no police officer should rightly need to endure.

Or some such.

They can say whatever they want, but to Harry it is like this: no one is taking him to task for what he did, much in the same way that Swarts was never taken down for killing Ntombini. And in the shadow of that truth stands his old commander, asking him whether the next time he draws his weapon he will do so again out of self-righteous anger, and keep firing until the magazine runs empty with a hollow click.

By the time Harry is at home again and staring out of the window at his daughter morosely marching around the garden, ripping rosebuds and daisies off their stems and lobbing unripe peaches into their neighbour's yard, his department is already writing up its investigation into what happened that night in a way that paints the Ballies as a bunch of good cops who simply lost the plot after a comrade was killed in the Maloney's bombing. That is close enough to the nature of a certain breed of police officers to ring true, Harry reckons. By the look of it, only Naidoo will take the fall for what happened in Tsolo and then in Alexandra, and this will be the end of it. No more questions asked about how deep the rot had permeated into the SVC, or why.

He rises out of his chair and opens the window to call Jeanie. She slinks over with a guilty look that manages to be defiant at the same time, even though she must have been aware he was sitting there.

'Will you stop that? What have those poor plants ever done to you?'

'I'm sorry, Dad.'

'Why are you doing that anyway? What's got you so upset?'

Jeanie stares at her shoes for a moment, then swings her body around on the axis of her waist before saying, in a tone that begs to be taken seriously, 'Dad, will you teach me to use a gun?'

He returns her gaze steadily, despite the shock at her words. 'You're a bit young for that, don't you think?'

'It's just . . . I don't like how those men took you away. If I had a gun like you do, I could have stopped them.'

'Baby, I had a gun in my hand that night, and I still couldn't stop them from hurting us.'

'*Ja*, but—'

'No buts, Jeanie. A gun isn't the answer. Hurting other people never is.' As he speaks these words, the feeling of being a liar shrouds his heart. He himself may shoot a man like Franklin with impunity while lecturing his daughter otherwise?

'But they hurt you!'

With that she storms off, heading towards the tyre swing at the far end of the garden, and no amount of calling will get her to pay any further attention to him.

In many ways policing and detective work is as political as any other government organization; it takes care of itself before anything and anyone else – mostly above board, of course. Whilst Franklin, always the loner and never a man to inspire liking, is now being blamed for just about everything the Ballies and even the Abasindisi ever did wrong, Russell Swarts is being put across by the PR men as a disillusioned hero, and the media, which always relished his gung-ho style, are lapping it up like thirsty dogs. Naidoo, who was wounded in the calf by Jacob Tshabalala and then spilled the beans about the fifty-four

AK-47s they managed to smuggle out of Tsolo during the confusion of rescuing Harry, seems to have quietly slipped off the radar as he awaits his fate. It takes the SVC nearly a month to actually suspend him, after union lawyers tough it out in court on his behalf, and then another month to charge him with a list of offences as long as a roll of toilet paper – the murder of Godun Phaliso being right at the top.

'What are you brooding about so seriously?'

He can smell the flowery fragrance of her shampoo even before her fingers curl around the handles of his state-issue wheelchair. He drags his eyes away from his troubled daughter, now sulking in the cold comfort of her old rubber-tyre swing, and glances up at Tanya Fouché.

'Nothing,' he lies.

The truth is, after all is said and done, and after his two days' worth of statements have been noted down by the CIS, ICD, SVC, NIA – and whatever you want to add to that goddamned list of abbreviations – after the investigations into the Ballies' operations and those killings in Alexandra, the reported routing of more Abasindisi now that the organization's populist leaders are gone and infighting has its members dropping out like a bunch of fumigated weevils, Harry still does not have a clue who it was that shot him in Tsolo. And there is no further evidence from which to start figuring it out, either. Naidoo remains as tight-lipped about who might have shot Harry as Swarts was, and the bullet removed from his stomach back in the Eastern Cape never actually made it to Forensics. Swarts had lied about that the way he did about so many other things.

'You look angry.' She kneels next to him and puts a slender hand on his thigh. 'What's up? Talk to me.'

Long earrings dangle from soft lobes, and a scarlet scarf bunches her curly raven-black hair in a ponytail. He wishes he could smudge away the lines of concern around her eyes and mouth, and restore her brilliant laugh.

'It's nothing,' he repeats, not wanting to bother her with an issue that is quickly turning into an obsession because he is afraid that he will never know how he ended up like this. 'I'm just frustrated, sitting in this damn thing while my daughter is out there stomping around in my garden and refusing to tell me what's really bothering her. It feels like I'm locked up in a goddamned prison.'

'Maybe she's just waiting for you to talk to her.'

'What about?'

'You.'

'Me?'

'The two of you.'

'You're not making any sense. We talk all the time.'

'Harry, anyone can yak away the day about bullshit that means nothing. Sometimes you have to throw a little of yourself into the conversation and see what happens. She can see you sitting in this room just staring out at the telephone wires for hours at a time. At night she can hear you and your chair creaking around the house like a rusty lawnmower that's lost its way. Jeanie knows you're scared and worried, and that scares and worries her too. But you keep telling her it's nothing, the same as you do with me. So cut the crap, Harry. We're not idiots. I'll give you the space for the moment, because you're not allowing me much alternative, but Jeanie won't.'

His cheeks glow like she has just slapped him.

'Sorry.' He turns his eyes back to his daughter, but Tanya grabs his chin and hauls his face around towards her so that he has no choice but to look her in the eye.

'Anyone can say he's sorry. Make it right, Bond. That's what matters.'

She leans over and kisses him on the cheek, then hooks her fingers behind his ears and pulls his mouth up against hers. He allows himself to succumb to the sensation of that deep kiss, until she eventually tugs at his bottom lip gently with her teeth and backs away.

'For a man your age, you have a lot to learn, Bond.'

'And if I wasn't stuck in this contraption, Auntie Tanya, I'd teach you a trick or two.'

'Yeah?'

'Yeah.'

'Well, you *are* stuck in it, you bloody juvenile.' She winks at him and grabs the chair handles to ease him away from the window. As she pushes him out of the door, the wheels of his prison rattle over the carpet. 'Are we going to Russell's funeral or not, then?'

'Suppose we are,' he says, reaching up to grab a jacket from a coat hook in the hallway.

2

It is an uncomfortable funeral service, not only for Harry Mason, who can feel many of the assembled eyes drilling holes into him from behind, but for Russell Swarts' family too. The man's widow, Bessie, is dressed in a frilly black lace outfit that ripples in the breeze, and her face is obscured by a veil. Occasionally a white tissue creeps underneath it to dab at moist eyes or a rose-red mouth. Her two sons, both of whom look fit to play university rugby, flank her like two square-shouldered sentinels.

The brass have awarded her husband a police funeral

and, despite all the rumours, they have cleaned up his name as best they could – for their own sake rather than his. They will doubtless also give him some last medal, and his widow a half-decent pension. There is that, at least. But the absence of any senior commander higher in rank than Chief Molethe sends out a clear signal to the assembled servicemen and their families: He was one of us and that is how far our relationship goes. From here on in, we do not talk about him, we do not want to hear about him.

Rumour has it that Bessie Swarts had already received a notice to vacate the three-bedroom house leased to her husband by the state while he was still alive, and just three weeks after her husband was pronounced dead. Harry wonders whether she will now have to sell the farm that Russell Swarts loved so much.

The day is already unpleasantly hot, despite the height of summer still being a few months away, and the mourners are discreetly wiping beads of sweat from their brows and necks. The pastor drones on in Afrikaans, his voice pitching high and low like a stormy sea, while Harry's thoughts snap back to just how he is going to prove that Franklin tried to kill him, if only to ease his own conscience about shooting the man.

Makhe, Khuzwayo, the Phaliso brothers, they are all gone, so there is no way he can find out more about what happened by following that route. And a lengthy interview with Moqomo over the phone has only helped establish that the local Tsolo commander and his men knew as little as Harry did. The news regarding the cache of weapons which was first smuggled out of Tsolo, then sold off by Franklin, took Moqomo as much by surprise as it did Harry. Whether any other of the locals knew about what was going to happen, he still does not know, but the way

Swarts had deliberately persuaded him to lead that team into a quadrant of the target village where the weapons were least likely to be found suggests that Moqomo and his men at least were innocent.

Swarts is dead, too. The first clods of dirt hit the redwood coffin, and a bugle accompanies Bessie's sobbing. He died with his secret, and the stubbornness of a man who was used to getting his own way. Knowing the type he was, loyal to his own above all else, Harry is certain Swarts would have wanted to protect Franklin at all costs. Franklin was his right-hand man, and had the connections to make them a bit of money on the side, especially with an expensive move to Lyons on the cards. Franklin was the person Swarts was closest to, so it had to be him who pulled the trigger. Combrink was not hard enough to shoot Harry, of that he is convinced; nor was Naidoo.

'Why did Franklin shoot at Mason!' Chief Molethe had personally thundered at his former captain in the interrogation room, while Harry sat and watched and listened in the observation area behind a one-way mirror, his hands clasped together as if in prayer. A lawyer with a briefcase was sitting at the head of the table, staring at his nails. Naidoo might have seemed a wimp around the other Ballies, but he was a sly player the moment the heat came down on him. He had even stopped drinking, and rumour had it he was suing Jacob's department for damages after getting shot in the leg, claiming he had not been adequately warned that a police officer was on the scene and about to fire on him. The bastard; the bloody cheek of him, thought Harry. 'Did he do it because he was scared Mason would uncover the gun-running operation, or was it because he owed Swarts a favour?'

'You know, chief,' Naidoo had replied in a calm

enough voice, though his hands were doing a samba and salsa all rolled into one, 'you don't have to shout like that. I'm co-operating with you, OK? I told you everything I know about Russie and Blondie, so isn't that enough?'

'You're not just some little geek that tagged along with them, you shit!' roared Molethe, leaning over, and his heavy boxer's frame threatened to collapse on the seated witness. 'You're a fucking embarrassment to us all. The SVC is crumbling all around our ears, and a month from now, good men, highly trained men, will be answering domestic incidents and running down DWIs like a bunch of ordinary uniforms, all because of you four. Doesn't that mean anything to you?'

Naidoo had merely shrugged in response, though shifting his own position away from the chief towards the scrawny lawyer. 'That shit was a long way coming. Don't blame me for it.'

'Mr Mason?' Harry is brought back to the present.

A large hand lands on his shoulder and the chief says, 'Harry, say hello to Bessie Swarts.'

He looks up from his daydreaming and makes eye contact with the short woman standing in front of him, tottering unevenly on high heels that keep sinking into the soft ground. Her heavily made-up lips glow red like a Stop sign through her veil. She is holding a stiff white envelope in the same hand as her small velvet handbag with its golden clasp.

'Mrs Swarts.' Harry shakes her petite hand. 'My condolences. Your husband taught me a hell of a lot in the time we worked together.'

'Is it true what they say about him?'

'I don't know what they are saying. I've been in hospital, as you can see.'

She lifts the veil away from her face, to reveal pale skin heavily powdered. The mascara around her eyes has run, and her lips have the puckered wrinkles of a lifelong smoker.

'Don't worry, I'll walk again.' He smiles. 'This is what you call a "temporary inconvenience" in the department.'

Relief crosses her face, and Harry has to wonder how much she knows about what her husband had been up to, or whether she genuinely cared for the well-being of other police officers. Or if she also worried about the number of people who had lodged complaints against her husband for his brutality. Her face, nevertheless, is hard underneath, her sons' even harder, and he has a feeling that she probably shared much of Russell Swarts' sentiments about crime in this country and how best to tackle it.

'I'm sorry about what happened to you. That was in the Eastern Cape, wasn't it?'

'No need to apologize,' he says, not quite knowing how to interpret her apology.

Bessie Swarts gives a smile, but it seems stiff on her face. Then she holds out the envelope to him. 'I found this in my husband's study while I was looking for some of our insurance documents. It has your name on it, so I think you should have it.'

The envelope is fairly light, but when he takes it from her he feels something hard slide down the inside of it.

'Thank you,' he says, his heart suddenly thundering. Russell Swarts' familiar bold scrawl covers one side of the envelope with Harry's nickname: *Bond*. 'I appreciate it, Mrs Swarts.'

Her eyes probe his further, and it makes him uncomfortable.

'I've always been rather curious about you, because

Russell seemed so fond of you. For what it's worth, I think he respected you in a way even more than he did his area commissioner. It's a pity I couldn't get to know you better.'

Harry turns the envelope over in his hand, round and round, feeling the mystery object inside it slide from one side to the other.

'Anyway, it was good meeting you, and I hope you're back on your feet soon.'

He smiles at her as she turns away, his tongue clicking drily in the back of his throat. He stands and watches as each of her sons takes hold of an arm so that she can proceed without toppling across the earth sucking hungrily at her heels.

Back home an hour later, Harry cannot contain his curiosity any longer than it takes to pull a steak knife from the kitchen drawer. At the table, he slices through one end of the envelope and upends its contents into his hand.

'Well?' Tanya asks, leaning against the doorframe as she takes off her beige boots with tassels on the side. 'What is it?'

He glances down at the object in his hand.

It is a 9mm copper jacket bullet, virtually without any deformations.

3

A week later, with a favour called in at the Ballistics Unit in Silverton and a fresh report on the passenger seat next to him, Harry heads into Fordsburg, looking for the one-bedroom flat in a run-down neighbourhood into which Naidoo moved after his parents apparently threw him out of their family home in shame. Everywhere around him paint is peeling off the walls like eczema, even the advertising posters look like they belong to a different millennium, and rubbish has collected thickly in the gutters. As a background, swallows sweep lazily across a sky the colour of Arctic ice.

Harry presses the button mounted next to the white door, and listens to a rusty mechanism ratcheting out a sound that can barely be called a bell. Kids are shouting, dogs are barking, and televisions blare as they do in all places where the unemployed congregate and just wait for things to happen. To add to the general air of neglect there is the smell of uncollected garbage in the second-floor corridor.

A momentary silence is followed by the heavy slap of bare feet over tiles, and then locks are unbolted. Naidoo looms over him, his bruised eyes stained darker than usual, his lips badly chapped, cheeks unshaven, the string vest covering his corpulent figure stained with oregano and melted cheese from a pizza slice he has eaten recently. A wet belch rises up in the man's throat by way of a greeting.

'What are you doing here?'

'I need to find out exactly what happened in Tsolo, Sammy.'

'I've told the department everything I can. Now fuck off.'

His breath smells like his teeth have not seen a brush in months, and behind him Harry can see a tiled floor strewn with newspapers and empty vodka bottles. So Sammy is back drinking again.

'I don't care about the police service. This is about you and Franklin, Swarts and me. Please help me.'

Naidoo's eyes drift towards the docket under Harry's arm, then he turns on his heel and heads back into a darkened flat that smells even worse than the corridor outside. Harry follows him in and closes the door behind him.

'How are things?' he asks, still feeling as uncomfortable about this meeting as he was when he first opened his eyes this morning.

'Fucked. How else can they be?' Sammy collapses back on to the couch and there is an ominous crack from the wooden frame inside it. 'What have you got there?'

Harry moves further into the room, stepping over occasional junk, and pulls out a single sheaf of papers. Microscope images are appended to it, showing the ridges and scratches that were found on the bullet Bessie Swarts had given to him. These are paired with a second group of images, with white lines to indicate the similarities between the bullets.

He hands this to Naidoo. 'You might want to take a look at these.'

Naidoo reaches for the report, though his eyes remain on Harry. More than anything else, he looks exhausted. Nothing like the passive-aggressive role he was playing with Molethe a few weeks back.

'A ballistics report,' Sammy says as he eventually scans the papers. 'But why are you showing me this?'

'That bullet on the right came from an envelope found in Russell Swarts' desk drawer at home. The residue of blood on it perfectly matches mine.'

'So?'

Harry exhales loudly and drops his hands to his side. He had hoped Naidoo would make things a bit easier for him. 'All of your service pistols were then tested: Swarts', Franklin's, Combrink's . . . yours too.'

Naidoo leans forward and chucks the report on a small

coffee table cluttered with dinner plates and whisky tumblers. He runs his hands through black hair that has grown long and oily with the time spent waiting in the dark for his trial to start. A huff escapes his lips; a sound almost like a laugh.

'Why?' Harry asks.

Naidoo sits back into the sofa and stares at the ceiling awhile.

'It was just an accident,' he eventually says.

'Bullshit!' Harry yells, suddenly furious. The bullet on the left, fired from Naidoo's gun into a drum of water for analysis, matched the one found in Harry's gut like they were identical twins. 'What did you owe Swarts that he could persuade you to shoot me?'

'Don't you talk about him like that, OK?' Naidoo roars suddenly, life springing back into eyes. 'I'm sick of it. He trained you up, he watched out for you like you won't believe. To save your life, he fucking ran a kilometre with you bouncing around on his back, your fucking blood ruining his favourite hunting khakis. The wallah, he had tears in his eyes when we finally caught up with you, you shit!'

'So he wants me killed, but then chickens out the moment he sees me lying there in a puddle of blood? What's good about that?'

Naidoo lets out a laugh and runs his hands over flushed cheeks. 'Fuck, Mason, but you are a self-centred son of a bitch. The world doesn't spin around you.'

'So enlighten me.'

Sammy gets up and walks over to a television propped on a chair in one corner of the living room, and fishes up a bottle of whisky from somewhere. He unscrews the cap and upends the final quarter of it down his throat.

'Won't have much of this stuff where I'm going, hey?' He stares lovingly at the label, lets a thumb run over it. 'Like I told the department, Franklin had a deal lined up for those guns your guy talked about, but he needed the rest of us in on it because he couldn't get them out of there on his own, and once back in Johannesburg, the AK-47s would be far too hot to simply lift from an evidence room. It wasn't hard for him to convince Kommie and me to help grab them while they were still out in the bush. We both needed the money, and we were taking them from a bunch of arsewipes anyway. Russie, he wanted nothing to do with it at first, because he'd been there with Franklin before and didn't like what he saw. But, you know, he was moving to France, and the rand–euro exchange rate isn't exactly Christmas time for us, hey? Eventually, between the three of us, we got him to play along.'

He sighed heavily. 'You were the problem from the beginning. You were the investigating officer with the tab, so we couldn't just dump you there and run off after those weapons. Combrink even thought you might come on board, but Swarts told him to leave that alone. He didn't want you in, that's my guess. Instead, he worked on you so that you would head off in a different direction, along with the local troops, while we could go after the guns by ourselves.'

'I was wondering about that.'

'Well, you're a dick for it. What kind of primary investigating officer lets himself be dissuaded from going after his own prize?'

Harry shrugs. 'I guess someone had to make sure the yokels didn't screw anything up. '

'You know how it was down there. The fog, and those fucking peasants shooting at anything that moved. Bodies lying around like on the set of a Vietnam War movie. I got wound up tight. I was scared shitless, I don't mind telling you that now. Franklin, he was already wired for that sort of thing before the devil shat him out, you know? But me, since I got shot, the idea of having another round put into me, it made me jumpy. So what? I don't care any more.

'We found those crates hidden in a shack in quadrant one, exactly where Motale had said they would be. First time lucky, we were. With the fog that thick we thought we could make it down to the vehicles before any of yous even noticed we were gone. So Blondie and I, we grabbed one; Kommie and Russie, they took the other, and we ran, *boet*. I tell you, there's been few times in my life that I was that shit-scared of getting shot or getting found out. And suddenly there's this guy standing in front of me, and he's turning in my direction when I bump that stupid crate against a tree stump. What was I supposed to do? Let him shoot me the way Moqomo got popped? I couldn't see it was you. How was I supposed to know you weren't still with your team? I shot first. Fucking miracle that I hit anything in that weather – a miracle that went the wrong way. Take it or leave it, *boet*, but that's what happened.'

Naidoo digs around under some newspapers tented over a drinks table, evidently scrounging for more booze, but he finds none. Harry watches him while he tries to keep a lid on the anger rising up inside him like bile. He does not believe the story, *cannot* believe it – but maybe that is just him wanting to know, *needing* to know, that he was shot for a more significant reason. That he had a reason to be angry with Swarts to the end.

'How far are you going to take this?' Tanya had asked him two days ago, after they had made love for the first time in what felt like decades.

He had reached over and run a fingernail down her arm, along her side, until he could rest his palm on a sculpted rump as smooth as marble. 'All the way to the end. It's the only way.'

'But what if there is nothing to learn?'

'I'll find it,' he told her. 'I have to.'

And here it is, a perfectly plausible explanation, and he still cannot accept it.

'What about those rifles you destroyed?' he growls, eager to find loopholes in Naidoo's story.

'Are you kidding me, Mason? It was a miniature army camp down there. There was enough hardware floating between Qumbu and Tsolo for us to get something together, pretend to the bosses that our raid was a success *and* sell off the real diamond wares.'

Harry's hands begin to clench into fists at his sides. 'You really killed Makhe just because you wanted information about more weapons to steal and sell on? It wasn't about an ambush, was it? You didn't ever believe that he set us up. It was all about greed.'

'The ambush thing crossed Russie's mind when all hell broke loose in Tsolo but, no, it was about the weapons. Fresh AKs fetch a better price than hot handguns lifted from evidence rooms, I tell you. The bank-robbery market is booming, and it kept the SVC in business, didn't it?' A girlish titter escapes his lips, but he quickly suppresses it at the sight of Harry's expression. 'Makhe was Franklin's idea. Russie knew nothing about it until the day we came for you, and by then he was already dead. Once we were in for that one deal, Franklin knew he could take it further with us helping.'

Harry stares down at Naidoo, perched now on the edge of his couch, his hands dangling between his legs, a blank expression that barely verges on relief. How does he interpret this, and what did he come here to find anyway? He finally had the truth in his hand the moment that ballistics report came through, so it is not really that. The truth will have its way in court. Does he now want an apology? Yes, he does – and he needs to know more about Russie too.

'You're a smug shite, Naidoo.'

'Come again?'

'Russie carried all that to his grave. His name is down a toilet bowl all because he covered for you right to the end, and yet you wouldn't relieve him of that burden. I've said it before and I'll say it again, you're a coward.'

'Hey, don't you blame me for that shit! What happened happened only because of you. It happened because of *him*. If the Ntombini business didn't exist between the two of yous, things might not have turned out this way, so don't you blame me, OK?'

Harry is about to say more, but he realizes the futility of continuing this argument. Naidoo has the same self-righteous stubbornness in him that Russell Swarts had possessed, the same faith that his actions can always be exonerated by those of others. He is not so much interested in his guilt or innocence as concocting the ideal alibi and, like a lifer, he will then remain convinced of it until the day he dies, despite the heavy burden of evidence against him.

Harry shakes his head resignedly and turns for the door. He can stand here and waste his breath for ever and a day, or he can follow Tanya Fouché's one simple piece of advice: 'Let it go, Harry. There are more important things to worry about.'

Naidoo gets up behind him. 'What?'

'Nothing, Sammy,' he calls over his shoulder. 'Absolutely nothing.'

'What!' he repeats.

Harry raises a hand without looking back as he gets to the front door. 'I hope you manage to live a charmed life up there in C-Max, that's all.'

EIGHTEEN

1

Jacob takes a step back and throws his eyes over the shrine he has put together in a darkened corner of the house, where the cupboard containing Nomsa's porcelain collection once stood. The *unsamo* is comprised of a small table of rough camel-thorn wood, on which rests a pot of the soil collected from his father's grave, a gourd with fresh sour beer poured into it, and some burning incense. Next to a lit candle there is a framed black-and-white photograph of his grandfather and father standing together.

There. Are you happy now?

Don't talk to us like you've done us some favour, boy, rumbles his grandfather. *Count yourself lucky we didn't throw a lightning bolt down on you that time you went chasing after your* umlungu!

It is good, Jacob, says another voice. His father sounds calmer than he ever did in life. *Now you must get yourself a decent wife.*

Jacob lets his shoulders slump as he looks up at the ceiling, silently praying to his God for some merciful peace and quiet. With Nomsa gone, and his two forebears nagging incessantly in his mind, he has seen no reason not to complete the mourning period for his father, after his mother had called him up about it. They are, after all, a part of him, as he is of them, and they will not miss a moment to remind him of that fact.

Besides, Nomsa had been right all those weeks ago, in the days immediately after his father died. Forgiveness is the one thing that primarily defines his faith, and if this is the only way he can truly show it to his father, then let it be so.

He turns around and takes stock of his house. It already smells dusty, looks empty the way a warehouse does when cleared of stock. Any noise and music sounds strange and unfamiliar as it echoes off the walls in these empty rooms. There are no longer any flowers on the wall unit next to the hi-fi, where Nomsa used to arrange them every Tuesday even though he might scold her over the expense. The kitchen dustbin is filled with fast-food containers, the fridge with beer and leftover roast chicken. He does not spend much time here any more, because what made this house a home has already moved out. Heated arguments about his possessiveness followed in the wake of his assault on Teddy Bakwena, even though Nomsa had then gone out of her way to convince that snake not to press charges. At the height of his fury, Jacob relished the thought of confronting Bakwena in a court of law and having it out in front of the judge, somehow convinced that he could justify what he had done, that the court would surely understand Jacob's actions in view of the other man's adulterous intentions. He thought this might be the only way Nomsa would understand how she was wrong here and he was right. His ears get inflamed with embarrassment just thinking about that time. Did he actually say all of this to her face?

Even Busi Mosetsane, who had gone back to headquarters but nevertheless came around to the office frequently for a week or two afterward for lunch with him, told him it was the stupidest idea she had ever heard. Something about his attitude in that time caused Busisiwe to restrict first their dinner dates, then the lunch dates at the office, until eventually she started missing his calls and not returning them.

Nomsa's father had turned up in a four-wheel-drive, with a few of her cousins and brothers, and they had quickly cleared out everything that belonged to his daughter, all the while glowering at Jacob as though he were a child molester or worse. When Jacob accidentally came across Nomsa drinking cappuccinos with Bakwena at a shopping centre in Orlando a week later, he had almost bolted for the nearest exit. He had then stopped phoning her house at night, stopped driving by in the hope of seeing her on the street outside so that he could speak to her without her father shouting obscenities or threats through the kitchen window. Up until then, Jacob had never thought himself capable of behaving so badly.

The house is empty, he tells himself by way of interrupting these troubling thoughts. *Which means it is a good time to paint it properly for when she returns.*

But will she?

Let it go, mfo, he chides himself in disgust, happy that she is nowhere near enough to see this ugliness inside him.

2

He is working on the far side of the roof, the sun blazing down on his naked back, the world around him stinking of paint and a small radio with poor reception to keep him company, when Jacob hears the diesel engine of a 4x4 that is turning into his driveway.

He wipes sweat from his brow and jogs the few steps to the other side of the tin roof, a cry of joy at Nomsa's return already bubbling to his lips.

A car door slams, and Harry squints into the sun as he looks up. 'Are you still painting?'

Jacob hopes the disappointment does not show too clearly on his face. He lets out a sigh and drops the paint roller from his grip. 'Yes,' he yells down.

'How long are you going to carry on doing that? You can't make things new over and over again every couple of months. That's just stupid, Jakes, and it's a waste of money apart from anything else.'

Jacob squats on his haunches, folding his hands on his knees. 'It wasn't the right colour. That's why I decided to redo it.'

Harry does not look convinced by this answer, and he allows his eyes to scan the rest of the front yard. 'Where's the rest, then?'

'Of what?'

'Normally when you're fiddling around with your house, you've got people from here to Dobsonville helping you out. It's a bloody neighbourhood party when Tshabalala starts to play at DIY.'

'I'm fixing things on my own this time. I actually prefer it that way. You could say the peace and quiet is doing me good.'

'Right,' says Harry.

'How are you, anyway?'

'I'm fine. Look, are you going to invite me up there, or are you just going to stare at me like the lonely bachelor recluse you've turned into?'

Jacob's mind goes blank as Harry holds his eyes, a mocking smile on his lips. The area of his head where doctors shaved off hair to stitch up the bullet grazes are still visible, but healing fast. An unexpected laugh erupts in Jacob's throat, and it keeps coming, like oil gushing from a newly drilled well. It feels good: relief and a return to some semblance of sanity all rolled into one joyous sound.

'Will you quit that?' Harry begins to laugh as well. 'People are going to wonder about this half-naked nutter running around up on the roof. And if the whole of Soweto doesn't decide you've gone crazy, I may be forced to arrest you for public indecency.'

'There's beer in the fridge.' Jacob scoops up the paint roller and begins to head towards the other end of the roof. 'And, please, help me finish this.'

They work all afternoon. Cicadas chirr in the trees, local kids shout and point up at the white man painting a black man's roof, while young men and women push supermarket trolleys through the neighbourhood below, shouting out their wares to potential customers during this lazy afternoon. For once Harry is doing all the talking as they work, and Jacob finds himself relaxing to the pleasant drone of a human voice talking about nothing to do with police work, a voice that communicates with him for no other reason than to reach out and reassure him that he is still remembered. Soon the man's pale skin and the puckered wound in his abdomen are glowing pink in the hot sun, and Harry is forced to put on his shirt. Eventually they are sitting on the edge of the roof like two kids fooling around after school, and Jacob's head is spinning like a top from all the beer and the sun and their hard labour.

'Jakes, what are you going to do about Nomsa?' Harry enquires at last.

'Nothing. She's made her decision. I can't change her mind for her.'

'Have you been to church?'

'No.'

'Why not?'

'It's *their* place now.'

'That doesn't sound at all like the man I know.'

'There's been some changes, in case you haven't noticed.'

Harry takes a long swig of beer; he now smells of sweat and deodorant and paint. His hands are stained terracotta.

'Maybe she's waiting for you to make the first move.'

'Me?'

'You chased her away, remember. You have to fetch her back.'

'I didn't chase her away. She left on the arm of that snake.'

Harry watches two distant hawks chase each other across the sky. 'Can I shoot straight with you?'

'Yes.'

'It's me that usually lies to himself, not you. You know you're the one who screwed up there, and you don't need me to tell you that.'

'I don't think I can do that,' replies Jacob.

'Why not?'

'*Mfo*, where do I start? Do you think it's sane and sensible for a man to drive past his ex-partner's house every half-hour at God knows what time every night? Is it fine to run Bakwena's registration on the office computer, and observe him for a week just to see if there's anything I can catch him out on? How many times can one person phone another's number and not know what to say when she eventually picks up and speaks in a voice sounding so terrified that you barely recognize her? How long do you think it takes before people start worrying you might just use your service pistol to do something stupid – and you start thinking the same thing?'

Harry looks at him in surprise, perhaps reacting to these details which Jacob has kept to himself until now, perhaps to the quiver that has crept into his voice. 'You did all that?'

'You have no idea.'

'Shit, Jakes, why didn't you say something about it?'

Jacob laughs, but it sounds hysterical. 'Who do you tell something like that to?'

Harry finishes his beer and stands up to stretch out a kink in his back. 'People do dumb things when they're desperate. And most other people understand because they know they can so easily end up on that side of the fence too, I guess.'

'Not like this.'

'Even like that, Jacob.'

'Her father will kill me.'

'You're not in love with her father, are you?'

Jacob drops his empty beer bottle on to the lawn below, and wonders whether he should tell Harry that life is not that simple, that Harry could not hope to understand the complexities of the situation. The fact is that he behaved like most husbands he has picked up in domestic murders; he is competing with a rich man who has no doubt promised Nomsa the world, a rich man who, incidentally, thinks about religion in a way that is much more closely aligned with Nomsa's upbringing than Jacob's own. And if he has to dig down deep enough, he has be honest with himself: he still loves a woman who has serious doubts about the compatibility of their religious and traditional choices. Her orthodoxy has no real room for his grandfather and father; it has no space for the *unsamo* his ancestors demand of him.

'What do you say?' asks Harry.

'I say there is a Sundowns and Ajax game starting in fifteen, and all that beer in the garage also needs to be dealt with.'

3

Sitting on the edge of the bed and facing the window, the mother basks in the sunlight dappling her skin through gauze-like curtains. The way the soft material occasionally streams in on a gentle breeze and brushes across her face reminds her of a time when she still had a mother and father, a period when her dad still had a job on the mines and they could afford the rent of a little brick house on the premises of some company she can no longer remember the name of.

She reaches out and runs a hand over the soft duvet that has been warmed by the sun, and breathes in the sweet scent of freshly washed linen. She grasps the lush nap of carpet between her toes and smiles at the pleasurable sensation.

Is this a dream, or what? she wonders.

The door to the small bedroom flies open and three girls, dressed in pressed white shirts and neat little blue skirts, race into the room, chasing each other first around the bed, then over it. Soon they are jumping around on the mattress, screeching with joy as if at some newly discovered miracle, but which they cannot yet articulate to her in their excitement. She cannot bring herself to shoo them off the mattress, and so joins in the laughter until tears threaten to well up in her eyes.

'I see you're all settled in,' says a female voice at the door.

The children immediately quieten down and slide off the bed. Their mother jumps up as though she has been sitting on a red ants' nest, and instinctively bunches her kids around her legs. She casts her eyes to the floor and looks away in shame.

'I'm sorry,' she says and wipes at her nose with a forearm. 'We won't make so much noise again.'

The woman at the door, younger and more petite than her, with a round girlish face and easy smile, just laughs. She walks into the room with some folded clothes in her arms and puts them on a dresser near the full-length mirror.

'Don't worry about it in the least,' she reassures her.

The mother glances shyly at the other woman, not quite trusting her generosity. But the younger woman catches the sidelong glance and approaches.

'My name is Nomsa. I'm one of the volunteers here. Those clothes I've put on the dresser, they're for you and your kids.'

'More clothes?' the mother asks disbelievingly.

'Yes,' she laughs. 'You can't just wear one pair, can you? What if they have to go into the washing?'

'Thank you. I don't know what to say.'

The woman called Nomsa glances at her three young daughters, then drops on to her haunches, both hands clasped in her lap. '*Dumela sisies.*'

The girls shyly press back against their mother's legs, but the youngest, whose scars are healing nicely, takes a hesitant step forward. 'Hello.'

Nomsa runs a hand up and down the girls arm, as if trying to warm her up. 'They are so cute.'

'They're mine,' the mother beams with pride.

The other woman gets up and brushes wrinkles from her summer skirt. 'I have to run a few more chores, but I'll see you at lunch, OK? Then you can tell me a bit more about yourself.'

The mother offers her a hesitant smile. 'That would be nice.'

Nomsa walks to the door, then grabs hold of the jamb and glances back. Though the smile on her face is ready enough, there is a distance in her eyes, even a sadness.

'By the way, how did you find out about us?'

The mother shrugs and averts her eyes again, feeling deeply ashamed of how she came to be here. 'There was this policeman. He gave me this number to call.'

Only I spat in his face and threw it back at him. She could only thank God that one of the paramedics had picked it up off the ambulance floor, that day of the evacuation, and insisted she keep the number in case she ever made it to Soweto.

Nomsa's eyes drift to her feet for a moment, and her eyebrows crinkle at the reference to a policeman. She seems to swallow hard, and her mouth twitches at some thought. But then she looks up again, and it's as if that smile has never left her face.

'Oh,' is all she says, before hurrying away.

The mother moves over to the window and pushes aside the white curtain which smells faintly of lavender. Dazzled by bright daylight, she squints into the garden outside, with its yellow lawn that nevertheless looks like the grounds of a palace to her. A smile comes to her lips at the sight of other single mothers sitting on benches, the kids playing on bars and swings or in a sandbox filled with plastic toys and mud pies.

This has to be a dream, she tells herself.

A small red pick-up pulls up to a low gate she can only see partly over to the left. She presses her cheek against the windowpane to get a better view of the new arrival, interested to learn more about the people who go in and out of this sanctuary. The man is still getting out of his car just as Nomsa strides out of the kitchen door with a basket full of washing for the line. She freezes at the sight of him. He looks up from his keys and makes eye contact with her. Then he too turns to stone. They stare at each other for a long moment, as children make a racket all around them, and a group of mothers chatter and laugh over sweet tea drunk from tin cups, seemingly oblivious to the new arrival. The mother is about to look away, as if embarrassed at participating in such an intimate moment, when the woman called Nomsa snaps out of the spell and takes one cautious step in his direction, then another, more self-assured this time. A name rolls off her tongue that reminds the mother of that policeman's hastily scribbled note, which she still keeps hidden under her pillow for a good luck.

She lets go of the curtain and turns back to her children.

'Come, girls,' she says. 'Let's go outside.'

Visit **www.panmacmillan.com** to read more about all our books and to buy them. You will also find features, author interviews and news of any author events, and you can sign up for e-newsletters so that you're always first to hear about our new releases.